Questionable Practices

Ruth Karen

HARPER & ROW PUBLISHERS

NEW YORK

Cambridge   London
Hagerstown   Mexico City
Philadelphia   São Paulo
San Francisco   Sydney

1817

FIRST EDITION

Designer: C. LINDA DINGLER

Library of Congress Cataloging in Publication Data

Karen, Ruth.
  Questionable practices.

  I. Title.
PZ4.K17527Qe   1980   [PR9286.9.A7]   823   79-2650
ISBN 0-06-012293-5

80 81 82 83 84 10 9 8 7 6 5 4 3 2 1

Questionable Practices

1

"We need someone we can trust to deal for us, to act as an intermediary when we need one. Someone who understands that we are handing him a very juicy plum, but doesn't figure that's a reason to squeeze us for more. You'd think that shouldn't be hard, but with hundreds of millions of dollars involved, it is. It's very hard."

The older man sighed in a short measured expulsion of air that left his face immobile and his eyes unclouded. He was a gray man, with gray hair cut very short, a gray complexion and a compact muscular body in a nondescript gray suit.

"There is von Stolzenfels," his companion said tentatively. "He doesn't know much about business—although he thinks he does and that might be a problem—but he is trustworthy. I can vouch for that." A half smile relaxed the determined mouth. He was a younger man, tall, slim and very handsome.

The older man shook his head. "No good, Jim. It can't be a relative. That wouldn't look right."

Jim Lindner still found it difficult to think of Helmut Werner Gottfried, Graf von Stolzenfels, as a relative. But the count was his father-in-law. Nevertheless, Ken Ward, Jim's boss and mentor, was right as usual. If the Department of Justice ever decided to trace the arrangement they were discussing, it would look fishy. Which, coming to think of it, it was.

"Ken," he said, "why do we need an intermediary? We can

1

sell directly from here to anyone, anywhere. Our production facilities are—"

"First rate," Ken cut in. He was not a man to waste words, but there was appreciation in his voice and a trace of affection. "But they are not big enough to take care of all the orders we get at headquarters that have commercial terms and conditions we can't handle at home anymore."

The two men were sitting in easy chairs facing a wide window that looked out over the Rhine. They could see the river below, a muddy brown under the pale sun of a late September afternoon, flecked with the spume of barges churning their way north to the sea. Along the way, the barges passed shores on which castles and vineyards, monasteries and villages blended gingerly with office buildings and industrial plants. One of the plants, on the outskirts of Mainz, was Copter GmbH.

From the house on the hill the two men could not see the extensive installations of their company, which were obscured by other buildings and, at this time of the year, by trees still dense with leaves. But their minds were focused on the company, probing what it could do to meet the worldwide needs of the parent firm in New York.

"Even if you supplied customers with special needs from here," Ken said, "we'd be vulnerable. Copter GmbH is a wholly owned subsidiary of The Copter Company. That makes it subject to a whole slew of US laws, among them the Foreign Corrupt Practices Act, which Congress in its wisdom gave us as a Christmas present last year." He crossed the legs he had stretched out over a hassock.

"Sometimes I wonder what goes on in their heads down there in Washington. They complain about our lopsided trade balance, talk about our need to step up exports, and then tie our hands with laws and regulations that make it impossible to compete." He uncrossed his legs. "Well, maybe not impossible. But awfully hard. You have to keep thinking of ways to deal with the curves they throw you."

"Outlawing corruption doesn't seem like such a bad idea."

"That depends on who defines corruption. One man's corruption can be another man's courtesy."

"You're losing me, Ken."

The gray man slid deeper into his chair. "I have this customer in Abu Dhabi. A customer. He says we're friends. I'm not sure that's how I would describe our relationship, but he's certainly acted like a friend. Anything I need or want in his part of the world, he tries to get. He never asks why. In his book, that would be a discourteous question among friends. He's done awfully well for The Copter Company with his ideas of courtesy."

"Even if he collects a commission that comes close to being highway robbery." Jim's resentment and suspicion were patent. He knew about the Abu Dhabi connection from the company grapevine. Ken's friend was The Copter Company's agent for all the Middle East and had indeed produced large orders for the firm. But the commission he was paid amounted to more than four times the percentage that was customary in the US or Western Europe.

"That money is no skin off our nose. We just add it to the price. And he needs it."

"I'm sure he can use it," Jim said contemptuously. "A couple of million a month for the personal piggy bank isn't so hard to take. But I wouldn't call it an urgent need."

"Not all of it goes into his personal piggy bank. He spreads it around."

"To other poor pals with multimillion-dollar piggy banks?"

"I didn't know you objected to money, Jim."

"I don't. But it does depend on how it's earned."

"They figure they earn it. Someone has to check out all the hungry folk who want a piece of the action down there. Someone has to screen people and deal with them. That's a job I wouldn't want, let me tell you. It would keep me awake nights."

"How did your pal check out The Copter Company? He's never even been to New York as far as I know."

"That's right. He hasn't. He checked me out. I came through for him when he was in trouble. And I didn't crowd him or drive a hard bargain. That's good enough for him. He figures I'm dependable and a good man to do business with."

Jim sat forward in his chair to face Ken. There was no questioning that assessment. Ken was straight, to the point of bluntness. When he said no to something, you knew that was it; and when he said yes it was better than a contract in which the lawyers had double-checked every paragraph. "He's right about that."

Ken did not stir. "He also points out that we don't pay any real taxes in their countries. Taking a slice off the top is their way of collecting some revenue on the lucrative deals we cut with them and letting the benefits percolate through their economies. They are pretty sharp. They have a good idea of what's in it for us." He laughed. It was a baritone sound that started deep in his chest and rumbled its way up through his throat. "I guess, all things considered, I still prefer the Internal Revenue Service—and that's saying an awful lot, as you know—but the Arab way of doing things isn't just a whim. It's a system. And it works for them."

"For how long?"

Ken closed his eyes. He looked weary. "How long does anything last? Even the best-designed copter goes to pieces after a while."

"I know that argument, Ken: In the end, we're all dead. But from where I sit, what happens meanwhile counts."

Ken opened his eyes. The weariness had vanished from his face. "Meanwhile," he said sharply, "you and I are in the business of making and selling helicopters. If you want to make laws, run for Congress. If you want to preach, become a preacher. The Copter Company supplies the world with planes, not morals."

They heard the key turn in the lock and the sound of the door being shut. The light went on in the hall. Jim rose. "Brigitte," he called. "I'm here, in the study."

"Coming, darling." Her voice ran through an entire scale of notes in just two words. "I've had a marvelous—" She saw Ken and stopped. Her face froze. "Good evening," she said formally.

Ken took his legs off the hassock and turned his head. "Good

4

evening, Brigitte. Sorry to be invading your home this way. We had some business to discuss."

"Not at all." Her voice had gone flat with a British intonation. Jim looked at his wife. He knew that she was always interested in his personal reports of what went on in the office, but she objected strenuously to business discussions on social occasions, and in her mind anything that happened in her house was a social event. Still, Ken had flown in from New York especially to talk about the important and delicate project of finding in Germany an intermediary to whom The Copter Company could entrust a sizable segment of its international business. Their discussion had required privacy. That's why he had brought Ken home.

"How about a drink?" he said easily.

Ken's response was swift. "If you have bourbon."

"I do. Brigitte found a liquor store in Bonn that stocks everything, even exotic stuff like Old Grand-dad."

"Marvelous woman. I'll have a double."

"Neat?"

"Yes, please."

"You, darling?"

She shook her head. The wide blue eyes signaled a plea. "No, thank you. I still have some calls to make. And I need to think about dinner. Papa sent a basket of Pfifferlinge. They smell glorious. We'll have them tonight." The color had come back to her voice, and she finished the sentence on a low, seductive note. Brigitte could turn a basket of wild mushrooms into an exotic encounter, and she was evidently planning to do just that. He turned from her reluctantly. "What are your plans, Ken? Are you free for dinner? Will you join us?"

Ken saw the look of disappointment on Brigitte's face. She made no effort to hide it. "I'm free," he said, "but I won't join you. I don't think that basket is big enough for three. And I'd be just as happy with a steak and another bourbon from room service. I could use a good night's sleep." A sobering thought occurred to him. "If they have bourbon at the hotel," he added doubtfully.

Jim's eyes locked with those of his wife. She turned to leave

5

the room. "I'll let you have what's left in the bottle," he offered, "if you promise to finish it."

"Sold, sight unseen. And I'll skip the one for the road. Can you take me to the hotel?"

"Of course. I have to go back to the office anyhow. Max Feld left word that he wants to see me urgently. It's always urgent when you have a plant with two thousand people, isn't it?"

The two men exchanged a look of understanding. "That's right," Ken said.

When Jim arrived at his office, Max Feld was already there, pacing impatiently, excitement oozing from him like an electric charge. Jim and Max had worked together for nearly five years, but Jim still could not predict what would erupt from his talented and mercurial 200-pound marketing manager. A Catholic from Bavaria, Max was anti-Communist by instinct. He was also warm-hearted and ebullient and loved life and all its pleasures. He liked to eat, drink and dance. He adored the Fräuleins, preferably buxom and blond, but thought redheads had Schmaltz and bru-nettes were classy. Blondes just were more gemütlich. They gave you something to hold on to. His kind of blonde, anyway.

But Max was a complex man. He also liked stalking deer in the forest, and could hide himself under a leafy tree, his rifle propped in the crook of a dividing branch for hours on end, not moving, concentrating on every rustle of leaves, the crunch of every twig underfoot. Behind his rifle, his eyes and ears alert, Max would let his mind roam, and his roaming mind could pro-duce interesting ideas. He had designed sales strategies for Copter GmbH that were inventive in a way his boss admired. Some of these ideas had produced estimable results. Others, however, had been absurdly grandiose. You had to watch Max without reining him in, keep him on a tight leash he didn't feel, play his game, but only up to a point.

"Okay, Max," Jim said, "I got your SOS. What's the tragedy today?"

Max lowered himself into one of the armchairs that faced Jim's desk. The movement was both bouncy and deliberate. For a second he closed his eyes. For him, life was theater; business, a movie. When he opened his eyes again, they were large and round. He seemed awed by what he had to say. "Not tragedy, Jim. Drama. The prologue is over. Act One begins." He blinked to indicate the curtain was going up. "The Iranians are coming. Indeed, they are here. I'm taking them to dinner and out on the town tonight. I believe they intend to cut the mustard this time."

Jim chuckled. It was amazing how Max picked up American idioms and adapted them to fit his own style. Max loved his native city's white veal sausages. Since their taste was rather bland, they had to be eaten with mustard. By immediate association in Max's mind, something desirable became something delectable. Jim decided to indulge his marketing manager in his metaphor. "That sounds appetizing, Max, but I'm skeptical. We've been expecting the Iranians to come across for two years. Two years and three months, to be precise. What makes you think they'll really deal this time?"

"This time I have a hunch. Here." Max put his hand under his jacket and allowed it to rest where he could feel the beat of his heart. "And here." He removed the hand and patted his voluminous belly. "These two never let me down. Not when there's harmony between them. Not when they speak to me in unison."

Jim smiled. The smile changed his face, softening the lean lines of his cheeks. His lips, usually clamped together, relaxed into a generous mouth. The smile was also reflected in his eyes, and the blue irises, which could appear icy, took on a shade of sky blue.

"I wouldn't dare come between those two, Max. Good luck to the three of you."

Max steepled his fleshy fingers and looked down at them.

Pensively? Jim was never quite certain what Max's poses were meant to portray. At the moment he looked like an overgrown choirboy, with his rosy face, his neatly combed wavy black hair, all set off by a white shirt and an expensive worsted wool suit, which on Max managed to look rumpled.

Max looked up from his steepled hands. "This will not be a simple business."

"A five-hundred-million-dollar order never is."

"True, but this will be trickier than most."

Jim's smile vanished. "What do you mean, trickier? That's not a concept I'm fond of, as you know. Business is complicated enough without making it tricky."

Max squinted at his boss. He never knew whether his General-direktor was deceiving himself, his staff or everybody with that rectitudinous stuff he handed out. It sounded all right when it came out of his mouth. It suited him. But Max didn't believe he meant it. As Jim would have put it himself, "It isn't for real." Just looking at my expense account, Max thought, with that precise analytical mind of his, must make clear that we aren't exactly boy scouts. And God knows they aren't angels in New York. He is as aware of that as I am. So why does he pretend?

Jim's eyes had narrowed. The two men stared at each other.

"For the moment, James, I mean only that the deal may require some unconventional arrangements." And when I discuss those tonight, he added silently, I don't want to be haunted by your Bible-quoting mother on her Pennsylvania farm and all the Puritan wisdom she poured into your head when you were four years old. Which you preach when it suits you, but don't necessarily practice, as I suspect we shall discover when the chips are really down.

Like every other executive at Copter GmbH, Max usually called the company president Jim. They did this at Jim's insistence, and Jim knew that when Max called him James—he pronounced it Tchames—something was up.

His voice took on a peremptory tone. "What are you telling me, Max? You might as well level. Neither one of us wants to mess up the biggest deal we've ever handled. That Iranian sale would really put this company on the map."

Max nodded enthusiastically, making his head look like a bobbing cork.

"With big pins on the map, in the shape of bonuses, for the select few responsible for pulling it off," he agreed, running a darting tongue over his lips. "Very inspirational."

Jim's eyes crinkled. "Mmm," he said. The tension between them subsided.

"I really have nothing to tell you yet," Max added after a pause. "I'd like to bring in the Iranians this afternoon and have you do your presidential bit. Then I'll woo them tonight. All-out seduction, Maxie style. And if my usually reliable sources are right"—he patted his heart and stomach—"we will have something to talk about in the morning. Talk about. Fight about. We'll see."

He bounded out of his chair—for a heavy man Max was very light on his feet—winked at his boss and was gone.

It was well past six—darkness and silence had settled over most of the building—when Liselotte Kestenmeier inquired over the intercom in her most mellifluous tone whether Mr. Feld could present to the Herr Generaldirektor the Messrs. Pishva and Esfandiary of Teheran. Fräulein Kestenmeier, Jim's prim, gray-curled secretary, thought of Copter GmbH as her castle, Jim as the reigning prince and herself as guardian of the castle's moat. Her voice conveyed that she was lowering the drawbridge.

Jim rose to greet the Iranians. They were swarthy, stocky and reserved. He wondered how Max would get them to open up or, more important, sign anything. With Jim they exchanged only banalities: The weather, crisp and moist at this time of the year in northern Europe. Almost like Teheran, they noted, although of course Teheran was drier. The polluted Rhine with all its traffic. Yes, Teheran was getting pollution as well. The price of industrialization. Too bad, but better than remaining backward. The problem of guest workers. Unlike the other oil-producing countries in the Middle East, Iran did have a large enough population to become a real power, but its people were not yet sufficiently skilled; Iran still had to import technical expertise. Not talent, mind you—there was a lot of that in Iran, including entrepreneurial talent—but know-how and technology, the latest and best.

They also talked about the need for law and order, anywhere and everywhere. That was as close as the conversation got to the topic of helicopters. When Jim tried to make a bridge from the subject of law and order to a discussion of Copter GmbH's product, world renowned for its quality and suitability for a wide range of purposes, Max flashed him a warning glance and cut in smoothly.

"We have a big program for this evening, Jim. Our guests may want to freshen up a little before then. We'll all get together again in the morning."

He rose, and the Iranians immediately followed suit. He marched them to the door, turned and, with a small formal bow in Jim's direction, added, "Until tomorrow then. Have a good evening."

Jim did not return to his house until well past eight o'clock, but Brigitte was used to late dinners and Jim had learned over more than four years of marriage to enjoy meals that filled an entire evening, or what was left of it when he got home. A sherry first, when the weather was cool, a Lillet when it was warm, or when the day had been tense a Campari or a Carpano to settle the system. No hard liquor, to make sure that the palate was fresh for the occasion to follow.

Dinner at the Lindners' in Mainz was emphatically not the wholesome meat and potatoes, ice cream and pie that Jim's mother had put on the table. The young Lindners' meals were light, eclectic and delicious. Asparagus vinaigrette, or mushroom in dill sauce as a first course; a thin slice of veal with lemon and a touch of paprika or a piece of rare beef in a flaky crust as a second course; a salad served separately—endives from Belgium or arugula from Italy; cheese and fruit to finish. Sometimes a sweet, a crepe or a Bavarian as course number five. Always wine—a German white or a red from France.

And conversation: intimate, leisurely. For Jim, that was the best part of the meal. During those two-hour dinners he would tell Brigitte about the events and demands of his day, and she would entertain him with the news she had collected in the course of her activities. While his reports were restricted mainly to company affairs, her news ranged from the latest political intrigues in Bonn to who was doing what to whom in the world of European society in which she moved. That world included not only jet-setters and fashionable young aristocrats, but also men and women engaged in some of the major arts and all of the minor ones. Listening to Brigitte at dinner, Jim had told her once, was like perusing a *Tatler* for the Age of Aquarius.

This evening she had regaled him with tales from Spain that revolved around the Duchess of Alba, a redoubtable lady who had built a social career on the claim that she was descended from more royal lines than anyone now extant in Europe. That included, the lady insisted on stressing, Lord Mountbatten, who came close. The duchess liked the aura of action that the mention of Mountbatten created. She herself had never done anything except cultivate her noble descent, the titles of which she trailed behind her like the train of a wedding dress. The latest about the Duchess of Alba was that she had dug up some Moorish ancestors, and that Sheikh Yamani of Saudi Arabia was amused but not convinced by the lady's attempt to deal herself in on the currently fashionable appeal of the Middle East. In the social circles frequented by the duchess, Sheikh Yamani had been the star of the 1978 season.

Jim in turn had told Brigitte about the Iranians, and she had been both intrigued and doubtful. Brigitte's half brother served at the German embassy in Teheran as cultural attaché, and his infrequent but long letters were replete with lore of Iranian intrigues past and present. His latest letter had hinted at considerable Sturm und Drang, but Brigitte had been more intrigued by his description of the crown jewels, including bucketfuls of emeralds, rubies, sapphires, diamonds and pearls, piled up in glass cases in a bank basement open to the public. It had made Brigitte's eyes glitter. "We must take a look someday," she had told Jim. "That kind of thing is vanishing from the world."

On the other hand, Brigitte occasionally delivered sermons about how that kind of thing should vanish from the world. Somewhere in her past she had picked up a spate of left-wing rhetoric, and when she got on her radical soapbox she could sound like a sustaining member of the Baader-Meinhof gang. It made no sense, and Jim had decided long ago not to take it seriously. Brigitte herself seemed unaware of the incongruity of her declama-

11

tions on those—fortunately rare—occasions and the manner in which she lived.

She was ready to launch on a tirade now. Jim had explained what it would mean to the company in Mainz, and to his own career, if the Iranian deal could really be put together. She had listened, but then her mind had suddenly veered off in another direction.

"That place needs a revolution, not helicopters," she pronounced.

She was pouring after-dinner mocha into the small, very thin maroon cups with a golden crest that she had brought from home shortly after they were married. Inattentive to her task, she spilled the coffee over the rim of the cup, making messy splotches on the embroidered linen tablecloth. Jim took the pot from her and filled the second cup himself. "The trouble with revolutions," he said, "is that you never know which way they'll go. They can leave people better off if they're rational and humane. They can leave people worse off if they're irrational and doctrinaire. In Iran I wouldn't want to bet how a revolution will come out." He shrugged and set the coffeepot between them. "Anyhow, everybody needs helicopters."

She stared at the stains she had made. Her eyes were wide and remote. "Why?" she demanded.

He put down the cup he was about to bring to his lips. "Why?" he echoed. "I've been telling you about it for four years, for God's sake."

"Tell me again. There are times I really don't know what I'm doing here."

Jim had never been able to fathom just how Brigitte's mind worked. It seemed to dart from gay frivolity to murky somberness, from intense, almost impregnable, self-absorption to brief but passionate concern with all mankind. When they talked, he never knew which Brigitte he would encounter; and what she said did not necessarily connect with why she was saying it. The changes and mysteries of Brigitte used to fascinate him, but increasingly he found them merely puzzling and sometimes disconcerting.

"Look," he said reasonably. "You take a helicopter to the

airport every time you catch a plane. A copter carries movies, magazines, liquor and who knows what else to your Italian friends who're putting up that petrochemical plant in the bush of Nigeria. Unfortunately those are not Copter GmbH craft. I only wish they were. And I know of copters, our copters, that fly blood plasma and penicillin to some godforsaken outer island of Indonesia." His voice softened. "In Indonesia our copters even deliver the pill!"

"Your copters deliver the pill?" Brigitte was the only person Jim knew who could manage to sound interrogatory and helpless at the same time.

"The Indonesian government," he said calmly, "believes in birth control. Rightly so, in my opinion. It also believes in giving critical students a tough time. Wrongly, in my opinion. But we don't live in a perfect world, Brigitte. We don't always get what we want. There are even times when it's better for us not to get what we want."

"Is that why you decided to saddle me with that revolting boss of yours for dinner?" she flared.

He had picked up his coffee once more and was about to savor the hot strong liquid Brigitte brewed so well. The venom in her voice startled him. He held the cup still in mid-air. "Ken may not be the most polished of men, but he is competent and kind and he taught me just about everything I know."

The thought of anyone she knew being beholden to Ken Ward seemed to drive her into a rage. "He's a bore and a boor," she exploded. "He spears his peas and he can't talk about anything except helicopters. And you're getting to be just like him."

Jim's fingers gripped the fragile handle of the cup so hard that it splintered and the cup crashed on the table in front of him. He paid no attention. "You seem to have no problem with the kind of life those helicopters provide." He was going to say, "for you." At the last second he changed his mind. "For us."

A flush suffused her face and turned the pale cream cheeks the color of a tea rose. How lovely she is, he thought. His heart expanded and pushed against his chest. But he said nothing. Nor did she. Minutes passed in silence. The house was empty and

13

still. An idea flashed through her mind. It's pregnant, this silence between us, and that's what he is talking about. The pregnancy. She felt the blood leave her face, course down her body, to the concave stomach in her close-fitting custom-tailored jeans. When he said, "You don't always get what you want," he was talking about the child we didn't have. The child he wanted and I did not. Is he hinting now that I was right? Why? But I can't ask him that, because we don't talk about it. There are a lot of things we don't talk about anymore.

The fight about the pregnancy had been their first real battle. Brigitte had come home late and drunk from Bonn, where the family gynecologist had told her with a congratulatory smirk that the test—"the rabbit test," he had added jocularly—was positive and that she was indeed pregnant.

She had exploded at the astonished doctor.

"Thank you very much, but I'm not a rabbit."

She had stalked out, her head held high, but then had searched desperately for the nearest bar and spent the next three hours thinking and drinking.

That she got home at all had been a miracle. She had been much too drunk to drive. But people saw the tall beautiful blonde in the sky blue Porsche weaving along the Autobahn, and gave way. Fortunately, it had been well past the rush hour, and traffic had been relatively light.

Jim had laid out supper when she arrived. His kind of supper: a big plate of cold cuts and two mugs of beer. It made her retch. In a drunk, broken voice, she had screamed at him, "Won't you ever learn to eat like a civilized person?"

The scream froze him. His arms, which he had held out to her, fell to his side. His mouth had tightened into a thin line. "What the hell is the matter with you?" he had asked coldly.

"I'm pregnant."

He hadn't believed her at first. "I thought you were on the pill."

"I am. I was. I don't know what happened. Perhaps those damn things aren't fail-safe after all. Perhaps I forgot to take them a couple of days."

14

Being with you, she had thought, makes me forget a great many things.

His mouth had softened, and his voice had become husky and tender. "I'm glad they aren't fail-safe, darling. I'm glad for us. But why did you get drunk all by yourself? We could have opened a bottle of champagne for the three of us. Too much alcohol isn't good for you now, or for the baby."

For a moment she had stared at him in disbelief. What gets into them, she had wondered, even the best of them? They think they're going to be fathers and suddenly they own you, body and soul. When they are nice, they get solicitous. When they're not nice, they get brutal. In either case you've stopped being a person and become a property. An investment.

"You can stop worrying about the baby," she had said, "right now. There will be no baby. I don't want one. I am not a brood mare. Hitler is dead, even if you and some other people haven't quite noticed. I have other things to do with my life than produce Aryan supermen, big, blond and beautiful as this one would undoubtedly be."

His eyes had gone sea blue, the way they did only when he felt deeply. There had been pain in his voice when he spoke, and it had made her shiver.

"Brigitte," he had said, "we won't have the child if you don't want it. There are good safe clinics in London that can take of it for you."

"For us."

"No, Brigitte. For you."

That had been two years ago, and he had never mentioned the subject again. Nor, she knew, made peace with the decision.

She looked at her hands and saw only a blur. "I'll clear the table." The safe, sane neutral chores of every day. So reassuring. So exasperating.

He rose with her. "I'll help."

They moved through their nightly routine without speaking. He handed her the dishes. She rinsed them and stacked them in the washer. She soaped the wine glasses and held them under the tap. He dried them. She tossed the broken coffee cup into

15

the trash can, the unblemished saucer after it. He followed her movements with his eyes but made no comment.

"It's useful having family china," she said, "the way we go through it." She had intended to sound uncaring, diversionary. It did not work.

"Yes," he retorted tensely. "We do dispose of china in peculiar ways." The last batch, he thought, was all yours. You smashed a complete setting—soup plate, dinner plate, bread-and-butter plate, dessert dish—neatly stacked, the way I always hand it to you. You raised your arms and crashed the lot into the sink. Götterdämmerung in the kitchen. Impressive, but weird. And for what? Because I didn't agree with your intemperate condemnation of the *Fidelio* production by Wagner's great-grandson.

"I know what you're thinking," she said.

"Do you?"

"You're pretty good on the guilt stuff, Jim. Virtuous James. Erratic Brigitte. James just crunched a little cup. Brigitte broke a whole stack of dishes."

Why, he wondered, does everybody in this country call me James when they want to hit me over the head? Nobody in the States ever did that. "That's right," he said coolly.

"It's my set, you know."

"That's true too."

"And you were wrong about that pretentious circus Gottfried Wagner staged, twisting Beethoven to suit his personal prejudices."

"I happen to share his prejudices. I don't think the fight for freedom is over. Certainly not here. Probably not anywhere. That's all he was trying to say. I thought he said it effectively."

"But he had to tamper with Beethoven to say it."

"For God's sake, Brigitte, let's not start that again. Beethoven isn't sacrosanct. He was a great musician, not a divine monument. Life and change do go on."

"Are you telling me . . ." She caught her breath and did not finish the sentence.

"No," he said wearily. "I'm not telling you anything. Not again."

16

The whole thing was nuts the first time, he thought. I don't need a repeat. Fighting over an opera production as if it were a matter of life and death. And fighting over life and death as if it were an opera production, he added bitterly. But of course that *Fidelio* fight wasn't about the opera at all. Not really. It was about ourselves and our values. And four years—four years and two months—of marriage have made miserably clear that we don't share many ideas of right and wrong, desirable and undesirable. Erroneous on the last count. She is still the most desirable woman I have ever known. Or, I suspect, ever will know.

He looked up from the glass, which he had been twirling slowly and wiping diligently for well over a minute. She was bent over the sink. Her trim buttocks curved against the jeans. From the slender waist, her back swept up and out to the sexiest shoulders he had ever seen. They were broad and sloping, carved like a Greek statue, but silken soft to the touch.

She turned and reached for a sponge to sop up the water that had dripped on the counter. As she stretched, her full breasts tilted up, her nipples pushed against the white see-through shirt. Nipples he knew to be rose-colored, shading into vanilla, delicious to the lips when soft, delectable on the tongue, dizzying as they hardened between the edges of his teeth.

"Brigitte," he said, his voice thick.

She twisted to look at him. Her eyes became opaque. She took the glass and towel from his hands and placed them on the counter. "Jim. Why . . ."

Her arms fastened around his neck. Her mouth tilted up. Her body pushed against his. "Let's share what we can."

Desperation edged her voice. He felt it too. It hardened him, gave a crystal luster to her straining body as they clung to each other seconds later in the round Hollywood bed that still made him feel giddy, as if he were on a carousel. His head spun as he covered her with his body, drove into her, sank his teeth into her shoulders. They lost themselves in their hunger to fuse, to be at one with each other, at peace with the world.

"You were wrong," she murmured afterward, her head resting on his chest.

17

He stroked the golden hair, cut short like a boy's. "About what?"

She laughed. "We don't, and I quote, live in a perfect world."

He sighed. "We could."

She lifted her head and looked up at him. "We do."

Minutes later her regular breathing told him she was asleep. She had a gift for sleep. She could be distraught with misery, driven with passion, consumed with anger; but when the time came to sleep, she could shuck off everything like a husk, stretch out her hands under the pillow above her head and be asleep in seconds. Her face in sleep was enchanting: the heart-shaped bones that led to the rounded chin with the tiny dimple that showed only when she was completely at ease or at rest (during the day the chin was usually pushed forward—Brigitte strode rather than walked—and the dimple vanished); the Cupid's bow mouth with an upward curl at the edges; the clear broad brow; the exquisite nose that trembled as she breathed; the fluttering lashes. She looked as if she were humming an inner tune. She had told him that quite often her dreams were filled with music: the music of water and wind, of trees and flowers, of psalters and piccolos.

He knew this to be true. The first time they had made love, he woke in the early hours of the morning to the strains of Schubert's Forellenquintett. He had thought at first that they had forgotten to turn off her stereo set, but when he had looked, the set was dark and silent. A late-owl neighbor, he had speculated sleepily, and then had realized where the music came from. Brigitte, stretched out next to him, was humming in her sleep. He had never been so charmed.

The evening that led to the enchantment of that first night had begun inauspiciously. Max had insisted that they put in an appearance at a cocktail party at the Saudi Arabian embassy in Bonn. Jim had had no desire to go. He had arrived in Mainz only a couple of months earlier and was putting in seventy-hour and eighty-hour weeks to take hold as quickly and completely as possible of the first assignment in his career where the buck unarguably stopped with him. He had begrudged the time and the effort for what had seemed to him an unnecessary diversion. He had never been fond of cocktail parties. As far as he was concerned, attending them was more like going to the zoo than engaging in human intercourse, and that Saudi party was likely to be worse than most. To begin with, there would be nothing to drink. Officially, the Saudis abjured alcohol. There would be no ladies among the hosts. The Saudis kept their women in purdah, even in Bonn. There would probably be no music either, just unrelieved mandatory and meaningless cocktail chatter.

Max had not only insisted, but insisted for what Jim considered the most irritating of reasons: "Everybody will be there."

"Who the devil is everybody?"

Max had looked at him levelly, blinked twice and pronounced, "In my lexicon, everybody is anybody who can buy helicopters."

Jim had been in no position to argue. Being so new a Generaldirektor, and still having so much to learn, he could not afford to discourage any eager beavers on his team.

At first the party had been as trying as he had expected: brittle politesse, cautious gossip, a reception line of men only, no liquor unless you knew the code. Fortunately Max did. He requested "a glass of the special milk, please." That turned out to be milk with a stiff shot of brandy in it. A revolting combination, Jim had concluded; but beggars can't be choosers, not at the Saudi Arabian embassy in Bonn.

Like everyone else, he had let his eyes roam discreetly until they had lighted on Brigitte. Brigitte: tall, casually voluptuous in an emerald silk sheath, and obviously bored.

They had homed in on each other like long-lost siblings. Within the next half hour three persons at the party had asked them whether they were brother and sister. To one of the young Saudis, who had made clear that he had ideas of his own about how Brigitte should spend the rest of the evening, she had said solemnly, "This is my brother. He promised our father that we would be home early."

The Saudi princeling had melted away, and Jim had grinned at Brigitte. "I don't know about getting home early, but I wouldn't mind leaving early."

19

When they were out of the door—it was a raw evening in March—Jim had suggested dinner, but Brigitte shook her head.

"Let's go dancing instead. All those languid eyes and somnolent rumps make me feel like wiggling to a hot beat. I know a club where they play good rock. Lively and not too loud. You can talk there too, if you shout a little. And the food is almost edible."

It had been difficult to talk, and they had eaten little. But they had danced a lot; and from the moment they began to move with the music, two feet apart but their eyes lost in each other, they knew they would make love that night. They also knew that something important had happened in their lives, something they did not want to let go.

They had not touched until they left the discotheque to walk to Brigitte's apartment. They had walked with their arms around each other through sleepy, respectable Bonn. Like two teen-agers, they had stopped at every traffic light to kiss. It was cold, but Jim had found himself wishing that Bonn were not just a decorous little capital on the Rhine, but a throbbing big city like New York, with lots of traffic lights and a higher probability of these lights coming up red.

Later he decided that there had been no need to wish anything that night. He never could recall how they got up the four flights of stairs that led to Brigitte's apartment—all teak and white leather, nestled under a gabled roof—or how they shed their clothes the moment the door shut behind them. What he did remember was how simple it had been, how irresistible. Inevitable, Brigitte had said when they talked about it the following morning. Her face had been soft, a little smudged with satiety and fatigue, but her eyes had been wide with wonder. He did not know what his face had registered, but knew he agreed with her. Brigitte and he together were inevitable and wonderful.

What followed was the most glorious spring of his life, and the lushest summer. Everyone—Brigitte's friends, his staff to the extent to which they thought it prudent to make the new boss's private life their business—had said they were inseparable. Indeed they had been. Not during the day—the job was too demanding to allow it—but at night. Every night.

There had been times when Jim felt that they spent an uncon-scionable amount of time at parties. He had not argued, though. Society was as integral a part of Brigitte's world as The Copter Company was of his. For him too the social whirl had been heady in its way. They had been Bonn's couple of the year that spring and summer of 1974.

Even Brigitte had been impressed by the way everyone fussed over them. Too impressed. Many nights they did not get to her apartment until two o'clock in the morning, and in those days he had to be back at the plant at seven. He did not sleep much that spring.

But, he decided, as he had many times before, what a way to run short on sleep!

He closed his eyes, stretched and let the sweet memory flood his veins. It left a taste of honey in his mouth. He felt like licking his fingertips.

That honey-sweet feeling had never changed and had become more intense as spring turned into summer and the Rhine, reflect-ing the rich foliage of trees along its banks, turned a deep bottle green.

In a way it was the river that had prompted their decision to get married. At least it had seemed so at the time.

Four months after they met, four months exactly after the boring Saudi party that had turned into such a delight, they had accepted an invitation to a masked ball, which the society pages had touted as the last and most glamorous event of the season. Schloss Rossheim, one of the oldest, proudest castles overlooking the Rhine, had been the setting, and the Middle Ages had been the ball's theme. The hosts had made clear that in their imagina-tion the period was not a dark age, but a time of knights and damsels in silk and laces, velvet and brocade, feasting at groaning boards lit by tall tapers, their beautiful faces reflected in silver goblets brimming with ruby-red wine.

Brigitte and Jim had invented their own theme to merge into this larger one. They had gone to the ball dressed as a line from a medieval poem: *Es waren zwei Königskinder, die hatten einander so lieb.*—Two children of kings there were who loved each other dearly.

21

They did love each other dearly. That night, to the consternation and envy of their hosts, they had danced only with each other. When the hookahs arrived with their chafed bronze bases decorated with the sensuous curves and curlicues of Arabic script, they had passed them up. They had no need for hashish. Later still, when couples had become foursomes, sixsomes, eightsomes, and had lost themselves in the castle's innumerable bedchambers, Jim and Brigitte had wandered off by themselves and found a room in the tower with tall narrow windows that looked out on the river.

The room had held a big oaken bed covered in heavy linen sheets worn smooth and soft with age, a damask bedspread filled with eiderdown, and a canopy with a coat of arms and golden tassels. They had laughed at the unicorn in the crest. "We can do better than that," Brigitte had murmured, her lips parted, luscious and very moist.

Dawn, laden with summer smells, had come early, too early for Jim and Brigitte, who wanted more of each other alone.

He had suggested that they move to his house. They could still see the river from there, he had coaxed. But Brigitte had insisted they go to her flat. When he had asked her why, she said, "I prefer my territory."

"We can make the house your territory," he had responded.

She had lain still for a while, her arms folded under her head, her beautiful breasts quivering, her eyes open, fixed on the canopy's crest. It had seemed an eternity before she had turned to him and said gently, "Our territory."

They were married the following Sunday.

But did it ever get to be our territory? he wondered. There had been moments when it seemed so; and days, weeks, months, when it did not.

They had talked about it during the first year of their marriage.

"We approach life in such different ways," Brigitte had said.

"And head in different directions," he had replied. "I believe in the future and want a share in shaping it. You're dedicated to cutting loose from the past. But you're riveted to it in a way and with a passion that I don't understand. I want to help you break those chains, but don't seem to be able to do it."

She had become sad and nodded assent, but said nothing. There was nothing to say.

He woke late, to a mélange of sounds: the chugging of barges on the river, muted and haunting up on the hill; Brigitte whistling; a closet door being pulled open; the snapping of a suitcase.

He opened his eyes. Brigitte, in jeans, a pale blue batiste shirt and a burgundy suede coat, stood gazing at him, travel case in hand.

He shook his head to make certain he was awake and sat up. "Where are you off to?"

Her mouth pulled down, creating two lines that curved toward the chin. The chin drooped. The lower half of her face looked crestfallen, but her eyes had a mischievous sparkle.

"I'm going to Italy. Armando Guido-Contini's villa in Capri. I can use it whether he's there or not. It's getting a bit chilly for Capri, but"—she tossed back the short blond shag falling over her forehead—"we don't live in a perfect world, do we? Not all the time, anyhow."

"When will you be back?"

She shrugged. "I don't know. I thought I should leave for a while. Give both of us time to think. Time and space."

His throat went dry. He would miss her badly, coming home to an empty house, an empty bed. Then he took a deep breath and felt a sudden lightness invade his head. Relief? Freedom? He leaned forward, bent his knees, laced his fingers on his shins and pulled. His muscles stretched. His mind cleared.

"That sounds like a sensible idea," he said. "Be—" He stopped short.

Once, early in their marriage, he had said casually, affectionately, "Be good," when Brigitte was about to leave for a couple of days to visit her father. Instead of the farewell hug he had expected, she had blazed in outrage: "You're not a clergyman,

23

Jim, and I don't need moral counsel. If you don't trust me, we should get a divorce."

He had looked at her aghast and never used the innocuous phrase again.

"Take care of yourself," he said.

She smiled. The down-curves in her face had disappeared. The smile was radiant. "I will."

Yes, he thought. You will.

She blew him a kiss. "Ciao," she called. The door closed behind her.

A half hour later he gunned his black Mercedes down the hill. As he took the turn that brought into sight the installations of Copter GmbH, the administration building caught his eye. Three flags fluttered from the roof. As usual, Copter GmbH flew the banner of West Germany and the Stars and Stripes but completing the trio today were the red, white and green colors of Iran. It was the custom of the company to run up the flag of any important foreign guest who came to call. The idea had been Max's. Jim thought it crude, but had discovered that visitors liked it. It was the company's version of rolling out a red carpet. It made callers from abroad feel appreciated.

The Iranian flag over Copter GmbH at this hour of the morning clearly carried a message. For his own reasons—mysterious, nefarious or both—Max had given orders the previous day that the flag not be run up when the Iranians arrived. Jim had learned not to question Max's judgment in such subtleties. Max had a sixth sense for seduction, pressure and the most effective combination of the two.

Miss Kestenmeier answered Jim's "good morning" with a warning look and a thumb pointed toward the door of his office.

"Mr. Feld," she said. There was a world of disapproval in her voice.

Max was indeed a sorry sight. He drooped in a corner of Jim's sofa, propped up by a pillow he had either borrowed or more likely purloined from Miss Kestenmeier, who kept it in her emergency drawer, which also held Band-Aids, iodine, a sewing kit, a pair of galoshes and a plastic rain cape that folded into a small transparent envelope. Max's eyes were shut and had dark blue circles beneath them, giving him the appearance of a cobra. His hair, usually neatly brushed back, fell over his eyebrows. He badly needed a shave.

But Max's looks could be deceiving. He was wide awake the second he felt Jim's presence. He sat up and patted the seat of the sofa. "Hi, Jim," he said. "Sit down."

That was a presumptuous gesture even for Max. A note of triumph, Jim thought. It had better be. He sat down facing his disheveled marketing manager.

"Jim," Max said sweetly. "We have it."

Max had sung in church when he was a boy and until he was twelve had had a lovely soprano voice. It changed into a resonant tenor when he grew up, but on special occasions he could recapture some of that pure, sweet soprano and its accompanying choirboy face. This was one of those occasions. Even Jim was impressed by the transformation. Cobra to choirboy in two seconds. Amazing.

"Okay, Max," he said. "Start at the beginning."

Max moved his head slowly from side to side and groaned. "Not at the beginning, Jim. The system rebels at the notion. Even my system. In short, I wined them, dined them, got them laid in all conceivable variations, even arranged for them to win big—reasonably big—at the casino. At four o'clock this morning they were feeling no pain. They had trouble holding a pen, though. I'm not sure they would recognize their signatures."

"On a purchase contract?"

Max looked wounded. "Jim, this is not America. On a memorandum of understanding for a purchase contract. Which I just happened to have had in my pocket."

Jim grinned appreciatively. "I bet. They signed as drafted?"

A note of caution crept into Max's voice. "With some amendments."

Jim's mouth became a thin line, very straight. "Okay. Let's have it. Chapter and verse."

Max plunged. "Chapter One. Over the next five years we

supply the Iranian defense forces with five hundred helicopters, produced and delivered by Copter GmbH. Payable in Deutsch-marks.

"Chapter Two. We overinvoice by five percent and deposit the difference in General Yeganeh's account at Crédit Suisse in Zurich.

"Chapter Three. We pay our Iranian agent, Taher Rezvani, the customary commission, but deposit half of it in his numbered account in Basel.

"Chapter Four. You go to Teheran as soon as they finish the paperwork at their end to sign the final contract.

"Chapter Five. We start delivery by mid-1979.

"Chapter Six. The Shahansha gets the best damn helicopters to be had on this planet.

"Chapter Seven. Copter GmbH has the prettiest bottom line anyone has ever seen.

"Chapter Eight. The Copter Company, New York, NY, loves us for ever and ever. Amen.

"Chapter Nine. It gives expression to this affection by present-ing us with a sizable stack of pretty green and white paper, en-graved with portraits of Benjamin Franklin."

He winked. "I'll even take my bonus in dollars, Jim. Chapter Ten. Max Feld celebrates carnival 1979 in Rio de Janeiro." He leaned back in his corner looking beatific. "Which he richly de-serves," he muttered.

Jim felt his temples throb and a cold sweat at the back of his neck. Alternating currents, he thought. Better make sure the fuse is in good shape.

"It's a terrific deal, Max," he said, "and you have my blessing to go to Rio dressed as a belly dancer as soon as all the loose ends are safely tied up. But—"

Max jerked forward. The cobra look had returned. "But what?"

"Chapters Two and Three trouble me. I don't believe they are necessary. I suspect they're illegal." He tried to sound objec-tive and seasoned.

Max attempted to match the tone. "They're *not* illegal, Jim.

Depositing half of the Rezvani commission in Switzerland is simply a commercial accommodation. It's Rezvani's money. If he asked us to put it in a chocolate easter egg tied with a pink ribbon, he would be within his rights."

"But isn't he evading Iranian exchange regulations? And tax laws?"

Max tried to sit up ramrod straight. "I didn't know, Jim, that we doubled as law enforcement officers for the Shah," he said nastily. "Nothing in my job description lends itself to that interpretation."

Jim glared. "There are times, Max, when your sense of humor doesn't do much for me. I take it that, by your reasoning, the overinvoicing for the general is also merely a commercial accommodation, *comme il faut.*"

Max's eyes narrowed to slits. "Correct."

"And Rezvani gets five percent in Teheran and five percent in Basel."

"Correct."

"Have you considered that the rather large chunk of change involved in all these commercial accommodations will make those copters horrendously expensive unless we take a serious cut in our profit margin? I assume you are not recommending that."

Max looked astonished, then baleful. "Of course not," he said reassuringly. "I've built all contingencies into the price, and the Shah can afford it. Our competitors would need the same markup. That's how business is done in Iran."

Jim felt a stab of pain in his head. That was what Ken had said about the sales he had made, and planned to make, through his friend in Abu Dhabi. That's why The Copter Company could offer a sweetheart of a deal to an intermediary who could get it out from under the Foreign Corrupt Practices Act. But that was Ken's baby. He had his own show to run.

"You really have thought of all the angles, haven't you, Max? But tell me, how do you propose we book these accommodations? I have no intention of letting anyone—I repeat, Max, anyone—tamper with our accounting systems or our financial controls. I can't afford to. We can't afford to."

Max lowered his eyes and looked at his pudgy hands, which he had cradled in his lap, fingers interlaced. He was trying to make up his mind. Is he faking again, this Mr. Clean of ours, putting on that act of innocence and virtue? Or does he mean it? I wish I knew. But you never do with Americans. On the one hand, they spread millions of dollars around the world bribing everyone in sight, not caring a whit whether they corrupt governments and corrode societies; on the other hand, they make speeches in their Congress reeking of fake morality and pass laws they don't really mean to enforce and couldn't enforce even if they wanted to. He dismissed the quandary for the present. Sooner or later reality would produce the answer.

"There's no need to tamper with anything, Jim. We have a chief financial officer who knows how to deal with such expenses. Günther Westphal gets along very well with the tax authorities."

Jim's stomach cramped. Had this kind of stuff been going on right under his nose without his ever knowing anything about it? But it couldn't have. He really kept his finger on the pulse of this organization. If anything, too much so. How come, then . . .

Max must have read his mind. "Westphal isn't doing anything illegal, or even unusual. German tax authorities do not wear blinders. They know that business practices are not the same everywhere. They also know that Germany must export to prosper."

Jim looked at Max. "So?"

"So, there is a rubric of perfectly legitimate business expenses known as 'Sonderspesen,' extraordinary expenses. A good description too. It covers such items as our general's not so little Swiss nest egg as well as Rezvani's commission, wherever it's paid. Sonderspesen are legal and deductible. There is no reason whatever why Westphal should not carry them on our books."

That's right, Jim recalled. He had seen Sonderspesen on the books and okayed them. But those had been reasonable amounts, another accounting technique for booking travel, entertainment and the customary executive perks. This Iranian deal involved millions. That was a different kettle of fish. Or was it?

28

Max was studying him. "Magnitude and principle," he said, "are not tied to each other by an umbilical cord. There's no integral relationship between some extra zeros and morality."

"You're being abstruse, Max."

"Perhaps. It's the kind of thing I think about while I wait for deer. Sun and leaves make the mind sway. Nevertheless—"

"Nevertheless," Jim interrupted, "if you indulge the general's whims and start playing the game the Iranian way, where do you stop? How do you know, for instance, that your own people won't get into the honey pot? Or at least want to get into it? And what does that do to the reliability of your staff? Or its morale?"

Max nodded. "That's right, Jim. Those are important questions. Real risks. There's no telling just what this deal will bring in its wake. I can see it churning the waters in many ways, making all kinds of waves: some attractive to contemplate, others dangerous to navigate. But then that's what this business is all about, isn't it? That's what you pay me for—to run my department successfully and control it effectively."

Right, Jim conceded. That's what being a manager was all about, and Max was a good one. It would be stupid to interfere with him. Stupid and uncalled for.

Max was heaving himself out of the sofa. When he stood, he was unsteady on his feet. The circles under his eyes had turned from blue to nearly black. It took an effort for him to speak. "I've already been in touch with Rezvani. He's following up. As soon as I hear from him, I'll let you know. At that time I think you should take the next plane to Teheran." His voice had turned very soft, but this time it was not the sweet soprano of the choirboy. It was the voice of the hunter who kept still for hours, his eyes fixed on the clearing where sooner or later the deer would appear.

"Reaching for the brass ring," Max said, "is not a game for children. Surely we all know that."

2

Jim's first encounter with Taher Rezvani was a pleasant surprise. He had expected Rezvani to be oily, swarthy and smooth. Rezvani was indeed swarthy, but heavy-set and solid, and gave the impression of a rock with sharp prominent ridges. His face was massive and seemed to belong on a monument rather than a man. The lips were large and fleshy and the nose enormous— a commanding peak setting off the narrow plain of his forehead and the two hills of his dark bushy eyebrows arching over wrinkled lids that were perennially lowered to shade the orbs of his eyes. His hair stood up in gray-white bristles, in a crew cut that badly needed a trim. His chin and the lower part of his cheeks were blue-black and looked as if his razor blade should have been changed three days ago. Large glasses with broad black rims perched on his nose. The spectacles looked light and small in a face that exuded a paternal power, the rugged charisma of a tribal chief. There was no mistaking the fact that Taher Rezvani was a magnetic man.

Rezvani's office was a comparable surprise. It bore a strong resemblance to Jim's own, a resemblance explained by the fact that Rezvani used the same German office supply house that Copter GmbH had employed in furnishing its headquarters. There were other parallels. Rezvani conducted his affairs, as did Jim, not from an office building in the center of the city but from a headquarters wing set in the middle of a sprawling industrial installation halfway between the airport and Teheran.

But there were differences as well. Jim's office at Copter GmbH had a carefully finished appearance. Rezvani's quarters looked as if everything in them and around them was still in the making. White dust speckled the leather furniture. The noise of construction rattled the panes. The view from the window was of bags of cement piled incongruously around a fountain, its delicate sprays playing in the frosty blue-white October air.

Dealing with Rezvani, Jim discovered within seconds, was congenial. When Jim had first walked into the office, Rezvani had given him an unabashed once-over and apparently had approved of what he saw. He had stuck out a large hand alive with blue-black fuzz and wrapped it around Jim's long cool fingers. "Welcome," he had said. That was all; but it sounded as if he meant it.

Talking business, they covered ground quickly. Delivery of 500 helicopters from the Mainz facility would be spread over two years. Jim knew that schedule would strain Copter GmbH's capacity, but it would also demonstrate what the company he ran could do.

Next Jim and Rezvani worked out the details of supplying spare parts and the training facilities that would be required for Iranian maintenance personnel. Some Iranian mechanics would have to be sent to Germany for on-site instruction. That raised language problems. Copter GmbH would set up an intensive language laboratory in Mainz. They agreed that Copter GmbH would also send a senior technician to establish maintenance facilities in Iran and supervise these facilities for the start-up period and that Jim would come to Iran himself at least once a year to make certain everything was working out as planned. When Jim promised his own presence, Rezvani looked at him speculatively. "That," he said, "is a very good idea. A very interesting idea. We will endeavor to make it worth your while."

Jim allowed himself to smile. He did not understand why Rezvani would think his appearance in Teheran once a year an interesting idea. It was, after all, a commitment to be expected from the managing director of a company making a very substantial sale. But he was not about to argue the point. Something in Rezvani's tone had indicated a warmth, a personal encouragement, that made Jim feel relaxed and made him conclude that now was as good a time as any to broach the troublesome aspects of this tempting deal.

"Right," he said. "May we proceed then to the commercial arrangements? I take it the terms stated in the memorandum of understanding are satisfactory to all concerned. I have only one problem and one question."

Rezvani moved his face from left to right and back again in an amiable gesture of agreement. "The problem," Jim said, "is the general. The five percent—"

Rezvani, who had slumped stolidly in his chair throughout their talk so far, almost shot out of his seat. With a curt wave of his hand he cut off Jim in the middle of his sentence, then laid a warning finger across his lips. He reached for a piece of paper, took a soft lead pencil from a copper container, silently scribbled a note and pushed it across the desk for Jim to read. When Jim had done so, Rezvani retrieved the paper, folded it and carefully pushed it deep into his breast pocket. The note had said, "We will talk about this at another time in another place."

The place Rezvani had had in mind was his home, the time later that evening. Jim arrived, as asked, at ten P.M. From the outside the house looked nondescript: another unattractive dun-colored Teheran building in a narrow alley off one of the city's main thoroughfares. Stepping through the door was a revelation. Inside, the Rezvani home was serene and beautiful, a magic amalgam of fantasy and comfort.

In the peaceful privacy of his living room Rezvani was quite willing to talk about the general. "General Yeganeh has his reasons. They are good reasons. Valiant reasons."

Do you have to be valiant to demand twenty-five million dollars to sign a purchase order for equipment your country needs? It was certainly a peculiar definition of valor. "I'm sure he does," Jim said diplomatically, "and I'd be interested to hear what the reasons are. But at The Copter Company we are not very comfortable with this kind of arrangement. I'm not. I don't like a payment of five percent off the top with no visible service rendered. And I'm particularly uncomfortable with covering this, uh, override, through overbilling. I really don't believe in doing business that way. It strikes me as unnecessarily complicated as well as risky."

Rezvani's eyes roamed to an indeterminate space in the far reaches of the room. "That is so," he said. "It is risky. For the general as well as for you. And me."

They were reclining on large cushions, their elbows propped on overstuffed bolsters. Rezvani had a hookah at his side from which he took an occasional meditative puff. The hookah's brass base glowed and the water in its glass throat gurgled softly.

The room had a high painted ceiling, and its walls and floor were covered with Persian carpets. No two were alike, and each had a pleasing pattern of jeweled colors. Four lamps of mellow brass, cut in elaborate designs, the interstices filled with colored glass that matched in richness and tone the hues of the carpets, hung from the ceiling. Sycamore screens crafted into open-work arabesques offered glimpses of an interior court from which heavy doors of sweet-smelling woods led to other rooms of the two-floor house. In the center of the court, goldfish swam lazily in a blue-tiled pool, flicking their salmon pink tails. Occasionally a firefly darted across the pool.

"Lights in camouflage," Rezvani said, watching a firefly weave its way from the pool to a spot above their heads, then take off again to the courtyard. "Nature has her ways. Subtle, intricate. We do well to emulate."

Was that an answer to his question about the general, Jim wondered. A Persian answer? It was difficult to demand anything in this profoundly peaceful room where concentration on a specific goal seemed inappropriate. His own voice sounded harsh to Jim against the harmony of the bubbling water pipe, the gentle splash of the goldfish in their pool. "What aspect of nature does the general emulate?" he asked.

Rezvani lifted the ivory mouthpiece of the hookah to his lips and drew on it twice, his eyelids lowered. Then he lifted them to their customary position halfway across his blue-veined eye-balls. "The general emulates fire. As he should. We were worshippers of fire before Islam embraced us. In truth, we still are. The fire of ambition, of glory. We play with it. We burn. We get burned."

Jim lowered his voice to a murmur. They were lying close to each other and the room was silent. He would be heard. "What are the general's ambitions?"

Rezvani allowed his somnolent glance to rest on the center medallion of a large rug covering the wall behind Jim's back. "The general is a patriot. He wants security and order for Iran."

Jim changed the position of his arm on the bolster to hold his head higher. "And why does the security of Iran require twenty-five million dollars in a numbered account in Switzerland to which only the general has access?"

Rezvani's hooded eyes had a pitying look. "You don't really know that, do you? You don't know who has access to that account. I might, for example." He lowered his eyelids and lifted them. "And I might not." He paused dramatically in the still room where one could hear the seconds steal away. Suddenly his voice picked up resonance. "The truth is that Iran is secure as long as the Shahansha is on the throne. What happens thereafter no one knows. A system has been devised for the succession, and it may work. It also may not. There are contending parties within the country and at our borders. All our borders. Land and sea: the rapacious Russians to the north; the vainglorious Saudis to the south; the militant Iraquis to the west; a fragile Pakistan to the east; the Afghans chafing at the bit of their frontier as they have throughout history; Kurds, Turkomans, Baluchis, Pathans, dreaming of independence, passionate, violent dreams.

"If something happens to the Shah, there may well be chaos. Two requisites are essential to contain chaos: guns and money. Twenty-five million dollars is nothing, a tiny nest egg." He snapped his index finger against his thumb, emitting a short sharp sound. Its echo ricocheted around the room. Rezvani listened. When the echo had died, he chuckled, a sound that came from deep within him and made his jowls shake. "I was thinking," he

34

said, "that Swiss bankers make very good mother hens. They preen and fluster, peck and straddle just like hens do. And, if you feed them carefully, they lay eggs. Golden eggs."

Jim smiled. It was an amusing analogy. It also made him wonder whether the other question he had on his mind was worth asking. Obviously Rezvani's insistence that half of his commission be paid into a numbered account in Basel was inspired by that nest-egg image. The Shah's demise would create serious dangers for men like Rezvani.

From the slit of white below his half-closed eyes Rezvani had been observing his guest. Jim appeared at ease, his lanky frame stretched out loosely on the plump cushions. It occurred to Rezvani that Jim looked more at home than any American he had ever brought to his house. He had not brought many. He could deal with them all right, but he did not like them very much. They were clumsy and cold. This one seemed different. He had a warmth to him and an agility of the heart that was pleasing.

"It was wise of you not to have asked the question," he said. "The answer is some of both. We are a large family and personal security is important to me. I am also an Iranian. A proud Iranian. Three thousand years of recorded history are in my blood, my mind, my imagination. We were great once. We can be great again. Our ancestors—Cyrus, Darius, Xerxes—inspired awe and admiration throughout the civilized world. I would like that to happen again. I have no objection to being a modern Cyrus myself, or even a Croesus in his service." His large lips loosened into an indulgent smile. He drew on his water pipe. The water swelled into bubbles. Under the colored light of the lamps, with their stained-glass bits, the ever-changing drops looked like soap bubbles.

Rezvani watched the bubbles dance in the bottle. He laid down the long drawing tube. It curled on the cushion beside him. "And then," he said, "there's always the tax collector. We negotiate tax payments here; at least we do in my tax bracket. It is a legacy from the days of empire. The Italians have the same legacy. Collecting tribute was always a diplomatic exercise, a fine balance between force and persuasion, requiring armies and ambassadors. Money that does not reach Teheran does not have to be negotiated with the tax collector. There is plenty to negotiate without it."

I bet there is, Jim thought. Rezvani must have dozens of balls in the air all over Iran and outside it. Behind this philosophic, paternal facade he's probably the smoothest, toughest operator I'm ever likely to meet. A matter of heritage and conviction. Like the Yankee traders that livened up Economics One in high school. Except that the Rezvanis of this world have been at it a lot longer. How far back was Cyrus? The millennium before Christ?

"When did Cyrus rule?" he asked. Something about Rezvani made him feel that there was no need to be methodical. Rezvani understood the leaps of the imagination. He was a devious man and perhaps a dangerous one, but he was also stimulating company.

Rezvani regarded Jim with brooding pleasure. "I would like you to do something for me," he said.

Jim shifted position. Instead of propping up his head with one elbow to face Rezvani, he supported himself on both arms, stretched out further and studied the painted ceiling: trellises of leaves and flowers in a fretwork of geometrics. "Yes?"

Rezvani was pleased. The young man was learning. His instincts were right. "I would like you to go to Persepolis. Pay tribute. Pay homage." He held up a hand to ward off the possibility of an awkward intrusion. "Not material tribute, tribute of the spirit. You will thank me in the end, whatever we decide to do or not do together."

Jim did not take his eyes off one particularly graceful arabesque on the ceiling. It was an intertwining of long lines softly curved at the end, like interlocked boomerangs, colored sienna red and rain-washed sky blue. So Rezvani wanted him to go to Persepolis. It was part of his price for the order from Mainz. As prices went, this one was a pleasure. Might be a pleasure. But why did Rezvani want him to go?

Jim let his elbows collapse so they formed an extended triangle under his head. His eyes remained on the ceiling. "I have to go to Isfahan anyhow," he said, "to see Colonel Sharif about

36

additional spare parts for the helicopters we delivered from New York last year. Apparently he needs more than the contract called for. We might be able to supply them from Mainz. Can I combine the two journeys?"

Rezvani pushed out his lower lip. It looked like half of a dried-out fountain, a reddish mud color, moist, ready to catch something, someone. Me, Jim thought, in some way.

"You can," Rezvani said. "It's perhaps not the best way to encounter Darius the Great, or to do business with Colonel Sharif. On second thought, it well may be." He measured Jim's recumbent figure. "Persepolis will reward you with many gifts."

Jim took his eyes off the ceiling and turned his head to look at his host. Rezvani had sat up, his legs tucked under him, the mouthpiece resting between his enveloping lips. He was drawing deeply and appeared totally immersed in the act. As Jim watched, it occurred to him that Rezvani was looking for the genii in the bottle. He would find it too!

Rezvani laid down the tube. It made a small wet spot on his sapphire blue cushion. "When you get back," Rezvani said, "I shall have something waiting for you."

The Teheran airport for domestic flights was a shambles, packed with snaking queues of people, the overwhelming majority of them men, who either hissed and shouted at each other or embraced and stood together with their fingers interlocked. Arrival and departure time of aircraft was erratic—the announcement of a three-hour delay caused no more than a shrug from the affected passengers—and the tempers of the clerks at the ticket counters matched the schedule. The clerks were sweetly solicitous, punctiliously competent, nastily rude and totally haphazard within a matter of seconds. It was another manifestation of the rhythm of the place. They were part of it.

When Jim's plane took off two hours late, the aircraft's muted interior, the neutral colors of its upholstery and the even drone of its engines seemed to him an oasis of sanity and peace. A sloe-eyed stewardess with opulent curves offered tea and a sweet cake that smelled of cinnamon. He declined and closed his eyes.

When he opened them the plane was over the desert. Below were undulating waves of tawny sand that seemed to flow into the horizon. Not a tree, not a drop of water, not an animal, not a sign of human habitation; just yellow-brown desolation as far as the eye could see. Teheran, bursting at the seams with buildings, traffic and people, had held no hint of this silent expanse, this enormous nothing which gave way finally to small valleys dotted with desert-colored huts and then to green foothills. The mountains beyond looked as unyielding as the desert. Harsh, massive and deeply ridged, they reminded Jim of Rezvani's face.

When he landed in Shiraz, his first impression was, This must be another country. Blue sky, a bright sun, flowers everywhere: in a planted oval that greeted him as he stepped out of the airport gate, in the traffic islands along the highway, in the gardens of villas sparkling in the clear clean light.

The gardens of the Darius Hotel, an hour's drive from Shiraz airport, repeated the theme: a profusion of colors, a luminescent grace of light, sky and air. The hotel itself was somber, grandiose and empty. In the enormous lobby the royal family—the Shah, the Queen and the Crown Prince, all in full regalia—looked out of their heavy golden frames, stern and serene. There was no one to return their glance.

The reception clerk who finally appeared took a good ten minutes to examine and copy into a big book the particulars of Jim's passport. Jim could not decide whether this protracted procedure served some secret purpose or was the result of the clerk's having nothing else to do. He watched impassively as the clerk checked, dawdled and rechecked. At last the clerk dropped a key on the desk. "I keep the passport," he said, "until you leave."

Jim's room, well appointed and silent, looked out on more gardens. The flowers glowed like jewels in a strong afternoon sun.

The taxi that took him to the ruins of Persepolis squeaked and groaned and smelled of leaking gasoline. The upholstery was dirty and had blotches of grease. In startling contrast, the driver, a slim young man with almond-colored skin, dark silken hair and eyes that looked like moonstones, was immaculate. He put the car into gear and swerved out of the gardens and onto a smooth, carefully maintained macadam highway.

Persepolis leaped out of the air. They made a turn and there, suddenly, was the ancient city of the Persians, an awesome spectacle of gigantic columns, enormous gates, horses carved in stone ten times the size of the real animal. Everything about the ruins proclaimed power. The only human beings depicted on the carved stone showed men bearing tribute, presenting their gifts to an emperor, haughty and aloof, surrounded by functionaries who all looked alike and as if they knew their business. The line of tribute bearers was long. Jim began to count.

"Twenty-two," volunteered a guide with a high, sharp voice who had been slouching against a pillar. "Twenty-two nations were subject to Persia in the days of Cyrus the Great." A sly expression spread over the guide's face. "Perhaps they will be again," he added, slowly pulling his hands out of his pockets.

Jim had wandered around the ruins by himself for the better part of an hour. He had not asked for a guide and did not want one. But the man was not to be shaken. He beckoned Jim. "And then there was the motto of Darius. It was this: 'I do not want the strong to do wrong to the weak, or the weak to do wrong to the strong.'" The guide smirked. "The Shahansha has the same motto." He held out his hand in a demanding gesture. "There are also the tablets of Darius. They say, 'God protect us from foes, famine and falsehood.'" He shrugged, raised his eyes to the sky and pushed his hand under Jim's nose. "That is all, sir. You owe me three hundred and fifty rials."

Three hundred and fifty rials, Jim figured quickly, was five dollars, for a three-minute walk and two pieces of information he hadn't asked for. But perhaps they were worth it for the lesson they had taught him. He fished out four hundred-rial bills. The guide grabbed them without a word, turned and walked away.

For ten minutes more Jim meandered among the gigantic ruins, set ablaze now by the afterglow of an orange-red sun that had sunk into the western sky. He felt small and cold, lost in time, space, power and history. It came to him that this was probably what Rezvani had intended.

As he prepared to leave, his attention was caught by a clump of trees he had not noticed before. Set in their midst was a scattering of white buildings in the shape of tents. They looked intriguing. As he walked down the hill toward them, he remembered reading about the sumptuous party the Shah had given to celebrate the 2500th birthday of the Persian empire. He had invited his royal peers from Europe, Asia and Africa, and everyone of them had honored the invitation. He had floodlit Persepolis for his guests and housed them in tents that faced the site, tents of poured concrete, equipped with plumbing and bathroom fixtures of pure gold.

Before Jim could reach the first tent, he encountered a fence topped with barbed wire. Behind it three armed guards watched him as he approached the gate in the fence. They looked brutal, mean and dirty. Their uniforms were slovenly, a mess of baggy, unpressed trousers and filthy, crumpled shirts.

Jim gestured to the gate. "May I go in?" In response, one of the guards spat on the ground. The second guard took his gun off his shoulder and held it up, the muzzle trained on Jim. The third guard took a saliva-covered sunflower seed out of his mouth and flicked it in Jim's direction.

Jim edged back, facing the guards, until he reached the path that led away from the fence toward the foot of the ruins. His driver was waiting there, glaring at the soldiers and the abandoned royal enclosure behind them. "The Shah and his murderers," he hissed. "I hate them." He turned abruptly and began to walk toward the car. "I will take you to the tombs," he said when Jim caught up with him.

What tombs? Jim wanted to ask, but didn't. It was hard to tell in this place how people would react. He nodded assent.

The tombs turned out to be graves of three ancient Persians of glory and fame: Cyrus the Great, who in the sixth century B.C. conquered the Medes, defeated the Babylonians and collected tribute from Croesus of Lydia, the man with the proverbial golden touch. The second tomb was that of Darius, the First and also the Great, who a decade later divided the empire, unmanageable by then, into provinces. He tolerated the cultures and religions of all the subject nations in the provinces and tied them to the center by a system of taxation and organized commerce, moving over roads he had built and waterways he had ordered constructed. One of the waterways was a canal that connected the Nile to the Red Sea. The Greeks defeated Darius at Marathon. His son Xerxes, occupant of the third tomb, took up the battle in his turn and defeated the Spartans at Thermopylae. In the end, however, the Greeks overcame the Persians, and Xerxes returned home to find solace in his harem. Disgusted by this unseemly behavior, one of his soldiers murdered him.

The history had been related by the driver as he pointed a thin hand at gigantic tombs cut into the living rock a hundred yards above their heads. They had arrived at the tombs after a drive of some forty minutes, along what looked like the rim of a large plain. The plain ended suddenly at a small chain of harsh hills hugging the cemetery of Persian potentates who had ruled a large slice of the known world 2500 years ago. Now the moon fingered the mountain that held what was left of their bones.

They returned to the car in silence. Jim was awed and tired. The driver seemed agitated. The aging vehicle moved creakily into gear. "Looks like you ought to get yourself a new car," Jim said conversationally.

"I have one." The young man spoke as jerkily as he drove. "A Jaguar. It's a beauty."

"A Jaguar," Jim said in surprise. "How can you afford it? And why don't you use it?"

The driver looked at him sideways out of his strange pale blue eyes. "I can afford it," he said. "But I keep it for my personal use."

Jim swallowed. What next? he wondered. Out loud he said neutrally, "I see."

The driver suddenly stepped on the gas pedal and sent the car hurtling down the highway. "You don't see," he shouted in a high, keening voice. "I want independence for my people. Real

41

independence!" He whipped himself around and pointed to a silver chain from which an amulet dangled on his chest. It had a crescent and a scimitar. He had opened his shirt to reveal an undergarment of bright green. "I am a green shirt," he said proudly, "a Mujahedeen. I want an Islamic republic, a pure country governed by the sacred laws of the Koran. I hate the moral filth we have now."

The car had skidded to the edge of the highway, its dilapidated tires crunching against the road's narrow shoulder. The driver spun the wheel. They swiveled off the shoulder and almost tumbled back onto the highway. Jim caught his breath. The driver let out a sigh. It sounded like an animal in pain. "Meanwhile," he said, "I will drive my Jaguar. It will teach me to pounce when the time comes."

The Shah Abbas Hotel in Isfahan could have been the set of a Hollywood spectacular. There had been a historic Shah Abbas, who ruled Isfahan during its golden age in the sixteenth century, built graceful palaces and one of the most beautiful mosques in the world. He would have been appalled by the garish edifice named after him, crawling with tourists sporting many modes of dress and speaking a plethora of languages: German, English, French, Italian, Arabic.

Jim found himself a place at the bar next to a man about his own age who looked like an American. They fell into conversation almost immediately. The American was an engineer engaged in the construction of a new port on the Persian Gulf, "where it's 120 in the shade twelve months of the year and there's nothing except us, our gear, the sand and the sea. And I do mean nothing. It's kind of peaceful at first, but it gets wearing after a while." Lovingly, he savored the whiskey he had ordered. "I've got plenty of nothin' all right," he said with a grin, "but I guess nothin' isn't enough for me."

Two whiskeys later he was explaining to Jim that he and the other guys—American engineers, technicians and construction supervisors working on the port—were doing something now about their plenty of nothin' situation. They had leased a helicopter. It was painted silver and carried the legend *Rendez-vous* on its sides. The propeller blades had red hearts daubed on their tips.

"What kind of a copter?" Jim asked, intrigued.

"Copter Company G-Four. A real cute critter."

"Yes," Jim said, "I know it well."

"How come?"

"I work for The Copter Company."

"You do?" The engineer looked genuinely delighted. He stuck out his hand. "My name is Henry McIver. Hank. Sioux City, Iowa. I'm sure glad to meet you. That copter of yours is a life-saver."

Lifesaver? Did they use it to fly medical supplies to their construction camp? To fly out men suffering from heat prostration, heart attacks, nervous breakdowns brought on by this strange country and its unsettling ways? Or by the loneliness Hank had hinted at? But they wouldn't paint hearts on the copter's blades if that were the use they made of it. Unless they were being engineer-type funny about bleeding hearts. "Has it saved your life?" he quipped.

"Just about. We use it as a spotter."

"Spotting what?"

"Girls."

Jim shook his head. "It's getting a little noisy here. What did you say?"

A broad pleased grin brought out every line and dimple in Hank's deeply tanned, sun-dried face. "You heard me, friend. We use your G-Four to spot girls. That," he added solemnly, "is why we christened the critter *Rendez-vous.*"

"You'll have to explain that one," Jim said. "I'm just a farm boy from Pennsylvania myself."

"I bet." Hank eyed Jim's custom-tailored suit, the fine cotton shirt, the Sulka tie. He had a surveyor's appraising glance. "But I'll let you in on the secret anyhow. As long as you don't print it in the company news sheet, if you have one."

He signaled for another whiskey. When he had drained half of it with one long gulp, he said, "I told you about our plenty of nothin'. One night, we were sitting around counting our money and griping about our life when one of the guys announced that he was going to Isfahan the next day. We all come here once in a while just to see people and keep sane, but he was sounding mysterious about it. We practically had to bang his head against the wall of our Quonset hut before he coughed up. He had a cousin, a nifty girl, kinda crazy, who had set out with a bunch of equally loony kids from all over Western Europe, who were traveling by lorry—that's a truck to you and me—east to Austria and then south across the Balkans and Turkey, to Iran, Afghanistan and Nepal. In Nepal, a couple of them had dates to join an expedition to one of the lesser peaks of the Himalayas. The rest were going to sell their truck, their tents and their sleeping bags to some rich Sherpas and fly home. Home was Britain, Holland, Switzerland and France for most of them. But for this guy's cousin and a couple of others in that crazy caravan it was the good old USA. Isfahan, he told us, had a trailer park. The cousin's caravan was expected to check in there shortly.

"Wild, right? We didn't believe him at first either. Thought he'd gone off his rocker in the heat. Well, the guy took off and didn't come back for a week, but he was in fine fettle when he did show up. What he had told us was true, he reported, and some of the girls were mighty nice. The only problem was that he had to hang around for five days before the trucks arrived. You can't make time on that route the way you can on US One. Things happen. That bunch, for instance, was held up by bandits who took all their canned food, their blankets and their gasoline. Someone had to hike to the next stop and bully or bribe a man to help them out with new supplies. Two of them started walking and the rest just sat there, in the desert, freezing and hungry. That's just one for instance. There's also the matter of sand in the gear box. That can slow you up. I know." He finished his whiskey.

"Anyhow, the cousin said that folk like herself made this kind of trip all the time. One a month at least, was her estimate. And they all check in at that trailer park in Isfahan.

"We have a draftsman in our crew who draws pictures of

44

everything. That's how his mind works. He picked up a pencil and said, 'The problem, then, is how do we find out when these lovely creatures are about to hit Isfahan.' He drew a map of Iran with a wiggly line from the frontier to the south. 'That's mostly desert,' he said. 'One could easily spot a truck from the air. All it would take is maybe two flights a week. A copter would do it.'

"So you see," Hank concluded.

"No. Not quite. How did you get the copter?"

"Right. That was a bit of a problem. We wound up leasing it from Colonel Sharif. He also suggested we paint it silver so it wouldn't get mixed up with other aircraft under his command. He runs the air base right outside this town."

"I know," said Jim dryly. "I'm seeing him tomorrow."

For a second Hank looked worried. "Don't say anything to him about the *Rendez-vous*. I'm not sure she's covered by Air Force regulations, even Iranian Air Force regulations."

Jim smiled thinly. "Don't worry. I have my own problems. And the colonel isn't likely to raise the subject with me, is he?"

"I most sincerely doubt it. Although the rake-off he's getting on the deal is small by Iranian standards."

"Cash? Or access to the girls?"

Hank grinned. "Some of each. Access only in civvies. And we tell the girls the truth, sort of. An Iranian pilot, we say. They get the message. They can take it or leave it from there. Those are savvy kids. Nice, too, most of them. Just a little crazy, bless their hearts. Makes them easy to talk to for the likes of us. We're a little crazy ourselves; have to be to take on this kind of job. They understand. Better than some girl next door in Sioux City." He looked at Jim thoughtfully. "Let me buy you a drink. I really wasn't kidding when I said that critter of yours was a lifesaver."

Colonel Sharif in his well-cut Air Force blues was a trim, dashing man in his middle forties. His luxuriant mustache was still coal black, as was his hair, except at the temples, where it was just beginning to turn a distinguished-looking gray. He had a clipped English accent with Teutonic overtones, the result of his studies at a university in Germany. Despite this personal association, he felt strongly about American technology. He thought it was the best money could buy, especially in his own field, the aircraft industry. "The British turn out beautiful engines; the French design an elegant craft; the Germans can make a machine so it lasts forever. But the Americans can make it fly, anytime, anywhere. And that's my concern."

Jim nodded appreciatively. "If you'll forgive a mixed metaphor, Colonel, we try to keep our eyes on the ball."

Sharif twisted the tips of his mustache. "I play polo, Mr. Lindner. I know what you mean precisely. It's not easy, but necessary if one wants to win." Sharif stopped stroking his mustache. He put his hands on the desk, an enormous slab of wood, crudely shaped and elaborately carved. The uncurtained windows looked out on a motley collection of aircraft uniformly painted in camouflage colors of khaki and beige that would blend perfectly into the desert and mountains of Iran. "I am pleased you called. I would like to talk with you about spare parts."

Jim sat back in his chair, which was as oversized and as crudely shaped as the Colonel's desk, but surprisingly comfortable. "That's why I came to Isfahan, Colonel. I am at your service."

Sharif's right hand began to tap a tattoo on his desk. "I don't mean the new order for additional spare parts. I will deal with Rezvani regarding that, in the usual way. I have something else in mind. More interesting perhaps for us both."

An alarm rang in the back of Jim's head. His eyes narrowed.

Sharif's drumming fingers came to rest. "I see no reason why we cannot produce spare parts in Iran. Indeed, right here in Isfahan. It would make much sense logistically. I have myself seen plants for spare parts in Germany and spoken with the managers and workers of these plants. They are not cleverer than our people. Our people need more supervision, but I can take care of that."

He laid his hands on the desk palms down, in a perfect parallel, and held them very still. "What I am suggesting, Mr. Lindner," he said smoothly, "is a co-production arrangement for spare parts in Iran, a joint venture between myself, you and Rezvani Enter-

46

prises. You could bring to it the technical capability and the know-how." He paused to indicate that he understood fully the meaning of that word. "Rezvani could handle the commercial and financial aspects. I would provide the market."

He looked down at his hands and nodded approvingly at the military precision with which he had placed them. Then he continued. "I could not, of course, participate in the venture in my own name, but my wife's cousin is a very reliable person and has some understanding of business. He has studied economics at the University of Southern California, in which the Shahansha takes a particular interest, and has taken law in Teheran. It would look most reasonable." His eyes, brown and brilliant, were fixed on Jim. "I am convinced it is. For all parties. And for Iran."

It occurred to Jim that the Iranians he had met in Mainz had been right. This was a land of enterprising people. A taxi driver who invested in a Jaguar to prepare for revolution. A colonel who turned entrepreneur to command spare parts for his aircraft. "An interesting idea, Colonel," Jim said. "Very interesting. I'll discuss it with my company when I get back to New York."

Sharif's hands abandoned their parade position. "The offer is extended to you personally."

"I appreciate that, Colonel, but it doesn't quite work that way. For such an enterprise to succeed, it would need ongoing infusions of technology. The Copter Company has that technology and will continue to have it: the latest and the best. I assume you want that."

Sharif turned to look out of the window at the serried rows of aircraft, extending as far as the eye could see. His gaze swept his dominion, then came back to his prospective partner. "Of course. We intend to be the Germany of this part of the world. We intend to catch up with Germany itself within twenty years, at the latest."

"Also," Jim said, "I don't personally have the money such an undertaking would require."

Sharif's right hand was back at his mustache. It alternately twisted up the far corner into a hook and smoothed it down into a neat line. "We used to think all Americans were rich." His voice

47

had a hint of derision. Jim could not tell whether the derision was for the demonstrated error of the thought, or for the fact that Americans were no longer rich in the eyes of countries that had oil. "We know better now," Sharif continued, "but there is no need for concern on this score. Rezvani will handle all of that. He is a very good financier."

"I'm sure he is," Jim said carefully. "Nevertheless, participation in such a venture would have to be a company decision, not a personal one. If only, as I explained"—he heard himself sounding lame—"for technical reasons."

The colonel shrugged. Suddenly he looked bored and impatient. "As you wish. Keep Rezvani informed." The last sentence was no longer a conversation. It was an order. And a dismissal.

On the plane back to Teheran, Jim allowed himself to toy with Sharif's proposition. It was flaky all right, but interesting. Very interesting. One could make an awful lot of money in a deal like that. The way those cards were stacked, it wouldn't take very long either. They'd all be rich: Colonel Sharif, Taher Rezvani and, yes, Jim Lindner. He looked out at the starry night. Dreams of glory, he thought. Seductive stuff.

It was ten o'clock at night when Jim landed once more in Teheran and discovered, on checking his wallet for the taxi fare back to the hotel, that he had run out of rials. He decided to walk the short distance to the international terminal, where exchange services were available around the clock.

He stepped up to the first teller's window he saw—a small counter with a clerk officiating behind horizontal bars. Jim countersigned a traveler's check for a hundred dollars and slid it under the bars. The clerk peered at it. He got off his stool, walked to what looked like a very large safe and returned with a round tin box. It had a blue and silver label that showed a darting fish surrounded by script in Arabic letters. The clerk pushed the tin through the window along with some coins. Baffled, Jim looked at him. "Your caviar," the clerk said irritably, "and your change."

Jim lifted the tin off the counter. It was a kilo of caviar from the Caspian. He set it down again. "I wanted rials." The clerk pointed his thumb to the right. "Over there," he said rudely.

He did not offer to take back the tin. Jim decided not to tangle with the imperious clerk. He would keep the caviar as a present for Brigitte when she came back, even though he did not know when that would be. She loved the stuff, and this was supposed to be the very best. He put the tin in his briefcase and collected his change. Each one of the coins, he noted, was embossed with a lion, a sword, a sun, a crown and a wreath of laurels.

At the hotel, a large manila envelope, addressed by hand and sealed with dark red wax, was rolled up in Jim's mailbox. His room was on the second floor. The hotel had an elevator, but its movements were unpredictable, and when it did decide to ascend it rose at a snail's pace. Jim took the stairs two at a time.

Upstairs, he stashed the caviar in the icebox that held pride of place in the room and sprawled on the bed. He ripped open the envelope at the top. Two official-looking typed documents fell out, one in English and one in what he assumed to be Farsi. There was also a handwritten note. "Dear Jim," it read. "Please peruse the enclosed carefully. I would like you to take dinner with me and my family tomorrow evening and receive your answer. Faithfully, Taher R."

The document was a contract offering Jim a position with Rezvani Enterprises at twice his present salary and an equity participation of 10 percent in any undertaking established under his management for Rezvani Enterprises. In addition, he would have a seat on the board not only of any such venture, but after a year of satisfactory collaboration, on the main board of Rezvani Enterprises. The contract was for an initial two-year period, cancelable with three months' notice at the option of either party.

Jim read the document twice and allowed himself to dwell on the possibilities it promised. Perhaps it was a serious proposition. Rezvani was not a man to toy with offers of equity, let alone directorships. Why was he being so generous? Or was he?

Jim rose and placed the documents on top of the refrigerator, where he could see them from his bed. They trembled as the old icebox wheezed.

He woke in the early hours of the morning with a dream

vividly in his mind. The dream had been dominated by an enormous Christmas tree covered with colored balls of glass, tied to each other with ropes of silver and gold. The star at the top of the tree had been very large and had human features, the features of Taher Rezvani.

The German embassy was a large squat building set in sizable grounds. Its trees were covered with dust—the brown dust of the desert and the white dust of cement—but inside it was meticulously clean. The office of the cultural attaché, Heinz Herbert von Stolzenfels, was a successful mixture of German efficiency in its furnishings and Iranian art in its appointments. Heinz Herbert, a career officer in the German foreign service, was Brigitte's senior by five years. His mother had died shortly after he was born, and his father had remarried three years later. Even though he and Brigitte had different mothers, the resemblance between them was strong. Heinz Herbert was tall, blond, blue-eyed and very handsome in a soft, highly polished way. He was delighted to see Jim.

"And how's my little sister?" he inquired. "She'd be furious if she heard me. My big little sister?" Jim suddenly felt awkward. "She's in Capri. Or was when I last talked to her."

"In Capri in October?" Heinz Herbert sounded incredulous. His voice intimated that for a civilized human being to be in Capri in October was about as inexcusable as eating fish with an ordinary knife.

"Well," Jim said defensively, "I've been traveling, and Mainz is not very entertaining alone."

Heinz Herbert blinked. His curling eyelashes flashed golden. Like Brigitte's, Jim thought. His fingertips tingled.

"I've never known my little sister incapable of entertaining herself," Heinz Herbert said doubtfully.

The tingling in Jim's fingertips converted itself into a sentence. He heard himself declare, "I'll be back in Mainz soon. And we'll be skiing in St. Moritz come December."

Skiing in St. Moritz was one of the delightful customs Brigitte had instituted in Jim's life. They had spent at least a week in that fashionable fairyland each year since they met. There was no reason to think Brigitte would want to tamper with this pleasurable tradition. Brigitte believed in pleasure, and in traditions that coincided with what she wanted from life.

Heinz Herbert looked relieved. The world had reassumed its proper contours. "Good," he said. "Schuss one for me."

Jim reached for his briefcase. "May I ask a favor? Small but confidential. You know Farsi, don't you?"

Heinz Herbert's mouth curled into a deprecating smile. "My one claim to fame. It's why I am here." His voice turned mocking. "I'm particularly good on Farsi poetry."

"This is poetry of a sort." Jim pulled out the two contracts and handed them to Heinz Herbert. "I've read the English version. I assume the Farsi is a true translation."

Heinz Herbert spread out the two papers on his desk. "Don't assume. This is Iran. Now let me concentrate."

Jim watched Heinz Herbert as he perused the papers. His head moved from one side to the other in a waltzlike rhythm. A slim golden pencil was poised in his hand. Two thirds down the page, he pulled close a pad of watermarked paper with the embassy seal engraved at the top. In his small neat hand he made a note.

"Impressive," he said when he had finished. "Are you interested?"

"An offer like this is never uninteresting."

Heinz Herbert furrowed his brow. Like Brigitte's, it was a broad, clear brow, and the furrows looked out of place on it. They vanished as quickly as they had appeared. "I'd love to have you here," he said, "but I doubt that my big little sister would like it for very long. Social life in Teheran is even duller than in Bonn. As you know, that's quite an accomplishment."

Jim nodded. "What's the note you made?"

"A small wrinkle. In diplomacy we call it a 'demarche.'"

"Enlighten me."

A supercilious expression crept into Heinz Herbert's face. "The two contracts are the same, with one exception. The English version stipulates that the agreement can be canceled at three months' notice by either party. The Farsi text says only that the contract can be canceled at three months' notice."

"Does that not imply it can be canceled by either party?"

"Imply? Perhaps. But you would have to establish that in an Iranian court, and that is not an exercise I would recommend. Also, the Farsi version takes precedence over the English translation in any legal proceeding here."

"Do you know what the court's presumption would be, working from the Farsi text?"

"I do not. But I can guess with a considerable degree of certainty. The court would presume that, uh"—he bent to look at the signature—"that Rezvani Enterprises and, more specifically, Mr. Taher Rezvani, has the right of cancellation. He is the primary contracting party. He is also an Iranian."

Does Heinz Herbert really know what he's doing? Jim wondered, or is he protecting his big little sister? "Maybe I should run this by the commercial attaché of my own embassy," he said. It occurred to him that his comment might have sounded churlish. "You've been a great help," he said and grinned. "I've always wanted a brother-in-law who is a whiz at Farsi."

Heinz Herbert smiled ingratiatingly. "I know the commercial attaché at the American embassy. We keep meeting at the same boring parties. Cahill's a bachelor too. I can ask him round for cocktails if you like."

John Cahill, when he arrived at Heinz Herbert's spacious residence, was edgy. The apartment was perched high on a hillside overlooking the valley that held the heart of Teheran. The building was surrounded by trees—cypress and sycamores—their leaves green and fresh. The dust that swirled around the bowl that contained the city was cleansed here by a cool sharp wind. A whiff of mountaintops was in the air.

"Goddamn place can drive you out of your mind," Cahill muttered after introductions had been made. Heinz Herbert nodded sympathetically and pointed to a tall pitcher of martinis. "But solace is near. Vodka martini. Help yourself."

Cahill headed for the pitcher. When he had drained most of his first glass, he settled himself in one of the soft leather lounge chairs and looked at Jim with patient exasperation. "Okay," he said, "tell me your troubles."

The comment irritated Jim. On the other hand, it was good of the man to turn up on such short notice, and his attitude might well be the voice of experience. Serving as commercial attaché at the American embassy in Iran could not possibly be an easy job.

"I don't really have any trouble," he said. "I'm here on Copter Company business. Someone made me an offer, a personal offer. Interesting terms. But Heinz Herbert seems to feel the terms aren't on the level. There's a little quirk between the lines."

"Yah. He told me. A discrepancy in the English and Farsi versions of the contract. A discrepancy that could mean nothing or everything. Sight unseen, you'd better figure that it means everything. D'you want to tell me who is making the offer?"

"Taher Rezvani. Of Rezvani Enterprises."

"Oh boy!" John Cahill rose, walked to the sideboard and poured himself another martini. "That one is a lulu."

Jim found himself bristling. "What is a lulu?" he asked sharply.

Cahill gulped down half of his glass and immediately refilled it. "Not what—who. Taher Rezvani. He's one of the smartest, richest, trickiest operators in this town. And that, brother Jim"— he waved his glass from Heinz Herbert to Jim, spilling a few drops in the process—"is really saying something."

He walked back to his chair, stretched and dug the tips of his shoes into the tiger rug under his feet. The rug was an acquisition from what Heinz Herbert called "an earlier incarnation," a three-year assignment to India. "You want a story?"

Jim's impulse was to say no. He refrained. Heinz Herbert cocked one eyebrow and said encouragingly. "I always want a story. Especially if it's Persian."

"It's Persian, all right. The hero, if that's the word, is one Taher Rezvani." Cahill looked at Jim.

"I'm with you."

"You know about the American senior executives who, after they retire, volunteer to put in stints in the developing countries,

53

advising nascent enterprises on the mysteries of management." Cahill's tone made clear that as a professional diplomat, he considered business management a minor art.

"I don't," said Jim.

"The organization is appropriately known among the cognoscenti as the paunch corps. Some of the people in it are quite good; others think they know how to run the world." He sneered. "After all, they all ran their own little empires." He sighed, looked affectionately at what was left of his martini and downed it. "Anyhow, we have to look after them when they're here. More precisely, I have to look after them." He sighed again. "And they do take looking after."

"Where does Rezvani come into this?" The asperity in Jim's voice was unmistakable. He was rapidly coming to the conclusion that John Cahill was a supercilious ass.

"Rezvani bought one of the paunch corps gentlemen—lend-leased him; hired him, I guess is the proper word—at, of course, about one tenth the money the man had earned in his last position in the US. The contract was for six months. When the six months were up, Rezvani asked to have it renewed. A fulsome letter came with the request, singing the man's praises. It was practically a paean. Heinz Herbert would have loved it." Cahill's hand, flashing a monogrammed gold ring on the little finger, waved in Heinz Herbert's direction. "We renewed the contract. A month later, a guy from the Voice of America came through. He was junketing around the world recording interviews with people who had made good use of the paunch corps. A laudable enterprise. He came to us for guidance, and I sent him to Rezvani. I should've known better. In a land of tricky gentlemen, Rezvani is one of the most."

He looked at his host and held out his empty glass. "Heinz Herbert," he said, "You look underemployed." The taunt in his voice was not altogether benevolent. "Cultural types usually are." He winked to indicate he was joking. Heinz Herbert rose to refill Cahill's glass.

After he had taken a few sips—he was drinking in a more measured manner now—he continued. "The interview was a disaster. Rezvani said the man was no good, incompetent, a nuisance and a fool. I still remember one particularly telling phrase: 'He knows nothing and understands nothing; my nephew's five-year-old daughter is smarter than he is and of more use to my business.' It was an all-out blast. The man from the Voice was shocked. Frankly, so was I. When I tried to reach Rezvani on the telephone, he was unavailable. To me, that is. A couple of weeks later I ran into him at a party and cornered him. I was still furious. He had made a fool of me, not to mention that poor guy from the paunch corps."

As Cahill had intended, both Jim and Heinz Herbert were now hooked on his tale. He paused dramatically and sipped at his martini. "Okay," he said. "Mark my words, because this is Iran in a nutshell. Rezvani came clean. The man was really very good indeed, he said, which is why he renewed the contract—at double the previous compensation, as he accurately pointed out. 'And you know I don't throw away money,' he added. Which is very true indeed.

" 'So why did you say all those awful things to the interviewer from the Voice?' I asked. Rezvani gave me his wiliest smirk. 'If I had told this reporter how good the man was, and the interview had been broadcast, every joker in this town would have been after my man. His price would have gone up five hundred per-cent.' "

Cahill finished his drink. "Okay, Lindner," he said. "I trust I have educated you about Taher Rezvani. I must go now. Diplo-macy calls." He nodded at Heinz Herbert. "Thanks for the mar-tinis, Stolzenfels. Best in town."

On the ride down from the breezy residential hills to the dusty center of the city, Jim considered three topics. The first was how much more pleasant and interesting he found Taher Rezvani than either John Cahill or his own half-brother-in-law. The second was how rich and encompassing was Rezvani's ap-proach to life, compared to that of Heinz Herbert or John Cahill. The third topic, and, he conceded, the most titillating, was how challenging and remunerative it would be to pick up the Rezvani proposition. If it worked out, he would make more money in two years than The Copter Company would pay him for the next twenty. Brigitte would be impressed. As would Heinz Herbert. As would their father. With all their anti-bourgeois pretensions, the three of them had a sound appreciation of the value of money. With a cool million salted away—and it might well come to that if he said yes to Rezvani—his stock with the Stolzenfels clan would zoom. They might even commission an oil painting of their hitherto dubious son-in-law and hang it in the gallery of ancestral portraits in that fraying Schloss Papa Stolzenfels rattled around in.

Besides, money like that was a handy key to all kinds of doors. It widened one's options. By a quantum jump, as the guys would have said at MIT.

To Jim's astonishment, Rezvani's immediate family consisted of five members only. Two boys, both away. One was at Columbia University getting a master's degree in business administration. "I don't believe in California schools," Rezvani explained. "And everybody and their nephew goes to Harvard." The other son was interning with a bank in Zürich. Mrs. Rezvani was present, a voluptuous woman who looked much younger than her husband. She had glossy black hair and snapping dark eyes and wore a floor-length dress made of a liquid-looking mauve fabric, cinched at the waist with a wide belt of gold mesh. The belt was clasped by an elaborate buckle set with green, red and blue stones. Jim suspected the gold was real, the stones rubies, emeralds and sapphires. The lady had a set of bracelets to match the belt, and dangling earrings.

"My daughter will be here shortly," Rezvani said. "She is attending a lecture at the university." He sounded mildly annoyed and proudly paternal. Ten minutes later the daughter appeared. They were sitting on cushions around the pool. A low brass table between Jim and Rezvani held mounds of caviar, bowls of vegetables cooked with almonds, a lamb dish with an aroma of marjoram and a taste of apricots, a platter of rice that was fried crisp at the bottom and a silver pitcher of red wine. The wine was a little raw, but its tartness set off nicely the succulent globules of beluga

56

malossol. The wine, Rezvani pointed out with a proprietary air, was Iranian. He had just poured a goblet for Jim when a figure floated through the door, fluttered along the edge of the pool and stopped in front of them. It was covered head to toe with a black shroud, the traditional chador of Moslem women. Jim tried to hide his disappointment. The girl must have watched his face from behind the black gauze of her veil. She laughed, a gay, tinkly sound, and ripped off the veil to reveal a pert face that looked like a younger replica of her mother's. The shroud came off next to display a pair of tight-fitting Levi's, wooden clogs with high heels and a T-shirt that had emblazoned on it THE PEPSI GEN-ERATION.

"My daughter," Rezvani said. "She is studying engineering. She will join me in the business as soon as she has her degree."

Mrs. Rezvani regarded her daughter's attire with a doubtful look. "Perhaps you should change," she said. "We have a guest."

"A guest who is used to ladies in jeans," Jim protested quickly.

The girl's eyes danced. "And who wonders why I wear a chador."

Jim had tried to rise from his cushion but had been pushed back firmly by Rezvani. "She wears it for safety," the girl's father said. "We have fanatics in this country who do not want women to work, or be educated, or share anything with a man except his bed. There are even some at the university who think that way. For such men a girl attending an evening lecture or walking home alone is fair game. When she wears a chador, they do not molest her."

"It's a nuisance," the girl added, unperturbed. "But it's unim-portant. The important thing is the new life—the revolution, the white revolution." She looked fondly at her father.

"How many colors of revolution are there?" Jim inquired teasingly.

Her answer came quickly. "Three. There's the red revolution everyone knows about: the Marxists of various stripes and shades. Then in our part of the world there's the black revolution, led by the mullahs, who want to turn back history and live again in the days of Mohammed. People who want to make the red and black revolutions are alike in many ways. They hate each other, but they speak the same language. They both believe they have the truth from on high; only the location differs. It's Moscow for one, Mecca for the other. But both are certain they know what's best, not only for themselves but for everybody else. And they don't much care how they stuff these truths of theirs down everybody's throats, even if people wind up choked and dead in the process."

The words had gushed out of her. Now she paused and looked straight into Jim's eyes. "Fortunately," she said, "there is also the white revolution, the revolution our Shah began, and his father before him. It's not perfect, of course, but it tries to move us, all of us, into the twentieth century as best and as fast as it can. That's my revolution. It will win." She swerved to scrutinize her reflection in the pool. Beside her, the chador lay in a small black heap.

For the first few minutes they reclined in silence. Rezvani concentrated on his hookah. Jim had crossed his arms under his head and was looking up at the ceiling. His mind was in turmoil. The longer he allowed himself to dwell on Rezvani's offer, the more tempting it became. Two years of building something from scratch during the day, living like this at night and emerging from it a wealthy man; it seemed too good to be true.

"How did you, eh, experience Persepolis?" Rezvani inquired. His voice was calm and sonorous but had an edge of intensity.

"Powerful." Jim kept his eyes on the ceiling.

"Yes. But the power is not power only. It is power with justice."

"Do you believe the twenty-two nations that paid tribute to Cyrus thought so?"

"History says they did. For a time. But I am a modern man. I do not believe in tribute. I believe in contribute."

"An interesting distinction."

Jim could hear Rezvani draw on his water pipe. "I believe other nations, other people, can contribute to Iran."

"And should?"

"And should. We will be a good power. A serious power. Tolerant. Responsible. As we were in the old days."

Jim thought of the brutal, primitive soldiers guarding the concrete tents; of the Mujahedeen driver in his bright green undershirt; of Colonel Sharif and his peremptory crookedness. "You have a ways to go," he said.

"I know. It is one of the reasons I sent you the sealed envelope."

Jim turned his head and looked at Rezvani. "Thank you. I appreciate the offer."

"But you want to know why I make it."

"Yes."

Rezvani kept his lids lowered so Jim could not see his eyes. Except for the occasional gurgle of the pipe indicating movement at the mouthpiece, Rezvani could have been asleep. He was not.

"There are circles of reasons. One is that you are an American, a man raised in a can-do civilization. We have become a namishe nation. Namishe: it can't be done. Which is not so, most of the time. I need someone who knows that it is not so, and can explain it. Not with patience, but with understanding. That is not easy. I have met many Americans. Most of them are good at what they do, but they cannot make the bridge—it is a bridge of the imagination—to people who are not good at what they do. Most Americans cannot comprehend that this apparent inability is not stupidity or laziness, but a mindcast shaped to a different patter. As your poet says"—his eyelids rose and fell twice in an indication of pleasure—"their hearts follow a different drummer."

Jim smiled. That was not exactly what the poet had said, but it was close enough.

"I will tell you a story," Rezvani announced. He waved his ivory mouthpiece. "No, it is not a story; it is a parable."

A land of parables. Parables and paradoxes. Jim looked at his host.

"A man I know," Rezvani proceeded in a storytelling tone, "a very clever man, started the first commercial bakery in Iran. He bought a big modern machine in Sweden. It makes many

59

loaves of bread per hour, twenty-four hours a day. The Swedes installed the machine, trained a foreman and a crew and instructed the foreman carefully in how much dough the machine must be fed to produce at full capacity. It all worked well for a few weeks. Then the foreman had an idea. If the amount of dough the Swedes had prescribed produced a thousand loaves a day, he calculated that doubling the dough would get the machine to make two thousand loaves. He could sell some of the extra loaves himself—on his own account so to speak—and tell his boss about the remainder. Everyone would profit. So the foreman doubled the quantity of dough to be fed into the machine. The machine broke down. The boss tore his hair and complained to the Swedes, who came running. They realized immediately what had happened—overload, they called it—fixed the machine and warned the foreman that he must not do this again.

"The foreman stuck to his instructions for a couple of weeks after the Swedes had gone home, then his enterprising mind started to work once more. 'Well,' he figured, 'maybe asking the machine to make double the amount of bread is too much. But how about twenty-five percent?' So he added a quarter more dough to the quantity the Swedes had stipulated. Once again the machine broke down. Of course. But the foreman was furious. It made no sense to him. The boss was furious too. The downtime was costing him money. Even the Swedes were angry, although with a Swede it is very hard to tell when he is angry and when he is happy. On this occasion the Swedes who came to fix the machine were certainly not happy. They had brought along their own aquavit, a lot of it. It was all gone when they left."

Jim chuckled and his response seemed to please Rezvani. He took three satisfied puffs from his pipe, making the bubbles in the bottle swell up and burst.

"This is what I mean," he said. "You understand—the second and the third circle. You would know how to manage the enterprising instincts of such a foreman and harness the skills and abilities, the hopes and ambitions that motivate men like him. There are many such men in Iran. Men and women. They need an engineer like you, a man who can build bridges of the mind, bridges with girders of know-how and empathy, expertise and imagination."

To Jim's annoyance, John Cahill's comment echoed in his mind: "A fulsome letter; a tricky operator."

"Thank you," he said, "I'm flattered. But what makes you think I can do all that?" There was a driving quality in his voice.

Rezvani's lids lifted like heavy blinders being pulled up slowly. "I checked."

Jim sat up. "Checked what?" he demanded. "Where?"

Rezvani's glance did not waver. "Your character. Your personality. Your adaptability. I checked when the transaction with Mainz became ripe. In Europe, mostly. I have sources there." Rezvani's eyes were fixed on Jim. "Most important, what I have seen myself confirms what the sources say. You will do very well."

Before Jim could respond, Rezvani added, "You have seen Sharif." It was not an inquiry. It was a statement. Rezvani certainly kept track. "The venture Sharif mentioned would be your first assignment with Rezvani Enterprises."

"The venture Sharif has in mind makes no sense."

"Oh? Why not?"

"I can't personally supply the required technology. Certainly not over the long pull."

"Of course not. We will make a licensing arrangement with The Copter Company."

"What kind of arrangement?"

Rezvani shrugged. "A percentage of sales. A small equity share. I will negotiate." He folded his hands over his belly. "For the terms of the license. And for you."

A spurt of anger and apprehension gripped Jim. He could see Taher Rezvani and Russel Knight, president of The Copter Company, sitting across a desk in New York or, more likely, at a discreet table in one of lower Manhattan's lusher watering holes, taking each other's measure. The two men would be at par. Knight would drive a hard bargain. Rezvani would realize he had met his match. Between them, they would deal with Jim as just another pawn in their game. Well, maybe a knight, who could move straight and sideways.

"By all means," he said, "negotiate for the licensing agreement if you like. But for me, for a piece out of my life, you'll have to negotiate with me."

"Good. Between friends, I can think of no better opportunity than here and now."

Jim realized that, in his way, Rezvani had just paid him an enormous compliment. He had called him, however obliquely, a friend. Jim was certain it was a word Rezvani did not use lightly, and he knew from Ken what the word could mean for someone doing business in the Middle East. He also knew that while Rezvani's proposition was tempting, it did not fit into the career path he had staked out for himself when he had decided to join The Copter Company. The rewards might well be worth the risks, but it was too wide and wild a detour.

"That's kind of you," he said. "But I'll have to think about it. And discuss it"—he hesitated a moment—"with my wife."

Rezvani looked at him sidelong. "I understand the former Miss von Stolzenfels is a most attractive woman. Will you speak with her when you return to Germany?"

3

Jim did not discuss the Rezvani offer with Brigitte when he got home. Brigitte was not there. Finding the house still empty startled and dismayed him. Brigitte was impulsive and was used to moving around the continent as if it were her personal backyard, but she had never been away this long without being in touch. She couldn't have reached me while I was in Iran, he told himself. But he knew better. Brigitte was very resourceful when she wanted to be.

It occurred to him that there was nothing to prevent him from calling her. He knew where she was, at Villa Mare, Guido-Contini's whitewashed honeycomb of a house poised on a rock that looked as if it might at any moment tumble into the sea. Brigitte and Jim had been there together once in early summer, before they were married. Armando had opened the season with a weekend party that lasted from Thursday to Tuesday. Jim could stay only for a couple of days, but those days were, as Brigitte would have said, divine. He was high all the time: on the sun and the sea; on swimming, dancing, wine and music. Most of all on Brigitte. Capri was her kind of a place. Her wardrobe consisted of bikinis and floor-length summer dresses, and it was difficult to decide which suited her better. By what had seemed a process of natural selection, Brigitte had become the unofficial hostess to the stream of elegant young Europeans that flowed in and out of Villa Mare. Armando was not married.

Jim walked to the telephone. He had not yet unpacked and used his suitcase to prop up his feet as he sat in one of the handsome but not very comfortable wooden hall chairs that flanked the telephone stand. The telephone stand was a fifteenth-century prie-dieu that came from what had been the private chapel of the von Stolzenfels family. In Jim's opinion, the ivory push-button telephone looked out of place on the medieval kneeling bench, but Brigitte had flanked the instrument with two tapers in pewter candlesticks and had declared the telephone directories she kept in the oak shelf designed for prayer books to be her equivalent of the scriptures. The directories were of Rome, Paris, St. Moritz and London. The shelf also held a gold and white Florentine box with cards listing the private numbers of her friends. Those numbers changed often and covered the world. Jim looked up Guido-Contini. The card had three listings; one of them was in Capri. He asked the overseas operator to ring it.

For the first five rings, no one answered. He looked at his watch: three-thirty in the afternoon. As he recalled, that was siesta time at the Villa Mare. After the sixth ring the receiver was lifted and a woman's voice said, *"Pronto."* The voice had the melodious roughness of people from peasant regions in Italy's south.

Jim's Italian was skimpy. *"La Signora Lindner,"* he said. Now what was the word for please? *"Prego,"* he added.

There was a prolonged silence at the other end of the line. Apparently one of the maids had picked up the telephone and was trying to decide whether she should acknowledge the presence of la Signora Lindner to a male voice she did not know, which was, in addition, not Italian. *"La signora dorma,"* she finally said.

That might solve her problem, Jim reflected, but it does not solve mine. *"Io sono Signore Lindner,"* he said authoritatively. He heard the intake of breath at the other end. *"Momento, signore."*

Within a minute Brigitte was on the line. She did not sound as if she had been asleep. Her voice was bright and a little brittle. "Hello, Jim. It's nice of you to call. I was going to—" The brittleness had shaded to a defensive undertone.

"Do what, Brigitte?"

"Find out how you are. Tell you about my plans."

"That's kind of you. What are your plans?"

"We're going to Morocco for the winter. Will you come? At least for a while?"

Brigitte's use of the first person plural was, for Jim, another of her unsettling habits. It could encompass one person or a dozen. She rarely elaborated and never explained. Jim had no idea whether in this instance the "we" encompassed only Brigitte and Armando or a whole passel of idle Italians who had a winter to fritter away.

"Thank you for the offer, but no thanks. I can't. I have a company to run." He was aware of the tinge of censoriousness in his voice. Well, damn it, it was true. Someone had to do the world's work. If only to make possible la dolce vita for people like Brigitte, who in return gave life— what? Charm? Style? Grace? He wasn't sure. Not nearly so sure as once he had been.

No one could accuse Brigitte of a lack of sensibility. She fought back. "I know that, Jim." Contempt and bitterness pushed her voice to a high hard pitch. "Nothing else matters."

Was that true? Not really, but it came close. "I've just come back from Iran. There really is an awful lot to do. And I have interesting things to tell you." He sounded conciliatory.

"You can tell me when I get back from Morocco."

"When is that?"

"I'm not sure."

He could hear her fingernails scratch the handle of the receiver. She did that when she was tense. He said nothing. After a few seconds the scratching stopped. "Would you do me a favor?" she asked casually.

He had never been able to resolve in his mind whether these quick changes in Brigitte's behavior were temperament or a controlled performance. Certainly she had a large repertory. This was her social charm number.

"Of course," he said politely.

He could hear her laugh. She appreciated a partner who performed well in a scene she had set. "Would you call Christine Kertner for me? I've been trying to reach her for a couple of weeks, but I don't seem to be able to catch her. She's never at home." Brigitte sounded aggrieved and it was Jim's turn to laugh. "Well," he said. "A classic case of the pot calling the kettle black, isn't it?"

Brigitte was not amused. "Tell Christine," she snapped, "that we will not be joining them in St. Moritz this year."

Jim stared at the receiver in his hand. Brigitte had hung up. He felt both let down and relieved. He really did have a lot to do. With Brigitte away, he would be able to concentrate. The proverbial silver lining? A golden lining if he handled everything right. He went upstairs to unpack.

He had no problem reaching the Kertners. It was Saturday, and when he placed the call to Bonn a couple of hours after his conversation with Capri, a butler picked up on the first ring. Jim could hear the sounds of a party in the background. Instinctively he asked to speak to Mr. Kertner. He had had enough for one day of servants wondering why he wanted to speak with the lady of the house. Besides, he liked Hugo Kertner. He did not know him very well, but Hugo had a worldly quality that Jim found relaxing and comforting. At the same time, he was clearly a solid citizen. The two traits made an appealing combination. As he waited for the butler to fetch Hugo, an idea took shape in Jim's mind: the venture Ken wanted . . . The necessary intermediary. Someone you could trust, who understood what you were doing for him and with him, and didn't consider that a reason to take you for a ride. It sounded like a profile of Hugo Kertner. Why not find out?

Hugo seemed neither surprised at hearing from Jim nor put out by having been disturbed in the middle of a party. Maybe he doesn't like parties, Jim speculated, and feels about them the way I do. He accommodates his wife, who cares about social life, but if he had his druthers, a little partying would go a long way.

"Forgive the interruption, Hugo. I carry a message, and I have an idea."

Jim's hunch about Hugo and his sentiments about parties turned out to be accurate. "There are times I don't mind being interrupted. Not in the least." Hugo sounded pleased. "It sounds intriguing—a mysterious message and an idea. I'm always interested in both."

"Good. But it's not a topic for the telephone; wouldn't be even if you weren't engaged in keeping a party going."

Hugo chuckled appreciatively. "Domestic duty," he said affably. "When would you like to deliver your message and discuss your idea?"

"The sooner the better. I should warn you, though. The idea concerns business."

"In that case, perhaps Monday morning would be best. Your office or mine?"

Jim had not thought of Hugo as having an office. Hugo was what the French called "a man of affairs." Just what he did, with whom or for whom, Jim did not know. He would find out soon enough if Hugo was interested in his proposition. It seemed plausible that he would be. "I'm going to be pretty rushed in the office on Monday. I've been away. You wouldn't by any chance have some time to spare tomorrow?"

It was an unusual request. In Bonn, people like the Kertners did not discuss business on Sunday. "For you," Hugo said smoothly, "I would. I have the impression that your idea is what you would call a hot one." His voice had lifted at the end of the sentence to make it sound like a question.

"It is," Jim said.

They met the next day in a restaurant on the river halfway between Bonn and Mainz. The restaurant had a broad stone veranda, and the creepers climbing the walls of the terrace were vine leaves. But low-lying clouds held the threat of rain, and it was too cold to sit outside.

Inside was not much warmer. European homes in the winter were considerably cooler than the temperatures Jim was used to, and since the price of oil had zoomed, Europeans seemed to be even charier of heating their buildings. They still drove their cars a lot faster than eighty kilometers whenever road conditions permitted, but they kept their thermostats turned down. Jim shivered.

Hugo noticed and spoke quietly to the maitre d', who seemed to know him. They were led to a corner table where it was warmer.

By unspoken consent they did not come to the point immediately. They were feeling each other out, making conversation that seemed to have nothing to do with the topic of their meeting. The conversation, although conducted in a light, almost bantering tone, was deeply serious and both of them knew it.

Jim told Hugo about his trip to Iran. Hugo was a big bear of a man with a soft growling voice, which delivered punctuation marks in all the right places: a grunt of assent where warranted, an understanding chuckle where that was appropriate, an abbreviated cough of a sound that indicated a question. He was relaxed but attentive. Jim found it easy to share his experiences. He was surprised, therefore, by Hugo's reaction to the deal proffered by Colonel Sharif. When Jim had spelled out the details, recounting the incident as a tale of Iran rather than a business opportunity to be taken seriously, Hugo's eyes suddenly ceased to concentrate on Jim and swept to the tall window at the other end of the room, now lashed with rain. The bare branch of a tree, wind-tossed, scraped the pane. Jim wondered whether Hugo had been distracted by the noise.

Hugo's eyes returned to the table. "I find the Sharif proposition interesting," he said. His growl had lost its softness.

"Oh. Why?"

Hugo wrapped his hands around the cordial glass in front of him. At Hugo's suggestion, they had been drinking Asbach Uralt, a pungent 100-proof schnapps brewed by Trappists in a nearby monastery, which looked like water and had a diamond sparkle when the light from the chandeliers struck it.

"The Iranians own twenty-five percent of Krupp. They tried to pick up a substantial slice of Daimler-Benz. They're making an intense effort to get control of our major petroleum distribution company. I think it would be politic if we had a piece of their aircraft industry." He kept his voice light, but the look in his eyes was deadly serious. "One chip deserves another, if you see what I mean."

"I think I do," Jim said slowly. "You mean just in case push comes to shove."

"Precisely."

"Are you speaking economically or politically?"

"Both."

Jim nodded. "I hope the shove takes a while," he said. "We're gearing up to produce five hundred copters for Iran."

Hugo looked impressed. "From here?"

"Yes. Made and delivered by Copter GmbH."

Hugo had heavy dark brown eyebrows that spoke a language of their own. One of them rose to describe an arc as he said quietly, "You're making sure, I assume, that your payment terms are nailed down. I would not consider the present government a reliable customer."

"Why not? It has money, God knows. For the Iranians, five hundred copters are a minor transaction."

"At this moment. Things change. Iran is not a stable country."

"There aren't many of those left in the world, Hugo. If we only did business with stable countries, our options would be very limited." Jim turned his head to stare at the window and the ghostly twigs that kept scratching at it, producing an eerie, disturbing sound. He ordered himself to concentrate. "In any case," he said, "I'm not sure that stability is a valid criterion nowadays. I can think of some very nasty regimes that are stable, or at least appear to be. I wouldn't want to do business with them if I could help it."

Hugo's expression lost its joviality, and the bantering tone vanished from his voice. "I am very glad to hear that," he said quietly. "Now tell me about your big idea. What did you have in mind?"

Crisply Jim explained the need for an independent German firm with which The Copter Company could do business at arm's length. Hugo understood quickly and completely. "It's a very interesting offer," he said, "but if you don't mind a frank question, why don't you do it yourself?"

"I can't. I'm an American." Jim winked at Hugo. "I am a

69

one hundred percent owned subsidiary, and as such subject to all American laws, including the Foreign Corrupt Practices Act." For a moment he looked bewildered. "I think I even approve of it. For us," he added quickly.

It was Hugo's turn to look baffled. "I understand that you can't do it in your own name. But the von Stolzenfels family is very reputable. You could—"

"I couldn't," Jim interrupted. "When the matter first came up, I did think of old man Stolzenfels, but New York said no. It can't be a relative. Also"—he winked at Hugo once more—"Gott von Stolzenfels is not exactly an easy man to deal with. You would be."

"Thank you." Hugo was thinking. Weighing what considerations? Time? Money? Other commitments? "How many countries do you deal with, Jim?"

"For Copter GmbH, the Iranian transaction is the first sale outside Western Europe. The Copter Company, of course, has a longer history and a much larger circle of customers. In breakdown by country, I guess the total would be about forty. I don't have the latest figures. That's the domain of the VP international, but he's a good friend and I can ask. Especially if you are interested in the offer." He smiled. "Kertner GmbH sounds good to me."

Hugo stared into his schnapps. "About forty countries, you estimate. Where exactly?"

"I'm not sure I understand what you want to know, Hugo. If the question is a geographic one, the answer is everywhere."

"Including Africa and the Middle East?"

Jim wished he knew what was going on in Hugo's mind. "Yes. Why?"

Hugo ignored the query. "If you'll indulge me," he pressed on. He sounded tentative and very polite.

"Shoot. Our man in Germany deserves indulgence." Jim was not joking. He wanted Hugo to say yes. Now. It would be a big feather in his cap to have come up with the right man so quickly. And the more he thought about it, the more it was clear to him that Hugo was the right man.

"Why not Brigitte? I understand the legal objection to a relative, but Brigitte's name could be left out of it. She has a great many friends who would be happy to do her this kind of favor."

"Brigitte's in Capri, and going to Morocco. In fact, the message I have is from her for Christine; it's that she—we—will not be coming to St. Moritz this year." He tried to sound factual. He did not quite succeed.

Hugo pretended not to have noticed. "I'll deliver the message," he said neutrally. "But there's not that much of a hurry about the . . . uh . . . new company, is there? Brigitte will be back."

"Probably."

Hugo's eyebrow lifted very high to become almost a semicircle. After it was back in place, he held out his right hand. "All right," he said. "I'll take it on."

When Jim arrived at his office the next morning, Max was once again waiting for him. He looked agitated. In reply to Jim's "Morning, Max. I have good news," Max pointed to a newspaper that had been flung on Jim's spacious chrome and glass desk. The paper, the prestigious *Frankfurter Zeitung,* still smelled of printer's ink, an acid smell that tickled Jim's nostrils. In a front-page box featuring late news, fat black letters proclaimed that US-made helicopters with nuclear capacity had been sold to Czechoslovakia. The box referred readers to a story on page three.

Jim turned to page three.

The Copter Company of New York, a leading international manufacturer of helicopters, the story said, had sold a consignment of its top-of-the-line craft to an Italian firm in Bologna. The Italian firm in turn had shipped the copters to Libya as part of a multibillion-dollar barter negotiated on a government-to-government basis that swapped a five-year supply of petroleum and natural gas from Libya for turnkey plants and transportation equipment from Italy. The transportation equipment included cars, trucks, buses, trolley cars and helicopters.

Somewhere in the Libyan desert, the New York–made helicopters, transshipped to Tripoli by the Italian firm, had been equipped to carry a nuclear payload. No one knew how or by whom. It

71

was known, however, that these payload copters were resold to Eastern Europe and flown directly from Tripoli to Prague, with the company in Bologna acting as agent for the resale.

The Bologna firm, responding to inquiries by the paper's special correspondent, pointed out that it no longer owned the planes when they were delivered to Prague. In New York, The Copter Company said it would have to investigate. For the moment, it had no comment.

Max followed his boss's eyes as he read the report.

When he had come to the end of the story, Jim looked up. "I don't believe it," he said calmly. "The Copter Company wouldn't sell craft with a nuclear payload to a Communist country. So let's not go off half cocked on this one. If there is anything to it at all, New York will have an explanation. If there isn't—and personally I don't see how there can be—we'll find out soon enough what really happened. Meanwhile, simmer down, will you?"

He sounded authoritative, and his appearance lent conviction to the tone. Broad-shouldered and slim-hipped, dressed in a well-tailored suit with a subtle gray-blue plaid and a center vent, he looked every inch what he was: the successful, young president of the important German subsidiary of a New York–based international corporation. The fashionably cut blond hair, blue eyes, straight nose and assertive chin completed the picture.

He looks like an advertisement for a Mercedes 220, Max thought.

Jim did not feel the way he looked. The tightness in his stomach told him that he was not nearly so confident as he tried to sound. The top team of The Copter Company moved in its own orbit and did not always choose to share its motives or methods with the people affected, even when these people were directly on the firing line.

He was doing much the same thing himself right now. He was not about to let Max know how perplexed and concerned he really was. Keeping your own counsel, he had learned, was an integral part of running your own show. Part of the challenge, and part of the price.

They don't teach you that at the Sloan School of Management, he thought. Problems in MBA programs always had logical solutions, and the competent executive arrived at them by making clear-cut decisions, which he communicated in a straightforward manner to those who had to execute them. But in the real world you were always trying to balance competing claims—of people, resources, goals. Most decisions were anything but clear-cut. They were made groping in gray areas. And the risks you took were real, not theoretical.

On the other side of the desk, Max watched Jim closely. Was he as cool as he sounded? If so, how could he be? This Italian fiasco, if true, was an unholy mess. Even if not true, or true only in part, it would make The Copter Company look bad, and be a nasty embarrassment to Copter GmbH. It might even queer the Iranian deal. The Iranians were touchy about security, understandably so. They shared a border with Russia.

"Jim," he said, "The *Frankfurter Zeitung* is a very good paper. It's accurate and dependable. It has an excellent reputation throughout Europe and beyond." An undertone of stubbornness and pride vibrated in his voice.

"I know that, Max. But even if New York—or someone in New York—had wanted to make this sale, they couldn't have. US export regulations prohibit it."

When will he learn, Max wondered furiously, that the US doesn't run the world. Not that it doesn't try! Or was he just playacting? That handsome all-American-boy look of his could be very deceiving. He had seen James H. Lindner make some tough decisions without a wrinkle creasing that broad, clear forehead. "US export regulations," he said, "cannot prevent an Italian company selling helicopters to Libya, especially if the transaction is buried, in that casual way the Italians have, in a deal so mammoth that no one can keep track of the details. And US law—let alone a set of unenforceable regulations—certainly has no jurisdiction over anything that happens in the desert of Libya. You can count on Colonel Qaddafi to make sure of that."

The long arm of US law. Jim had heard Europeans complain about it almost from the day he set foot on the continent. US tax law, US anti-trust law, US export regulations, and now the

Foreign Corrupt Practices Act attempting to end by fiat from Washington the millennia-old business of greasing the wheels, big and small. Not that the Europeans were consistent in their attitude to the long arm of US law. When it interfered with something they wanted to do, they were outraged. When it crippled US companies and blunted their competitive edge, the Europeans were more likely to be pleased. But always they were shocked. As Max was now, or pretended to be.

"Look, Max," he said, "there's nothing we can do about this immediately. So why don't we just go about our business until we find out what really happened and how it affects us. The Iranian deal is on. We have a lot of work to do."

Max's eyes hooded. He leaned forward and lowered his voice to an ominous whisper. "I can tell you right now how it affects us. This Italian mess means two things at the very least. One, the less unpleasant, is that the Communist Party in Bologna will have no financial problems for the next couple of years. The Party got a rake-off, a percentage commission on the value of the deal. That's standard operating procedure in Italy for all exports and imports that move between Italy and the Communist countries of Eastern Europe. The company in Bologna paid off, even though the transaction was routed through Libya. There is no doubt in my mind"—his finger stabbed the newspaper—"that the Italians in Bologna sold and resold those copters. It's these commissions that make it possible for the Communists in Italy to be free of financial corruption. Unlike the Christian Democrats, who have to hustle for their money, the Communists just collect a piece of the action. Every time. And you and I know that helicopter sale must have provided a very substantial sum to their coffers. It'll be interesting to see what they do with the money. Finance Red Brigades on the sly, I wouldn't be surprised. So you or I can get shot in the legs next time we're down there."

Jim tilted back his recliner. It was made of soft tobacco-colored leather and chrome, to match the understated elegance of all his office furnishings. When Max became agitated, as he clearly was now, everything about him got wet. Beads of perspiration formed on his wide low forehead; droplets collected in the folds of his neck, above the starched collar of his shirt. His speech got wet too. The hiss emanating through his widely spaced, slightly crooked teeth was accompanied by a spray of saliva. Jim preferred that moisture to land on the *Frankfurter Zeitung* rather than finding its way to his face.

As he leaned back, Max bent further forward. "The second thing it means, Jim, and that's what really gives me nightmares, is that someone on the other side of the Danube can now load up *our* copters with nukes and drop them on our heads any time they choose. It's not very far, you know, from Prague to Munich, where my parents live. Or, for that matter, from Prague to Mainz, where you and I live." He straightened up, pursing his rosebud mouth. "I don't know about you, Jim, but the idea of going to heaven in a mushroom cloud does not appeal to me. Not yet, anyhow. There's too much going on down here that I enjoy." He took a handkerchief from his back pocket and wiped his forehead and his neck. When he had finished, the handkerchief was sopping wet. He stared at it and stuffed it back into his pocket. "Call New York, Jim, will you please, and find out what happened."

When Max had left, Jim flipped the switch on his intercom. "Liselotte," he said, "get me New York as soon as they open. I want to speak to Mr. Ward." Ken would know what had gone wrong in Italy—if the story was true. And he could tell Ken about Hugo. Ken would be pleased, and so would Russel Knight.

Promptly at 3:01 P.M. Miss Kestenmeier rang through. "New York on the line, Mr. Lindner. Mr. Ward's secretary. I could not get Mr. Ward himself. Perhaps he has not yet arrived in his office. It is only just after nine o'clock in New York."

Liselotte Kestenmeier could be annoyingly officious, particularly about time. She lived by an inner clock that was exact to the minute. She expected the rest of the world to function the same way.

"Thank you, Liselotte. I'll speak with Mr. Ward's secretary." He picked up the phone. "Hi, Mary. How are you this beautiful November morning?"

There was no response. He thought he heard a sob.

"Mary? Are you there?"

"Yes, Mr. Lindner." Her voice sounded fragmented. The satellite relaying transatlantic telephone calls sometimes had that effect.

"You don't sound like a beautiful morning, Mary. It's probably pouring cats and dogs where you are."

"No." Another silence.

Boy, he thought, these devoted elderly maiden ladies. They all go off their rocker sooner or later. I'll have to watch Liselotte.

"Mary," he said, a commanding edge to his voice. "Put me through to Ken, please."

"I can't." Her voice still sounded strange.

"Why? Is he in a meeting? Unless it's an awfully important one, you can connect me. I won't keep him long."

"No," she said, "he isn't in a meeting anymore." He thought he heard her cry.

"Where is he?"

"He's passed away. Mr. Ward has passed away."

Jim Lindner's fingers gripped the telephone. Passed away? What the hell did she mean? "Mary, I'm not sure I heard you right. This seems to be a bad line. What did you say?"

"I said Mr. Ward is dead. I found him this morning when I came to the office. He was slumped over his desk. Dead." Hysteria, shock and grief mingled in her voice.

"Have you called a doctor?"

"Yes. And the police."

"The police?"

"The doctor insisted."

"Why?"

He could hear her hesitate at the other end of the line. Then she blurted, "It wasn't a heart attack. I figured he was due for one, the way he was pushing himself, but it wasn't."

"A stroke?"

"No." She began to sob again.

"Mary." He tried to put support into his voice, while his own head was whirling with distress, anxiety, doubt and questions. "What was it, Mary?"

"He killed himself. He took his own life."

4

A shadow crossed the craggy features of Russel Knight as he faced Jim in the pale blue light of a New York autumn dusk. The shadow deepened the creases in the gaunt face, and filmed over the shrewd brown eyes behind their steel-rimmed glasses.

They had been talking about Ken.

"I still find it hard to believe. It's so out of character for the man I knew, and I've known him for almost forty years. But then you can never really tell about people, can you, even when you think you know everything about them." Knight shook his head brusquely, trying to banish a ghost. But the ghost stayed with them. "I brought Ken to the company back in the late forties. Had a hard time prying him loose from the big aircraft company on the West Coast where we both started out. This outfit was a struggling organization then, with everybody doing everything. We all wore at least two hats, one of them a hard hat. We worked as engineers, operated as managers and had a great, tough time."

He turned to look out of the windows that took up two sides of his corner office on the 106th floor of the World Trade Center. One of the windows faced across the East River to the defunct Navy Yard in Brooklyn, where The Copter Company had been launched. The original facility had been expanded many times and was still one of the company's major plants.

In profile, Knight looked like an American Gothic painted by Rockwell Kent. Nostalgia tinged his voice as he continued his

77

reminiscence, speaking as much to the plant across the river as to the man sitting on the other side of his desk. "We were heading into the Korean war and needed someone who knew what he was doing. Ken was the man, then and later." He swung around to face Jim.

"It was take-off time for this company," he said in his customary metallic tone. "Ken's wife wanted him to stay where he was. She felt safer with a big corporate family. I don't blame her. But Ken was tempted by the challenge and the opportunity, as I figured he would be. Especially when I offered him his own production line from design to finished product. I knew he wouldn't be able to resist that." Even in retrospect, the triumph of that coup brightened Knight's features. "Ken was a member of the take-off team; it was a great crew."

Once more Knight turned to peer out of the window, across the river and back in time. He had known how to bait the hook for Ken because Claude Asherton, the company's chairman, had held out to Knight the same temptation: the opportunity to start from scratch and to run one's own show. It was an offer no man worth his salt could refuse, and Asherton had been keenly aware of it. The chairman had collected a fine board of directors, and not once interfered in company operations. That had been the understanding between them from the beginning, and they both realized it made sense. You picked a man who knew his business and then let him run with it—even if it took more than either one of you had bargained for.

Knight took off his glasses, rubbed his lids and swiveled around to face the composed young man who had been his audience.

Jim willed himself not to sit up ramrod straight in response to the penetrating gaze. The voice that came at him matched the look. It was commanding and brisk.

"Well, Jim, we need a VP international. You're young for the job, but you have a track record with us. Ten years now, isn't it?"

Jim nodded and moved back farther in his chair.

"You've done a good job in Germany. I know that wasn't

78

easy. It's our biggest operation outside the US. Biggest and, thanks to Ken and you, best. I think you can give us our money's worth."

Had there been a tentative cadence to the last sentence? Jim was not sure. He felt his chest expand and his head go light. "Yes," he said, surprised at the confident sound of his voice. "I think so too."

"Right. I hope our mutual judgment proves sound." Knight made no effort to hide his sarcasm. Jim caught it, but did not respond.

Cool customer, Knight noted approvingly. His voice changed and became collegial. "Okay then. Decision number one. The German operation. Do you think it can be handled from here for a while, until we decide whom to send over to fill your Gucci loafers?"

When Knight wanted to be ingratiating, he could be. On such occasions his manner was a mixture of dynamism and charm. He could turn on the combination like a spotlight. It was very effective and he knew it.

Jim felt the pull of Knight's personality. He had to make an effort not to sound too eager. "We have a first-rate group in Mainz at all levels, but especially at the top. I've been thinking anyhow that the time has come to let a German take over. A German running the show has a great many advantages. It looks better too."

Knight growled agreement. It *would* look better at this point to have a German run with the Mainz operation. The Germans were competent. They didn't have good old Yankee ingenuity, that all-around inventive know-how of Americans—which was probably just as well, all things considered—but they certainly could keep an operation going once it was set up. He had meant what he said about the facility in Mainz. Thanks to Ken Ward and Jim Lindner, it had a hum and a whir that sounded good to his experienced fine-tuned ears. Even Asherton had thought so, and said as much at a board meeting after he had paid a call on the Copter GmbH facility in Mainz when he was in Europe on some fancy law business for his firm. And Asherton did not hand out bouquets lavishly; not in business, anyway.

"Whom do you have in mind?"

Jim hesitated. "My candidate doesn't quite follow the rule book. In fact it isn't one candidate; it's a consortium. My suggestion would be a president's office, not a Generaldirektor."

Knight raised his eyebrows. "Why?"

"You know how the Germans are about titles. Especially that one. Herr Generaldirektor. It makes their heads swell." Jim grinned and pushed the palms of his hands against the sides of his face in a compressing movement. "I had to let some of the hot air out myself occasionally."

Not bad, Knight observed. He's got a sense of proportion. That's a good beginning. "Yes," he said. "Go on."

"I thought we might split the job between Günther Westphal and Max Feld. Westphal is smart and precise. He thinks lean. Feld is ambitious and imaginative. He thinks big. Together they'll make one fine Generaldirektor." He paused. "And they'll keep a check on each other. That would be an important fringe benefit of the arrangement."

Knight looked beyond Jim to the world map on the far wall of his office, with its blue-headed pins for Copter Company manufacturing, assembly and licensed facilities, red-headed pins for countries to which the company had made major sales. The map was getting to look good, he thought, and this new VP international he had just recruited would certainly do his damnedest to put in place many more Copter Company pins, red and blue. His plan for the German facility was very smart. Westphal and Feld would not only keep a check on each other, they'd compete as well. It was a clever way to put both on their mettle and get the most out of each. Young Lindner was not as green as he looked. That was a help. He would need someone who could take the heat if it came—when it came. He couldn't afford another Ken Ward.

"Okay, VP International," he said. "That sounds like a good plan. We'll give it a try. Now let's have a little libation to celebrate your promotion." He switched on the Knight charm. "If you play your cards right, I might even buy you dinner."

At Delmonico's, resplendent in red plush, gleaming brass and mellow wood, everyone knew Russel Knight. The maitre d', in his immaculate tails, produced what in Manhattan passes for a bow. The waiter waved. No one asked what Mr. Knight wanted, but the two men had barely settled into a corner banquette when a martini appeared: clear, with the merest hint of vermouth, cold enough for crystal drops to form on the outside of the glass, and unblemished by olive, onion or lemon peel.

"I like mine without garbage," Knight said, regarding appreciatively the outsize funnel-shaped glass set before him. "How about you?"

Jim did not drink martinis. He found them lethal to his mind and his stomach. He liked the whiff of juniper berry in the gin, but gin went straight to his head and made him very thirsty. All the same, he decided this was no time to demur. He could handle one.

"Same, please."

Knight nodded approvingly.

While Jim had cherrystone clams on the half shell, rare roast beef, baked potato with sour cream and chives and a creamy New York cheesecake, Knight downed three more martinis. He skipped the first course, picked at his roast beef, ignored the side dishes and refused dessert. The waiter arrived with coffee. For Knight he also brought a Hennessy Five Star brandy and a wood-lined silver box of cigars.

"Montecruz?"

Knight nodded.

When the waiter had snipped and lit the cigar for him, Knight inhaled deeply and watched the blue smoke curl up to the old-fashioned glass chandelier. "Cuban," he said. "Tastes like the real McCoy."

"How do they get them? I thought we don't trade with Havana."

"We don't. These are made by Cubans who started over again in the Canary Islands. But an expert is an expert in any field. Those guys know their business." He drew again deeply, with satisfaction reflected in his face.

Jim decided it was a good moment to broach the Italian deal. Trading with Cuba, or rather not trading, could serve as a bridge for his question. "Castro," he said, putting a chuckle into his voice, "moves my peculiar mind to Qaddafi. I think they're birds of a feather. Which raises the question of the Bologna caper. What really did happen? We read some strange speculations about it in Mainz."

The satisfaction vanished from Knight's face.

Had the question been a mistake? Would it make for a nasty end to what had been an eminently satisfactory afternoon and evening? "It was all over the European press," Jim added quickly.

"Not a caper at our end," Knight replied curtly. "We had nothing to do with it." He exhaled and watched the smoke rise and dissolve. "We know the Bologna company as customers, of course. Know them quite well personally. They've been over here, and both Ken and I have been over there. But we have no equity in that company—majority, minority or even a portfolio investment. We have no control over them whatsoever, nor any way to exercise influence. I so told the boys from Washington when they came to call."

The bluish-red blood vessels in Knight's sunken cheeks seemed to swell and pulse. "I had to prove to them that there was absolutely nothing we could have done about the whole damn thing. We don't license the Italians and don't give them technical assistance. Truth is, they don't need it. Those fellows in Bologna are smart and imaginative. As we all found out."

"You mean they really bought, sold and resold our copters?"

"Yup. And fixed them to carry the payload. And made money on each transaction. A lot of money, if I read our best Italian customers right."

If Knight had any objection to what had occurred, it did not show. It appeared almost as if he had a sneaking admiration for those wily Copter Company customers in Bologna. Didn't he care about the planes winding up in Prague?

"What happens now?" Jim asked.

Knight shrugged. "Nothing, is my guess. Our Department of State will deliver an official protest, over a champagne dinner

I wouldn't be surprised, or by murmuring a polite something into the ear of an appropriate flunky at the Italian foreign office. The Italians will then sooner or later express their official regret, and the boys in Bologna will take care of whoever they need to take care of to make sure no one gets in their way. And go about their business."

"Do we sell them any more copters?"

Knight shook his head in a motion that looked truncated. "Not to the Bologna firm, we don't. But we have no reason not to fill orders from Italy, if we can get them. It's a friendly country, with a government friendly to the US for the time being. The Italians are our allies in NATO. We sell all kinds of stuff these days to countries and governments whose friendship is considerably less dependable. By 'we,' I don't mean The Copter Company either. I mean the United States. And if we won't sell, someone else will. That applies to our corporate competitors in the industry, and to our political competitors in the world. I don't believe that all these regulation and control games we play serve any purpose. The only answer I know is to stay strong so no one can clobber you. It's certainly true about the company. From where I sit, it looks just as true about the country." He flicked a long end of ash into his empty brandy snifter and signaled the waiter for another.

In his corner of the banquette, Jim quietly took a deep breath. "Speaking of competition," he said, "a problem came up in Mainz just before I left. I'd appreciate your advice." He saw the alert light go on in Knight's eyes. It seemed to pierce the soft smoke of the cigar and the mellow mood of the room.

"Fire away."

Jim made an effort to sound precise and analytical so that Knight would not detect the tension beneath. "You know about the sale to Iran out of Mainz. We've finally got it landed. There are two sticking points. One, Rezvani wants half his commission paid in Switzerland."

"He always did," Knight interrupted. "I would too if I were Rezvani. Iran is an explosive place in more ways than one. I am not even sure that sale is safe, although I suppose whoever runs

83

that country will need helicopters. They might as well be ours."

Jim swallowed. "I suppose so," he said, hurtling to his next point. "The big hook in the deal is General Yeganeh. He wants a five percent override."

Knight deliberately reached for his snifter. "On the whole transaction? That's a lot of money."

"Exactly what I figured. Yeganeh wants it handled through overbilling, with his check deposited in Zürich."

Knight set down his glass abruptly. The amber liquid swayed. "What, exactly, is General Yeganeh's claim to Persian fame and our money?"

"He's the adviser, or at least an adviser, on procurement to the Iranian defense forces. A cousin of the Shah's, or his wife's, I'm not sure which. Anyhow, intimately connected with the royal family. Impossible to ignore. Dangerous to buck. Our French competitors have made clear they would be happy to honor his wishes."

Even in the dim light of their protected corner, Jim could see the lines deepen in Knight's forehead. There were three of them, horizontal furrows of almost equal length that looked as if they had been etched with a penknife. "I don't doubt that for a minute. We've come up against the French in quite a few places. They're as amoral about commercial competition as they are about everything else. I know. I served in France during World War Two. How did we put it? 'In the US, anything that isn't expressly forbidden, is allowed. In Germany, anything that isn't expressly allowed is forbidden. In France, anything that is forbidden is allowed.' "

Jim made certain his astonishment did not show. If Knight decided to tell war stories, all that alcohol must have got to him after all. "From what I can make out, the French business attitude is that they do whatever local custom requires. They just do it more elegantly than anyone else. That's how they see it. They have a point, judging from the occasions on which I have seen them operate."

"Are they bidding on the copter order for Iran?"

"They are, and their government is helping them negotiate. Which is more than ours does."

"You can say that again!" Knight cut in vehemently. He paused to calm down. "Not that I'd want them to. They'd just screw things up and turn a straightforward transaction into a three-ring circus. What about the German authorities, though? Can't they help?"

"They do, in their fashion. They don't negotiate for us, but they 'facilitate,' I guess, is the word."

"Meaning?"

"Meaning *they* have no problems with the general's piece of the action. Not the why, or the how. There's a gimmick in Germany called 'Sonderspesen.' "

"I know about Sonderspesen. What's your problem, then?"

Jim's stomach contracted, sending a sour taste to his mouth. "No problem in Germany," he said. "But what about this end? Don't the US tax folk have their own somewhat different views? Less, shall we say, accommodating?"

"They do. A delegation from the IRS descended on us immediately after the news of the Bologna transaction broke. But they were on a fishing expedition, on which they had no right to be. They're supposed to collect revenue, not rattle around in people's closets. People's or corporations'. I handed over their nosy questions to corporate counsel, who will deal with them. The guys I really worry about are the eager beavers in the Department of Justice. They can make real trouble."

He raised his hand and a waiter appeared almost instantaneously. "Another Montecruz, Carlos," he said.

When the waiter had come and gone, Jim sank farther into the soft upholstery of his seat. "I take it Justice can prosecute under the Foreign Corrupt Practices Act. That's why a lot of companies are writing themselves codes of conduct." He had phrased the sentence as a statement, but the question was implied and he left it hanging between them.

Knight's reply was swift and emphatic. "Yes, that's the corporate fashion nowadays: codes of conduct. Only I've been around awhile. That sort of thing comes and goes. It's like the length of women's skirts. Personally, I'm too old for that stuff. Never did believe in it, as a matter of fact. A good product, a fair price, dependable delivery—that's what it takes, and that's all it takes."

He took a determined double puff of his cigar. "I also figure that if my executives don't know what to do when the going gets rough, or when a deal becomes difficult, I don't want them in my company. I don't run an institution for incompetents, innocents or nervous nellies." He exhaled, and his tone became more thoughtful. "I know that if you write down a mess of don't's, good people will use their brains to find ways around restrictions that ignore where the real world lives. As far as I'm concerned, that way of operating is a waste of good brainpower, and there's not enough of that around for me to want to participate in wasting any of it. When it comes to ethics and morals, if you have to spell them out to people in your company, you might as well forget about 'em. Anyhow, I can't improve on the Ten Commandments."

Jim felt a rush of relief. So that's how it was. He was on his own. He could make the rules as he went along, and take the rap if need be. He didn't mind that. The feeling of exhilaration that had welled up in him when he landed in New York earlier in the day surged through him again.

"I'm with you on that," he said.

"I'm glad to hear it, Jim. It's what I figured you'd say. In that case, I can get us a check." The dynamic charm flashed out once more, attenuated now by fatigue. His? Or Knight's? Both, most likely.

"It's been a long day," Jim said. "Which reminds me . . . ."

Knight looked up from the bill the waiter had placed in front of him.

"If you don't need me for anything special tomorrow, I thought I'd pay a call on Edith Ward. She and Ken were awfully good to me when I first showed up in Mainz. Edith insisted I stay with them at the house. I wasn't married then, and she said I needed initiating. She was right too. The initiation included her supply of Brillo and crocheted potholders. I'd like to see whether there is anything I can do for her."

Knight concentrated on his bill, pretending to double-check the figures. Risky, he thought, but I can't stop him. That would look odd. I can make sure, though, that Edith knows he's not coming without my knowledge and consent. That'll keep her from spilling the beans, if she has any to spill. Who knows what Ken told her.

He signed the bill in a forward-slanted scrawl and handed it back to the waiter. "That's a good idea," he said. "We're looking after Edith financially, of course, but women need other kinds of attention as well at a time like this. Be careful, though. Edith is a sensible woman, but there seem to have been personal reasons for Ken's doing what he did, which none of us know anything about. Including, I suspect, Edith. Certainly it was a great shock to her. It was to all of us."

That was true enough. Really left us up the creek. Unless this bushy-tailed beaver here builds us some dams pretty quick. "I'll call Edith in the morning, and tell her you're coming. You can take one of the company cars and my driver. He knows his way around those fancy Jersey suburbs. I get lost the minute I cross the George Washington bridge." He looked at his watch. "The driver is waiting now. I don't like to keep him too late if I don't have to. I'll drop you off at your hotel. It's been a good evening."

For Jim too it had been a good evening. Heading up the international activities of The Copter Company at age thirty-six was nice going. A lot sounder than the Rezvani deal. Rated at least a paragraph in the "Who's Who" column of the *Wall Street Journal.* He tried to be deprecating about the notion, but the truth was that it warmed the cockles of his heart, and would do the same, he knew, for his mother and father when he told them about it. He would visit with them on the weekend and give them the news in person. He had not seen them since he left for Germany. Spending time on a Pennsylvania farm was not Brigitte's idea of a holiday, and he had found it hard to argue the point.

What pleased him most was that he had made it to VP international in his own way. A number of his friends at MIT, where he had studied engineering, and particularly some of his classmates at the Sloan School where he got his MBA, were also doing very well for themselves. But they had arrived at their desirable

87

spots by parlaying initial job offers into the maximum head start on the fastest track, and they had speeded up their progress on the track by job jumping. It was the approved method of career crafting for his generation. Nevertheless, he had decided while he was still in Cambridge that it wasn't right for him. He had had a number of job interviews with the company recruiters who came to the campus in the late spring of 1968 and he had enjoyed them. They demonstrated, he had thought at the time, that there was a big wide world out there with all kinds of intriguing opportunities. But he knew what he wanted. He wanted a company with which he could identify for the long pull. A company that was of his own time. To him that meant a high-technology product, a modern style of management, an international outlook. He also wanted a company that was of his place, and, as far as he was concerned, that meant a company headquartered in New York.

The first time he had seen Manhattan was as a teen-ager, on a field trip that took his high school sophomore class to the Museum of Natural History, Times Square and Wall Street. He remembered all of it vividly. What he had seen that day represented such a range of experience, such a variety of ambition and accomplishment, that it stayed engraved in his mind. And the people crowding the sidewalks, midtown and downtown, were so diverse and colorful that it seemed to him the little island with its tall towers must be the center of the world.

Perhaps that had been teen-age hyperbole. But it was as true today as it had been then that the city sent his blood racing. He liked its rhythm, its pace, the emanation of what he felt to be life's most meaningful secret: It was the reach that mattered, not the grasp.

And so he had followed none of the corporate pied pipers he had seen at Cambridge. Instead, he had responded to an advertisement in the *Wall Street Journal* and wound up on the Brooklyn waterfront on a sweltering summer morning looking for The Copter Company.

He had spent five happy years in Brooklyn, walking to work from a one-bedroom apartment on the parlor floor of a brownstone in Brooklyn Heights. The first year he had worked mainly with Ken and had been sorry to see Ken leave for Germany. But by then the Mainz plant had been ready for expansion from an engine factory to a full production facility, and The Copter Company felt that only Ken could be trusted with that undertaking. Ken and Jim had polished off half a bottle of scotch in Ken's office the day before the Wards took off, with Ken leaving a trail of instructions and a few nuggets of advice. Finally, Ken had winked at Jim and said, "You do what I tell you, Jim, and do it right, and in a few years yours is the Rhine and all that's on its shores—or at least the section of those shores that I have anything to do with."

When Jim had left for Germany five years later to collect his share of the Nibelungen loot, as Brigitte described his transfer to head up the Mainz facility, the sleek corporate headquarters on the penultimate floor of the World Trade Center had been only a gleam in Knight's eye. But, as everyone at The Copter Company knew, gleams in the eye of Russel Knight had a way of becoming reality. That was another reason Jim felt fine this splendid November night. He believed in men like Knight, who set themselves a goal, staked themselves a claim and then gave it all they had. Jim's father was the same kind of man, on his own small scale. And so was Jim. On a big scale, he hoped, bigger than Dad certainly, and maybe even bigger than Russel Knight. But there was time for that, and surely this evening he had climbed an important rung on that slippery ladder, so seductive, so compelling, if only because, like Everest, it was there.

The next morning Knight arrived in his office early. Despite the useful evening with Lindner, who looked like a cool customer and a comer; despite the martinis and the brandy, which usually added up to an effective sedative, he had not slept well. He had dreamt and tossed, and in the morning his wife had told him that she had heard him carrying on a conversation with Ken Ward in his sleep.

Must have been that parting shot of Lindner's about seeing Edith, he thought. The whole business with Ken is distressing. Who would have figured he'd kill himself? I certainly didn't. Nor

89

did Morse Clark, and he's the sharpest calculator we have in this place. I'd better let him know about Lindner's visit to Edith, just in case.

The office of Lawrence Morse Clark, chief financial officer of The Copter Company, was next door to that of the company's president. The contrast was startling. Except for the view from Knight's window, which encompassed most of Manhattan Island, the Statue of Liberty and the Brooklyn and Jersey shores, the room occupied by The Copter Company's chief executive officer was undistinguished. An expensive decorator who specialized in corporate headquarters had designed it. The only touch Knight had added was the map of the world with its pins demonstrating The Copter Company's growing presence around the globe. Knight had discovered quickly that what lay beyond and below his windows took care of any additional effects he wanted to achieve. The vista made some visitors dizzy, enchanted others and impressed all.

Morse Clark's office offered a segment of the same view, but his visitors rarely had the opportunity to see it. Most of the time Morse Clark kept his drapes drawn. They were custom-made of a beige taffeta shot with flecks of pale green, and provided the color-keyed background for the rest of the furnishings. These furnishings were mostly exquisite eighteenth-century antiques that, in Knight's view, belonged in a museum, not an office. They were heirlooms bequeathed to Morse Clark by an aunt whose death had led to the dismemberment of the family mansion, which no one could afford to maintain anymore. Morse Clark had casually informed his boss that he would be bringing some of these heirlooms to his office and Knight had nodded absentmindedly. Interior decoration was not one of his interests. He had always left that kind of thing to professionals or, at home, to his wife, Elaine, who had very definite ideas on the subject.

Still, the metamorphosis of Morse Clark's office was more than Knight had bargained for. It suited Morse Clark all right. LMC, as he was known in the company, with his sandy hair, pale brown eyes, sandy eyelashes, long pointed nose and a skin that matched the drapes, looked as if he had been sent by central casting. Knight did not find LMC's museum congenial. It seemed to thumb its nose at the functional no-nonsense spirit of the company which he, as president, had established and intended to maintain. LMC's office proclaimed an affectation that was as irritating as it was uncalled for. Like Morse Clark himself much of the time.

As always, therefore, Knight's stay in Morse Clark's office was as brief as he could make it. He walked over to the antique desk and picked out of a green morocco holder one of the engraved personal memo sheets on which Morse Clark, in his neat small hand, practiced the financial wizardry for which the company paid him. He wrote on it, in his own bold scrawl, "See me when you come in."

Morse Clark did not respond to the summons until an hour later, well after the secretaries had arrived and the silent tower of the early morning had turned into an anthill. In his Groton-Princeton accents, the voice pushed out parsimoniously from a half-closed mouth, he mumbled a perfunctory apology. Knight ignored it and impatiently waved him to a seat.

"Two points, Larry. First, I've decided to appoint Jim Lindner VP international. I spent about eight hours with him yesterday afternoon and evening, and he looks like a good bet to me. I've told him he's on."

Morse Clark looked down at his meticulously manicured fingernails. "A trifle precipitate, don't you think?" he drawled.

"If you have any comment, Larry, speak up," Knight said, irritated. "You know I can't hear you when you go into your preppy act."

Morse Clark looked up. "Lindner is rather young for that post, isn't he?"

"I was younger when I became president of The Copter Company."

"It was a different organization then, Russ, from several points of view."

"True. But I'm not making Lindner president." Knight's eyes bored into Morse Clark's. His voice sounded like a hammer striking metal. "Yet."

Morse Clark did not flinch. Once more he looked down at his fingers with their sand-colored fuzz on the first joint. This time he raised his head before he said judiciously, "I was not referring to chronological age, Russ. We all know about Mozart and Alexander Hamilton. My concern is with maturity. Lindner makes an excellent appearance, but there's a naiveté about him that worries me. I don't have to tell you that this is a job for a man, not a boy. As this company, uh"—he cleared his throat, carefully covering his mouth with his hand—"matures, and joins the big league"—his eyes did not swerve from Knight's face—"we will need"—he coughed again—"genuine sophistication and, if you don't mind my saying so, real breeding. As far as I know, young Lindner has neither. Comes off some farm in Pennsylvania, doesn't he?"

Knight regarded his colleague. Morse Clark was only in his mid-forties, but there was something about him that made him look like a smooth-faced old man. He had probably looked much the same as a boy and would not look very different when he was seventy. It was that kind of a face: bland, contained, giving nothing away.

"You forget, Larry," he said, and there was a quiet, almost contemplative menace in his voice, "that I'm a Pennsylvania hick myself. I come from the wrong side of the tracks in Pittsburgh, or what you would consider the wrong side. I'm not sure it is. There are men and women with guts on that side of the track— guts and conviction. Which is more . . ." He left the sentence unfinished, the implications of it clear. Morse Clark did not pursue the topic.

"The other point," Knight continued after a pause, "is Ken Ward. Lindner is going out to see Edith this morning. They know each other quite well, it seems. The Wards put up Lindner in Mainz during the changeover. They also visited around some, I now remember, when Jim worked for Ken in Brooklyn. I don't expect any real trouble, but in this type of situation you never know."

"Does Edith know Lindner is coming?"

"Not yet. I told him I'd phone her and let her know."

Their eyes met, and this time Morse Clark's controlled, almost passive face did register a reaction. His narrow nostrils seemed to contract further. "That's commendable," he said, "consider-ing." He had not really intended to finish the sentence. In any case, Knight's curt rejoinder prevented him from doing so.

"Thank you," Knight said, his voice caustic.

A silence fell between them, each aware of the other's thoughts. They were casting their minds back to the same scene: the morning they had spent three days earlier in the same office, talking to Ken Ward.

It had been a protracted, tense meeting. Ken had asked for it, wanting originally to talk only with Knight. But Knight had insisted Morse Clark join them.

A two-edged sword, that insistence, Morse Clark had thought. Makes clear I'm next in line, but also means he wants to make sure I take my share of the repercussions, if there are any. Well, there won't be if he follows my lead. I'll see to it that he does.

There had been no polite exchanges and no preliminaries. Ken had immediately come to the point. "That Italian fiasco looks dangerous. It may blow, and a lot of other stuff with it."

"It's blown already," Knight had said reasonably. "But they really can't get at us with that one. It was demonstrably out of our hands."

Ken had shaken his head. "Not quite so simple, Russ. To begin with, two of the guys who doctored the copters in Libya are former Copter Company employees. Former, true. They're getting paid three times as much as they ever made with us, or could ever have made with us. But we did train them. It's our expertise they took to Qaddafi."

Knight's face had gone gray. He had looked at the ash of the cigar he was puffing. Normally, it was too early in the morning for him to have lit up. "That's unfortunate, Ken, I grant you, but it's still out of our hands. We run a company, not a jail."

"I know that, Russ," Ken had said, "only too well. More important, those guys in Libya know it. But that's not the point. The question is, does the SEC know it, or the IRS for that matter. I have already heard from both."

At the mention of the revenue agency, Morse Clark had per-emptorily cut into the conversation. Taxes were an important ingredient in the company's financial picture, and management of the company's finances—complex, multilayered, intricate and very profitable—was LMC's preserve.

"Why didn't you refer the IRS inquiry to me?" he had demanded.

Ken had looked at him and in his firm, husky voice replied, "They weren't looking for numbers, Larry. They were looking for culprits. They were after what in Washington these days is called questionable corporate payments abroad. I sent them to Grant Barlow. He's corporate counsel. That's what we pay him for."

Knight had nodded assent. "You were right, Ken. So far, so good. But I'm worried about the SEC. They have clout. They can subpoena just about anything they want and ruin you with publicity if you don't play along. And those guys think they have a mandate straight from heaven."

Ken's salt-and-pepper eyebrows had contracted. "Yup. Or the stockholders, which in Washington or Wall Street is the next station down the line. Washington especially. Stockholders spell votes."

Ken and Russ had looked at each other knowingly. The aircraft company at which they had both started out as engineers had been involved in an SEC investigation that had subsequently brought in the Justice Department and ballooned into a major scandal which bedeviled the company for years. Heads rolled, people went to jail, the company's bankers got skittish and the stock took a precipitous dive.

Morse Clark had lashed out at the unspoken understanding between Russ and Ken. It annoyed him because it left him out. If he couldn't, yet, have star billing in the company, he was in a position to insist on a key role. "What exactly did the SEC want?" he had asked sharply.

"They wanted to know whether we were planning to file one of their tell-us-all Eight-K forms to explain our participation in the Bologna transaction." Ken's voice had become ironic. "And anything else we might want to disclose. That's a quote."

"Were they specific about anything besides Bologna?" When Morse Clark was on a scent, he was like a greyhound, which in any case he strongly resembled: lean, persistent, his long nose to the ground.

Ken had shaken his head and sighed. "Not yet. But it won't take them long to turn up something. We're vulnerable. There is Abu Dhabi, and all our other sales in the Middle East; Jakarta, and the rest of Southeast Asia; Nigeria, I am pretty sure; and, of course, Basel. That's why I am trying to set up the arm's-length deal in Germany. Trying. I haven't got it yet."

Once again Morse Clark had lashed out. "For god's sake, Ken," he had said nastily, "don't sing us your song of woe. We know. In addition, I, at least, had reason to believe you would have learned to be more discreet."

Knight had intervened then. "He's right, Ken. You never know these days who's listening. Or what." Knight's keen eyes had swept the room. "I don't think we've got any bugs planted on us yet, but it never hurts to be careful. Anyhow, what did you tell the SEC?"

"That I had no reason to believe we had any disclosures to make that warranted filing an Eight-K, but that I would discuss it with you."

Morse Clark had taken a Benson and Hedges out of his thin gold case and tapped the cigarette insistently against the case. "That wasn't very smart." He had made no effort to hide his disdain.

Knight had looked down on his blotter. "That's true." He had looked up again and his eyes had nailed both men. "I hate to agree with Larry twice in a row, but that buck has to stop with you, Ken."

"You mean . . ." The full significance of Knight's verdict had seeped into Ken's brain.

"I mean," Knight had said, his voice hard, "that there's no point in sticking the company with any of these shenanigans. You, Ken, are going to have to run with this ball. You are VP international. There is no reason why anyone except the man in charge of international operations should know about questionable foreign arrangements, unless of course it's someone further down the line. Someone, or ones, actually involved in making the arrangements."

Ken's voice had become even huskier than usual. "I see," he said. He had looked directly at Morse Clark. "Larry," he added, "your signature is on the account in Basel that we use to make these questionable arrangements." It had been an appeal for support, but the underlying threat had been patent.

Larry had pulled out the du Pont lighter that matched his cigarette case and elaborately focused on its flame as he finally lit his cigarette. "No, it isn't, Ken," he said. "There is a countersignature on that account all right, but as you know, it is not my name. You'd have to prove it's my signature, and that would not be easy to do."

Ken had got out of his chair and moved his solid body to the window, his trunklike legs planted three feet apart. He had stood there for some time staring out at the Jersey suburbs where he lived and at the Brooklyn plant where his career with The Copter Company had begun. The two sites had come together in a blur, which moments later was illuminated by a painful message. "They're hanging it on you," the message said. "They're finking out. And there is nothing you can do about it. Or is there?"

He had turned to face them. "Okay," he had said. "I got the message." He had walked to the door silently, quickly, on the balls of his feet like the athlete he had been, and slammed the door shut. The sound had startled Knight's secretary, Grace Hartung, who was not used to anyone slamming her boss's door. Other people in the corridors of the executive wing had picked up their ears in surprise. Knight and Morse Clark had looked at each other, each drawing on his cigar or cigarette.

Morse Clark had been the first one to act. He had shrugged, slouched back into his chair and crossed his legs. "Unpleasant," he said, "but we don't really have much choice."

Knight too had settled back into his chair. His had been an abrupt slump, almost a contortion. "No," he said. "We don't."

It's hard to believe, Knight thought, that Ken was alive only seventy-two hours ago. He blinked and pulled himself forward into the present.

Opposite him, Morse Clark reached inside the double-vented gabardine suit, with its silk paisley-patterned lining, for his cigarette case.

"Don't make yourself comfortable," Knight growled. "I'm not planning to discuss this. I'll handle it. I just thought you ought to know."

He picked up his private telephone, consulted a small black address book and dialed. "Edith," he said in a paternal voice, "this is Russ. I'm calling to announce a visitor, if you want to see him."

In his quiet room at the Waldorf Jim woke with a start. The euphoria of the evening had evaporated. He felt disoriented. His tongue was coated. The idea of breakfast seemed incongruous and revolting. His body told him that lunchtime had come and gone. He decided to settle for juice, coffee and toast. The toast, when it arrived under a heavy silver-plated hood that was too hot to handle, tasted like buttered straw. He gave up on it after one bite.

The taxi that took him downtown crawled through the cross streets. On the East River Drive traffic was dense, and fog lay like a shroud over the water and the highway. When he finally arrived at the World Trade Center, considerably later than he had intended, the lobby, so charged with energy and glamour the day before, now resembled a rather shoddy railway station. Shooting up on the express elevator to the 106th floor made his empty stomach contract. The sleek receptionist with shiny blond hair who had given him the eye the previous afternoon, now assayed him without a flicker of recognition. When he told her that he had come to see Mr. Knight, she looked vaguely perturbed. In the far corner of the room, streamlined and sterile with its four carefully positioned Barcelona chairs flanking two glass tables on brass bases, the bulky security guard tried, with noticeable lack of success, to be unobtrusive. He ran his eyes

97

over Jim searchingly. Jim felt he was being frisked.

Knight too had shed much of the previous evening's cordiality. He was preoccupied and short. "Edith is expecting you," he said. There was an undertone in his voice that Jim could not define but knew he did not like: a caution; a warning; the touch of a threat.

He had no cause to feel threatened by Edith, nor she by him. Unless there was, after all, something about Ken's suicide that was deliberately being hidden.

If there was any information about the tragic event floating around corporate headquarters, Knight's driver either was not talking or was not privy to it. The driver was about the same age Ken had been and had known Ken well.

"I had my own little machine shop on the Brooklyn side of the river when The Copter Company moved in," the driver told Jim. "The company needed space and Ken came to see me about selling out. It was a good shop. I had workmen who had been with me for years—machinists who really knew their trade and cared about it. Ken liked what he saw and offered to take it over, lock, stock and barrel. Everything except me. He said there couldn't be two bosses running one place, and he had to be the boss of this one. I was welcome to work for him, of course, but he warned me I wouldn't take to that kindly. "When you've run your own show as long as you have,' he told me, 'it's hard to turn yourself inside out and become an employee.' He was right. I tried it for a few months, and it didn't work.

"Besides, he gave me a very fair price. That, plus what I had put away myself, added up to enough of a nest egg for the wife and me not to have to worry about money for the rest of our lives. The kids were out of the house and on their way. I decided to take off for Alaska and do all the hunting and fishing I'd been promising myself since I was in high school. But how long can you hunt and fish? After a year of hanging around, I'd had enough. Couldn't stand it anymore. Nor, to be honest with you, could the wife.

"When I came back, I went to Mr. Ward and told him my troubles. He fixed up this driving job for me. Told me it would

98

keep me busy and moving, going places and meeting people. I'd be working, and have a kind of permanent vacation at the same time. It was good advice. This is just about my speed now. I'm having a good time. He was one smart man."

Jim nodded agreement. This man is my father's age, he thought, and ran his own little workshop, just like Dad does. Would Dad be happy being a driver? Now? Ever? I doubt it. He'll die working in his own place. He wouldn't sell out if they offered him a cool million. Wouldn't know what to do with it in the first place. Nor would Mother. The farm and the shop is what they want, and it's all they want. I wish I were as certain of where I'm going—how and why—as they've always been.

"Pleasant country," he said. They had emerged from the Lincoln Tunnel and driven steadily along the suburban sprawl of billboards and shops, restaurants, motels, shoddy houses and old factories that crowded against the turnpike. Now they were off the highway, moving in secluded lanes lined with trees, their crimson and golden foliage lighting up the dreary November day. The houses were stately, set back from the lanes on sizable lots.

"There's quite a lot of industry around here," the driver commented, "but you wouldn't know it. They disguise it in these parts. Those new plants look more like big high schools or a college campus."

Jim could not decide whether the driver approved or disapproved of this development. It was certainly different from the way he had lived and run his business.

"He was a nice man too," the driver said suddenly, as if the conversation had never strayed from Ken. "Thoughtful. When my daughter was married, he brought her back one of those Indonesian screens, batik print and lots of fancy woodwork, a special kind of thing you don't see around. He didn't ship it, either. Brought it home himself."

The driver concentrated on negotiating the gentle curves of a leaf-spattered road running along a murmuring brook. "We're almost there," he said. "This is Saddle River."

The village of Saddle River was more than a suburb or an expensive bedroom exurb. It was a community with houses that

99

expressed the individuality of their owners. Some were colonial, painted white, some were deep brown Tudor. There were ranch houses of cedar wood, and one property sported an octagon building of rose-colored brick with very large windows, its residents sheltered by white gauze curtains.

Jim found Edith Ward in her garden minding the flowers. She was studying them, deciding what they would need now and later in the year. Every so often she snipped off a late-blooming rose or aster and laid it in a wicker basket that she carried on her arm. She was totally absorbed in what she was doing and looked up with mild annoyance when she heard the car's crunch on the gravel. Her face brightened when she saw it was Jim.

He bent to peck her on the cheek. "I'm so sorry, Edith." She moved her head as if to shake off—what? Sympathy? Pain? Memory? He could not tell. Externally nothing had changed. She was the same brisk, efficient Edith he had known. The neat curly hair was perhaps a touch grayer, the bounciness a bit subdued, the sparkling blue eyes a little duller, and somberness lay on her face like heavy makeup. It was unmistakably there, but it was not part of her real self.

"Edith," he said solicitously, "is there anything I can do for you? Anything at all. I'm going to be here for a while. So if there is something you want, just ask. Please."

She ignored the offer but responded to the announcement. "Oh," she said. "Are you going to take Ken's job?"

"They've asked me," he replied, feeling awkward. "It won't be easy. Ken Ward is a hard act to follow." Damn, he thought, that wasn't a very felicitous way of putting it. "I mean . . ." he mumbled.

She held up a small pink hand. "I know what you mean, dear. Congratulations. I think they made a fine choice. How does Brigitte feel about it?"

Jim studied his shoes. "I haven't had a chance to tell her yet. I didn't really know myself until last night. It was too late to call then. I didn't want to wake her."

Edith was concerned. "That was wrong, Jim. Brigitte wouldn't have minded. Not with that kind of news."

"I guess you're right." He couldn't very well tell Edith that

100

Brigitte was spending the winter in Morocco with Armando Guido-Contini. She wouldn't have understood. He was not sure he did either.

Edith had continued her gardener's stroll, and he had kept pace beside her. She bent to cut another flower. "It's hard on the wife," she said. "I had the house and the garden and good neighbors after they made Ken VP international. But he was away an awful lot, and I never knew just how safe he really was. He went to places where they think differently, do things differently, where life itself has a different value. I was always worried that something would happen to him. And it did." She sounded puzzled and sad. "He was a different man in the last few years." She shook her head. The gray curls stayed in place. "He was the same Ken in a lot of ways, but there were changes I didn't understand. Even before he . . ." Her voice trailed off. The hand that held the cutting shears trembled.

He took the shears and the basket from her, put an arm around her shoulder and held her close. "Edith," he said, "let me help."

She sagged against him for a moment. Then she pulled herself up and turned to face him. Her voice was clear. "It's dear of you, Jim, and it's good to know you're just across the river. If there's anything I need, I'll be in touch. I promise." She let her eyes roam the garden, the house and along the other homes on each side of the lane. "The company has taken care of everything." She said it matter-of-factly, without bitterness or gratitude. It was what she had expected.

She reached for her basket. "How about some coffee?" she asked. "The children are here. They came home for the funeral. Lisa is in the shed. I'll see whether I can find Stephen. He may want some coffee too. And he'll want to say hello. He hasn't seen you since Brooklyn Heights, has he?"

Unlike his mother, Stephen Ward had changed. Dreamy and withdrawn, he had always seemed a mutant in that energetic, outgoing family. He was a lawyer now, he told Jim, for an environmentalist organization, in charge of a campaign to persuade farmers to switch to windmills for their power. "It drives Mother batty," he said apologetically. "She keeps telling me that the greatest

101

day in her father's life was when the county laid electric lines to the family farm in Iowa. So we don't talk much about what I do. But I think it's important. Wind is a renewable resource and it doesn't pollute anything—not the air, not the water, not people's lungs, or their lives."

"What did your father think of your project?" Jim asked.

Stephen seemed to shrink further into his dark turtleneck sweater. "I don't really know. I can't imagine he approved, considering the kind of man he was. His idea of a better life was more things for more people. But . . ." Stephen pushed his long hands deep into the pockets of his corduroy trousers, lengthening the tear on one side. "He called me, you know, the night before he . . . the night before he did it."

"And?" The question was put gently, but Jim could feel his heart begin to race. Would Stephen offer a clue to his father's incomprehensible act?

"I hadn't seen him in about a year," Stephen replied. "So he asked about my beard, first. I'd shaved it off meanwhile. That seemed both to please him and puzzle him. Then he wanted to know about the windmills. I told him we were getting someplace slowly. I expected him to laugh. Instead he said, and this is exactly what he said, 'Well, good luck, Stephen. Keep at it. A man without a beard has to shave, and the most important thing in life is that when he looks in the mirror in the morning and sees that fellow looking back at him, he doesn't want to spit him in the eye.'"

"What did you answer?"

"Nothing. His comment took me by surprise. As you know, he didn't talk that way as a rule. Before I had digested what he said, he'd hung up."

"Just like that?"

"Well, not quite. He said, 'Good night, son.' He hadn't called me that in a while either."

"Did he speak to Lisa too?"

"No, he didn't. He may have tried to reach her, but she was out that night. We asked Mother whether he had phoned Lisa, but Mother didn't know. He called from the shed, not the house.

It was close to midnight. I asked him what he was doing in the shed so late. 'Oh, just trying to figure out something,' he said. I thought he was talking about an engineering problem. He was always designing copters, or pieces of them, in the shed." Stephen stared into space. "It isn't a shed at all, really. That's what Mother calls it, because she likes to think of it that way. It's a workshop, a fully equipped engineer's lab. It reminds me of those garages they write about in Horatio Alger stories, or in *Forbes* magazine, where big businesses have their humble beginnings." He sounded bitter.

"Their creative beginnings, Steve," Jim said. Stephen blinked. "Okay, their inventive beginnings," Jim amended. "You'll have to grant that much." He smiled. "I know about workshops. I grew up in one. Can I see your father's?"

"Yes," Stephen said, his mind no longer on the conversation. "You can look at it if you want. Just follow the path at the back of the house to the circle of dogwood and forsythia. It's inside that circle. You can't miss it this time of the year."

Jim walked to the shed. In the spring and summer the shed would be well hidden by bushes. Now its weathered wooden walls and roof were exposed, as brown and bare as the big trees beyond the shed would be in another couple of weeks.

Lisa Ward sat in her father's chair in the far corner of the workshop scrutinizing a piece of paper. "Hello," she said. "I knew you were coming."

Lisa did not believe in small talk. In fact, Lisa did not believe in conversation. She had been eighteen when Jim first met her at her parents' house in Brooklyn Heights. She had been at Barnard then, a firebrand crackling around every issue igniting co-ed consciousness. At home, her father had confided to Jim, she was a pain in the neck. She never came off her soapbox. It had hurt Ken to admit that. When Lisa was small, a button-eyed, bubbly creature with a mind like quicksilver and movements to match, Ken had doted on her and she on him. But she rebelled early and with a vengeance, mainly against her mother. Anything Edith was, Lisa did not want to be. Edith had always wanted a home, a husband, a family, a community in which she could find some-

103

thing useful and congenial to do, and neighbors who either helped her do it or appreciated her for what she did and how she went about it. Lisa thought volunteer work degrading, considered a family an obstacle to more important commitments, and regarded a husband—if and when—as a luxury, not a necessity. She wanted a career that served a cause. She was living in Chicago now, working for a counterculture newspaper.

While Lisa went back to staring at the paper in her hand, Jim looked around. This was neither a shed nor a workshop, he decided. It was Ken's castle. The center of it was taken up by an enormous workbench flanked by two drawing boards. The walls held a graded array of saws and screwdrivers on neatly spaced hooks. There was a large sideboard with trays of nuts and bolts. The room had neither carpets nor curtains. A transistor radio was perched at the corner of the workbench. The chair occupied by Lisa was a big rocker with a cane seat and a faded blue pillow tied to its back. Above the chair, within comfortable reach, was a shelf of well-thumbed books. An old-fashioned black wall telephone hung on the near side of the shelf.

"Any ideas?" Lisa demanded, holding out to Jim the paper she had been studying.

Jim looked at the sheet. It showed three lines of varying length, all perpendicular to a horizontal base. The lines were drawn with a heavy blue pencil. From the two ends of the base line a tall triangle rose to enclose the perpendiculars, none of which touched the triangle's sides. The triangle was drawn with a thick red marker.

"No," he said. "But this is no time for puzzles, Lisa."

"Isn't it?" She pushed the paper under his nose. He took it and examined it closely.

"Dad left this," she said. "I found it by the side of the chair, neatly clipped to a lapboard. The blue pencil and the red pen were lined up alongside."

"It looks like just a doodle to me, Lisa. A Ken Ward doodle. He was always designing, as you know. Designing planes was his hobby; making and marketing them, his job."

"Hobby, hell. It was his passion. It's what he lived for."

104

Jim put his hand on her shoulder. "Lisa, haven't you come off the soapbox yet? Your father lived for a lot of things."

"Name three."

"You. Your mother. Stephen."

She shook her head vehemently. "A noble try, Jim Lindner, but not true. I'll give you my three, and they come a lot closer. His life consisted of copters, the company and the corruption it took to cope with both."

"That's a dreadful thing to say, Lisa."

"That was a dreadful thing he did, Jim."

He could hear the shakiness underneath the determined voice and understood that the angry stance was an effort to hide her searing feeling of abandonment. Her fingers gripped the rocking chair and she began to swing it back and forth, back and forth, with mounting violence.

"Stop that," he said sharply. "You'll topple over."

"And one deadhead per family is enough," she retorted nastily.

"Lisa, for god's sake. I came to find you and see whether there's anything I can do."

"You found me," she said, bringing the chair to a halt with a jerk, "as you found me. Don't try to make me over. Everybody has tried that. It hasn't worked. It won't work." She grabbed the paper away from him and squinted at it with half-shut eyes. He thought he saw the eyes become moist.

"If you really want to help," she muttered, "you can figure out what this means. I have a hunch it's my father's real will and testament, as Stephen would say. I'm certain it has something to do with his death. And his life."

5

"Just what is the situation in Indonesia? I understand we're doing well there, and that's quite an accomplishment. But the files are not exactly informative on the country's problems or on our sales success. I'm told you would be. Informative that is. And knowledgeable."

Jim regarded the young woman sitting opposite him with interest. He had been told that Anne Gregory, The Copter Company's chief of corporate planning, held her job by dint of achievement. "Smart and perceptive" was the way Ken had described her shortly after he hired her in the summer of 1975. "A handy gadget" had been Russel Knight's assessment when he had mentioned her shortly after Jim had settled in at corporate headquarters as VP international.

At first glance, she did not look like a knockout. Her charcoal gray flannel suit, with a man's white silk shirt, lent her the appearance of one of those photographs that appeared occasionally in *Business Week* depicting the new young women executives who were giving their male counterparts a run for their money: prim, determined, cool.

But that impression changed when you looked longer and closer. The first surprise was the eyes. They were large, brilliant, slightly myopic and an astonishing emerald green.

The second surprise was her voice. It was a melodious alto and had a throaty chuckle in it when she challenged him: "I'd be interested in your sources. Gray eminences who tell tall tales worry me. They cast gray shadows."

An acute observation, even if the phrasing was cryptic. This streamlined headquarters with the windows on the world, as the builders described it, seemed to have all kinds of gray shadows lurking in its corners and corridors. And cryptic comment appeared to be the style of the house. The Indonesian file with its irritating gaps was a prime example.

"That's a good way of putting it." He hesitated for a moment. What the devil do I call her, he wondered. Miss Gregory? Or is she Mrs. something? "Anne," he said, "I feel the way you do about shadows. That's what troubles me about these files. I sense more shadow than substance. Take this one." He pulled closer the folder marked "Indonesia." "It's so anemic, I wonder whether it won't just fade away someday when no one's looking."

Annoyed and impatient, he rapped the folder with the knuckle of his middle finger. The folder was so thin that the energetic gesture sent a small spasm of pain through his hand. "Ouch," he said, looking surprised.

The chuckle that had been in her voice earlier now worked its way into a smile. She had a wide mouth on which she wore no lipstick. Her lips were pale, her skin alabaster with a smattering of freckles. The straight brown hair came almost to her shoulders but was meticulously curled under at the ends.

"Did you hurt yourself?" The concern was genuine.

He massaged the knuckle with his left hand. "I'll live," he said, "but I need help, Anne. I would appreciate your working with me on this."

The green eyes rested on him steadily. She looked pleased and watchful. "I'd be happy to. Where shall we start?"

"With Indonesia."

She picked up an old-fashioned gold watch with Roman numerals, which she wore at the end of a long gold chain. Her hand, with its well-kept nails and no polish, toyed with the timepiece. "It's a fascinating country in many ways. Its people look gentle, but don't necessarily act gently. The landscape is lovely, but most of the people who see it every day do not live very

107

lovely lives. There are layers and layers of problems—political, economic, social—that will keep festering for a long time to come."

"Then why is there nothing about all this in the files? Don't any of these problems affect our operations?"

"I'm sure they do. But we don't have to worry about it here at headquarters."

"Why not?"

"We have Cathy Quon."

"You'll have to elaborate on that statement, Anne. Let me tell you, though, that you're the second person who thinks it's a satisfactory answer. The first was Mr. Knight, who also advised me that Cathy Quon was a crackerjack. His words. But I really do need to know a little more about this mysterious woman and her operations."

The hand that had toyed with the watch dropped into her lap. She sat up straight. The warmth that had been in her voice earlier was gone. "Cathy Quon," she said, "is The Copter Company's representative for Southeast Asia. All of Southeast Asia. She runs our regional corporate headquarters out of Singapore. She has done very well for us throughout the area."

What's got into her all of a sudden? he wondered. What did I say that brought this on? "I know. That information is in even this file." He looked at the thin folder with distaste. Instead of rapping it, he patted it cautiously.

When he looked up again he saw her lips twitch into a pixie grin that added a new dimension to her face. It gave her a gamine quality, a startling note of contrast to the understated poise, the air of thoughtful balance she projected most of the time.

Anne's grin had been prompted by Jim's cautious pat. He was an attractive man, she decided, even if he did seem to have all the usual prejudices about women, Asia and probably everything else that was outside his own experience. And who knew how wide—or more likely narrow—that experience was?

"The files," she said, "really do contain all the data we need here. They contain no more because, as I'm sure you know, Mr. Knight is not given to asking unnecessary questions."

He looked up, startled and pleased. She was not only knowledgeable but also cued in on who was who and what was what
in the company.

"But," he said, "Miss Quon reported to Mr. Ward, not Mr.
Knight."

"Yes. She did this directly, verbally. Mr. Ward went to Singapore at least four times a year, in some years more often than
that."

The voice had been punctiliously informative. Nevertheless,
he detected a hint hidden in the statement. Was she suggesting
that there had been additional reasons for Ken's frequent journeys
to Singapore? Personal reasons?

"Well," he said lightly, "it looks as if I'd better collect my
briefings directly from the source as well. I'm planning a trip to
all of the places on which I don't find the files informative enough
for my requirements. I'll make Singapore my first stop."

"Where else will you be going?"

"Nigeria. That file troubles me for the opposite reason. It's
as fat as the Indonesian one is thin, but all it seems to say is
that we owe this person, uh . . . ."

"Pascal Udoyen."

"Thank you. That we owe Pascal Udoyen a hundred thousand
dollars per annum, apparently for all eternity, and for reasons
that completely escape me."

Her hands fluttered up in a gesture of resignation. "Udoyen
had Mr. Ward stumped too. He never could figure out whether
Udoyen was taking us for a ride or whether things in Nigeria
really work the way Udoyen claims they do."

"What do you think?"

"Mmm," she said. The pixie grin had vanished utterly. "I
think both are true. From an operational viewpoint, Nigeria is
really dreadful. Everything that should work doesn't: the port,
the roads, the telephone, electric power, the water supply. On
the other hand, the armed forces work overtime making life difficult, I gather, for a lot of people in a lot of ways. Whether they
make life difficult for Udoyen, I don't really know. He says they
do, which is why he hasn't produced any results. But he also

109

claims that some of his best friends are important officers, which is why we should pay him—and keep paying him—the very handsome amount he collects from us. Cathy Quon gets a lot less for producing a lot more." The last sentence had come out in a rush. The disparity clearly annoyed her.

"Speaking of producing," he said, "another stop on my itinerary is Abu Dhabi. Someone is certainly producing for us there. I don't understand what a country with a population of 250,000 people can possibly do with all the copters we've sold them. And the commission is awfully high. I'd like to find out why and just who it goes to."

Her hands had returned to her lap, laced lightly, palms up, offering two rosy hollows. "I don't know what they do with the copters either, but with their kind of income they probably used them to fly baby food to the bedouins. The commission is standard for the area. And I can tell you where it goes."

"You can?"

"It's a pattern. It goes to an agent designated by the customer. Each of the Emirates, in fact every country in the Arab Middle East, has a law stipulating that the agents of foreign companies must be local citizens. Not residents—citizens. The local governments want to have unquestionable control of the agents, legally and physically, in case any problems come up. Most of the Middle East countries also have a set scale of commissions established by either law or commercial custom. The agent then spreads the money around in the appropriate government circles. The art—and it is an art—lies in finding an agent who doesn't only collect a commission but renders real service. Fortunately, we do all right on that score in Abu Dhabi. Our agent was designated by the ruling family itself."

She really was well informed. Everything she said about the Middle East dovetailed with what Ken had told him in Mainz. But he wanted to know more. "How did we manage that?" he asked.

"I'm not sure 'managed' is the right word. It happened in Monte Carlo."

He tilted back in his chair and looked at her encouragingly. "Okay," he said, "tell me."

110

Her face changed expression. The eyes seemed filled with troubled wonder. "It really is a story," she said, "straight out of Scheherazade. It happened in the fall of 1974, about a year after Abu Dhabi, more accurately the Emir of Abu Dhabi, had unexpectedly and, I suppose from his point of view, miraculously come into a fabulous amount of money as the result of the OPEC-engineered price hike of oil. Just what made the Emir decide that some of this money should be spent on helicopters I can't say, but he did make that decision and word got to Mr. Ward that a nephew of the Emir's, with duly authorized purchasing power, would like to talk with The Copter Company."

"That was fortunate," Jim commented dryly.

She stiffened. "I don't believe it was entirely a matter of luck, Mr. Lindner. Mr. Ward had a network of friends, colleagues and employees that effectively covered the world."

He had touched a raw nerve, and he did not want to antagonize Anne Gregory. He smiled. "Please call me Jim. For tales from the *Arabian Nights,* Mr. Lindner doesn't sound right. Especially since it appears that I will be involved in some strange nights of my own." That remark had more of a double entendre than he had intended. "Or days," he added.

"Yes," she said flatly, "you will."

"In that case we have a cautionary tale here, don't we? Back, then, to Monte Carlo."

Was it a cautionary tale? she wondered. Had The Copter Company learned anything from it? Would Jim Lindner learn anything from it? It had killed Ken in the end, in its circuitous way. But she couldn't say that to this cool new vice-president. To begin with, he wouldn't believe her. Besides, he was clearly a man who went his own way. In a hurry.

"It was the Emir's nephew who chose Monaco as the meeting place," she said. "Mr. Ward thought it a bit odd—this was the company's first negotiation in the Middle East, and we weren't familiar then with the area's operating procedures—but Monaco isn't hard to get to, or hard to take when you are there. This was September, when the worst of the tourist crush is over but the harbor is still full of yachts and the sun still dances on the Mediterranean."

I know, he thought. I was there with Brigitte that same autumn. But how does Anne Gregory know? Was she there with Ken? Unlikely. She didn't join the company until the following year. But how long had Ken known her before that? And how well? His impression that the relationship had contained elements she was not prepared to discuss was strengthened when she switched unconsciously to the use of his first name as she continued. "Ken's first business meeting with the nephew of the Emir of Abu Dhabi took place at five o'clock in the morning. Ken was grouchy, because even he and Elaine don't rise that early, and the nephew was groggy with fatigue and beset by misfortune. He had spent the entire night in the casino and had managed to loose a round million at roulette. He explained to Ken that, as a result of the events of the night, he was in urgent need of recovering his losses. Unless he did, his uncle, the Emir, just might decide to cut off the hand that had dispersed the chips. Therefore he had a proposition. He would place an order right now, as soon as they had finished their coffee and croissants, for an initial consignment of twenty-five helicopters. The standard commission would be paid to an agent whom he was in a position to designate and who would represent The Copter Company from now on in what he confidently expected to be a continuing relationship profitable to all parties. On this particular occasion there would also be a negotiation fee—a finder's fee, if Ken preferred—of one million dollars that would not appear in any official papers that reached the Emirate. He would not presume to tell Ken how to handle the fee at his end of the business. The million was payable in a lump sum. Now.

"At that point he fished out a large alligator wallet—Ken remembered it because of its extraordinary size and because it had no compartment for credit cards—opened it, and held it under Ken's nose. The wallet was empty. 'You see what I mean,' said the nephew to Ken. 'There are times when a man needs a friend who helps without asking questions. That's how we do business in our part of the world. It's a good way. I recommend it.' "

Jim leaned forward. "And Ken took him up on the proposition?" Disbelief registered on his face.

"Yes. I know it doesn't sound like him. He was not a gambling man. Not that way."

Now what the hell did that mean? The Ken he had known wasn't a gambling man in any way. He took a businessman's calculated risks, and those only after very careful analysis. What did this girl know that he didn't?

"That's right," he said. "So why . . . ?"

He thought he detected a defensive tone in her voice as she proceeded to explain. "You have to remember," she said, "this was 1974. The Middle East market was just opening up, and everybody, certainly in the aircraft industry, was in hot pursuit. No one knew much about it except that it had its own ways and operated by its own rules. The nephew had laid out some of those rules for Ken. Friendship was a two-way street. He had friends in the other Emirates, as well as in Saudi Arabia, and if Ken and he saw eye to eye, he could have a word with those friends about the special qualities of The Copter Company. That was a self-evident courtesy."

Jim found his throat going dry. Had Max been right, after all? Different worlds. Different ways. He swallowed. "Go on," he said. She peered at him. Had she noticed his worry? Probably not. She was too near-sighted and not wearing glasses. Bless vanity, he thought gratefully.

Her voice returned to its narrative tone. "The nephew turned out to be as good as his word. As you know, there have been two additional orders from Abu Dhabi since then. We've beaten out our competitors in most of the other Emirates, and the first order from Saudi Arabia is in house."

"We do have the best product."

"I know. But I'm not at all sure that would have been a convincing argument for the nephew in fear of losing his hand."

Jim tried to keep his voice impersonal. "What did Ken do?"

"Some quick figuring, first. On the transaction itself, and the market prospects. Twenty-five copters were worth about twenty million dollars at the time, so a finder's fee of one million wasn't all that much out of line. If you added the possibility of the deal opening the door to other Middle East sales, it was a risk worth taking. Cheap at the price."

That was one way of looking at it. Ken's way? Knight's? "So?"

"So Ken handed over all the cash he had on him, which the nephew stuffed into his alligator wallet quickly and appreciatively. Then Ken wrote a check for the rest."

"A personal check?" Jim asked, surprised.

"No. I don't think Ken had that kind of money. He wrote a check on the Basel account."

The Basel account evidently served more purposes than Jim had realized. "Yes," he said, probing, "there was no reason to run that transaction through New York. Basel, incidentally, will be my last stop on this swing." He let his voice drop expectantly.

"There isn't much I can tell you about that. Switzerland doesn't require analysis from my department. All the variables there—social, political and economic—check out stable. The action in Switzerland is purely financial. That's Morse Clark territory." Her tone made clear that she had nothing to add to that statement. Or chose to add nothing. Whether this was because she knew no more, did not like what she knew or was simply accommodating herself to LMC's rigorous assertion of his territorial imperative Jim could not tell. He sat forward and pushed the Abu Dhabi folder to the side. "Scratch Abu Dhabi," he said.

She uncrossed her legs and put her feet on the floor. He had noticed her calves and ankles when she walked in. They were nicely articulated but thin, and gave her a gawky quality when she walked or stood. Deerlike.

"I think you can. The men in the Emirates like doing business abroad, unless it's a negotiation to set up a venture in their country. In that case they want to see the whites of your eyes, in situ. For straight purchases they'd just as soon do business in London, Paris or New York—or, of course, Monte Carlo." She looked speculative. "I guess they haven't discovered Reno yet. That may be because they don't need it for divorces."

Now what had that to do with anything? The girl had an interesting mind, but it did jump around. "Explanation, please," he said.

She grinned. The perky nose with its uptilt at the end twitched. "That's another story," she said, "not relevant to your trip."

"Okay, let's save that one then. But I do need takeouts on Southeast Asia and Nigeria before I leave. Say Friday afternoon. I take off Saturday morning."

She nodded. "Can do, and just in case the takeouts leave you with any questions, I'll let Mary know where I can be reached Friday night."

"Thanks. In fact"—the idea crossed his mind and he voiced it as it came—"why don't you have dinner with me on Friday if you are free? I can take a look at the material in the afternoon, and if I have any questions, we can talk about them in the evening." He got up and smiled. "That way you won't have to tell Mary where you can be found. I'll know."

She had risen with him. Fast work, she thought, and neatly done. But what does he really want? He seems nice, although I have no doubt there is more to this I-am-as-you-see-me stance than meets the eye. I'll have to get along with him, so I might as well find out what he's like as soon as I can.

"I'd be delighted," she said in her best Vassar voice.

When she had gone, Jim did not sit down again. Questions chased each other in his head. Anne Gregory had been informative all right, up to a point. But discreet. Too discreet. Discretion was a vital ingredient in a manager's job, as was the ability to make decisions. He had no quarrel with that. It was the proportions of the mix that bothered him. The quotient of discretion was too high throughout the headquarters of The Copter Company, where management style seemed to consist of keeping mum. He had been in his new job for over three months now and still had not been able to determine just who was setting the style. It could be simply a matter of temperament. Companies had personalities with their own traits and characteristics in the same way individuals did, and personalities either suited you or they didn't. There was no point in running the whys and hows through a computer. You just got a shambles if you tried to break down style into computer bits.

115

He began to pace. His office, despite its stupendous view, was both smaller and less elegant than that of The Copter Company's Generaldirektor in Mainz. There was not nearly so much room, and pacing set his mental juices flowing, especially when he needed to bring his thoughts in line with his intuition. Right now his intuition was telling him that a subtle message had been conveyed, intimating he should remember the old adage that what you did not know couldn't hurt you. He did not believe this. What you didn't know, he was convinced, could hurt badly.

A meeting with Knight the previous day had deepened his unease. He could not put his finger on just what it was that had made him feel uncomfortable. He was certain it had not been Morse Clark's senior VP charade. That was office politics. He expected that and could deal with it. What nagged at him was what Knight had said, or rather not said.

It had been an early morning meeting, called at Jim's request. He had walked into Knight's office at eight-thirty to find Morse Clark already ensconced in the larger, more comfortable chair facing the president's desk. Morse Clark generally kept banker's hours. The explanation was that he entertained often and late, and he generally did not appear much before ten. Also, Jim had not requested Morse Clark's presence, and Knight had said nothing about wanting Morse Clark there.

Knight did start the meeting by explaining that he had asked Morse Clark to join them "because your lines cross his in a number of places. I want to be sure you keep him fully informed."

Informed of what, Jim had wondered. Morse Clark was copied on all financial transactions as a matter of routine. "Of course," he had responded blandly. Morse Clark had made no comment. He had sat in his chair, legs crossed at the ankles, looking abstracted. His posture had indicated that he was there only as a presence, uninvolved in whatever grubby operational detail Jim had insisted on discussing with the president of the company.

"Okay, Jim," Knight had said, "what's on your mind?"

His brusqueness had jolted Jim. He had come to talk about some of the baffling omissions in the files, expecting Knight to fill him in on the gaps, or at least tell him why they existed.

116

Three minutes into the meeting, his instincts had told him that he would get nothing from Knight. He would have to proceed differently.

"I'm pretty well set now," he had said easily. "And I've gone through all the files."

Knight's shrewd eyes had seemed to contain an unspoken challenge. "Yes" was all he had said.

Jim had struggled to keep his voice unperturbed. "There're a couple of situations that I don't quite get a feel for, and I thought I'd check them out personally."

Again Knight had surprised him. He had expected Knight to inquire just what the situations were. Instead, Knight had taken his cigar out of his mouth just long enough to say, "That's a good idea." He had said it quickly, too quickly.

After that there had been a brief awkward pause. Jim had felt as if he had been handed his marbles and was expected to pick himself up and go. But he had been wrong again. Knight did have something more to say.

"When you get back," Knight had instructed, signaling the meeting was indeed over, "I'll want a report. I'm not a paper shuffler, so a verbal report will do. I'd like you to bear in mind that I would prefer not to file an Eight-K with our friends at the Securities Exchange Commission. I'll be looking for your assessment of that on your return."

At that point Morse Clark had spoken for the first time. "You should go to Basel," he had said, "and introduce yourself to our bankers there. They knew Ken Ward very well. They don't know you. I'll send you over what I think you'll need."

It had sounded more like an order than an offer of cooperation. Jim had understood that Morse Clark was making a point: He was an established senior vice-president; Jim was only a newly baked VP. Morse Clark was nailing down their respective standing in the corporate hierarchy.

Jim's response had been carefully calibrated. He could be as adept as the next man at corporate gamesmanship. He did not take to it with a passion, but if someone set up a board, he could play.

117

"Thank you, Larry," he had said. "I'm sure that will be helpful." Jim, knowing that in The Copter Company Morse Clark was addressed as Larry only by Knight, had been pleased to see annoyance register on Morse Clark's face.

When Jim had left, Morse Clark had looked at Knight. "Overplays his hand," Morse Clark said. "That can be, uh, inadvisable."

Knight concentrated on choosing a cigar from the humidor on his desk. "We'll find out soon enough," he said. "Anyhow, I don't see where we have much choice. Ken isn't with us anymore."

That afternoon three pieces of paper were delivered to Jim's desk. The first was the carbon copy of a letter from Knight to the enforcement division of the Securities Exchange Commission informing it that he had instructed the executive in charge of international operations to conduct an investigation into the company's activities abroad to see whether any of them warranted an Eight-K report. If, contrary to expectations, the investigation should turn up data calling for such a report, it would be made as soon as the relevant facts were available. The letter indicated that a copy had gone to James H. Lindner, Vice-President, International.

The second piece of paper to arrive was a sealed white envelope of very good stock marked PERSONAL AND CONFIDENTIAL. Jim's first reaction had been to wonder whether the erratic blonde at the reception desk had decided to make her move. Picking up the malachite-topped letter opener he had inherited from Ken but had had few occasions to use—Ken's secretary had decided to stay on and not only opened but knowledgeably presorted Jim's mail—he carefully cut across the top of the linen-textured flap. He was taken aback by what he saw. Inside was a small piece of paper typed on a machine different from the late model IBM's that were standard in the company's executive suite. The slip read:

BANK: Freie Strasse, Basel
ACCOUNT NUMBER: 23684KW
IDENTIFICATION: Chopper
BANKER: Jürgen Zwirli

He turned the envelope upside down and shook it, but there was nothing else. He thought for a moment, then folded the slip in the middle and put it in his wallet.

The third piece of paper Mary handed him just before the end of the day was a hand-scrawled memo from Knight. It said, "Suggest you have AG brief you before you leave. She knows her business." It was signed "Russ."

The restaurant was called Once Upon a Stove. Warm, crowded and cozy, it consisted of two long and narrow rooms. The back room had once been the vestibule of a tiny neighborhood church. It had very high ceilings, and a wooden railing ran about two thirds of the way up the paneled walls. Piled on the balcony behind the railing was a motley collection of mahogany music stands, wooden chests that had held vestments, a voluminous wormeaten wardrobe, a potbellied stove, stools, benches and half a dozen pews. The feeling was of an attic clean enough to make possible dining in it in comfort and style.

The restaurant had been Anne's choice. It was in the east twenties, within walking distance of her apartment in Murray Hill.

When she entered, Jim's impulse was to hug her. She looked lovely. The tailored businesswoman had become a girl in russet wool slacks, an enormous yellow turtleneck sweater and a deep green velvet jacket that made her eyes look like ferns in a forest.

It occurred to him that it had been almost four months since he had had dinner with an attractive woman. Just before Christmas there had been a postcard from Brigitte postmarked Tangier. It had said only, "New year in the sun really *is* different," and was signed, *"Auf Wiedersehen,* B." But it had said nothing about when she expected to see him again or where. He had not replied. There had been no return address.

The owner of the restaurant eyed Anne and Jim approvingly and conducted them to a booth in the back room. Two steps led up to the booth, which had burnished wooden benches, curved in the back, and an oblong table covered with a red-and-white-checked cloth, held in place by a small glass lamp. It was like having a picnic in the middle of February in the heart of Manhattan.

Over cocktails they talked shop. He did not have many questions. The takeouts had been concise and complete. As Jim had been told, Anne Gregory's department did good work. Their business done, he proposed that since she knew the restaurant, she order dinner. They had mussels cooked with raisins, a moussaka that melted in the mouth and a big salad that came in a wooden bowl, with black olives, carrot sticks and feta cheese. They also had a lot of Chianti.

After dessert—an apple pie baked on the premises, with a double scoop of vanilla ice cream—she sighed with contentment. "I've never had the thank-god-it's-Friday feeling, but there can be something nice about the end of a full and fascinating week."

"Yes," he said. "If someone scratched my back right now, I think I'd purr."

The green eyes considered him. "And what," she bantered, "would you do with your claws?"

He put his hands on the table and stretched back into his bench. "Good question. I guess that depends on who does the scratching. And how."

"I bet."

He came out of his stretch. "Which reminds me. You owe me—"

"What?" Her voice tightened.

"A story. The story of why Middle East potentates don't need Reno."

"Ah." Her mouth turned up at the corners. "Once upon a time there was . . ."

"Yes," he urged.

"A gentleman from Qatar," she continued, "who came to call on The Copter Company. He was a friend of the Emir's notorious nephew. Mr. Knight talked to him all morning. Mr. Knight and Ken took him to lunch, upstairs on the 107th floor, and Ken talked to him all afternoon. That was business. The problem arose of what to do with him in the evening or, really, who would be doing it. He had already made clear what he wanted. He wanted to dine at Twenty One. He had heard about it from a good friend in Kuwait, who was another friend of the Emir's nephew.

120

"At around five o'clock Ken came to my office and laid out his problem. 'A hot customer,' he said, 'who, I gather, at this point would greatly appreciate some female company. Are you free to join us for dinner? We would appreciate it. Him and me.'

"Ken, as perhaps you know, wasn't very fond of nightlife. After a long day's work he liked going home, and places like the Twenty One were not his kind of thing to begin with. 'They take themselves seriously,' he once told me. 'Too seriously for my taste. I like good food as much as the next man, but they make me feel they expect me to get up and salute every dish they put in front of me. Come dinnertime, I want to sit back and relax, not stand up and salute.'

"Anyhow, Ken wanted me to come along, and I did. I too had heard about Twenty One, and hadn't yet been there. Besides, I like meeting people who look at the world in a different way. I like to hear what they think and observe how they behave.

"Our guest that evening was worth watching. At the restaurant, he wanted to know who in the room was famous and nodded acknowledgment when he recognized a name. He recognized surprisingly many. He also seemed to order from the right side of the menu. For every course, he chose the item with the highest price. I don't know whether he was testing the generosity of The Copter Company, a serious consideration, I understand, in the Middle East, or whether he was conducting an experiment of some other kind. Ken never said a word, and I decided to be gracious in proper Middle East fashion and joined him in everything he ordered. That really went down well. Too well.

"When dinner was over, he thought the evening had just begun. He had also heard of El Morocco. Could we go on there? Ken had had enough by then. It was ten o'clock. He mumbled something about last trains—which was a misstatement, to put it tactfully, because Ken drove in—and thought that would get us off the hook. It didn't. Abdul el Selah Rahman just looked at Ken—not, mind you, at me—and said, 'Perhaps Miss Gregory would accompany me.'

"I have to say for Ken, he was crestfallen. He really had not meant to saddle me with our corporate guest for the rest of

121

the evening, but I was feeling rambunctious and decided that there wasn't much that could happen to me at El Morocco that I didn't want to happen.

"So off we went. When we arrived, Abdul Rahman slipped the headwaiter a hundred-dollar bill, which produced a ringside seat right at the edge of the dance floor. Mr. Rahman ordered, very quietly, 'the best champagne in the house, if you please'; and that, with another rolled-up bill, this time a twenty, brought us Veuve Cliquot. For a while he sat and watched the dancers. The men, I noticed, got short shrift. I think he was interested only in what they were wearing. But he really studied the women from the ankles up, back and front. I'm not sure he looked at their faces, but he did take in everything else. Finally he asked me to dance. He was soft and pudgy and made me think of a cream puff. I figured he'd try the cheek-to-cheek bit, shuffling around in the dim light under El Morocco's fake palms. I was wrong on both scores. He didn't try anything, and he danced like a dream. He seemed to melt into what little melody the orchestra produced, and with a rhythm of his own managed to gentle down the beat of the band. I really enjoyed myself. So, it turned out, did he.

"When we sat down, he ordered some more champagne. After it had been poured—we got very good service that night—he asked me how I would like to come to Qatar. I said I'd like it fine, and perhaps I could build two or three days into my next European trip and stop off to pay a visit. This left him genuinely puzzled.

" 'Two or three days? But you cannot even say salaam in that time. Anyhow, you do not understand me. I would like you to come to live in Qatar. I would give you a villa of your own, all the servants you need and anything else you want. I have other European ladies living with me in the same way, and they are all enjoying themselves.'

"It was my turn to be puzzled. I guess I gulped and murmured something about being certain my father wouldn't like the idea. Nor would The Copter Company.

" 'Your father is Christian?'

" 'Yes. Catholic.'

" 'Ah.' Another mediation. 'I could not marry you now. I already have four wives. But I could divorce number four. It would be expensive. Her dowry is invested in very good real estate in London.'

"I nodded gravely and concurred that London real estate was a good investment.

"He took me home in a chauffeured Rolls-Royce—he must have asked El Morocco to order it for him while I was in the ladies' room—and never even got out of the car when we arrived at my house. I did feel his eyes on me as I climbed out, traveling up and down my back. The last I saw of him, he had tucked his feet under and was sitting cross-legged like a Buddha on the pearl-gray upholstery of the Rolls. He looked awfully comfortable."

She seemed to be conjuring up the man in her mind, relaxing pasha-fashion in his rented Rolls in the silent streets of Murray Hill. A look of fond amazement flooded her face.

"The rest of the story is secondhand. I wasn't there, but I did hear all about it."

"Go on," Jim prompted.

"Late the following morning, Abdul el Selah Rahman telephoned Morse Clark and asked for an appointment. He wanted to discuss a personal financial matter not connected with the purchase of helicopters.

"You know Morse Clark. If there is such a thing as a seventh heaven for LMC, he was in it after that call. He had visions, I imagine, of petrodollars rolling around the 106th floor of the World Trade Center in large clinky amounts, and a vista of himself as the discreet and indispensable adviser on the billion-dollar funds someone has to guard for the Emir and his entourage. Only it didn't work out that way." Mischievous delight sparkled in her eyes.

He felt an urge to hold her face in his hands and get as close as he could to those amazing emeralds. Instead, he smiled. "I find it hard to imagine Morse Clark in any kind of heaven. How did he come back to earth?"

"How, I don't know; but I can tell you when. They had made

123

polite preliminary noises to each other, Morse Clark expressing his pleasure at the opportunity to be of service in any confidential financial matter Mr. Rahman might have in mind. Then, from friend Abdul: 'How much would it cost to have Miss Gregory come to Qatar?'

"Morse Clark, sounding mystified but in managerial control: 'Miss Gregory? Well, we don't generally make her available for consultation outside the company, but I suppose there is no reason why, as a special accommodation for a valued customer, this could not be arranged. I will need to check what the daily rate would be for her professional services, but I estimate that it would not exceed five hundred dollars a day. Plus, of course, transportation and other out-of-pocket expenses.'

"Abdul, thoughtfully: 'Yes. I see. That seems reasonable. It would come to about 120,000 dollars a year.'

"At that point, it seems, LMC turned on a recording cassette he keeps hidden in one of those antique boxes on his desk. The rest of the story comes directly off the tape.

"Morse Clark: 'I really doubt that we could spare Miss Gregory for a year. She, uh, does valuable work here.'

"It must have cost him to say that. In his heart, I am sure, LMC thinks strategic planning is unnecessary, and costs the company too much money. He also thinks that having it headed by a woman is asinine, as well as an affront to the company's image."

Anne looked at Jim. He held up his right hand. "I plead not guilty. Having a woman head up strategic planning is okay with me, if she knows what she's doing. I gather this one does."

She grinned. "Okay. Back to the tape. Abdul: 'Could I not acquire Miss Gregory outright?'

"Morse Clark, temper snapping: 'Mr. Rahman. This company sells helicopters, not women.'

"Rahman: 'I told you this was a confidential financial matter.'

"Morse Clark: 'Indeed you did, Mr. Rahman. But your inquiry exceeds my area of expertise. Or experience.'

"Rahman: 'I see.' The sound of his rising from the chair. 'Well, thank you very much. I regret we cannot do business. Good day.'

"End of tape. Which Morse Clark practically ripped out of its box. Tape in hand, he tore down the hall to Mr. Knight's office, sputtering that he wanted to talk about Qatar. The Middle East was known to be Ken's special bailiwick, so Mr. Knight called in Ken. Together they listened to the tape and roared. That made Morse Clark hopping mad. I don't think he has talked to me since."

"But," Jim protested, "Qatar bought a consignment of copters. I saw the record of the transaction in the files."

She winked. "Why, sure. We make the world's best copters. Rahman didn't say he wouldn't do business on planes. It was Morse Clark's incompetence in the other transaction he regretted."

"You mean the transfer of the assets of Anne."

She gurgled, sounding like a little girl at play. "That's a fine way of putting it. The transfer of the assets of Anne. Only they didn't get transferred."

"All things considered," he said in a judicious tone, "that's just as well."

Anne snuggled into her corner of the booth. She was pleased with herself. If that was how the new VP international felt about the chief of strategic planning, that was fine. He did sound as if he meant it. Still, it wouldn't hurt to make sure. She uncurled and sat up straight. "I'm glad you think so."

"Doesn't everybody? Given the inevitable exception." Something in his tone indicated that he shared her attitude toward the unnamed exception.

"I believe so. Now. But it wasn't always that way."

"Oh?"

"When I started out in the company, strategic planning was known as 'Ken's folly,' and when I was safely out of earshot, they referred to me as 'Ward's ward.'"

His eyes narrowed with amusement. "Yeah," he said. "I remember now. That one even made its way to Mainz. Max Feld had some fun with it."

"What kind of fun?" The sense of isolation, of subtle but constant embattlement that had marred her first years at The

125

Copter Company, gripped her again. Was he, after all, identifying with those cheap shots she had seemed to attract endlessly when she first came to the firm?

He sensed her distress. "It wasn't all that funny," he said, putting what he hoped would be a comforting distance between himself and the sense of humor of Max Feld.

"What did he say?"

"You may remember he was in New York for a few days early in 1976. I guess you hadn't been with us very long. When he got back to Mainz, he reported, 'Weni, Widi, Ward's ward.' " Jim exaggerated the German mispronunciation of the V's. The impersonation made her laugh. It sounded funny on Jim Lindner.

"Vell"—she joined the game—"that wasn't too bad. There vas vorse in New York."

"I bet," he said encouragingly.

"There was, for instance, Robert Clayton the Third, who, along with his other charms, insisted that he not be called either Bob or Rob, but Robert. In full. All the time."

Was the slight quaver in her voice anger? Bitterness? Hurt?

"And what was Robert Clayton the Third to Ward's ward, or Ward's ward to Robert Clayton the Third?"

"He was after me."

"That's understandable."

She waved. It was a gesture of dismissal. "I don't mean that way. He wasn't after me personally. I don't think it ever occurred to him that I was a person. He was after my job."

"That happens to all of us sooner or later."

True, but what was he really telling her? That she was a crybaby? Or that they were all in the same boat?

"Yes," she agreed. "I suppose so."

But there was a difference, her mind insisted. There shouldn't be, but damn it, there was. And there was no point pretending there wasn't. Robert Clayton would never have done to a man what he did to her.

Her memory darted back to the day Robert Clayton III arrived at The Copter Company, a pink-cheeked Harvard MBA, with longish hair calculatingly balanced by a Brooks Brothers suit. She

126

had been with the company for over a year then and was just beginning to work with Ken on mapping out the objectives and resources of a strategic planning unit. Robert Clayton had in fact been recruited for that nascent enterprise.

When he discovered who A. Gregory was, he decided she represented no obstacle to the meteoric career of Robert Clayton III. He began, immediately and systematically, to demolish her at meetings. The way he did this was by smiling tolerantly whenever Anne spoke, and ignoring everything she said. He thought nothing of interrupting her in the middle of a sentence, not, as he invariably pointed out, to be rude, but because, he would imply, what she had said simply did not matter. Or as he put it, was not genuinely relevant to the topic under discussion. He assumed that all the other men around the table shared his view. Anne was always the only woman in the room.

Robert's trench warfare culminated in a frontal assault one afternoon during a discussion of Indonesia. The Copter Company was eying the country not only as a market but as a possible investment site. Anne had attempted to convey the complex and nebulous amalgam of social and political factors—nebulous certainly to the group of engineers by training, mind cast or both who were attending the conference—that would have to be considered if the company were to make a long-term commitment in that country.

Robert had cut her short. "What we need, of course," he had said authoritatively, "is a systems approach, a risk index that quantifies the commercial, financial, economic, political and, if you will, social factors, and juxtaposes them to quantified opportunity indices which we will construct. The opportunity cost picture will shake out of this exercise very precisely."

That was the way Robert talked. At first, a great many people in the company had been impressed. It sounded savvy and scientific. If they did not always catch the gist of what Robert was saying, they figured it was probably their fault. They weren't as up on this kind of stuff as he was, and they probably should be.

During the meeting on Indonesia everyone had gone along as usual with Robert's suggestion. Ken had said, "Okay, Robert.

Why don't you do your thing and let me have a look at it." To Anne, who had left the meeting feeling both badgered and betrayed, he had added curtly, "I want one of your country profiles too. Before the week's out."

Well, that worm had turned all right! Robert had delivered his report two weeks after the meeting, and Ken had mulled it over for a couple of days. Then he had written across the top of Robert's paper, "I think this is bullshit"; on Anne's country profile he had noted, "This makes sense"; and he had sent both submissions to Knight. The following day the two papers had come back to Ken with a typed note from the company president. "I agree," the note said.

Three months later the strategic planning unit was formally slotted into the company's table of organization. A five-year forecast for the growth of the unit was hammered out and budgeted. Anne was promoted from research analyst to corporate planner, and moved from a cubbyhole at the end of a long corridor to an office of respectable size three doors down from Ken Ward.

Jim had watched the lights and shadows chase each other on Anne's face. He was not certain whether they were effects created by the pink bulb of the lamp at the far end of their table or whether they reflected memories passing through her mind.

"Whatever happened to Robert Clayton the Third?" he asked. "I don't see him around."

She pushed her hands into the pockets of her jacket. "He dropped out of the race. Went to look for bluer skies. Come to think of it, he probably went to look for bigger computers. Anyhow, he left us after the strategic planning unit was structured and staffed and I was appointed head of it. He couldn't take that. He had figured the job was his by right of regression analysis, meta-development and matrix organization, not to mention systems approach."

Her voice vibrated with latent fury. The girl could fight when provoked. "How about some more coffee to celebrate the timely departure of Robert Clayton the Third from The Copter Company?"

The wide mouth stretched to a grin. "That celebration," she said, "calls for an Irish coffee."

128

When the coffees arrived in tall glasses piled high with whipped cream, she started on hers by scooping up the crest of the cream with her tongue. It was small, pink and agile, and launched Jim's mind in a direction he thought it should not take.

"How long did the metamorphosis take?"

She looked up from her coffee.

"From Ward's ward to chief of strategic planning," he amplified.

She reached for the straw on her saucer and dropped it through what was left of the cream, deep into the coffee. "I joined the company in the summer of 1975. I became head of the unit early in 1978. Just about this time last year. After the Brazil deal."

He put his palms against his glass. The glass was warm, the coffee fragrant, and the whiskey, when he took a swallow, burned pleasantly on the tongue. "I know about the Brazil deal. But I didn't know you were involved in getting it off the ground." He had no objection to sounding impressed. He was.

She drew deeply on her straw. A glow spread over her face. "Ken sent me down to Rio to shepherd the papers through the investment approval apparatus. He said that if he'd sent one of the men, they wouldn't have come back until carnival was over. This was in January." She looked at him, surprised. "Only thirteen months ago. It's hard to believe. It seems a lot longer."

Where had he been thirteen months ago? In St. Moritz with Brigitte. But Anne Gregory was right. It did seem a long time ago. Even the three months that had passed since he tried to reach Brigitte in November to tell her that he would be staying in New York seemed a very long time. There had been no reply at the Villa Mare when he called. He had telephoned the house in Mainz every weekend until the postcard from Tangier arrived, forwarded by Miss Kestenmeier. He had spent the New Year with his parents, and in January had written Brigitte a letter with the news of his transfer, asking her to call New York when she returned. He had mailed the letter to the house in Mainz but had heard nothing yet.

"International types like us," he said, intentionally creating a bond between himself and Anne, "develop a different sense of time. It seems to matter less and mean more."

The green eyes lit up. "You mean we learn to forget about the clock and pack a lot into the moment."

"Yes," he said. "Whenever. Wherever."

Her mind raced back to Rio. He was right. Certainly that's what had happened in Brazil.

She had arrived at the government investment office in Rio at ten o'clock on Monday morning. She had been told there was no point in getting there earlier; she would find no one to do business with. That had turned out to be true. João do Lira did not appear until close to eleven, but when he saw her in his waiting room he was all apologies and ushered her into his office immediately. They worked the rest of the morning. He was attentive, alert and expert: expert at his work and expert at life.

It had been close to two in the afternoon when they finished the first review of the papers, and by that time her stomach had begun to rumble. She never found out whether he had actually heard the sound or whether his invitation was just another sign of his extraordinary empathy. "Are you free for lunch perhaps?" he had asked. "Lunch, and a little time after lunch?" His eyes, bright and concentrated while they had been working, had turned the color and consistency of molten chocolate.

She had shaken her head. "Thanks, but I can't. I have another appointment." That had not been true. She had been told that between two and five on summer afternoons—and it was deep summer in Rio—anyone who had to be in the city did not spend that time working, if it could possibly be helped. She hadn't been ready then for what João obviously had in mind. He had been very relaxed about it. "Ah," he had said. "A pity. I'll see you tomorrow then." And he had bent over and kissed her lightly, teasingly on the lips.

He had agreed to work with her again the following afternoon. The work went swimmingly. By five o'clock all the blanks on the papers had been filled in, discussed and double-checked.

"Bom," João had said. "Or, as you would say, that makes all systems go."

Anne had felt a wave of elation and attraction. Elation because she had been warned that it would be difficult to do business in Latin America, that it would take a long time, and that it would be replete with unexpected problems. None had appeared. Attraction bounced around the charming and clever young man who had so effectively disposed of all the dire predictions. She felt like celebrating. Can I buy you a drink? she had been tempted to ask. But she had caught herself in time and amended: "Would you care to have cocktails with me?"

At that, João had smiled. "That would be a great pleasure. An early cocktail so we have some time afterwards. I would like to show you a little of Rio. Eight o'clock?"

In Rio eight o'clock was the beginning of the cocktail hour, and the bar of Anne's hotel, the Ouro Verde, was crowded. It was a delightful bar: a sidewalk array of comfortable chairs, small tables and a lot of lush greenery facing Copacabana beach. The hotel was known for the excellence of its food, the generosity of its drinks and the finesse of its service. Anne could vouch for all three. The hotel had treated her, an attractive woman alone, as if she were a treasure of the house. Whenever she appeared in the dining room, whether it was for breakfast, lunch or dinner, they had ushered her to the best table and lavished her with attention. In the morning they gave her a quiet table near the window so she could start the day looking out at the sea. In the evening they seated her in the center of the dining room so she could see and be seen. They had made her feel pampered and precious.

João, when he arrived for cocktails, had steeped her in more of the same treatment. He had made clear that he was proud and pleased to be with her. When they had left the bar to go to dinner, he had offered her his arm. To her own surprise, she took it.

They had dined in a candlelit restaurant tucked away in an alley downtown. The place specialized in the regional cuisine of Brazil's Northeast, offering delectable dishes with exotic flavors and fragrances. Dinner was served by copper-colored mulatto women with scrumptious figures and beautiful faces. A strolling trio of young men with rippling muscles played and sang sensuous music with simple melodies and complicated rhythms.

131

It was well past midnight when they left the restaurant, and Anne wondered where the time had gone. It seemed incredible that she had been in Rio barely forty-eight hours, that she had accomplished everything she had hoped to do, and that this luminous moon over Sugarloaf Mountain was real and so was the sinuous scallop of the beach.

João had insisted they go to a typical Brazilian nightclub after dinner, and they had done so, watching a long show of Brazilian dances, international comedy routines and dollops of intricate capoeira wrestling. They had held hands while they watched, and when the show was finally over he had suggested a stroll on the beach. "We can look for candles for Yemanja." Yemanja, he had explained, was the goddess of the waters, worshipped by Brazilians who were drawn to macumba, the mystic cult that had its roots in Africa but still flourished in Brazil's Northeast and had millions of devotees throughout the country. At certain times of the year, Yemanja's disciples lit votive candles for the goddess at the shore of the sea.

They had not found any candles, although they had looked for an hour. But the sand had been soft under their bare feet—at João's suggestion they had taken off their shoes and stockings—and the wind had been warm, moist and caressing. Anne had been elated by success; by heavy, heady Brazilian wine; and by the extravagant attentions of João do Lira. At three o'clock in the morning they had made love on the beach, with the sound of the sea in their ears, the rhythm of the waves in their bodies. It was an act of obeisance, João had whispered, to Yemanja, the goddess of the waters.

"And did you?" Jim asked. She looked at him and blinked. "Shepherd the papers, I mean."

She picked up her glass and sipped at her coffee. "Yes, I did. I was back in New York before the week was out. The investment was approved a couple of months later. As you know, we have a joint venture there now."

Knight's decision that Anne was a handy gadget probably dated to that period.

Her mind had moved along the same track. "After that,"

132

she said, "Mr. Knight wasn't embarrassed anymore when he met me in the corridor. He actually knew who I was. He even introduced me to the chairman one morning when I ran into the two of them on the way to a board meeting." There was a caustic note of triumph in her voice. The image of Anne Gregory talking with Knight and Asherton made Jim shake his head. It could not have been easy for a girl straight out of Vassar to make her way in the very male world of The Copter Company. Come to think of it, it was a strange choice for both The Copter Company and Anne Gregory. What had prompted the choice on her side? Jim realized with a rush of regret that he knew very little about this competent, very appealing girl sitting on the other side of the narrow table, absorbed, it appeared, in examining closely what little was left of her Irish coffee.

"What made you decide to come to The Copter Company? Did you find us, or did we find you?"

"You found me. Ken came to Vassar when I was in my senior year and we got to talking."

"What on earth was Ken doing at Vassar? Lisa wouldn't have been caught dead in a place like that, I would have thought."

"I know Lisa, and you're right. Vassar would have driven her out of her mind. Or at least up its ivy-covered walls. Actually, it was Morse Clark's daughter, Jennifer, who was responsible for Ken's appearance in Poughkeepsie. She was a sophomore at Vassar when I was a senior."

An image presented itself to Jim. He saw Anne in slacks and a big sweater, much as she looked now, strolling, as he had almost a decade earlier, under the rainbow-colored foliage of the campus. Pacing probably, as he had done also, trying to sort out her life and her future. His heart went out to her.

"How do we get from Jennifer Morse Clark to Ken Ward?" he asked.

She caught the warmth and interest in his voice. Vivaciously she responded, "Jennifer has her father's instincts for the advantageous. A special seminar had been scheduled at school with glamorous outside speakers. The topic was 'The Multinational Corporation on the Global Chessboard: Queen or Pawn?' I remember the title because it was so quintessentially Vassar. Anyhow, Jennifer wanted to be in that seminar for status reasons and volunteered to recruit the corporate speaker. She did not suggest her father, but she did procure a candidate from her father's firm. That was Jennifer's description of The Copter Company. Mr. Knight, I gather, doesn't do that kind of thing. He doesn't communicate easily with young people. His own kids have really struck out on their own. Gone way off the rails, from his point of view. So Ken was volunteered for the assignment."

Her head dropped and he had difficulty hearing her as she continued. "Ken didn't mind. He had his own problems with the generation gap, but he was interested in young people and curious about them. 'Like to find out how the other half thinks,' he used to say. I thought he did awfully well at that seminar. He explained what multinational companies really are, and what they're not; what they can do, and what they can't; what they're good at, and where they make mistakes. His presentation was straight, practical and unpretentious. He wasn't patronizing and he didn't hand out propaganda. 'The workhorses of the world,' he called the companies. I liked that, after our more high-flying, if not necessarily high-minded, speakers had painted multinational corporations as either devils or the saviors of mankind. I also got some good sensible answers from Ken in the question period that followed. At the end of the evening there was a reception for the speakers at Alumni House, and some of the seniors were invited. I was close to getting my degree, a combined bachelor in economics and political science, so I was a natural. Ken and I got immersed in a conversation over the dreadful punch they serve at Vassar on such occasions." There was a twinkle in her eyes. "I suspect what really got us going is that we both preferred our conversation to what we were drinking."

"In the matter of drink," Jim said, "you've been nursing the last of that coffee for half an hour. Let me get you another."

She shook her head. "No, thanks; no more room. I was savoring it, not saving it; letting the coffee and the whiskey really get together. That's good Irish whiskey. And pretty good coffee. A fine combination, surely."

There was a lilt to the way she pronounced "surely." Irish, of course. It hadn't occurred to him until now. That accounted for the spunk and the dander beneath the soft voice and the casually classic clothes.

"There isn't much more to tell anyhow. Ken said to check in with him after I graduated. I did. He hired me."

"He hired me too," Jim said, "fresh off a New England campus. We worked together until he went to Germany in 1969. He taught me some fundamentals that my brilliant professors had neglected to mention."

She eyed him questioningly. "Such as," he spelled out, "it all starts on the factory floor, and involves people every step of the way."

She said nothing for a moment, but her mouth quivered. Her voice had a choked quality when she spoke. "Ken Ward," she said, "was a good man. They had no business . . ." She caught herself and did not complete the sentence.

Jim felt the hair at the back of his neck stiffen. Who are they? he wondered. And no business doing what? He couldn't push her for answers to these questions. He wouldn't get anywhere if he tried. Someday perhaps. The prospect was more pleasant than it had any right to be. It made him feel all of a piece. "Last call," he said. "Coffee? Or home?"

He hoped she would choose coffee and tell him what she knew about Ken's grim way of calling it quits.

She understood what he wanted, but she did not trust him yet. She did not trust herself. After all, she couldn't be sure. And this was too serious a matter for guesswork. "Home," she said. "You're leaving tomorrow morning, aren't you? And I have some work to catch up with. The VP international kept me kind of busy this week."

He bowed from the waist as well as he could, sitting in a booth. "The VP international is most grateful and looks forward with anticipation to further fruitful collaboration with the chief of the department of corporate strategic planning."

She picked up her glass with both hands and slowly drained it. As she set it down, she said quietly, "You might want to have a word with Cathy Quon about Ken. I believe she knew him very well."

6

Singapore was sultry. Sodden clouds strolled across the sky, and the city was covered by a blanket of humidity. To Jim it felt like one of Brigitte's silk-covered goosedown comforters under which one could laze away not just nights but days.

Sky and air, however, were the only somnolent elements on the island. The people, and every aspect of the society they had devised in their tiny city-state, moved lickety-split. Jim's plane, which had arrived exactly on time, was met on the tarmac by two smart-looking and smartly moving young men, sensibly dressed in light trousers and open-necked white shirts, who expeditiously cleared the aircraft, its crew and its passengers. Two minutes later the passengers were filing down the mobile ramp and into a bus, neither new nor air-conditioned, but clean and well maintained.

The processing inside the arrival building was quick and courteous. The young woman at customs gave Jim and his olive briefcase and neatly packed two-suiter an experienced glance and waved him through. "Welcome to Singapore," she said. It sounded practiced and conventional, but her exotic eyes seemed to speak a language of their own that lent an intriguing implication to the perfunctory phrase.

When Jim turned his head to double-check the impression, he witnessed a quite different encounter. The bearded young man who had followed him in the customs line was getting considerably

136

less promising treatment. The young man had long blond hair, slightly dilated blue eyes and the bronzed skin and sculptured muscles of a California surfboard rider. The pert customs agent's eyes had narrowed to slits and her tiny button nose was engaged in a spasm of sniffs as she took the measure of the man nearly twice her size. Jim hesitated long enough to hear her order the young man to empty the entire contents of his duffel bag on the counter and see her signal a bulky male colleague, who walked quickly in her direction.

Jim remembered the briefing material Anne had prepared. As an illuminating sidelight on the social environment of Singapore, there had been a note that hippies were not welcome in the city and were shorn of their locks before they were allowed to enter. The haircuts were administered by order of Singapore's Prime Minister Lee Kuan Yew, who considered slovenliness next to ungodliness, and indulgence in drugs an un-Singaporean activity. Mr. Lee, Anne's briefing said, was convinced that it took wit, guts and discipline for his embryo nation to survive, and was therefore inclined to run his state not as a liberal democracy but like an efficiently organized and administered corporation. As a result, Singapore was not the lotus land that its balmy climate and luxuriant vegetation indicated it could be. Instead, the tough and tight management of Prime Minister Lee had managed to procure for the people of Singapore the second-highest per capita income in Asia, behind only Japan. And as a Japanese businessman had once told Jim at a cocktail party in Bonn, "We're not really the Far East. We're the Very Far West."

The Shangri-La Hotel, where a taxi deposited Jim within the half hour, also did not conform to his idea of the romance of the Orient. The hotel was a big pile of marble and glass, with giant crystal chandeliers that assertively proclaimed their status as Intercontinental's finest. The lobby they illuminated seemed stocked with gray-haired men in crew cuts, their cheeks too red, their stomachs too voluminous, their shirts too florid, accompanied by lithe and lovely Chinese girls. The girls' willowy silhouettes were displayed to perfection in clinging satin gowns, tight-fitting and high-necked, with slits on the sides that offered calculated glimpses of shapely legs well up the thigh. The men acted proprietary, the women deliberately demure. Would Cathy Quon look like that? It seemed unlikely. From everything he had heard, Cathy Quon was anything but demure. She might well be lovely, though, in that dimunitive Chinese way. Like the girl at customs.

Jim had arranged to meet Cathy Quon in the vestibule of the Shan Palace, the Shangri-La's well-known Chinese restaurant. The dining room of the Shan Palace was large and high-ceilinged, ornate in brilliant red and gold, with paper lanterns tasseled in crimson silk swaying over the tables, its walls decorated with calligraphed ink drawings of mountains, rocks, bridges and trees curving to the wind.

He recognized her the second she came through the door. She was slender but not willowy. Instead of a tight-fitting sheath, she wore a crisp white piqué suit with a cropped jacket. Her hands were delicate but strong, their nails neither long nor enameled. To his relief, Cathy Quon also did not look demure. Jim did not like demure women. In college dating co-eds, and in New York as an eligible bachelor, he had discovered that demure women were a dangerous species. They stuck to you like caramel on your fingers, which was okay for a lick or two but quickly became cloying; often the demureness also turned out to be the cover for a very tough-minded creature ruthlessly on the make.

Cathy Quon's voice was low and a little curt at the edges. She too had recognized Jim immediately. They had nodded at the same time. As he stepped forward to greet her, she had put out her hand and said, "I'm Cathy Quon." She had not added "Good evening," "How are you?" or "Did you have a good trip?" She was waiting, perhaps with proverbial Oriental delicacy, for him to set the tone.

"I'm Jim Lindner," he said. "Good to meet you, Cathy. I've heard a lot about you." Had that been a felicitous way of putting it? Her eyes narrowed. "The Copter Company thinks highly of you," he added quickly. He had meant it to be reassuring. It emerged sounding stilted.

Her eyes flicked to the headwaiter, who had recognized her and was bowing them to a table.

"You have a reservation for Lindner," Jim said, feeling superfluous.

"Yes, sir," the maitre d' replied blandly. "Thank you, sir."

He seated them in the center of the room near a tall pillar. All around them was the clatter of dishes and the babble of voices, a mixture of staccato Chinese, booming American and hissing Japanese. To the ear it was a nasty mix, irritating and inundating.

Squiring Cathy Quon at the Shangri-La Hotel seemed to be inundating in itself. Just about every other person entering the dining room either nodded to her, exchanged a polite greeting or stopped at the table to talk.

"You know a lot of people," he said, trying to keep the comment noncommittal, even though the interminable interruptions both annoyed and interested him.

Her voice in retort was equally flat. "Yes. It's a small place, our Singapore. And we're involved in it in many ways."

"We?"

"The family. Father went to school with some of the men who run Singapore, politically and economically. They don't necessarily approach what you would define as life, liberty and the pursuit of happiness in the same way, but they all have the same goal."

"Which is?"

"To have Singapore succeed. It's also my goal." The last sentence was delivered in a tone of crisp assertiveness, which made clear that the sentiment expressed was not subject to either challenge or debate. "Cathy is not really my name."

Was there an intrinsic connection between her name and her city, he wondered, some subtle bond that would have been evident to someone more knowledgeable about both? Like Ken perhaps.

"What is your real name?"

"Chih Min. It's a boy's name. My father wanted me to be a boy. But Chih is hard to pronounce for Westerners. It usually comes out 'she,' and that's very inappropriate."

Jim, eying the delicately molded figure, did not think it inappropriate. "Why?" he inquired.

139

"Chih means knowledge or will; Min means people. In English, I suppose, that would translate into public service."

"But you're in business."

"In Singapore business is public service." It was a declarative statement with a cadence at the end that implied "Your turn now."

Jim put his hands to his ears. "This is really no place to talk. Would you mind if we went someplace more quiet for dinner? Is there a restaurant you'd like to go to where we can hear each other?"

She looked pleased. "Yes, of course."

The first impression was tumbledown Victorian in the tropics: faded, fraying, graceful and lush. The people who ran the establishment were evidently glad to see Cathy. The man behind the reception desk bowed, and the bartender beamed. "Miss Quon. What may I make for you this evening?"

She considered. "Singapore sling, please. Two. But should we not have them outside?"

The barman nodded, regretful at losing her. "Yes. It's a nice evening. The trio has just begun to play."

Jim followed her to a low settee of honey-colored bamboo facing a white wrought-iron table that also had grouped around it two chairs with curved Victorian backs and curlicued arms. A half dozen of these arrangements were scattered across a spacious lawn. Voices were only a murmur and died gently amid palms, potted bougainvillea and the muted sounds of the city, yards and worlds away.

"I like this," he said. "Where are we?"

"At Raffles. Glamorous imperial Raffles of gossip and history. I shall miss it."

"What do you mean, you'll miss it? Are you going away?"

He must have sounded anxious, because there was an amused smugness in her voice as she replied, "No, I'm not. But Raffles is. It won't be here much longer."

"Why not?"

"It sits on a valuable piece of real estate near the heart of the city. It takes too much room. It gives too much room. We can't afford it."

"Pity."

She looked out to the empty swimming pool at the far corner of the garden, a bitter-sweet smile on her face. "Yes and no. It's a place where my two worlds collide. I love its grace and resent its Victorian pretension. I know it doesn't make economic sense, but I feel deliciously at home in it." Her voice held both mockery and longing. "You see," she said, "knowledge and will do not always coincide."

That was a perceptive comment. He was about to say so, but the words froze on his tongue. Her face had changed terribly. Like the woman in the movie about Shangri-La, when she steps out of the magic valley into reality and the young radiant face instantly turns to a dust-colored mask, Cathy Quon suddenly looked grim and ancient. Her skin, which earlier had had the luminescence of polished ivory, now resembled old parchment ready to crumble.

"Ken knew that," she said in a cracked voice.

Jim swallowed. "We all do."

She stared at him, and her face changed once more, to a cool concentration. "You're his successor. You came to talk business."

"Yes, but we can do that tomorrow and the day after. Tonight I just want to have dinner with Cathy Quon. Chih Min Quon."

The concentrated look on her face softened. "In that case," she said, "the time has come to order."

It was a gracious dinner, as she had intimated it would be. They sat under a stately palm, its crown swaying fifty feet above their heads. The starched damask tablecloth glowed under the light of a candle, and the candle in turn was reflected in a chafed silver bowl that held a bouquet of small mauve orchids. Dinner arrived on plates displaying the blue and gold Raffles crest. The wine glasses were cut crystal and the cutlery monogrammed silver.

The trio the barman had announced was playing at the far end of the lawn: a violin with a warm if slightly thin tone, a deep vibrant cello, and an upright piano, a little on the tinkly side,

141

addressed by a girl in purple satin. Her floor-length gown was the color of the bougainvillea spilling over its pot to curl around the barrel-chested trunk of a short palm with large leaves that fluttered over the piano like a giant fan. The trio played good oldies from around the world: "La Vie en Rose," "The Umbrella Waltz," "Good Night, Sweetheart," "South of the Border." When the musicians thought no one was listening, they played Mozart minuets for their own delectation. And Jim's. He thought the minuets made a lovely counterpoint to the cotton-ball clouds that had not changed their tempo since he first saw them at the airport.

"You must be tired," she said. "It's high noon for you, isn't it? Ken always . . ." She stopped. "You can drop me at the house on your way back to the hotel. It's only a very small detour."

He rose to hold her chair as she got up. "I would have preferred it to be a big detour," he said gallantly. Over her shoulder, she threw him a questioning look. Or was it a luring one? The moon was milky, and the candle did not offer much light. He could not be sure. But he found himself hoping that it had been what he had thought: luring. The image of Chih Min Quon in his arms, or better still underneath him in bed, delicate and durable, made his nerves tingle.

The taxi stopped at a rather sizable house half-hidden by a whitewashed cement wall. There was an iron gate. She would not allow him to leave the car and take her to the door. She pushed down the handle on her side and when he moved to get out after her, put her hand on his shoulder and firmly pressed him back into his seat. The hand was sinewy and had amazing strength. "I'll see you tomorrow," she said. "Thank you for a pleasant evening. Sleep well and sweet dreams."

He did not sleep well, but he did have sweet dreams: of orchids and polished ivory and a tall palm that pierced the moon.

The next morning when the driver pulled up at the address Jim had given him after consulting his itinerary, the house looked oddly familiar. That's absurd, he thought; must be jet lag. He went to read the small brass plaque on the right side of the gate.

"The Copter Company," it said. "Regional Headquarters, South-east Asia."

The bell was answered by a young man in an open-necked white shirt and trousers that looked vaguely like a uniform. "This is Chou," Cathy said by way of introduction when Jim and the young man had reached the front door of the house, where she was waiting. "John to visitors from America. He doubles as guard and courier."

Jim's initial confusion about the house had not been the result of jet lag. Cathy explained that the villa doubled as the company's regional headquarters and her residence: offices downstairs, living quarters on the second floor. She used the living quarters frequently for business entertaining. It was very convenient.

On the lower floor, four offices took up the left side of the building. They were crowded with equipment, secretaries and book-keepers—two women and two men. They all looked very young. The offices were small but airy and cool, with windows that faced the side of the grounds offering a view of a brownish lawn, palms, bougainvillea and hibiscus. The office equipment was functional and spotless: standard typewriters that were noisy but moved at a rapid pace, first-generation Xerox machines that smelled of acid and ink, and old-fashioned steel filing cabinets.

The right side of the first floor was taken up by two larger rooms. At the back was Cathy's private office. She indicated it with an explanatory phrase but did not take Jim there. She ushered him into the front room, which was furnished with a large round table of heavy mahogany surrounded by ten matching chairs. The chairs had high backs and broad armrests. They were evenly spaced around the table and looked very solid. Two walls were occupied by equally solid sideboards. One had a large brass tray with the glossy pamphlets of the company's product arranged in lotus blossom fashion and a smaller tray that held calling cards. A modern watercolor of Singapore, showing fishermen and factories in lively juxtaposition, topped the two trays. The second side-board displayed a decorated bowl of red lacquer and a classic blue and white Chinese vase. On the wall between the two hung a scroll—a misty landscape of craggy mountains, small huts and

143

two tiny bridges—brush-sketched in muted tones of gray on a cream-colored silk with an undertone of gold. It was framed in bamboo.

"Tea?" she inquired when they had settled at the table facing each other. The tea arrived, before he could decide whether he wanted it, in delicate porcelain cups. It was a pale gold and smelled of jasmine. He watched her sip it daintily.

She set down her cup. "I'm at your service." She looked at him, a half smile lightening the interesting planes of her face. "Or, as you would say in America, what can I do for you?"

He rested his elbows on the carved arms of the chair. They were not comfortable. The wood that looked so mellow was hard to the touch; the carving, with all its gentle curves and curls, cut into the fingers. The chair's back was ramrod straight. Jim gave up doing the proper thing. He put his arms on the table and leaned forward. "What you can do for me first is to fill me in on our operations throughout the area."

She kept her eyes on him, but they had gone blank.

"I don't mean numbers," he continued. "Those are in the files in New York, and very nice numbers they are too." The compliment, delivered emphatically, aroused no reaction. Her face remained opaque. "I mean our procedures. I know firsthand how we operate in the US and in Europe, but management styles differ and so do methods around the world." The scene of Ken and the Emir's nephew dealing at dawn on a café terrace in Monte Carlo flashed through his mind. "I'm sure you know that. Ken must have—"

At the mention of Ken's name, her eyes turned alert and her face hardened. "Yes," she interrupted, "Ken did tell me about his operations around the world, and he knew how we manage in my part—in this part—of the world. I will tell you, if that is what you want." Her voice had assumed a Chinese tempo and ring. Jim also detected an undertone that struck him as subtly sinister.

"Yes," he said, "I do."

"All right." Her hands curled around the ends of her arm-rests. Unlike Jim, she did not seem to find the wood hard. Her

144

back, very straight, was a perfect parallel to the back of the chair. "I will start with Indonesia." Her voice had the same impatient, slightly didactic tone she had used the previous evening when she had talked about her father and the men who ran Singapore. "In Indonesia, three layers of payments must be factored into the cost of doing business. The first and smallest is grease. That, I understand, exists everywhere in one form or another. Ken enlarged my vocabulary in this area. It is called 'baksheesh' in the Middle East, 'mordida' in Latin America, 'dash' in Africa. These are the words used by the people who collect. The people who pay—and especially people in North America who pay—have a more elegant description. They call the money 'facilitating payments.' From their point of view that's an accurate description. Grease does facilitate. In Indonesia, for example, it would be impossible to get anything done without it. And I do mean anything. The daughter of our associate in Jakarta, who is a very smart young woman in business with her father, once put it to me this way: 'In my country, you can't get a bobby pin out of customs without paying someone something.' I should perhaps add that the girl wears her hair short and has no personal use for bobby pins."

Was he supposed to be amused? Was she making a point, an Asian allusion that escaped him? The core of the message was clear enough. You had to pay off to live. The image made him feel queasy.

She had watched him carefully. "Shall I continue?"

He found himself tightening the muscles surrounding his stomach. "Yes."

"The second layer, involving amounts that are not very large in themselves but are substantial in the aggregate, is a payment for services. That is, payments to lower- and middle-level bureaucrats to do what, in theory, and here in Singapore in practice, their government pays them for: clearing goods through customs, issuing import licenses, inspecting production facilities—that kind of thing. In Indonesia there is a complete shadow system for these services. It functions with much of the same steadiness and devotion to duty that the shadow cabinet displays in the political life of the United Kingdom. One must know the people in the shadow system, their requirements and their abilities. This knowledge—it involves both procedures and individuals—can secure very good service."

He tried not to let the distaste he felt color his voice. Rezvani, of course, operated the same way, as did Ken's legendary friend in Abu Dhabi. But their ways had style, imagination and a rationale of sorts. This was blatant, brutal corruption. "What happens,"he asked, "if you play it straight? If you simply insist on getting the service to which you are entitled without additional payments under the table?"

The blank look returned to her eyes. "I know a company that tried it. The company makes a precision product and needed a small part for one of its complex machines. The company sent the part by air from its main facility in the United States. The part was so important to continued production that the company assigned one of its technicians at headquarters to fly to Indonesia with it. The customs man at the Jakarta airport asked for his usual fee for special service. If he was not appropriately compensated, he told the American technician, it would take six weeks to clear the part through regular channels. The technician was a young man from the Midwest who knew everything about precision machinery but nothing about Indonesia. He exploded and threatened to inform the agent's superior, the head of the customs service, the president of the republic of this outrageous demand for a bribe. The agent calmly collected the package that contained the vital part and put it away. 'Come back in six weeks,' he said. 'It will be ready for you.'

"The local manager of the company knew better, of course, but did not dare initiate his colleague from the home office into the facts of life in Jakarta. It was one of those squeaky-clean companies. The part was cleared by customs exactly six weeks later, the day the agent had told the technician he would receive it without paying the fee for special service. Meanwhile, the machine stood idle. Six weeks of production were lost. The visiting technician had to be housed and fed. He tried to make himself useful while he waited, but there wasn't very much for him to do. Fitting the part, when it had finally cleared customs, took him one day.

146

The total cost to the company of this indulgence in virtue came to about seventy thousand dollars. The customs agent had asked for two hundred."

"I take it The Copter Company does not indulge in these virtuous exercises?"

"It does not."

"And what are the going rates at the next level, the third ring of this Indonesian circus?" He heard himself sounding snide. That was uncalled for. He had, after all, asked for what he was getting.

If his tone had conveyed his sentiments—and his mind as well as his fingertips told him that Cathy was alive to every nuance—her demeanor did not show it. "That depends on the product, the competition and the size of the sale. In our industry we start at six figures."

"And stop?"

"At nothing."

She had looked like ancient parchment the night before when she had first mentioned Ken. Now she looked like an ivory carving: precise, immutable, ageless. Jim's skin crawled. Or did it tingle?

"Who does all this? Do you go to Indonesia often?"

"No. Very rarely. For what you call the third ring of the circus, the generals—they usually are generals—prefer Singapore. They like privacy for these transactions, which our arrangement here offers."

Was she telling him that she slept with the generals? That this was part of the very efficient service she rendered The Copter Company? It was a disturbing thought. But if she did, he might as well get in on the action. Certainly that was what his body was telling him, hard, throbbing and insistent. He bent further over the table.

"They also don't like to be seen doing business with a Chinese," she continued calmly. "We're not very popular in Southeast Asia. Except here."

"I've heard as much. Why is that? In your opinion?"

Her hands tightened around the chair. It occurred to him that she must be cutting her fingers. If she was experiencing pain, she gave no hint of it. "Envy, mostly," she said. "We work very

147

hard. We use our heads. We help each other."

"I take it the associates you have—we have"—he corrected—
"are Chinese?"

The correction had been politic. His use of the identifying
"we" relaxed her. Her fingers loosened their grip on the chair.
"Yes. In Indonesia, the Philippines, Malaysia, Thailand and, of
course, Hong Kong, our associates are Chinese. Mostly they are
relations; not in your sense perhaps, but in ours."

"The difference being?"

"We count third cousins and their in-laws. We know who
they are, where they are and what they can do."

"And what do they do in the Philippines? For The Copter
Company, I mean?"

"They make contributions to the appropriate charities."

"Who defines appropriate?"

She shrugged. "People who get a piece of the charitable action. Wives or daughters of men who place orders for helicopters."

The queasy feeling inundated him once more. He tried not
to let his discomfort show and to keep his voice casual.

"Malaysia?"

A look of contempt fleetingly shadowed her face. "Our former
partners in nationhood. Not very efficient but easygoing. We pay
for luxury trips around the world for certain personages, and
we are sending two very nice young Malaysians, the nephew and
niece of one of these personages, to college in the US: the boy
to MIT, the girl to Smith."

Jim's mind leaped back to his college days. There had been
a number of Asians at MIT, including his pal Sumaryo. Sumaryo
was Indonesian, very bright and very nice. Jim and Sumaryo had
double-dated several times. They had even talked of rooming
together. But Sumaryo had switched schools before they could
make the arrangements to share an apartment. He had gone to
Berkeley. Now Jim wondered who had financed Sumaryo's education.

"That sounds friendly," he said, "and what do we do for
our man in Bangkok? Or is it a woman?"

He saw her pale under the ivory patina of her skin. She looked

148

pinched. "Chinese women have a long tradition of adroitness in business affairs," she said, "but our agent in Thailand is a man. Two men, in fact. They are brothers. We compensate them, in addition to the customary commission, by managing their financial affairs in Hong Kong. My father's brother has a small private bank in Kowloon."

"I see. And how do our Thai associates get their money from Thailand to Hong Kong? I gather it is not money they can transfer through regular banking channels."

Her eyes darted to the window. Through the window one could see the gate. It was unattended. "We supply courier service. Chou is the courier. You met him when you arrived. We don't require a guard here. Singapore is a secure place, the most secure in Asia. But 'guard' serves as a satisfactory job description. For all parties."

Who the hell were "all parties?" The Singapore authorities to begin with, he assumed; Cathy and associates throughout Southeast Asia; and, most likely, The Copter Company in New York. He could not see anyone at corporate headquarters cottoning to the idea of having a cash-toting courier on the payroll, even if it was the Singapore payroll. The SEC, if it ever found out, would certainly be perplexed by The Copter Company's regional headquarters for Southeast Asia having a full-time courier on its staff of six. He leaned back in his chair. The hard wood pressed against his shoulders. The queasiness that had washed over him twice before now suffused him from head to toe. The earlier flush of passion for the intriguing woman sitting across the table had disappeared.

"Is there really no other way?" he asked.

Her hands let go of the chair. She put them on the table as close to his as she could reach. If he stretched forward, their fingertips would touch.

"Perhaps there is, but that is how it is done, how everyone in this part of the world builds his house of success. It is risky to be different, foolish to be different unnecessarily." She turned her hands over, withdrew them and looked intently at her palms. "There is a Chinese proverb," she said quietly, "that is both practi-

149

cal and profound. It points out that the rafter that is exposed rots first."

And you, Cathy, he thought, prefer to rot last. I can see that, but it still leaves the question of whether there is need for rafters to rot at all. At least the rafters of my house. He pushed back his chair. It grated on the floor. She rose from her seat in one lithe, soundless motion.

"I'll want to look at the accounting procedures," he said heavily. "For my education, if not necessarily edification. I want to know how these interesting transactions are booked."

"Do you?"

Now what the devil was that question about? What boxes within boxes did it contain? "Didn't Ken?" he demanded.

A faint flush suffused her cheeks. "Yes. He did. And so does . . ." Her voice had risen to a Chinese staccato and stopped midsentence at a high pitch.

"And so does who?"

She did not reply. Instead she gestured in the direction of her office. It was an elegant artifice, the hand turned back at the wrist in a dancer's pose. "I keep the ledgers in a safe in my office."

He followed her to the office and watched her twirl the lock of a fair-sized safe. Under her ministrations the padded steel door swung open to reveal two shelves. The lower shelf held a large tin box and an octagonal lacquer casket. "This"—she indicated the tin box with another of her dancer's gestures—"is cash, mainly US dollars, but there are other currencies as well, all in large denominations. There are situations in which it is important for me to have immediate access to cash." A strange smile pulled down her mouth. "Immediate and intimate. And that"—she waved at the casket in a dismissing motion—"is jewelry."

What jewelry? he wondered. Does The Copter Company deal in rubies and emeralds in this part of the world? From what I've heard already, it wouldn't surprise me.

She cut short his speculation by pointing to the upper shelf. "These are the ledgers. One for each year that I have been with the company."

There were five of them: tall traditional English ledgers, the kind he remembered from illustrations of novels by Charles Dickens. Ken must have hired Cathy Quon the year he got back from Germany.

She reached for the last ledger in the row and handed it to him. It was heavy. "This is 1978. You will want to start with the most current accounts, won't you?"

"Thank you, yes. But I want to see all of them."

She nodded. "It will be easier for you to work in the conference room. I'll send in the others."

Chou-John brought the remaining ledgers barely a minute after Jim had settled himself once more at the mahogany table. The young man, Jim noticed, had no difficulty carrying four of the heavy books. Under his short-sleeved white shirt, wiry muscles bulged and stretched. The Copter Company's courier in Southeast Asia was equipped to hold his own in foreseen or unforeseen encounters.

Jim studied the ledgers. They were accurately kept, and all their entries were logical. In Indonesia a long series of sums, each less than a thousand dollars, was booked as "social services" or "community contributions." Those, he realized, were the facilitative payments. An array of expenditures ranging from $1000 to as high as $100,000 were booked as legal fees or consultancy payments. The books listed all kinds of consultants: engineering consultants, consultants for government relations, consultants for promotion and advertising, consultants for personnel services. All expenditures were covered by rendered invoices. The invoices were numbered and their numbers recorded in the ledger.

The large sums, ranging from $100,000 to $3,000,000, were booked as commissions. The $3,000,000 commission was for an order of fifty helicopters, billed out at $50,000,000. That amounted to 6 percent, high by US and European standards, but eminently plausible by the yardsticks of the Middle East. The problem with the commissions was that in no case had they been paid to anyone identified as The Copter Company's representative. They had gone to an array of local firms with meaningless, phony-sounding names: Electrom Indonesia PT, Thai Aerody-

151

namics, Manila Agro-Industry, Capital Company of Malaysia. He had no way of telling what these firms were or did. His instinct told him they did nothing; they were corporate shells to collect money for whoever the local power brokers were: generals in Indonesia, freewheeling businessmen in Thailand, politicians in the Philippines. He would have to ask Cathy. If he wanted to know.

Did he want to know? After he had digested ledgers covering five years of The Copter Company's operations in Southeast Asia, he was not so sure. Her question had been subtler than he had realized when she asked it. There was nothing wrong with the books as such. All expenditures were documented in ways that made commercial sense and could provide plausible explanations to any government agency that might want explanations. Even the SEC. All the same, they hid a mess of corruption, evasion and double-dealing that made him ill. The room was close.

He felt a sudden panic, a fear that he would suffocate if he did not leave quickly. He slammed shut the last of the ledgers. It closed with a thud.

She must have heard the sound. He had just begun to pace, in a room too small, with a ceiling too low, when Cathy blocked his stride. She had materialized in the soundless way that seemed to characterize her movements. She stood there like a small tree, swaying a little; but to uproot her one would have to dig deep. He halted and looked down at her. Her head arched back and the supple body stretched sinuously. I want her, he thought, I want to . . . I want . . .

Her lips parted. The teeth were small and pointed, the color of baroque pearls. The voice had a seductive hush. "May I offer you a meal tonight?" she breathed. "There is a dining room upstairs."

He found it difficult to speak. "Yes," he said. "Yes, please."

Getting through the remainder of the day was an agony of anticipation. When he attempted to organize the notes he had taken while reading the ledgers, his mind went soggy. He decided to take a cold shower and get some sleep. He managed to drop

152

off but woke in a sweat, his pillow moist, the sheets tumbled and his body making very clear what it wanted.

Chou-John opened the gate and showed Jim upstairs. She was waiting for him on the landing, dressed in a floor-length sheath of patterned black. Her hair was swept up and held in place by a jade comb. She wore earrings and bracelets of gold with glinting green stones. Emeralds from the jewelry casket in the safe? The company's? Hers? He bent to kiss her hand. Her skin smelled of ginger and gardenias. He felt the blood pound in his ears. It seemed to be pounding a phrase: gold-and-black, black-and-gold.

The landing led to a hall furnished with two low chests and a Chinese rug in pale blue and rose. On one of the chests a statue covered in sea blue glaze sat in the lotus position, eyes closed and a mysterious smile on its lips. The expression made the Mona Lisa look clumsy.

Cathy had accompanied Jim's meditative gaze. "It's Kuan Yin," she said, "the goddess of mercy. She is my most treasured companion."

He could appreciate Cathy's sentiment, esoteric as it was. There was a resemblance between the woman and the statue, a resemblance not limited to the similarity of the features. It was in the expression on their faces—worldly, wise, but abstracted and distant at the same time. Two beings that could be touched but not held, that would always beckon and never come within reach. He looked from one to the other. A shiver went up his spine.

She turned to open a door to her right. "This is the dining room. I use it to entertain for the company, but we won't eat here tonight. It's too big for two." It was a large room of Victorian dimensions with Victorian furniture. The oblong table could have seated twenty.

She closed the door and beckoned him to follow. Behind her, he stepped into a beautifully proportioned space furnished with low settees, small tables, scrolls, pillows and vases. The settees were upholstered in yellow silk. The rest of the furniture

153

was red and black lacquer. Yellow silk curtains framed the window. They were drawn aside to let the moonlight bathe the room.

She served him from a tray of decorated covered bowls. Using ivory chopsticks, she searched each dish for the best morsel and placed it on his plate. A hot strong liquid in a tiny cup accompanied the meal. She kept refilling his cup from a porcelain bottle at her side.

The moonlight played on her fingers as she held the throat of the bottle. She held it lightly, moving her hand up and down. He caught her wrists, took the bottle from her hand and put it on the table. "I envy the bottle," he said. "I would like to feel your hand move just so."

She looked at him, her eyes tantalizing jet slits. Slowly she slid toward him across the floor, pushed his knees apart and sat between them. Her right hand played, stroked and caressed in an expert motion. I'll burst, he thought. Now. He took a deep breath.

She looked at him, a luring query in her eyes. He stood and pulled her up close. Her mouth was on his chest. He could feel her hot breath through his shirt. "Where?" he said huskily.

The room they entered had what looked like a large bed but was merely a mattress resting on curved lacquer feet. The corners of the mattress were round. "Round corners," she said, "make for harmony—in life and in love." He hardly heard her. His senses reverberated to the sound of the sheets. They were crepe de chine and seemed to emit a sigh as she turned them back. The scent of joss sticks was in the air.

He could feel his blood throb in every inch of his body and knew that he had never been so big, so erect, so ravenous. When he saw her on the bed, doll-like, her legs drawn up in two glowing triangles, a tiny black wisp parting into ivory lips in the center, he wondered how she could take him. She arched toward him, and he entered her hard. It was like being in a vise, excruciating and exquisite. A spasm of delicious agony convulsed him.

Her voice reached him from far away. "You really didn't know," she murmured. "Did you?"

He tried to struggle back to consciousness. "Know what?"

"The ledgers. What was in them."

For a moment his mind came alert. The ledgers, those sickening, beautifully kept books. Not now, he thought. I'll deal with that tomorrow. "No," he said, and allowed a gold-threaded blackness to enfold him again.

She stretched underneath him, gently but firmly pressed her hands against his shoulders and rolled him on his back. The pillow smelled of ginger and gardenias, of joss sticks and the musk of Cathy Quon. She ran her nails over his belly in a drowsy rhythm. It was a circular motion, without beginning or end. "Sleep," she said.

When he woke, he did not at first know where he was, knew only that it was dark, close and exotically fragrant. His head ached faintly and an alien lassitude enveloped his limbs. He lay still to let his mind recapture what had brought him here, what had happened. When it was all in place, he turned his head. Cathy lay beside him, curled up in the fetal position, looking like an ancient infant. Her hair was down and fell over her face, hiding most of it. Her breathing was shallow but even.

Her comment echoed in his head: "You really didn't know?" His reply to that question was what Cathy had been after when she invited him to supper, to her sitting room and to her bed. She had played him, expertly, for her own purpose. A flush of fury coursed through him.

He turned to glare at her. She was oblivious. She had procured what she wanted. Or had she? He had certainly not been much of a lover. What pleasure the encounter had provided her must have come from her own will, her own secret desire. Fair enough, he conceded reluctantly. I guess we're even.

He sat up and swung his legs over the side of the bed. His eyes, accustomed now to the dark, searched the room and found the door at the far side. He headed for it, walking silently in long strides. As he had expected, the door led to the bathroom, a spacious place with a large square tub of black tile and a row of tall closets. A sink in matching tile was topped by a mirror-

155

faced cabinet. He clicked open the mirror door, looking for tooth-paste. He found it, and in the shelf above it, shaving equipment: a can of Palmolive Rapid-Shave and a man's razor. The faint ache he had felt in his head when he woke pressed against his temples. He decided not to shave in Cathy's bathroom. He didn't like using another man's razor, especially when he didn't know who the man was.

He rinsed his face, neck and hands and looked for a towel. There was none in sight. He slid open the nearest closet door. On the left, shelves held fingertip towels, hand towels and bath towels. They were made of soft terry cloth, some green, some white. The other side of the closet had a bar across the top that held two dressing gowns on brass hangers. One of the gowns, made of gold-patterned silk, was Cathy's size; the other, polished blue cotton with white piping, was a man's, cut like a long pajama jacket with a monogram on the breast pocket. Jim peered at the pocket. The monogram read KW

Chou-John materialized out of the shadows when Jim reached the front gate. Noiselessly, Chou lifted the iron bar that held the gate shut and lowered the bar into place when Jim had stepped out into the street. "Good day, sir," Chou said.

Was it day? Jim looked at his watch. Four o'clock in the morning, Singapore time. Five o'clock in the afternoon in New York. He could not fit himself into either chronology. He decided to go to the hotel, draw the blinds, sleep and let his body adjust to time and place.

The telephone jangled him awake. Still, his head was clear when he reached for the receiver, the air was cool and antiseptic and the air-conditioning unit emitted a familiar reassuring hum.

"Jog Lindner," a cordial male voice boomed over the wire. "This is Curt. Curt Stiles. I just heard from usually reliable sources that you're visiting our little island. How's about getting together for an evening of booze and bull and fond recollections of adventures on the banks of the Charles? I haven't talked to anyone about those for too damn long."

Jog had been Jim's nickname at Sloan. The name had been

a Cambridge compromise. Jim had not been sufficiently devoted to athletics to be called a jock, but he did do a lot of running and pacing. So he had been tagged Jog Lindner. Curtis Stiles, classmate at both MIT and Sloan, had occasionally jogged with him along the esplanade that bordered the river.

"Curt," he said. "I'll be damned. This is a pleasant surprise. And a great idea. Three questions."

"You haven't changed much, Jog, have you? The man who likes an orderly agenda. Okay, fella, fire away. I'll throw in an allowance for a fourth. That's for auld lang syne."

Jim packed the pillow into the small of his back and sat up. "Okay. First question: How did you find out I was here? Second question: What are you doing here? Third question: Where are you? Fourth question: When do we have our bull session, and do we jog first?"

Curt laughed. "That's five questions, or at least four and a half. Same old Jim. The extra reach, the extra smile. The answers are: One, this is a small island and I get around. Two, one reason I get around is because I'm general manager of a manufacturing sub of Garrett-Royce. Three, it, and I, are in the industrial park on the outskirts of the city, about twenty minutes from your Shangri-La. Four, how about tomorrow night? Four and a half, thanks, but no thanks. It's too darn hot."

"Curt, I'd sure as hell like to see you, but tomorrow is too late. I'll be in Lagos. I'm leaving early in the morning."

"Ah, hell." The regret in Curt's voice echoed Jim's sentiments. "I really can't make it tonight. There's a meeting of the Singapore-American Chamber of Commerce and I'm president this year. I've got to be there. You wouldn't want to come? Nah," he answered his own question. "I wouldn't if I were in your place. With only one night left."

"A drink then, before you do your patriotic, commercial and presidential duties?"

"Won't work. I don't leave here much before seven, and the meeting starts at seven-thirty. But I'd hate like hell not to see you. Why don't you come out here? We can talk in my office. I'll put out a genius-at-work sign."

Jim laughed. "That sounds like the nifty old days. Genii and

157

other spirits. You're on. How do I get there?"

"I'll send a car for you. Three o'clock in front of your door. It'll be marked 'G-R Electronics, Singapore.' The driver's name is Sun Lee. Sunny, to you."

"Fine, Curt. See you soon."

Sunny turned out to be a thin elderly man with a very toothy smile. As they drove through the town, he pointed out the sights: a large new refinery, gleaming steel blue; an old pagoda painted a brilliant red, its pointed upturned corners touched with gold and hung with tinsel; blocks of new housing, simple structures of whitewashed concrete livened up by clotheslines hung with garments every color of the rainbow; the busy quay and the crowded port; the solid office buildings guarding the quay, some old, brown and squat, others new, glass-fronted and tall, all clean and functional, with a hardworking air about them.

They passed several rows of apartments just before they turned into a paved driveway leading to the industrial park. The flats looked new, low-cost and uncompromisingly utilitarian. "Government built apartments for workers same time it laid out industrial park," Sunny explained. "Lee Kuan Yew good planner." Sunny stretched his lips to signify approval, displaying his tobacco-stained teeth with prominent silver fillings.

Curt's plant was sizable and spotless. It worked three shifts, and most of the employees were women. They were, Curt explained, dexterous and dependable. A ticker in the main lobby of the plant's office wing ran the latest quotations from Wall Street. The Garrett-Royce company had a subsidized salary deduction plan through which employees could buy stock in the parent firm. The Wall Street news ticker was therefore a popular place, more popular even than the Coke and coffee machines.

Curt's office had the Singapore touch. It was spare and functional, with everything an up-to-date executive required and nothing else. It suited Curtis. He was from Maine and had no taste for frills.

It did not take long for Jim and Curt to catch up with the near-decade that had elapsed since they had last met. The old shorthand still worked, a mixture of engineering terms and business school buzz words, with an admixture now of corporate reference points.

"VP international, eh? That's pretty good going. Great company too."

Jim shrugged. "Yah, but—"

Curt cut in. "Headquarters stuff is getting to you. I know what you mean. Find it hard to take myself whenever I get back. Wouldn't really want to work at headquarters. But I guess one has to, sooner or later. It's where the action is."

"Yes," Jim said. "I'm not complaining. It's just a different ballgame."

"Yup. More politics. More Mickey Mouse. More money."

"And a bigger pond."

Curt looked at Jim. "Bigger and dirtier. All kinds of effluents, as they call them nowadays. Back home in Maine we called it sewage—when we were being polite, that is."

Were they talking about the same thing? One could level with Curt. Jim decided to lay it on the line. "Speaking of which—I mean crap, corruption of all kinds—how much of it do you get here?"

Curt shook his head. "None. Not me. Not here."

"Does that sentence have a 'but' at the end?"

"Yes, it does. We have plants in a lot of places, but Southeast Asia is really all I know firsthand."

"And?"

"We accommodate if possible, pull out if necessary. We don't pay off. Anyone, anywhere."

Jim pointed to the thermos bottle on Curt's desk. "What d'you have in there?"

"Water. But there's scotch at arm's length." He bent and reached for the lowest drawer of his desk. Jim held up a hand. "No, thanks. I think I had too much last night. Of something. I'll take the water."

The cool liquid felt good in his mouth and throat. He had been thirsty ever since Curt's phone call woke him from what now seemed like a deep, drugged sleep.

"What d'you mean, 'accommodate'?"

"I mean the national predilections, whatever they are. In Malaysia, for instance, where we have another good-sized plant, almost as large as mine here, we go with the government about hiring Malays instead of Chinese. The Malays are not nearly as good, smart or reliable as the Chinese, and they need a lot more training. They used to be the boondocks people, and now they want their place in the sun. The economic sun. To many of them that means a job in an office or a factory. We do our best. The quid pro quo is that they—they of the pervasive government—don't put the bite on us in any other way."

"Does it work?"

"Yup. It works in Malaysia. That's why we're still there. We had the same deal in Indonesia, where they have a comparable problem. It didn't work there. We kept our side of the bargain and employed only a minimal number of Chinese, but they didn't keep theirs. Everybody wanted to get paid off for everything. And I do mean everybody. The last straw, if you don't mind a mixed metaphor, was a road. The road that led to our plant needed fixing. It was wrecking our delivery vans. This being Jakarta, we didn't even bother to ask the authorities to do the repair work. They don't in Indonesia. We offered to do it ourselves. Mind you, this wasn't off in some remote island or some outer rim of the city. We were right in the heart of Jakarta. We had to get a permit to repair the road. When we applied for it, a colonel appeared, said he would designate the contractor and collect ten percent of the contract price. From us. To begin with."

Jim held out his glass for a refill and drank it down in a long gulp.

"That must have been quite a night," Curt said.

"It was. How did you handle the colonel?"

"We said, 'So long, Charlie; it hasn't been good to know ye.' "

"You mean—"

"I mean we closed down the plant, folded our company and went home."

"And just blew the investment?"

"Yup. It was not a negligible piece of change either. Writing it off didn't look very nice on the balance sheet that year."

"What about the competition?"

Curt nodded. "Right the first time, Jog. The Japanese took over. They've set up shop in our building. They paid off the colonel, fixed the road and are beating the pants off us in the market. In Southeast Asia and at home." Curt grinned.

"Why is that good news?"

"That's the bad news. The good news is that we're coming up with a new product which I'm pretty sure will beat the pants off them. The better mousetrap. Better, not bigger. Smaller and better." He poured a glass half full with water, took a bottle of Johnny Walker Red from his drawer and added two good slugs to the glass. "You lose some, and you win some." He raised his glass. "Here's to both, even though I prefer the latter."

"Me too," Jim said. He pushed his glass toward Curt, who picked it up, blended a drink to match his own and handed it back.

"Bottoms up, Jog. Like the man said, 'It's a good life if you don't weaken.' "

Jim raised his glass but put it down again.

"Do you have a policy on this stuff? I mean at headquarters?"

"We sure do. In spades. Written and enforced. From the top down, all the way. Some of the guys find it a pain in the you-know-what. Personally I like it. Makes things easier. I can get drunk in peace, without worrying about what I'll say, or to whom, that can get me into trouble. Me or the company." He held up his glass. "Your good health."

"And yours." The mellow scotch went down smoothly and slaked what was left of Jim's thirst. "I'm sorry about tonight," he said. "I'll catch you for a real one next time around. It's been good to talk with you."

It had been good to talk with Curt in more ways than Curt could possibly know. It had made clear in a practical, realistic way that getting stuck in the morass so accurately depicted in Cathy's meticulous ledgers was not inevitable. There were other ways of doing business. At a cost, of course. The question was whether The Copter Company was prepared to carry that cost. Was it? Was he? Riding back to the Shangri-La Hotel in the dark

161

blue station wagon of the Garrett-Royce Company, Jim squinted into the setting sun. He couldn't really answer that question. Not with certainty. Not yet.

At the hotel, the room clerk handed him a telephone message. It was from Miss Quon. Would Mr. Lindner be good enough to call the office at his convenience?

It was nine o'clock in the evening, safely past dinnertime, when Jim made the call. Cathy answered on the first ring. Where was she taking the call, he wondered. In the drawing room? The bedroom? He had not noticed a telephone in either, but then he wouldn't have, even if there had been one. "Copter Company Regional Headquarters for Southeast Asia," he said, "has a very prompt switchboard."

Her reply was curt. "I am in my office."

"Good." There was no need then to play games. He could sound and act as businesslike as he felt. "There're a couple of things we still need to talk about. As you know, I leave in the morning. May I come over to discuss them now?"

"Certainly."

This time she opened the gate herself. She was dressed in a business suit, much like the one in which she had met him the day he arrived. It was cut the same way but made of raw silk. She wore no jewelry.

Her office matched her appearance. He had been too preoccupied the first time he saw it to notice its sternly functional atmosphere. It had a steel desk with a steel chair behind it and two plain chairs facing it. One corner was occupied by a low wooden table unadorned except for Copter Company catalogues and a large metal ashtray. Two steel chairs flanked the table. Behind Cathy's desk, presiding assertively over its own corner, was the safe.

She indicated the chairs at the table. They were placed so the people sitting in them could either face each other or look out into the neutrality of this utterly noncommittal office.

"Business procedures," he said. "I'd like to see a change."

162

He did not look at her. Deliberately he directed his eyes to the safe. He could hear her catch her breath. "Have you . . . ?" she asked but did not complete the question.

He turned to face her. She looked stern and concerned. Another face of Cathy Quon. "Have I what?"

"Discussed this at headquarters? With Mr. Knight and Mr. Morse Clark?"

"It is my area of responsibility."

"As it was for Ken." Her head drooped like a flower too heavy for its stem. Under his eyes, the stern face turned soft and sad. He wanted to reach across the table, put his finger under her chin and lift up her face. "Yes," he said gently, "as it was for Ken."

She did what he had not done: lift her face with her two hands. She kept them there, loosely balled, under her chin. Emergency support. She had loved Ken.

She read the understanding in his eyes. "Ken," she said, "acted on instructions."

A sinking feeling swept over him.

"They murdered Ken," she added.

His head snapped up. "Who did?"

"The instructions," she said tonelessly.

"Whose instructions?"

"Russel Knight's and Lawrence Morse Clark's. They told Ken what to do and how to do it. They left the details to him, but they set the policy and hounded him with it. There were times it made him ill—ill in his body and in his soul. I nursed him back to health. At least I thought I did. But I was wrong." Her fists fell forward. Her shoulders shook.

He reached across and put his hands over hers. "I don't think so, Cathy. It's never wrong to be kind."

She looked up at him. "I have no regrets. I only mean that I failed. I could not make him healthy enough. He's dead. He killed himself for them."

Jim's hands broke into a sweat, but he did not want to remove them. "For whom did Ken kill himself, Cathy?"

He felt her fingers tremble under his palms. "For Russel

163

Knight and Lawrence Morse Clark. They must have pushed him into a corner where he saw no way out."

Jim felt his spine crawl. Was she right? Did Russ and Larry muscle Ken into a corner from which there was no escape? And were they plotting the same strategy for him? Or was it all the feverish imagination of a woman who had lost a lover and felt bereft and betrayed? "You don't really know that, Cathy." He tried to sound comforting and reasonable.

Her voice was corroded with bitterness. "But I do."

He removed his hands and wiped them surreptitiously on his trousers. Did she really know? And if she did, did he want her to share the knowledge with him? Before he could decide, she said, "Ken kept a diary. It's all in there: names, places, amounts, instructions, procedures. I have seen some of the pages."

He blinked. "Pages?"

"The diary is just a loose-leaf notebook in a ring binder. I bought it for him. He wrote a page on each deal when it was completed. Facts only: no more, no less. But naming all the names. It was dangerous stuff."

Dangerous, he thought, is putting it mildly. Explosive is more like it. The unvarnished truth, with names attached, could blow the roof off The Copter Company and a slew of prominent people in a score of countries. He stared at the safe. His heart hammered. "Is the diary here?"

The sadness stole over her face once more. "No. I offered to keep it here, but Ken wouldn't let me. He didn't want to expose me, he said, to pressure or blackmail. He felt that if anyone ever found out about the diary, there was no telling what they'd do. He wanted it kept safe without running the risk of anyone getting hurt. That's why he didn't take it to Saddle River either."

It sounded like Ken. In his own way, gruff and old-fashioned, Ken had been a protective man. He might not even have told Cathy where he had decided to keep the diary. But Cathy had her own ways of getting what she wanted, and she would have wanted to know.

164

He gripped his knees. "Do you know where the diary is?"

Her hands on the table closed into fists once more. "Yes, I do. Unless he decided to destroy it before . . ." Her fists were cramped so tightly the nails cut into her palms. She did not seem to notice. "Before he destroyed himself."

"Can we find out?" he asked thickly.

"You can."

"How?"

"I will tell you. I will help you. If."

"Yes?"

"If you will pay my price."

Images tumbled through his mind: Cathy acknowledging greetings from a stream of people at the Shangri-La; Cathy being gracious at Raffles; Cathy presiding in the conference room; Cathy standing behind her steel desk twirling open the lock of her safe; Cathy supine on the bed with its rounded corners, enveloped in incense and crepe de chine. What could she want from him that she could not get for herself? A replacement for Ken? He couldn't do that. Wanting her was one thing, becoming a corporate gigolo another.

"What is your price?"

Her face turned grim and ancient, the way it had looked for a moment in the garden at Raffles. "Revenge," she said. "Revenge for Ken. That is my price."

"But," he stammered, "Ken is gone. Revenge will not bring him back."

Her face remained masklike, and the voice coming from deep within her did not sound like her own. "The ancestors want it. If evil is not punished, virtue dies."

He leaned across, put his hands on her shoulders and shook her hard. The haunted look dropped from her face. Their eyes met.

"Cathy," he cajoled. "Whatever happened to your treasured companion the goddess of mercy?"

Stubbornly she shook her head. "Kuan Yin is a Buddhist and a goddess. I am neither. We are companions, not twins."

Her voice was her own again. The obsession had left her.

He let go of her shoulders. "I'll do what I can," he said softly. "Where is the diary?"

"In Switzerland, in a safety deposit box at the bank in which the company kept its numbered account."

Her voice had the clipped tone that had grated on his ears at the Shan Palace. He had not imagined that he would ever welcome that high-pitched staccato sound.

"I'll find it," he said.

"When?"

"I'll be in Basel before the end of the month."

A half smile lifted the corners of her mouth. It fused into an expression of otherworldly satisfaction. The resemblance to the blue-glazed goddess became pronounced.

She rose and walked to a garish calendar tacked to the wall behind her desk. With a red felt pen she circled the last week of February. "I will burn a joss stick every night. For good fortune and success."

7

Singapore to Lagos is a long ride. It gave Jim the time and solitude that international executives have come to treasure: a time when the telephone cannot ring, a solitude that can be safeguarded from loquacious fellow travelers and attentive stewardesses by business documents spread out on the tray and the adjoining seat. Behind this protective facade, Jim reviewed what he knew of the Nigerian situation and came to the conclusion that it was ridiculous. The Copter Company was paying Pascal Udoyen the same amount of money that it paid its outside counsel in New York, who devoted considerable time and knowledge to the company. In the two years The Copter Company had retained Udoyen, at $100,000 a year, he had drawn three perfunctory legal documents and produced no business whatsoever, not even a serious nibble. In New York the argument for this peculiar arrangement had been that Nigeria, with all these people—no one seemed to know exactly how many, but the guess was around 90 million— all that oil money, and a government interested in sophisticated hardware, was a major potential market. Udoyen was supposed to have the right kind of connections among the military.

So far, Udoyen had insisted that commitments of the magnitude involved in a sale that would be worthwhile for all parties— he included himself among the parties—take time in Nigeria, and that the colonels were more important than the ruling elite of generals, because the future was in the colonels' hands. Not necessarily all that far off, either. Generals got killed in Nigeria easily and regularly, and anyone who believed that the future of Nigeria would be shaped by civilians did not know the Yorubas, the Hausas and the Ibos, let alone all those lesser tribes scattered around this large and populous place. The future, Udoyen had assured Ken, belonged to the colonels. If The Copter Company wanted to plug into the Nigerian market, the colonels were the ones to cultivate.

Anne had disagreed. Her analysis was that local civilian government, in cities and states, was lively and responsive and could become the base for a cohesive national government that would not require a military presence to whip everyone into line. She believed the generals, at least the more responsible among them, knew this. It was the colonels who worried Anne. She thought it was their hunger for power and money—the unappetizing but probably accurate metaphor she had used was "their time at the trough"—that might undermine a civilian regime.

Going over the papers once more, Jim decided that, whether Anne's analysis was on target or Udoyen's prediction proved out, the fact remained that $100,000 a year for a minimal amount of work and no discernible results was too much money down a rat hole. Udoyen might well be taking The Copter Company for a ride. Anne's briefing had indicated that a lot of people got taken in Nigeria.

Anne's takeout had also warned Jim that the ripoff started the second one entered the country. Nigerian bureaucrats were likely to hold up a visitor at the airport, demanding a payoff for health, immigration, currency control or customs checks. If they tried it on him, Jim resolved, he'd tough it out, if only to get in trim for Udoyen.

The resolve turned out to have been a waste of adrenaline. What Jim encountered as he got himself processed by a series of jauntily uniformed men and women in neatly pressed khaki with elaborate badges was a kind of somnolent smugness, a peremptory edge to tone and gesture. But no one bothered him beyond the standard formalities, and no one asked him for anything.

When he got through the customs barrier, he found himself face to face with an ample black woman holding up a piece of paper with his name penciled on it. She wore an ankle-length gown of brilliant marine blue, and around her head a bandanna patterned in bronze and maroon. The costume suited her. He held out his hand. "I'm Jim Lindner."

She crumpled the paper, dropped it on the floor and gave his outstretched hand a very firm grip. "Welcome to Nigeria. Mr. Udoyen asked me to fetch you. He sends you this." She handed him a closed white envelope. He opened it and found two ten-naira notes, the equivalent of thirty dollars. No explanation was offered either in a written message from Udoyen or from the woman who had handed him the envelope. Bafflement prompted him to inquire, "How much does a taxi to the hotel cost? I was just going to the bank to get change."

"The bank is closed at this hour of the night. You don't need taxi money. I am taking you to your hotel." Her tone made clear there was no arguing with her, or at least that it would be better not to try. And why not have her drive him? It might amortize .001 percent of the money The Copter Company paid her boss.

He handed back the envelope. "I won't need this then. Thanks very much."

She looked at him, said nothing and took the envelope.

Her car turned out to be a sturdy little Volvo, and she drove it with smooth competence. Traffic was light, and drivers signaled each other politely with eloquent hand gestures when they wanted to pass or be passed. The Volvo made good speed along a well-paved highway and across a macadam-surfaced bridge. "I was told traffic is terrible in Lagos," he said, his tone conversational. "I guess that was a piece of what the intelligence folk would call disinformation."

She kept her eyes fixed on the road and her hands firmly on the steering wheel. Her reply came close to being a bark. "It is terrible. You just arrived at a lucky time."

He decided to try again. "I was also told that you can drive a car in Lagos only on alternate days: even license numbers on

169

Monday, Wednesday and Friday, odd numbers on Tuesday, Thursday and Saturday. Is that true?"

This time the nastiness in her voice was unmistakable, as was the implication Why the hell don't you mind your own business? "It's true. What happened is that everybody bought another car. We're back to square one."

He suspected the solution of acquiring an extra car for alternate days had been beyond her financial reach and that therefore the regulation angered her. But she was clearly not a woman to encourage well-meant probes. His briefing had pointed out that when the police caught someone driving a car with the wrong license plate for the day, they had been known to take out the driver and horsewhip him. He had found that hard to believe. After all, this was 1979. It was evidently not a good idea, however, to check out the information with this most unwelcoming welcome committee Udoyen had dispatched to greet him. Was Udoyen making a point?

They drove on in uncompanionable silence for some twenty minutes, until they pulled up in front of the Federal Palace Hotel. At the desk inside they encountered a shifty-eyed, mean-looking reception clerk whose manner was as unpleasant as his looks.

"You have a reservation for Mr. Lindner," Jim's escort said. The clerk did not trouble to look up from the splashy tabloid in which he seemed immersed. "We have no rooms."

She rummaged in her pouchlike handbag and came up with a paper that had several official-looking seals and stamps. "I have a letter of confirmation from the manager. The reservation was made by the office of Pascal Udoyen. Chief Udoyen, Junior." Her voice held an undertone of threat.

The clerk sat up. "How much for me?" he demanded, but faltered as she stared at him coldly, pushing the stamped letter under his nose. Sullenly he turned, took a key from its hook on one of the room slots—there were at least a dozen hanging above empty boxes—and threw it on the desk. "Fill this out," he ordered, pushing a long registration form at Jim, and slumped back into the chair, his head buried once more in the tabloid.

Jim did as he had been told and reached for the key. Obviously no one was going to show him to his room or help him with his luggage. That was all right. He never took more luggage on business trips than he could comfortably manage himself. He picked up his suitcase. "I'm Gloria Amoypola," his escort said. "I'll pick you up here at eight tomorrow morning. Mr. Udoyen expects you at nine." He wondered whether he should offer her a drink or a cup of coffee, but she had already turned to go and he found himself looking at her high, firm rump. "Good night." She tossed it at him over her shoulder like a small hard ball and was gone.

His room, when he found it, was depressing. The walls were painted a dirty yellow, the bed covers and curtains were grimy chintz, with a bilious green as their predominant color. The room was filthy and smelled rank. It looked out over a parking lot.

When he turned on the shower, a cockroach the size of his thumb crawled out of the bathtub drain. He stepped aside and turned the shower on hard and hot to flood the cockroach down the drain. But he felt itchy even after he had soaped and splashed himself for the better part of ten minutes, and his dreams that night were full of crawly, menacing creatures. He woke in a sweat.

At eight o'clock sharp, after eating a foul breakfast, he was in the hotel lobby, where the newsstand man was just laying out his papers, including a stack of copies of the Paris *Herald Tribune* that turned out to be six days old. The sullen clerk of the night had been replaced behind the reception desk by a dapper young man with a quizzical look and very mobile eyebrows.

Gloria Amoypola appeared a minute later. Once again there was no conversation between them as she negotiated the traffic, which now was everything Jim had been warned it would be. The distance to Udoyen's office could not have been more than thirty blocks, but it took them an hour to get there.

What Jim looked at as they stalled and inched, swerved and got nudged, was awful. Most of the buildings they passed were scabrous. There were a few new skyscrapers, but they were already melting into the parade of older buildings with their peeling paint, blotchy doors and splattered windows. Open sewers ran in shallow ditches along the gutter. Just behind the ditches were rows of

171

little stalls with one person, usually a woman, selling just about anything an ill-assorted grab bag might hold. The women looked both animated and content. He wondered how they could possibly make a living. There were literally thousands of these tiny stalls. Who bought what from whom?

Udoyen's office was startling in a different way. It was in a tumbledown four-story building with cracked walls. Steep stone stairs led to an air-conditioned room jammed with rickety wooden furniture, except for a thronelike chrome and leather swivel chair which was occupied by Udoyen. Udoyen himself was almost too much what Jim had expected: a lithe young man, polite, charming and exquisitely turned out in a manner that somehow produced the effect of being a caricature of a fashionable Park Avenue banker. Everything Udoyen wore was exactly right: the carefully tailored lightweight gabardine suit, the shirt boldly striped in pale green, the discreetly patterned tie that pulled the ensemble together. He shot his cuffs in a neat abrupt gesture, displaying initialed gold cufflinks. It should have looked elegant but didn't; it looked slick, and something about it didn't work.

Udoyen's desk was a large table with an intercom, two telephones and no papers.

"Mr. Udoyen," Jim said, "as you know, I have taken over from Mr. Ward, and I've come to discuss with you—"

"Call me Pascal," Udoyen interrupted, flashing a smile.

Jim nodded. "I've come, Pascal, to review the situation of The Copter Company in Nigeria and to renegotiate your fee."

Pascal's eyes glittered. "You mean you'll finally take my advice and make a serious effort to capture this very promising and lucrative market? With a commensurate recompense for me." He shot his right cuff. His voice became deprecating. "I've tried for years to persuade Ken to give this market the commitment it deserves." He clicked his tongue in disapproval. "This is a VIP." He flashed his smile. "I don't mean me, or at least not only me. In my dictionary those initials stand for a Very Important Place. And getting more important all the time. We will be the dominant power of Africa. Soon." He checked himself, but the glitter in his eyes intensified.

172

Why did Udoyen refer to Ken by his first name? They had never met personally, and Ken had been old enough to have been Udoyen's father.

"That's very interesting, Pascal, but I like to start with first things first. From where I sit, the first question that needs to be answered is, Why have we not yet sold a single helicopter in Nigeria, and why is this costing us a hundred thousand dollars a year?" He saw Udoyen's face close up sharply. "We can go on from there," he added.

Udoyen's face changed again. He looked at Jim deliberately, thoughtfully almost, with an expression not unlike the one Jim had seen on Gloria Amoypola's face when she had dealt with the obstreperous reception clerk the previous night. "You find my fee too high?" Udoyen inquired in a voice meant to be deceptively calm.

Jim cleared his throat. "I find it steep for the amount of work done. It's comparable to what we pay outside counsel in New York."

"And New York counsel, of course, is entitled to a higher fee than Nigerian counsel." The voice was cold now and had a stiletto ring to it. "I take it New York counsel is white."

Jim stared. "What's that got to do with anything?"

"You know very well what it has to do with everything. You just don't see paying a black man what you pay a white man."

"Don't be absurd," Jim said, but he could hear the defensive tone in his voice. "It's a question of demands made, time put in, work done."

"The quality of work, you mean."

"Quality is part of it, but I'm talking mainly about the amount of work and the results achieved."

"And a black man can't produce the quality a white man can. And therefore doesn't get the results." Pascal's voice was pure poison now.

Jim sat back, his shoulders pressed against the hard frame of his chair. Pascal was curled up in his thronelike recliner on the other side of the desk. "Look, Udoyen, I am not here to discuss race relations. I want to talk to you about The Copter

173

Company's prospects in Nigeria and your role in these prospects: past, present and future."

"And the first item on this worthy agenda is that The Copter Company is paying too much money to that little black Nigerian, Pascal Udoyen."

Jim's hands gripped the not very sturdy arms of his chair. His knuckles showed white. "The first item on the agenda is, Why has The Copter Company no results whatever to show for two years of effort and two hundred thousand dollars of expense in Nigeria? The next item is, What can we do to get results? We. The Copter Company and Pascal Udoyen."

Pascal's eyes narrowed to near slits.

"I will start this 'agenda' "—he put ironic quotation marks around the word agenda—"with Pascal Udoyen. And I suggest you listen to me carefully. The message is that Pascal Udoyen does not work for white masters for groundnuts. Let me translate this for you to make certain you understand. It means I don't work for white bastards for peanuts. My father did that, and his father before him, and his father's father before that. You bullied and squeezed us for three hundred years, looted our country of its resources and made us think at the same time that we should be grateful to be allowed to serve your superior civilization. Let me just advise you, Mr. Lindner—and it is good advice, worth every puny penny you have paid me—that this shit isn't going to stick anymore. I don't believe it and I won't put up with it. More important to the fate of The Copter Company, to which you are so devoted, the people who now rule this country will have no part of your exploitation or your pretensions. Not anymore. If you can't get that through your square white skull, you can forget about Nigeria, or any other black country on this continent." He jerked a thumb toward the door. "You can go peddle your copters to South Africa. They're your kind of people."

Jim's stomach cramped. The man might be right. He might just have blown any potential Nigeria held as a market for The Copter Company. On the first try too. But something in him reared. "I had, and have, nothing to do with your colonial history, whatever it was. I come from Pennsylvania. My folks left Germany in 1848 because they were fed up with class exploitation in Europe, óf Europeans, by Europeans. And, I remind you, the United States was the first country to fight colonialism, and the first to free itself from it. If you must gum up a business discussion with irrelevant history."

Pascal's eyes had become flinty. In a voice that mingled patronizing smugness with mock compassion, he said, "Listen, Jim. My forebears were Hausa chiefs when yours were peasants digging up the earth with wooden plows in Germany, or wherever it is you come from. My father is a Hausa chief now, governing the lives, the property and the fortunes of some ten thousand people and more than a hundred thousand acres of land."

"And my father runs a repair shop in Lansdale, Pennsylvania. What's that got to do with anything?"

The mock compassion turned to mock pity. "Everything, Lindner, everything. It explains why I won't work for a pittance for the likes of you. I suggest you seriously consider this. I give you until this evening. I'll meet you at your hotel at six o'clock to get your commitment to raise my fee to one hundred thousand naira per year. That's one hundred and fifty thousand dollars. Our money is worth more than yours. The commitment becomes effective tomorrow. If you want to do business in Nigeria. And this consultation is concluded." He held out a bony well-made hand, drooping it slightly as if he expected it to be kissed.

Jim pushed out of his chair, struggling to keep his muscles and his voice under control. "I'll see you tonight," he said. It came out sounding calm. He was glad to hear it.

He did not feel calm when he got down to the street. The air was hot and muggy. His palms were moist and his stomach felt queasy. He did not know whether this was due to the slightly redolent breakfast he had been served on the terrace of the Federal Palace Hotel overlooking the huddle of ships on the river, or whether it was due to his encounter with Pascal Udoyen. It did not matter much. The important decision he had to make was where he should go from here. Did he have any choice? Was there an alternative to Udoyen? How could he find out?

A taxi pulled up at the curb. It was unkempt, but the driver was wearing a gleaming white lace shirt. He had pulled in behind a black Mercedes 220 parked in front of Udoyen's office. Jim felt certain the Mercedes belonged to Pascal.

The driver had been watching Jim. "Where to?" he asked when Jim stepped forward.

"The American embassy."

The driver nodded. It figured. "Eight naira."

Jim sighed silently. He was sure he was being taken. Again. But there wasn't much he could do about it. He didn't even know how far it was to the embassy. "Okay," he said.

The embassy was located about two thirds of the way back to the hotel, and it took half an hour to get there. Traffic was still murderous, but the meter showed only N 1.25 when they pulled up at the embassy door. Jim forked over a ten-naira note, took all of the change, got a contemptuous look from the driver in white lace and stepped into the building.

Inside, it was cool and clean but chaotic. The embassy seemed to partake of the same kind of shambles that characterized all of Lagos.

The economic attaché was free to see him, even though Jim did not have an appointment. Not really free, but he would interrupt what he was doing to talk to Mr. Lindner; that's what he was here for, after all. He was middle-aged and wore thick rimless glasses. He was also serious and knowledgeable.

Painstakingly he explained the economics of Nigeria: the enormous potential; the frustrating problems; the political, social and economic bases of these problems; the operational agonies of doing business in Nigeria; the possible rewards. The country had nowhere to go but up; and it had the money, the people and the resources to go up. It would do so in a messy way, from any and every point of view, but it would do it, and America, American companies, could and should play a role in the process. Nigeria needed the help: technology, know-how, managerial expertise. For its part, America had a stake in black Africa. In many ways Ambassador Andrew Young was right. If the vacuum wasn't filled by America, there were others more than willing to step

176

into the breach. Economically, Europeans—the Germans, Italians, French—were all active in Nigeria, as, of course, were the British, who were dug in deep. Politically, there were always the Russians and their stand-ins from Havana. True, this was a partly Moslem nation, and Communism didn't sit well with most Moslems. Besides, the way individual Russians behaved in Africa did not exactly endear them to the black population. The Cubans did a lot better, though. Anyhow, the Russians would certainly keep on trying to gain influence on this continent, and they had already chalked up some real successes, directly or via their Cuban Charlie McCarthys. To wit, Angola, Mozambique, Ethiopia. In sum, for American companies to establish a constructive presence here was good for Nigeria, good for America, good for the free world. What, specifically, could he do to help?

Jim had listened to the attaché's disquisition with a mixture of discomfort and boredom. He never went to US embassies for help in doing business if he could avoid it. If that was a prejudice, his encounter with John Cahill in Teheran had reinforced it. In Jim's experience, and with some notable exceptions—the exceptions tended to be agricultural attachés, labor attachés or men detailed to the embassy from Treasury, guys with real, concrete jobs to do, in a real, concrete world—foreign service officers always seemed to know the answers without ever listening to the questions.

"Thanks for filling me in on the big picture," he said with just a touch of sarcasm in his voice. "But what I need is some practical assistance. Does this embassy have a commercial officer who can identify a possible representative for my company so we can take that constructive action you advocate?"

The attaché nodded. "Yes, indeedy. I'll send you right over." He rang for his secretary. "Take Mr. Lindner to our commercial officer, will you please?"

Jim thought he saw a supercilious smile pull up the corners of the attaché's mouth. "Good luck, Mr. Lindner," he said. "I suspect you'll need it."

When the secretary had knocked and pushed open the door with the sign that read G. HENDERSON BENNETT, COMMERCIAL OFFI-

177

CER, Jim did a double take. Behind the desk sat a handsome black woman with a figure and carriage much like Gloria Amoypola's.

"Is Mr. Bennett in?"

"I'm Grace Bennett." The voice was firm and flat. Jim caught a Midwestern note, twangy on top, tough underneath. "I know what you're thinking," she said. "Everybody does. Nevertheless, I am the commercial officer of this embassy, have been for the past three years. Which is too long."

Grace Henderson Bennett certainly said what she thought, and said it straight. It made a welcome change.

"Yes," she concurred, although Jim had not spoken. "It's easier that way. Now what else is on your mind?"

"I need a representative in Nigeria for my company. A serious professional, preferably honest. He has to have good contacts among the guys who run this show, whoever they are, or will be."

She shrugged. "Everyone wants that. What're you selling?"

"Helicopters. The best in the world, bull aside. For civilian and military use. Examples: offshore oil exploration, spotting submarines."

"Oh," she said. "You really aren't—"

"Whistling Dixie?" he interrupted with a wink.

She winked back. "Playing tiddlywinks, I was going to say. I've been here awhile. One catches things, in more ways than one."

"Tell me."

"You tell me first."

"There isn't much more to tell. We've had a fellow here—I guess we still have him—who's been giving us the business for two years, producing nothing."

"For how much?"

"A hundred thousand."

"A hundred thousand what?"

"Dollars. US. Now he wants to jack it up to a hundred thousand naira."

She looked thoughtful, and a frown chased across the mahogany planes of her face. "For doing nothing, that's a bit stiff even for Nigeria. Do you really mean nothing?"

"Just about. He drew up three legal papers. My guess is that was about five hours' worth of work. He probably had his clerk do it, whom he pays a hundred dollars a month."

"Two hundred," she corrected. "This is Lagos after 1973. I take it he's a lawyer, and you need a lawyer."

"Not necessarily. A good representative can always farm out the legal work. But it looks better on the books if he's a lawyer. The SEC understands legal fees. It has more trouble with commissions, especially in our industry. And some congressmen have even more trouble than the SEC. It's known in the business as The Lockheed Inheritance. Nevertheless, representatives really do have to be paid."

"How much could a good person make representing you in Nigeria?" He noticed she had said person, not man.

"Depends on how much he or she sold. It could be a handsome income. In fact, given the way I understand this country works, it could be a hell of a lot."

"Does Nigeria really need your helicopters? I mean, should they be buying them?"

Jim studied the map of Nigeria tacked up on the wall behind her. The map was flanked by framed photographs of President Carter and Ambassador Young, signed Jimmy and Andy. The picture of Young had a dedication. He strained to read it. "To Grace," it said, "who knows where it's at." I bet she does, he thought.

"There's a case to be made," he said deliberately, "that they need houses and hospitals, schools and roads before they need military hardware of any kind, ours included. But it doesn't work that way. Do taxi drivers in Lagos need white lace shirts? I hear the lace is smuggled in, costing wads of foreign exchange. Should this town be crawling with Mercedes 220s? Should it be just about impossible to get a local beer, which I understand is pretty good, while you can get any amount of imported whiskey at twenty dollars a bottle?"

"Okay," she said. "I get your point. But—"

"I've thought about the 'but,' " he interrupted. "And perhaps, mankind being what it is, here and now, it does take muscle to change a tribal society into a nation: modern military muscle,

179

the kind we furnish. Also, copters do have important civilian uses: transportation, communications, the delivery of services to areas and people who can't be reached any other way. Even rescue. Helicopters have been known to save lives."

She nodded. Her mouth curved down. When she spoke again, her voice was sad and had an undertone of bitterness. "You may be right. About mankind being what it is, here and now." A small hole of silence opened between them. She filled it. "This is a dog-eat-dog society. St. Louis, where I come from, is gold compared to this. What they admire most here is what they call cleverness, by which they mean how ruthlessly you can cheat someone and get away with it. I know. I get insights into this place that white people can't get. So does my husband. He's an engineer and installs wells all over the country. I run fashion shows on my own time. African fashion. I think some of it is great and has a real potential back home. But in wells or clothes, everybody here tries to give everybody the kind of deal you got."

"Are you telling me that I might as well settle for what I have?"

"No. There are good people here like anywhere else. But, as you know, they—"

"Finish last?"

"I don't really believe that. Do you?"

"No. But they don't necessarily make out either. Do you have a good guy I could try?"

"Yes. He has a music degree from Juilliard."

"What?"

"And an economics degree from London, and a law degree from Ibadan."

"That's quite a combination."

"He's quite a guy. Do you want to take a chance?"

Jim thought of Udoyen, and the nausea of the morning returned. "I'd certainly like to talk to him."

"Okay." She wrote two lines on her memo pad, tore off the page and handed it to Jim. The heading read, "From the Desk of: Grace Henderson Bennett, Commercial Officer, US Embassy, Lagos, Nigeria." The official US seal was on top. In neat penmanship she had written, "Michael Smith Oni. 54 Anifowoshe Street, Victoria Island."

"Where's that?"

"Residential section, not far from here. A five-minute taxi ride."

"Five naira?"

She nodded. "One naira on the meter."

He rose and put out his hand. "Thanks a lot," he said. "You restore my faith in the United States foreign service."

Her eyes twinkled. "I know what you mean." She took his proffered hand. "Keep the faith, Mr. Lindner. We need it. We all need it."

The taxi ambled down the alley. By Lagos standards, the street was wide and clean but unpaved. Many of the houses had national seals over their entryways or flew flags.

The driver stopped in front of a high wall with a small iron door. There was no bell. There was also no number and no name.

When Jim pushed the door, the hinges creaked but the door gave easily. He found himself in a very large courtyard facing eight Mercedes cars of various sizes, all of the latest vintage, and one Silver Cloud Rolls-Royce. Four of the Mercedeses had license plates with even numbers, the other four had plates with odd numbers. The Rolls had one of each and a movable metal piece that could cover either one of the plates. At the far end of the courtyard a door stood ajar and he could hear voices speaking English. When he got to the door, he saw that they belonged to two people, an enormous black man weighing at least three hundred pounds, wrapped in a sheet and lying on a waterbed, conversing with a trim, muscular brown man of medium height, who was immaculately dressed. He wore a summer-weight pin-striped charcoal-gray suit, a white shirt striped in blue, a silk tie of matching blue with a Countess Mara crest, and large silver cufflinks of a dull gray. As Jim got close enough to see, the links turned out to be old coins with cursive Arabic script. The brown man looked as though he would feel perfectly at home on Wall Street or in the City in London.

"My name is Lindner," Jim said at the doorway.

The two men looked at him encouragingly. "Grace Henderson Bennett sent me."

They exchanged a glance, and the large man on the bed turned to peer at Jim. As he did so, Jim noticed that there were four telephones lined up alongside the waterbed—white, red, purple and green. A telex machine clattered in the corner and the Wall Street type was checking figures in what seemed to be a small ledger bound in red morocco. He looked up also. "Yes, sir," he said, in an accent that sounded Indian to Jim. "You're welcome. Why have you come?"

"I am looking for Michael Smith Oni."

"Oh," said the Wall Street type, sounding disappointed. "You've arrived at the wrong house." He bent his head over the little ledger. The man on the waterbed stuck out a fat thumb slanted to the right. "Next door," he said. His voice was gravelly and resonant. He raised it a little to call out, "Mary."

The head of a slender, very pretty girl appeared in the door. "Yes, Father."

The big man nodded toward Jim. "This brother is looking for Michael Oni. Take him over there."

The girl held out a small hand and beckoned imperiously. "Follow," she said.

"Thank you," Jim muttered at the two men, who had gone back to their business.

Walking toward the gate, past the extraordinary assembly of cars in the courtyard, Jim could not resist inquiring, "Who're you?" It came out sounding peremptory, and he immediately regretted the tone. But the girl did not seem to care.

"Mary Arogundade," she replied. "My father is a Yoruba chief. He's in business."

"And the man with him?"

"Is his financial adviser. He's a Pakistani. Went to Oxford."

Her English was flawless. It had an American accent, with just a touch of New Yorkese.

"And you?" he asked.

"I have an MBA from New York University. Now I help my father."

182

The touch of New York was reassuring. Jim smiled. "Any more at home like you?"

She smiled back. "Lots. There are thirty of us. My father has six wives."

Jim gulped. "Where?" He stopped, his eyes appraising the compound. There seemed to be residential quarters on two sides.

"Oh," she said airily, "not here. Five of the wives are always in the village. Only one at a time is in residence in Lagos."

"Your mother?"

"They are all my mothers."

She led him out of the iron door to the next house, where a considerably larger gate permitted a view of tended lawns, neat beds of flowers and, behind them, a modern whitewashed bungalow. She pushed the bell at the gate. "This is Michael's place," she said. "He's nice."

She waited with Jim until a handsome black man with a full well-trimmed beard showing the first flecks of gray came across the lawn. He was wearing a tan-colored safari suit with short sleeves. "Hi, Mary," he said. "What, or rather who, have you brought me?"

Mary produced another imperious wave of her hand. "Don't know, Michael. He was looking for you." She turned and walked back to her house, leaving the two men eying each other.

"Actually," Jim said, "Grace Henderson Bennett sent me. I'm Jim Lindner of The Copter Company, New York."

Smith Oni nodded. "I know New York. I don't know The Copter Company. But if Grace sent you, come on in."

The house, a combination office and residence, was as neat and clean as it had appeared from outside. The study looked much like a good lawyer's office in New York: well-made wooden furniture carefully polished, comfortable leather chairs, lots of books, file cabinets tucked away in one corner, a few etchings. What made it different was an enormous oil painting in vivid colors on the wall behind the desk.

Smith Oni had followed Jim's gaze. "Yes," he said. "It is Nigerian. We do well in the arts here. Have done long before the bronzes of Benin. Look at that." He pointed to a corner. Mounted on a brass block, the stone sculpture of a young woman's head looked out into space. It was an exquisite carving of an exquisite face. "Beauty, isn't she? Ife. That's a tribe not far from here. They've been doing that kind of thing for a thousand years." Reluctantly, Michael Smith Oni turned his head away from the girl's face.

Jim found himself sharing the reluctance. "How do you get any work done," he inquired, "with her in the room?"

Smith Oni's face lit up. "It's hard," he said, settling in his chair and motioning Jim to sit opposite. "But let's try."

Jim briefed him succinctly. Michael Smith Oni, he felt, didn't need selling. In fact, probably couldn't be sold. So Jim just told him about The Copter Company, its products, its record in Nigeria, its experience with Pascal Udoyen.

"I know Udoyen," Smith Oni commented. "Not a graceful loser."

"Dangerous?"

"Could be. He'll try."

"Can he do any real harm?"

"Possibly. Some."

"Should I risk it?"

"Do you want to?"

"Yes. Very much."

"Then what's your proposition?"

Jim hesitated. A fair deal was what he wanted. Well, at least a reasonable arrangement. Not being taken by a buggy little twerp on the make.

"Okay," Smith Oni said. "Let me put it to you this way. Do you have a representative in Holland?"

"Yes, of course. Why?"

"What are your arrangements with him?"

"A retainer and a two percent commission on every copter sold in the Netherlands."

"I'll take it on the same basis. At least, I'll give it the old school try. I'll need to know what a retainer comes to in figures, but whatever you pay your Dutchman, I'll settle for."

"Why? I mean why Holland? We do business in dozens of countries around the world."

184

"Dutchmen are the squarest folk I know."

"You don't look square to me."

"I'm not. But I like doing business that way. It makes life simpler and more pleasant. Gives me time and mind for my girl"—he nodded toward the statue in the corner—"and my music. Grace told you about that, I imagine."

"She did." Suddenly, Jim's mind turned back to Brigitte and the stupid, unsettling row they had had about the production of *Fidelio*. "I think I envy you," he said.

"Don't. It's a bad habit. Besides, I have my own problems."

"Having spent all of one night and one morning in Lagos, I imagine you do. And having delivered myself of that tactless but true remark, I'd like to ask you something that is also none of my goddamn business."

"Business is an elastic concept. Everywhere. Very elastic in Nigeria. Ask."

"Where does the Smith come from?"

Smith Oni shook his head. "No. It's not what you're thinking. I'm one hundred percent black and beautiful. But one of my grandfathers made it back here from the Caribbean, where his grandfather had been shipped as a slave. At the time my granddad returned, the British, who, as you know, governed this place for some time, had a rite of manumission which they offered to people like my prodigal ancestor. In that rite a man became officially free and could pick a new name. The consul who presided over my grandfather's manumission was a man called Smith. My granddad thought that was a fine name, given the occasion. All things considered, I think so myself. That's why I use both names. Oni is the real one, of course. But Smith is Smith. Or was, anyhow."

Jim reached for his wallet and fished out a card. "Okay, Michael Smith Oni. It's a deal. I'll send you the back-up material on the company and our products as soon as I get back to New York. And a contract exactly like the one we have in Holland. In fact I'll send you a copy of the Dutch contract along with your own. Don't frame it though. Keep it in your desk drawer. Or have your girlfriend over there keep an eye on it. She looks mighty smart to me."

"Not smart. Knowing."

"I guess that's right. An important difference. And speaking of knowing women, I may have to send Grace Henderson Bennett a bunch of posies. I think she did me a real favor. The problem now is to peel off Pascal. I'm meeting him at six. I don't cherish the prospect."

"Why don't you wait a couple of days before you talk to Udoyen? He's a volatile guy."

"I can't. I'm leaving tonight."

Smith Oni frowned. "Fast on the trigger, aren't you? I'm not sure that's necessarily the best way to get things done."

"I'm not either, but they tend to think so in New York."

"New York can be wrong, all propaganda and considerable evidence to the contrary notwithstanding."

"Spoken like a splendid legal eagle. And I agree with you." New York can be murderously wrong, he added silently.

"While I'm offering opinions," Smith Oni said, "unsolicited and non-reimbursable, here's another. When you see Udoyen this evening, don't turn your back to him in any way."

"Thanks. I consider that first-rate counsel. It augurs well for our mutual future. You keep your head down too. Your girlfriend over there likes it, I'm sure. And I need it."

Driving back to the hotel, his stomach still fluttery but his head clear, Jim noticed two phenomena that struck him as quintessentially Lagos. One was a large truck built up in the back and on the sides with wooden boards that were painted in primary colors. The back board showed a very yellow, very ferocious lion on the left, faced by the legend, painted in pale blue, JESUS LOVES YOU. Above that an enamel sign read, GOODS ONLY. The truck was jammed with people who chattered, laughed and, when traffic stalled progress, bought glass bottles filled with cashew nuts from girl vendors, who had the bottles piled up on straw trays on their heads.

The other Lagos phenomenon he observed was a large sign in a cramped empty lot wedged among four small stalls selling splashy cotton textiles, oven thermometers, yams and electric steam irons. The sign read, NO DUMPING, and was stamped at the bottom, BY ORDER OF THE LAGOS CITY COUNCIL. The sign looked down on an enormous garbage can heaped to the brim with trash, which had overflown like a dirty river. Empty cans, broken bottles and rotting peels looked straight up at the order of the Lagos City Council.

It was twelve minutes past six when Udoyen swept into the lobby of the Federal Palace Hotel. He was dressed in a gauzy material of pale blue, delicately embroidered around the loose collar and the hem of the sleeves. The material was starched and hissed as he walked. He wore a Nigerian cap that fitted snugly around the skull like a crown, then fell softly forward. It was made of brocaded velvet, with gold threads glistening in the deep blue.

He sparkled amiability. After a quick glance around the cavernous lobby, which to Udoyen's evident surprise contained no one he cared to see, he took Jim by the arm and steered him toward the hotel entrance. "Dreadful, this Federal Palace. Let me take you away from all this." He smiled mischievously, then insinuated a sober tone. "Really, I know a better place."

When the hotel doorman had bellowed the number of Udoyen's car and the driver had brought it around, it turned out to be the Mercedes 220 that Jim had seen parked at the curb in front of Udoyen's office. They climbed into the back. "Eko," Udoyen said.

The Eko was a hotel built by Holiday Inn near the beach of Lagos. They drove close to a stretch of the shore to get there. The sand was pale brown, strewn here and there with cabanas made of plaited straw. Waves rolled in gently, with a soft, even rhythm; and the rising moon played its own games with them, making and unmaking patterns of shadow and light as the water embraced the sand.

It was a seductive sound. It occurred to Jim that the choice of route, with its romantic detour, had been deliberate. Udoyen could be subtle when he wanted to be.

The cocktail lounge of the Eko resembled a stage set: wood,

187

straw, bamboo and phony Caribbean-style rustic appointments to hide the plastic and plywood efficiency underneath. The lounge looked out on a swimming pool occupied by a dozen bikini-clad white women and their pre-teen offspring. The breeze carried a whiff of chlorine to their table from the noisy frolickers in the pool.

Udoyen ordered a suffering bastard. "Appropriate," he said, flashing the charm.

Jim asked for a beer.

"Harp?" the waiter inquired.

It took Jim a second to catch on. Harp. Odd name for a beer in Nigeria.

"Try it," Udoyen said playfully. "You might like it." Then, his voice suddenly sober and with an edge to it, he added, "You might like Nigeria too if you learned how to operate in it—with people who know their way around because they belong in it, because it's their country."

"That plural, I take it, includes one Pascal Udoyen, attorney-at-law?"

"It does. And he cannot be shylocked."

It was dark enough for Jim to be able to hold on to his knees under the table without Pascal being able to see what he was doing. He could hear the surf slap the beach. "Then let's not go through unnecessary and unpleasant motions. Let's just call it a day and part friends."

"It's night, and people who cross Pascal Udoyen are not friends and are not treated as friends in Nigeria." The threat was blatant in his voice and face.

Jim could feel his stomach knot again. The little bastard, he thought. How does he do it, sitting there, half my size, dressed like a girl going to a birthday party and scaring the hell out of me? He forced himself to sound calm. It took doing. "I guess I'll have to take my chances on that."

Udoyen pushed the table away from himself and rose from the chair in a quick, abrupt motion. It made Jim think of a switchblade. The candle in its coconut shell casing listed, fell, sputtered and died.

188

"Indeed you will," Udoyen murmured. He turned, and in a second the night had swallowed him.

When the waiter brought the drinks, Jim used the beer he had ordered as a chaser. First he polished off the suffering bastard. He was feeling a little woozy and remembered that breakfast had been barely edible and that he had had no lunch. He decided a suffering bastard was an appropriate drink, and that the smartest move he could make was to get himself the hell out of this place as quickly as possible.

Half an hour later he was on his way. It was just as well, he had concluded. He would rather spend a couple of hours in the international lounge at the airport than in his room or in any other part of the Federal Palace Hotel. The drive that had taken less than half an hour coming in dragged on endlessly going out.

On the bridges and wherever traffic merged, hopeless snarls developed with trucks, cars and motorcycles darting and careening in and out of the mess. Jim's driver too played the chicken game. It was not a matter of money. The deal the driver had demanded when Jim had told him he wanted to go to the airport was a time arrangement: ten naira per hour. Jim had thought it surprisingly fair, considering his previous experience with Lagos taxis. He had been wrong.

When they finally got to the airport, departure was barely forty-five minutes off. Waiting in line to check in, Jim glimpsed a giant of a man, about six foot six, ebony black and all muscle, with a handsome handlebar mustache. He was dressed in tailored khaki and had a peaked military cap on his head that was tilted, but only to a still eminently proper angle. A swagger stick was tucked under his arm. The British legacy was patent and impressive. The man looked as if he knew who he was and what he was about.

That turned out to be an acute observation, although not in the way Jim had assumed. He had run the gauntlet of exit barriers to the last stage of outgoing customs. Jim had never understood the point of outgoing customs, but he knew it was a procedure in some Asian and African countries where there

189

was a lot of smuggling in and out. With his simple case neatly packed with nothing but clothes, toilet kit, shoes and papers, nobody had ever given Jim any trouble at customs. Until now.

When he had identified his luggage on the counter, a porter suddenly rolled his eyes, lolled his tongue and did a little two-step, half singing, half whining, "I could use a Harp. I could use a Harp."

Puzzled at first, Jim soon remembered that Harp was a beer and reached into his pocket for the last of his Nigerian change. He handed it to the porter. "Go and have one then."

The porter looked at the coins and shook his head. Jim shrugged, turned back to his luggage and found himself facing the big man in khaki with the swagger stick.

He lowered his head to look into Jim's eyes. "How much money do you have?"

Jim blinked. "I just went through currency control."

The man did not take his eyes off Jim's. The voice, as quiet as before but insistent now, repeated, "How much money do you have?"

"About a thousand dollars, US. A few Nigerian bills. Some Singapore currency."

"Are the dollars cash or traveler's checks?"

"Some of each."

"How much of each?"

"Five hundred. Approximately."

The big man looked thoughtful for a moment, then said, his voice still unchanged, his eyes never flinching from Jim's, "I want some of the cash."

Jim's mind raced through a calculation. It was less than thirty minutes for his Pan American flight's departure. The big man could easily find a reason to delay him or his luggage for a half hour and make him miss the plane. Getting bookings out of Lagos was not easy. When one could get out. If one could get out. There was no telling what they could hold him for, or for how long. This might, in fact, already be Udoyen at work, in which case anything was possible. And the big man did not look as if he could be crossed.

"How much is some?"

190

The man shrugged. "Oh," he said easily, "five percent."

Jim took out his wallet and held out a twenty-dollar bill. The man stared at him. He held out another twenty. The gaze stayed where it had been. Jim added a ten and snapped his wallet shut.

Next to him, the porter again rolled his eyes and went into his jig. Jim looked at the big man behind the counter, who took his swagger stick and flicked it at the porter as he would at a fly. "Never mind," he said, addressing Jim in a man-to-man manner. There was the trace of a Sandhurst intonation. "I'm the boss. I'll give him change." He marked Jim's luggage with a check of white chalk and gestured at the porter to carry the suitcase through the barrier. Jim followed.

The flight was called exactly on time. Two pert Nigerian girls, wearing the forest green miniskirts and rakish berets of Air Nigeria, processed the boarding cards. At the top of the ramp, a raw-boned blonde with heavy legs said, "Hi. How're you this muggy night?" Her voice was nasal and grating. Jim was glad to hear it.

"Okay now," he said. "And welcome to the world of Pan Am."

She gave him that resigned I-guess-it-takes-all-kinds look which, Jim suspected, stewardesses practiced in front of their mirrors at night. "You have the window seat in the fourth row." A no-nonsense girl. All-American. He followed her directions. His seat was soft and upholstered in red and blue. The pillow on the head rest was a spotless snowy white. Jim buckled up, closed his eyes and leaned back with a sigh of relief. He was home.

Ten minutes later, when they were airborne, the man next to him lit a cigarette, and Jim heard the clinking of ice on the bar cart coming down the aisle. It seemed a long time since he had first met Pascal Udoyen, or peeled off bills for the boss of outgoing customs. That all this and everything in between had happened in little more than twelve hours did not seem possible. Nevertheless here he was on his way from Lagos, Nigeria, to Basel, Switzerland. Some pretty improbable things happened there too.

The clinking had come close. He opened his eyes.

"What'll it be?" the big blonde asked.

8

Basel was dreary and depressing. Darkness fell early, and the Rhine looked murky and small. The huddled houses along the river and in the city's center exuded a steaming air, like the sweat of people hunched over a fire and covered by too many layers of clothes. Only the diamondlike glitter of the neon sign atop the naked tower of the Ciba-Geigy building seemed to pierce the opaque sobriety of the town.

But there was comfort inside. The taxi that transported Jim from the airport was another roomy Mercedes. In reassuring contrast to Lagos, this one was spanking clean. Its radio worked, emitting classic opera, Swiss style: measured, predictable, soporific. At the Hotel Drei Könige, the doorman had departed for the night, but the hotel's tall doors, their thick panes rubbed to a shine, opened and closed by themselves with startling rapidity. The young lady behind the reception desk, equally scrubbed and shiny, gave Jim a brief look and after a barely perceptible shrug addressed him in three languages, which she managed to pack into one appropriate sentence. *"Bon soir, mein Herr,* how are you?" Jim decided to let her off her multilingual hook quickly, although she was clearly capable of coping in any of the languages in which he might have responded. "Fine, thanks."

She moved toward Jim a brief registration form, also trilingual, encased in a black leather frame, gold-embossed at the top with the historic symbol of the house: three kings, bearded,

192

crowned and brandishing their scepters at the arriving guest.

The Hotel Drei Könige claimed to be the oldest inn in Switzerland and managed to purvey an atmosphere of both history and luxurious comfort. The history was carefully preserved and offered up as stock in trade. The lobby had a trompe l'oeil of Basel in the Middle Ages and a mural of the yeomen dressed in velvet and iron who fought to create the country and keep it secure.

Jim's room, carpeted with a genuine Aubusson rug, was draped and upholstered in heavy silk the color of tarnished gold. The ceiling was molded, with a cupola in the center, and painted cerulean blue to resemble a piece of sky. A medieval chandelier hung from a link chain, its candles converted to tapers of white metal topped with tiny incandescent bulbs. The one picture on the wall was a gold-framed aquarelle of Napoleon at Austerlitz. A color TV set was hidden discreetly in a cabinet of dark wood, and the radio and alarm clock on the bedside table were streamlined in design and unobtrusively small.

Hotel literature on the Louis XIV desk informed Jim that his own presence in this historic hostelry had been preceded by such luminaries as Voltaire and Prince Metternich, the Princess Victoria before she became England's Queen, and a firmament full of stars in the contemporary international social scene, including ex-King Farouk of Egypt and the Maharaja of Baroda.

More history, albeit of a different kind, was spread out on the desk. The hotel's stationery was enfolded in a cover furnished by the city's leading financial institution, the Swiss Capital Union Bank, founded more than a century ago. The Copter Company's bank now and Ken Ward's bank.

Jim stared at the bank's trilingual assertion of its confidence-inspiring capacity for survival. Unlike Ken. The thought came unbidden and with it a sour taste that rose from deep inside him, leaving his gullet parched and his lips dry.

The house bar to which he repaired was cozy: dark woods, solid brass, a handsome array of bottles containing the best of everything from everywhere. He did not have to explain what a Rob Roy was; it arrived strong, cold and tart, and obliterated quickly the dry acidity that had almost made him retch in the

193

solid comfort of his room. But the company was uninspiring. To his right, three middle-aged men were engaged in concentrated conversation. They wore heavy wool suits with vests that strained around the bulges above their belts. They spoke German and were talking business. On his left, two even more rotund men of the same age seemed bouncier. In English, they informed the bartender that they were from Mexico, had just arrived and were here on a business trip. The bartender had heard of Mexico City. The Olympics were held there once, weren't they? When the men told him that their home town was Guadalajara, his face went blank. He had never heard of it, could not pronounce it and did not want to try. Still, the men were customers. He served them the tequila they had asked for and had not really expected to get. They raised their glasses to each other. *"Por mañana,"* one of the Mexicans said, *"buena fortuna."* The other looked into his glass, then up to the ceiling. *"Con dios,"* he responded and knocked back his tequila in one gulp.

Jim had watched them and silently joined in their toast: To tomorrow, with luck and providence. He drained his drink. The barman looked at him, a question in his eyes. Jim shook his head; he did not want another. But he did not want to go back to his room either. The sourness had given way to a nervous itch that he could feel in his palms and in the joints of his knees. Too much sitting, on too many airplanes. He had an urge to stretch his legs.

Outside, the street was dark and dead. Suddenly a motorcycle sped toward him with a young man on the front seat gripping the handlebars and a girl behind him, her arms around his waist. Both had hair long enough to flow out under their bright red safety helmets. The girl's hair was longer. It was black and streamed in the wind as the cycle clattered down the street.

Jim watched the pair pull up at the far corner of the building that bordered the hotel, park their motorcycle at the curb and vanish down a staircase. He walked toward the spot. By the door a small sign read CHEZ PIERRE, and a brightly lit stairway led to a basement filled with sound and young people, tightly packed at the bar and even more tightly packed on the dance floor. They were gyrating to a rock and roll record that seemed to pound at them from the four walls, the ceiling and the floor. It was not exciting electric rock, but it was insistent and demanding and they obeyed. They were mesmerized by the beat.

At the bar, some of the young men and women looked at Jim briefly, surprised but unconcerned. They were busy with themselves and each other: boys and girls, boys and boys, girls and girls; black, yellow, every shade of olive and pink. Next to Jim a tall skinny blonde smiled.

Jim smiled back. *"Prost, à votre santé,* cheers and *skoal."* The language-shopping bazaar that was Switzerland had its own challenges. The girl's fjord blue eyes opened a little wider. "Are you Swedish too?" She sounded expectant.

"No. American." The answer seemed to disappoint her.

"Are you on holiday?" he inquired politely. She shook her head violently. They were standing close to each other at the crowded bar, and as she tossed her hair, it touched his cheek. It felt like sand. "I wouldn't be in Basel on vacation," she said contemptuously.

"Where would you be?"

"Fez. Marrakesh. Dakar."

"Then why're you here?"

"My parents." The voice was antagonistic. "They're tax refugees."

"Come again."

Her answering smile had a salacious quality, then turned quickly into a resentful pout. "My father makes films. My mother designs textiles. In Sweden taxes are too high. So they live here."

Jim studied the girl more carefully. She was younger than he had thought at first glance. Eighteen perhaps. Rebellious, bored, hungry for something. The mouth was avid, and the eyes dilated under his scrutiny. "And you?" she challenged. "What brings you to this burghers' paradise?"

"Business."

"Ugh! How can you? You look like such an attractive man." She had lowered her voice to pronounce "man" and rolled her tongue around the word. The tongue flicked out. She was wearing jeans and a red and white T-shirt that clung. It would take less than a minute for her to reach for the zipper of her pants and pull them down. She was probably wearing nothing underneath. Not on top certainly. Her nipples were making eyes at Jim. Beneath the jeans there just might be a wisp of a bikini. That would come off quickly enough.

She was watching him. Her tongue slowly washed her lips.

Christ, he thought, she's young enough to be my daughter. He put out a hand, pulled her out of her slouch against the bar. "Want to?"

She smiled at him knowingly. "Why not?"

On the dance floor she vanished into her own world. This was not the kind of dancing he had known at her age: no cheek-to-cheek romance, no holding hands and twirling to a shared tempo. These couples didn't touch or even look at each other. They were separate and alone in a world of driving rhythms and colored lights that flickered over their bodies and faces and shredded them into jagged bits. The dance floor became a kaleidoscope of light and sound. He found his own body easing, his joints losing their tension, his feet, arms and shoulders moving, merging into this swirling barber pole that seemed to be turning around and up, around and up, forever.

He had no idea just how long it had been since he pulled that rangy blond child onto the dance floor, but slowly the eased tension of his muscles turned into lassitude, the repetitive rhythm into boredom. He caught her flailing hands and pulled her toward him roughly. "Let's go."

Outside, his eyes searched the street. "What are you looking for?" she demanded.

"A taxi."

She shook her head, and once again the ends of her hair whipped his cheeks. "No. We walk."

He held her hand as she strode rapidly in the direction of the river, then up a hill toward a small park surrounded by old houses. She allowed him to interlace his fingers with hers, but she was not there. Through her fingers he could feel her blood pound to that other fragmenting and isolating rhythm. Her head was turned away from him. A cold wind blew from the river.

She lived in one of the many morose gabled houses that bordered the park, in a tiny attic with one round window. The heavy furniture that apparently came with the room had been pushed against the walls to leave a central space that was occupied by a large foam rubber mattress, sheeted in swirls of violet and mauve. A sheepskin served as a blanket. The rest of the space on the floor was spattered with books.

"What do you do?" he asked, puzzled.

Her hand had already reached for the zipper of her jeans. She left it there. "Study."

"Study what?"

"Chemistry, of course." Her voice was sarcastic. "Doesn't everybody in Basel?" The voice changed to an imitation of a radio announcer producing mellifluent pear-shaped tones for a commercial. "Basel, world capital of the pharmaceutical industry, nestled unobtrusively on the leaf-shaded banks of the Rhine, where men of science push back the frontiers of knowledge to bring more health and wealth to all."

The imitation was perfect. She noticed the effect she had produced on him, and a slow smile invaded her mouth. The eyes dilated once more. The zipper came down. It was a large one, made of steel, and produced a metallic sound. He never found out whether there was anything underneath. It all came off in one quick, impatient motion. A tearing off, almost.

I should have done that, he admonished himself.

She was ahead of him all the way. Her body pulsed the minute he entered her and rapidly worked itself into a crescendo. She came before he did, and her moans of pleasure swept him along. But there was no merging at the end. She had moved off, as she had on the dance floor, into a world of her own in which he had no place.

When she opened her eyes, the look on her face was almost one of surprise. "Oh," she said. "You."

"Who did you think it was?"

She moved beneath him, wet, itchy and uncomfortable. "It doesn't matter. I had a good time."

197

He stared down at her. "Thank you." He felt her eagerness to get away from him. "And what's my serial number in your regiment of lovers?" He sounded bitter and hurt.

Impatience and distaste made the young face look hard. "Don't go American on me. I don't like sentimentality or pretense. You knew what you were doing. You did exactly what you wanted. Don't give me a hard time now."

The sour taste of the early evening was back in his mouth. He swallowed to banish it. It didn't help.

She reached up and touched his cheek. There was compassion in her eyes. "No need to give yourself a hard time either. It's unnecessary and stupid."

The girl was right. But that did not prevent Jim from feeling shoddy, empty and suddenly very tired.

Jürgen Zwirli rose from his desk to meet Jim halfway across the large high-ceilinged room. Zwirli moved with athletic strides that had a skier's grace and control. The muscles of his legs bulged against the trousers of his gray flannel suit, and his broad shoulders pushed against the top of the sleeves. His assertive body made the suit seem skimpy.

Zwirli had a skier's coloring as well. His face had the subtle brown of a winter tan, except for the eyes, which were ringed in a pallor that showed the pattern of goggles. The pattern was cut oddly by his gold-rimmed glasses.

The hand he held out to Jim was tanned, and the grip he offered was muscular and sure. "Good morning, Mr. Lindner." His voice matched his grip. It was both strong and eager.

They sat facing each other at a marble-topped table in the center of the room. The room, thickly carpeted, paneled in dark wood and curtained in heavy silk, breathed solidity and a wealth so sure of itself it could afford the luxury of restraint.

Zwirli himself did not quite fit into the ambience of his office. To begin with, he was astonishingly young to occupy such clearly authoritative quarters. He was in his mid-thirties, and there was an avidity about him that his assiduously conventional attire covered but could not obliterate.

198

"I am at your disposition." The formal phrase was offset by a smile, but the smile was thin and weary—an old man's smile in a young man's face.

Jim reached for his briefcase, took out a closed manila envelope and placed it on the table. He extracted a business card from his wallet and put it next to the envelope, his name and title facing Zwirli. "As I believe you know, I have taken over from Mr. Ward."

Zwirli glanced at the card, then let his eyes rest on the envelope but made no move to reach for it. "A premature death, wasn't it? Unexpected." His voice held neither warmth nor sympathy. The comment was a statement, with the hook of a question attached to it.

"Yes." Jim's fingertips touched the smooth paper, and the touch sent a wave of sadness through him.

"I have brought the document," he said. He flattened out his hand so that his fingers, palm and wrist lay on the plain envelope that held the death certificate of Kenneth Ward.

Zwirli had been observing Jim. "In that case, we can arrange now to have your signature replace Mr. Ward's for access to the account." The brisk voice hesitated for a second. "I understand Mr. Smith will remain as co-signator."

The tiny pause pulled Jim back to the present. So that was what Morse Clark called himself in Basel. One would have thought he'd pick something a little more imaginative. Morse Clark was emphatically not a Mr. Smith. On second thought, that was probably the reason he chose the name. It made a convenient and convincing cover because it was so bland and common. No one who knew anything about Morse Clark would make the connection.

"Yes," he said. "That's correct."

Zwirli strode to his desk in the corner of the room and returned with two small pieces of paper. The forms were made of heavy stock and printed in old-fashioned lettering that looked vaguely Teutonic. An account number had been entered in a flowing European hand, with the sevens crossed and the ones hooked on the left. The number matched the figures Jim had memorized from the typed slip that had arrived on his desk in New York the day before he left. He nodded and reached for the slim gold pen Zwirli had placed across the top of the two forms. As he signed, his stomach turned a somersault, making his fingers tremble. He gripped the pen hard. When he was finished, it seemed to him that his signature was practically unrecognizable. His customary easy scrawl looked rigid and alien.

Zwirli had remained standing, waiting for Jim to hand him the signed forms. His eyes shifted to the manila envelope on the table and back to Jim. Jim straightened up in his chair. "The safety deposit box," he said. "That needs to be transferred as well."

If Zwirli had any doubts or suspicions, he hid them successfully. "Yes. We can substitute your signature for Mr. Ward's on the basis of this, uh, documentation. His eyes rested for a moment on the still unopened envelope that held the death certificate. "But you'll need the lady's consent before we can let you have a key. Her consent must be conveyed to us in person. As you know, the box is registered in her name."

So it was another woman! Ken had been a more complex man than anyone had imagined.

"Yes, I'm aware of that. I was going to see her immediately after our meeting. Are there any specific instructions I should convey to the lady from you?"

Zwirli's hands remained at his side, loose and controlled. An image raced through Jim's mind of Zwirli's hands resting on a ski pole, tightening for a quick stab in the snow as he executed a sharp smooth turn on the slope. "No," Zwirli said. "The lady is experienced. That's why we recommend her."

So it had not been a romantic association, after all; just a helpful hint from the bank, probably from Zwirli. Jim rose, his heart hammering in his chest. "I can walk there, can't I? I understand it's not far from here. I don't know Basel very well." He looked at Zwirli. "Yet."

Zwirli's thin old man's smile reappeared. "If we can be of assistance in any way . . ."

Jim reached for his back pocket and pulled out his wallet. With a show of intensity, he searched its compartments, failed to find what he was seeking. "Damn! I seem to have mislaid the address."

Zwirli's smile vanished.

Jim repeated his performance. Demonstratively disconcerted, he spread out on the marble-topped table an assortment of currencies from Singapore, Nigeria and the US. The colorful notes looked like well-worn playing cards. "I had it on a slip of paper that I put in my wallet for safekeeping. I can't imagine where it could have gone."

He looked again at the currencies, let his eyes stop suddenly at the collection of naira, stared and brought his right hand to his forehead with a sharp slap. "That's where it must have happened!" he exclaimed.

Zwirli's expression was bland and remained so as Jim launched into the story of his exit from Lagos and his hassle with outgoing customs. "I must have pulled out the address when I paid that man, and dropped the slip. I trust no one from Lagos will trouble the lady." He sounded embarrassed and concerned. Will it work? he wondered.

While Jim had gone through this act, Zwirli had kept his eyes on the currencies. He had appraised them appreciatively, almost affectionately. Now he took his eyes off them and looked at Jim. His voice gave away nothing. "I have the address." He reached inside his jacket to pull out a walnut-colored notebook, its smooth leather cover matching the hue of the paneling in his office. The notebook had alphabetic indentations with the letters marked in a dull gold. Zwirli slowly turned the pages until he arrived at the letter S. He put the book on the table, face down. It lay next to the envelope that held the death certificate of Ken Ward.

What do I have to do to make him turn the damn thing over? Jim wondered desperately. I need that name and address. Jim's eyes were riveted on the little leather volume. Zwirli followed his glance, allowing the tension to mount. Jim did not stir, and Zwirli's efficient voice finally cut the silence. "If you can spare me a few more moments," he said, "there's another piece of business I would like to discuss with you."

Zwirli's eyes returned to the tabletop. As if by instinct, he

201

began sorting out the scattered bills, dividing them into stacks by currency, then ordering them by denomination. This accomplished, he lifted his head. "I was wondering," he said nonchalantly, "whether you had ever considered transferring The Copter Company's European account to Switzerland?"

Jim's heart stopped hammering. Zwirli was driving a bargain. He wanted The Copter Company's account for all its European operations. It would be a substantial account, solid and prestigious, and would look very good on Jürgen Zwirli's record. Jim raised his eyes and let them sweep the impressive room. He understood now how young Zwirli had got so far so fast. He had done it by producing business for the bank in his own way, unorthodox but effective. Swiss banks were scrupulous about the manner in which they handled money for their customers; they were considerably less scrupulous about the methods they used to get that money.

"The account is in Mainz at present, as you know. It's a convenient location for me."

"The financial services you receive are competent, of course." Zwirli's voice was neutral.

"We find them satisfactory."

Zwirli's hands moved from the currency stacks to the address book. He did not turn it over. Instead, his two hands pressed down gently on its spread pages. "I'm sure you do, but wouldn't it be a good idea to, ahem, improve them? With the, uh, additional sophistication, the extra dimension, we can offer here in Switzerland?"

He had a point there. It was certainly an extra dimension. Whether one called it sophistication or crookedness depended on the eye of the beholder. Jim looked at Zwirli. "I've thought about moving the account to Zug. Some of my colleagues in other multinational companies have already done so."

Zwirli had rearranged the piles of currency in front of him and set them up in one straight line. A notion entered Jim's head: Swiss yeoman, latter-day version.

Zwirli ran the index finger of his right hand across the regimented currency stacks. The nail had the yellow-brown stain of a cigarette addict. "Zug is an attractive location," he conceded, "but the special tax advantages it offers are marginal for a company like yours. We have compensating attractions in Basel."

A sharp trader, Zwirli, and ambitious. He didn't merely want the account for his bank. He wanted it under his own management and control, here in Basel.

Once more Zwirli moved the stacks of bills on the table. This time he arranged them into a pyramid. His tobacco-stained index finger slid along the sides of the triangle he had constructed, from the base to the peak, tapping a stack at a time as he enumerated the charms of his city. "We have theater here, good music, excellent museums, interesting galleries, the world's best zoo and, uh, contemporary entertainment that cannot be found in Zug." His finger had arrived at the pyramid's apex. For the first time in the encounter, his mouth had relaxed, revealing lips with a sensuous curl, indulgent and appreciative. They suited his face and figure better than his thin old man's smile.

He probably meant Chez Pierre and its counterparts. Apparently there was more of that in Basel than met the eye. "Yes," Jim said. "That would be an advantageous move."

Advantageous for Zwirli certainly and, Jim admitted, necessary for him. He had to get the key to that safety deposit box. Zwirli knew it, even if he did not know why. He probably figured there was a nest egg in it of some size that Ken had stashed away for reasons of his own. Which was true, in a way.

"It's an interesting suggestion, Mr. Zwirli. I'll have to discuss it with my colleagues in New York, of course, but I can see no compelling reason why they wouldn't concur."

Zwirli had begun to tap the stacks of currencies at the base of the pyramid. He played them like piano keys with one finger running back and forth. "I rather think Mr. Smith would appreciate this kind of initiative."

Smith being Morse Clark, Jim translated. Appreciate the initiative? Morse Clark probably would. Especially if he could duck responsibility should anything go wrong. Which it might, given the increasing curiosity and expertise of the IRS. If the IRS ever got on the scent of the whole Basel business, Morse Clark could point out quite accurately that moving the company's European account to Basel had been Jim's idea. He had just accommodated the VP international, who presented logical operational reasons.

And Russel Knight? What would be his reaction if Jim proposed such a move? Knight would insist on knowing why the move should be made. Or would he? With all his toughness in managerial matters, there was a Pontius Pilate air about Knight. "You have to go along to get along" was the way he felt about most actions that didn't impinge directly on his own domain. He would probably shrug off this Zwirli bid as typical European shenanigans, the kind you can't do much about. In his mind's eye, Jim could see Knight looking over his steel-rimmed spectacles, and saying, "If it doesn't make a dent in the bottom line, play it their way. It's their continent."

"I'll take it up with New York as soon as I get back," Jim said. Zwirli waited. "I will recommend that we make the change." Zwirli continued to wait. "To Basel," Jim added. Zwirli's face registered no reaction. But there was a glitter in his eyes, which looked for an instant like a winter-blue sky reflecting sunlit snow. Perhaps the glitter was just a trick of light played by Zwirli's glasses catching a ray of the pale yellow sun that was trying to break through the curtained windows. Zwirli bent his head. The glitter disappeared. Zwirli reached for the address book, turned it over, peered and read out loud, "Frau Clarissa Stauffinger. Totentanz five."

Totentanz turned out to be a continuation of the street on which Jim's hotel was situated. The street sloped up from the hotel, climbed a small hill on which fifteen houses were perched, two- and three-story buildings, narrow but deep. Their fronts faced the street, where the smoothly humming electric tramway ran from a park at the top of the hill to the center of the city. Their backs looked out over the river. On the river side, each house had window boxes painted white but filled only with brown earth at this time of the year.

When Jim had called, Clarissa Stauffinger had asked him to come for coffee at four o'clock in the afternoon. Frau Stauffinger was a buxom lady in her fifties, dressed in a durable tweed suit, completed by a silk blouse in muted colors. Her graying hair was neatly coiffed. She wore sturdy Swiss shoes. The moment she opened the door, the fragrance of coffee caressed Jim's nostrils. She poured the coffee from a china pot decorated with wildflowers, and served with it rich Swiss cream and home-baked cake that was light, marbled with chocolate and covered with a white icing that had an almondy taste. They sat in the back room, which was lit by the sun just preparing to sink into the river, giving a glowing if evanescent patina to the four bridges that span the Rhine at Basel. From Frau Stauffinger's warm and fragrant back parlor the bridges looked like paintings.

Frau Stauffinger's first concern was Ken Ward. She shook her head sadly. "Such a nice man. So solid. So reliable." She paused and sighed. "His family must be very distressed."

Jim thought of Stephen and Lisa, and of Edith pottering in her garden in Saddle River. He thought of Cathy Quon, and the bathrobe that still hung in her closet with the initials KW embroidered on the breast pocket. "He was a loss to many," he said quietly.

Frau Stauffinger looked out of the tall narrow window to the other side of the river. But she saw nothing there. "I also lost my husband prematurely." The voice, warm and sturdy, had a quaver at its edge.

Jim set down the coffee cup he was about to lift to his lips. "I'm sorry," he said. Frau Stauffinger nodded, but her mind and heart were with the man who had died. When was that, Jim wondered. Does she want to talk about him? With me? "How did it happen?" he asked.

Frau Stauffinger lifted her shoulders and let them fall. They were broad shoulders but rounded, right for the solid softness of her face and form. "It was cancer. All our great and famous pharmaceutical firms could do nothing." Once more her gaze wandered across the river, where two of Switzerland's world-renowned pharmaceutical companies had their headquarters and maintained extensive research facilities. She turned her head to look at Jim. "There are limits to what man can do. That's what my husband used to say." She reached for the silver cake knife with its weighty handle and sank the knife into the softness of the cake. "You will have another piece, yes? That much a man can do." The smile that went with the offer was maternal.

Jim nodded and moved his plate toward her. The design on the rim was a trellis. The wildflower decorations scattered over the entire coffee service seemed to reach for the trellis and disappear in it. "What did your husband do? He sounds like a philosopher."

Frau Stauffinger was grateful. Jim had paid the late Mr. Stauffinger the greatest compliment she could fathom. "He was a philosopher in his heart," she acknowledged proudly. "By profession he was an official of the Basel stock exchange."

"That's an unusual combination," Jim said courteously.

Frau Stauffinger refilled his cup and hers. She still wore her wedding ring, a plain gold band, but on the left hand she displayed a creation of gold and diamonds that looked as if its appraised value might go to the upper reaches of five figures.

"I thought so when he was"—she hesitated a moment—"when he was with me. But he's with me still. I support myself in a manner of which he would have heartily approved."

"You support yourself?" The question escaped Jim, sounding as incredulous as he felt. Frau Stauffinger did not convey the image of a self-supporting woman. He would have guessed that she lived on her husband's pension, plus whatever property he had left her, carefully invested. Everything about Frau Stauffinger and her house made clear that there was no need here to pinch pennies. Or even solid Swiss francs.

Frau Stauffinger set down her cup. A proud and pleased smile played on her lips. "Indeed I do," she said.

"May I inquire how?"

"Certainly. It was my husband's conviction that Switzerland cannot be the policeman of the world for the conduct of financial affairs. But we can offer asylum to those who need it. He did this professionally. All our financial institutions do. As you know." She regarded Jim affectionately. "I do it personally. It gives me great satisfaction."

Jim bent over his coffee and breathed in the strong stimulating smell. That was one way of looking at it, although he was not sure how Morse Clark would feel about being regarded as a financial refugee in need of Frau Stauffinger's care and protection. "Do you have many, uh . . . ?" He fumbled for the word.

"Clients," Frau Stauffinger helped out. "But I think of them as guests whom I can render a service. Some of them have become friends. They enrich my life." She looked contemplative for a moment, then the warm smile reappeared. "As I do theirs."

Jim held out his cup for a refill. She poured. He wondered how he could broach the subject that had brought him.

"Some of your guests," he said, "must travel quite a way for the services you provide." To take the edge off his leading comment, he gestured at the starched white tablecloth, the gay china, the freshly ground and brewed coffee and the mountainous cake.

"Oh yes." Frau Stauffinger's nod was so emphatic that it caused a minor dislocation in her freshly set hair. "They come from everywhere. Every continent. Many countries. The best, the most interesting, the most charming people." She looked out of the window, her gaze fixed once more on a ghost she saw there, a vision on the horizon across the river. She nodded. "Yes, dear," she murmured. "I do business only with the best."

Was she conversing with the memory of her husband? Or was she addressing him, client-guest Jim Lindner? "Then I'm in good company," he probed.

"Indeed, yes. I cannot give you names of course, but my guests are princesses and dukes, millionaires and military men, famous artists and great entrepreneurs, beautiful women and successful gentlemen." Her voice was pitched high with excitement. She sounded like a little girl talking about the select few she had invited to her birthday party.

"But why?" Jim faltered. Why do they need you? he was going to inquire. That would not have been kind, nor was he entitled to the interrogation, all things considered. And that brought up the question he had come here to ask and had not yet managed to pose.

Frau Stauffinger, however, was not yet ready to talk business. "Men and women have needs, private needs, that cannot be fitted into rule books," she said. "If, for example, a beautiful woman gets a diamond necklace from an admirer that could make her husband jealous, her friends envious or perhaps thieves ambitious, what can she do to keep it safe?"

Jim had the impression he was being prompted. Like a schoolboy. "She can come to you," he volunteered.

Frau Stauffinger's affectionate smile became almost an embrace. "Quite right. She can. I will take for her a safety deposit box in one of our splendidly reliable banks, and all will be secure: the bracelet, the husband, the lady."

That's right, Jim commented silently. All will be as secure as in a grave, and the lady will be able to wear her necklace when her husband is safely dead.

"It is not only ladies who need me." Frau Stauffinger pursued what was clearly her favorite topic—the rich and famous, successful and glamorous, who beat a path to her door. "A man may have good reasons to keep from his family knowledge of property he owns or gains he has made. He may have the property earmarked for a special purpose that he wants no one to know, that perhaps he needs to keep inviolate, that may be dangerous for his loved ones." She raised her head. In profile it looked like a woman's head on the prow of a ship. "They're all safe with me."

Dreams of glory! There were probably as many of them as there were people on the planet. Frau Stauffinger's dream seemed to Jim to be bizarre, almost grotesque. And his own? He shifted in his seat.

Frau Stauffinger had left her position at the ship's prow and was returning to land. "Well," she said briskly. "We must now discuss our arrangements."

Meaning what? Jim had to be careful not to give Frau Stauffinger any reason to suspect he was on a fishing expedition. She would grab the net out of his hands so fast he would wind up with nothing: no key, no diary, no information.

"That," he said, "is why I have come."

She pushed aside her coffee cup and the cake plate to which a few honey brown crumbs still clung. Her voice became competent. "We must," she said, "adjust our account for inflation. It's low here in Switzerland, but as you know, I am a person of the world."

Jim nodded. "Of course." What on earth was she leading up to now? She was quick to enlighten him. "I have raised the fee for my services to all my clients this year to offset the inflationary factor."

So there was a fee for Frau Stauffinger's encompassing humanitarianism. But how could he find out what it was without giving himself away? Jim reached into his jacket and pulled out his personal checkbook and his pen. He too pushed aside his coffee and cake and put the checkbook in their place.

"You'll get no argument from me, Madame Stauffinger, on the ravages of inflation. And I know I'm in good hands. Why don't you just fill in what you consider appropriate?" He dated and signed a check and handed the entire book to her along with his pen. To his relief, she took both from him promptly, placed them on the cleared space near her and wrote. Then she turned the checkbook around so he could see what she had written. The check was made out to Clarissa Stauffinger, for the amount of $550. He tore out the check and pushed it toward her, tactfully placed wrong side up.

"I'll have to go to the bank and tell them about the new owner," she said. "Do you have the key?"

Jim's palms turned moist. "I'm afraid not. It couldn't be found among Mr. Ward's effects. No one knows where it is."

Frau Stauffinger understood. "That does happen. I can give you my key and get a new one from the bank. Mr. Zwirli has told me that all the formalities are in order."

Jim put his checkbook and pen back into his jacket. So that was how it worked. A smooth system once you knew how to push the buttons. "Yes," he said politely. "When do you think you could go to the bank?"

"Tomorrow."

Jim's heart begun to hammer once more. Why tomorrow? Was there anything else she needed to do? Anyone else she had to check?

"Wouldn't it be possible today? I was planning to leave tomorrow." Instinct prompted him to add, "I'm meeting my wife. We have a date in St. Moritz."

He did not know how the inspiration had come to him, but it was obvious that he had made the right move. Frau Stauffinger was all motherly solicitude. "How lovely! I would certainly not want to delay you. I've been invited to a dinner party tonight and can't get to the bank before that. But our evenings end early here in Basel. I could go to the bank when dinner is over. That would certainly be no later than eleven o'clock. The safety deposit department is open twenty-four hours every day. It has to be, of course." Her mind was traveling again to other people, other places, living in their own time zones. "Excuse me a moment." She walked to the far corner of the room where a heavy credenza had been converted into a desk, its lower shelves serving as a file cabinet. Neatly stacked folders crowded the cabinet. Jim calculated that there must be close to a hundred. At her rates, that added up to $55,000 a year. No wonder Madame Stauffinger served excellent coffee.

On the credenza's top lay what looked like a directory. Frau Stauffinger consulted it. "Anton Schermerhorn is on duty tonight," she remarked over her shoulder. "After my dinner I'll leave a key with him in an envelope addressed to you. I will tell him to expect you after eleven. Is that all right?"

Was it all right? That would depend on what he found in the box guarded by Herr Schermerhorn. Jim rose from his chair. The upholstery was so thick and soft it was difficult for him to get up. "That'll be perfect, Frau Stauffinger. Thank you very much."

At eleven o'clock at night the city was bone-chilling. Jim turned up the collar of his Burberry, which was too light to protect him from the icy gusts snapping at his face. When he reached the bank building, only a short walk from the hotel, it seemed to be a sanctuary from the elements. It was a massive building, squat and solid, with an air of permanence. Nothing identified it as a bank. There was no plaque, no sign over the door, not even a number. Tall letters above the main entrance said only LAGERHOF. Evidently, anyone who needed to know, did. It was like a numbered account: not secret, just discreet. He pushed the bell.

The guard who answered was a small thin man with sparse ash-colored hair. Everything about him was ashen. His uniform, his eyes, the tinge of his skin. He looked frail, as if he couldn't hurt—indeed couldn't cope with—a fly. What would he do if two determined terrorists decided to break into the bank? Or even a lone thief? There was no telltale bulge anywhere in his thread-bare jacket or below it. Did he keep a weapon in his desk? The desk was as small and unpretentious as the man, placed incongru-ously in a corner of the imposing main hall, a large space with marble floors, marble walls and a very high vaulted ceiling.

"Lagerhof," translated literally, meant camp court, headquar-ters perhaps, once upon a time, for those citizen soldiers in velvet and iron who provided Switzerland with its security in centuries past. Now its financial institutions did that, in their own way. *"Herr Schermerhorn, bitte,"* Jim said.

The guard gave him a quick sharp look, then straightened up smartly and inclined his head in the Swiss version of a German heel-clicking bow. He secured the outer door, turned and led the way.

They walked through a dark corridor until they arrived at a flight of broad stairs that led downward. The stairway had an elaborate iron railing, and the guard indicated to Jim that he should hold on to it. There was little light. Two flights down, they arrived at a heavy wooden door. The guard knocked, two short raps and a long one, then waited in silence. When the door opened, he motioned Jim forward. "Herr Schermerhorn," he mumbled and disappeared into the shadows of the darkened stairs.

Herr Schermerhorn was almost the antithesis of the guard. The same age perhaps, but Herr Schermerhorn was a round and rosy man with pink cheeks and bright blue eyes behind a pince-nez perched on a small nose. His mouth was full and pink as well, as were his hands with their carefully cut and shaped fingernails. He wore a pin-striped business suit, a white shirt with a starched collar and cuffs and a dark tie patterned in the bank's emblem: a pair of crossed keys. The keys, Jim had been told, stood for dependability and discretion. If the bank needed a person to incorporate that concept, it could have done no better than Anton Schermerhorn.

Herr Schermerhorn was expecting Jim. Frau Stauffinger had stopped in earlier to make arrangements, and Herr Schermerhorn had an envelope for Mr. Lindner. It contained the key to the safety deposit box. All Herr Schermerhorn needed from Jim now was his signature on the admittance card. Jim signed, and Herr Schermerhorn took the card to his desk and compared it with a form that lay in the center of his green felt leather-framed blotter. Jim recognized the form as one of the papers Zwirli had asked him to sign earlier in the day. A tightly run ship. All that marble was misleading. Most likely, so was the mousy watchman. The place probably had a security system that was twice as sophisticated as anything The Copter Company's sleek headquarters had to offer.

Herr Schermerhorn was satisfied. He preceded Jim along another corridor, a short one that was brightly lit. It led to a set of sturdy vertical bars with a complex lock, which Herr Schermerhorn opened by turning a large key back and forth. Behind the bars was another wooden door, covered on the inside with dark red padding. Herr Schermerhorn stood aside to let Jim pass.

The room they both entered was lined with safety boxes on four sides. Herr Schermerhorn indicated a row on the far right and pointed to the numbers. He moved toward one of the boxes. It was high up, and he had to stretch to reach the lock. He produced a key of his own which he inserted and turned twice. Then he held out his hand. What did he want? Jim wondered anxiously.

"Your key, please," Herr Schermerhorn said. "In the envelope."

"Of course." Jim reached into his pocket, pulled out the envelope Herr Schermerhorn had handed him earlier and tore it open.

It contained a small slip of paper with a number on it. A key was taped to the slip. He looked at the number. It was the same as the one over the box Herr Schermerhorn was stretching to reach. Jim detached the key from the slip and handed it over. Then he took out his wallet and carefully slipped the piece of paper with its precious number into the last folder for credit cards. It lay there alone, sticking to the plastic.

Meanwhile, Herr Schermerhorn had inserted Jim's key and turned it twice counterclockwise. The lock clicked open softly, and Herr Schermerhorn pulled out what looked like a long narrow velvet-lined drawer. From it he lifted an oblong tin box, which he passed to Jim with a ceremonious bow. "I will take you to your room," he announced.

With the tin box tucked under his arm, Jim followed Herr Schermerhorn out of the chamber. The padded door closed behind them. Jim heard the snap of the lock in the bars.

The room in which he found himself a minute later was located on the other side of Herr Schermerhorn's office. It was about twelve feet square and furnished only with a small desk and a comfortable armchair upholstered in forest-green leather. The arms had small brass decorations that looked like the heads of thumbtacks.

Jim walked to the desk and set down the tin box. It was a short walk, no more than three paces, but he could hear his footfall on the floor, and his heart seemed to echo the sound of every step he took. In the airtight basement room the sound was overwhelming. Jim was certain the entire building reverberated with his steps.

As he leaned over to open the box, his throat tightened. The metal interior revealed several thick papers, rolled up and held in place by rubber bands. Underneath them the diary was wedged tightly, touching the sides of the box. It was a medium-sized loose-leaf notebook, lined, with a hard cover of marbled black and white. Jim reached for it, but found himself suddenly reluctant to open it and read its contents. He lifted instead one of the rolled-up papers. Securities? Did Ken, after all, have a little private nest egg? And, if he did, what did he mean to do with it? Give it to Cathy? What do I do with it? The question made Jim's stomach jump. He pulled the rubber band off the scroll and opened it to find a blank piece of paper. He unrolled a second and a third. They were all blank. His stomach had stopped jumping. It was now a tight knot. What the devil? Then the idea struck him: decoys for Frau Stauffinger. Ken wanted his maternal Swiss cohort to believe the box contained securities. She would understand that. A safety deposit box with nothing in it except a notebook would have puzzled her and perhaps made her curious. Ken wanted that notebook sheltered and safe, even from Frau Stauffinger's discreet and dependable eyes.

Jim lifted out the book and opened it. The entry on the first page had a date on the upper right corner: "September 1974." Entered below, in Ken's neat, determined hand, was a heading: "Abu Dhabi." Details followed of the initial arrangements with the Emir's nephew and the sale that resulted from it; further sales; the skim off each; to whom, when and where. Exact figures, and alongside each figure the notation "Approved by RK" and a date; alongside that another notation, "Arranged by LMC," and a date.

Jim's hands shook as he turned the leaves. He steadied them on a page of the diary. The sweat of his hands smudged three lines in one of the entries. So Knight had known about every one of these transactions! Had known and approved. And Morse Clark had made the arrangements to siphon off and reroute the money that was needed. Cathy Quon had told the truth. Come to think of it, Ken, being the kind of man he was, would not have done this any other way. Ken was loyal to the company and all its credos. A corporate soldier. He might have stuck his own neck out, but he wouldn't have taken risks for The Copter Company. Not without approval from the top.

And where does that leave me? Jim wondered. For a moment he thought he smelled and tasted the coffee of Clarissa Stauffinger. It was bitter now. He could feel beads of sweat form on his temples and on the back of his neck. The room was silent, airless and close. He was about to slip off his jacket and loosen his tie when it occurred to him that he did not have to sit in this tomb of a place to get the information he wanted. He could take the notebook with him. As far as the pink, pince-nezed keeper of worldly wealth in the outer office knew, the notebook was Jim's. By right of signature, double-checked.

He rerolled the empty papers, slipped them again into their rubber bands and returned them to the box. Then he rose and walked into Herr Schermerhorn's office.

Together they moved once more through the ceremony of locked bars and padded doors. Inside the vault, Jim looked around while Herr Schermerhorn replaced the box in the drawer. It occurred to Jim that each one of these drawers probably contained a tale of wealth or woe, deceit or hope, tragedy or triumph. The room was clammy. He took a deep breath, but it did not ease the constriction in his chest.

Herr Schermerhorn had finished his task, and this time Jim reacted with alacrity. Herr Schermerhorn turned Jim's key twice counterclockwise and passed it back. They walked out of the vault in single file.

Do I say anything about taking the notebook with me? Jim wondered nervously. No. That would only make Schermerhorn suspicious. As far as he is concerned, it is my property. And in this place, property is sacred.

"Thank you, Herr Schermerhorn," he said. "Good night."

Herr Schermerhorn opened the outer door of his office to let the light shine through long enough for Jim to find his way to the stairs. When he reached the first landing, Jim thought he heard the click of the lock on the bars. But it was probably his imagination.

In Jim's room, the bedcovers were turned down and the pillows fluffed. He kicked off his shoes and peeled off his jacket and tie. He half sat, half lay on the bed and read. The pages on which transactions had been registered were numbered. There were fifty-six of them. The deals they recorded spanned the globe, and the sums involved made the payoffs he had discovered in Singapore look like small change. These figures ranged from $500,000 to $50 million. Arrangements ran the gamut of every devious trick and elaborate maneuver he had read in Cathy Quon's

215

ledgers, plus half a dozen more. In Mexico, he learned, there existed a special agency run by a trio of enterprising attorneys that did nothing but issue fake invoices, for any amount and almost any kind of service. The cost of the invoices was fixed on a moving scale: 1 percent of the deal, if it was a big one, up to 10 percent if the deal was small. The schedule was as precise as the tax table issued by the Internal Revenue Service and as soundly based on reason, plausibility and equity. Knight had approved and Morse Clark had covered each expenditure listed in the book. The last one was dated October 24, 1978. There the diary ended.

Jim had turned the pages slowly, picturing in his mind every transaction registered, every situation set down. They were all noted briefly, brusquely almost, but Jim's experience of the past few months—his battles with Max Feld and Cathy Quon, Anne's story of the Emir's nephew, his own encounters in Iran and Nigeria—conjured up images of needs and ambitions, furies and frustrations, daring and danger. When he got to page fifty-seven, unnumbered and empty, his head felt light. As he stretched out on the immaculate linen, his back surrounded by soft pillows, vertigo assailed him.

He pulled himself together and walked to the bathroom. There he let the tap run, then gulped down a glass of water, clear, fresh and ice cold. A frigid spasm shook him, the vertigo departed and he walked back into his room, changed into pajamas and got into bed. The alarm clock on his bedside table read four A.M.

He tried to go to sleep but couldn't. For what seemed like an eternity, he tossed, testing every position that might help induce slumber. He stretched out on his back, breathing deeply; lay on his stomach spread-eagled; turned on his side, his arm tucked under the pillow. Nothing worked. When he switched on the bedside lamp again, he felt hopelessly disheveled but wide awake. It was six in the morning. He reached for the phone and dialed the house in Mainz.

Brigitte's voice sounded sleepy, cuddly and sensuous.

"Was it a nice dream?" he asked. He could see her on the other end of the line, snuggled into the big bed, stretching luxuriously. Brigitte had a trick of clamping the phone to her ear, holding it up with one shoulder and murmuring into it. Endlessly, he used to think. Now he wanted badly to hear that murmur and keep hearing it.

"Yes," she said, "it was. But not as nice as this." She sounded delighted. "How are you, darling?"

"Better now." He felt a wave of warmth lap over him. It started in his chest, moved up into his head and down past his thighs and loins to his toes. It drowned completely the troughs of nausea and crests of vertigo that had kept assaulting him with such insistence when he had tried vainly to sink into sleep.

"Where are you?" There was a tremor in her voice. He recognized it with a thrill. It was the voice she used when she wanted to make love. "Are you here?"

I should be, he thought. I sure as hell would like to be. "Not quite, but close."

"How close?" The tremor had become throatier and softer.

"Up the river a piece."

"Bonn?" The excitement and magic of their first night and of their first spring together in Bonn sang over the telephone. He lay back and smiled. He pictured her breasts peeping out over the blanket, her beautiful shoulders framed in the pillow, even the right one, which she had raised to clamp the telephone to her ear. Her eyelashes would have a grain or two of sand-colored sleep at the outer edges. He wanted to lick them off with his tongue, then kiss the eyes, the nose, the mouth.

"Unfortunately not." The regret in his voice was palpable. He could hear her sigh, then catch her breath. "If it's up the river, it can't be too far." The voice had a tease in it now, a rich, ripe temptation.

"It isn't. I'm in Basel. How would you like to meet me here?"

"In Basel?" It occurred to him that she sounded very much like Heinz Herbert had when Jim told him that Brigitte was in Capri. He reassured her quickly. "I'm here on business. But if you meet me, I thought we could go on to St. Moritz together."

He could hear the sheet rustle. She must have sat up to lean against the pillow, half of her body naked and luminous in the

217

predawn dark. "Now that," she murmured, "is a civilized idea."

"How long will it take you to pack and drive down?" He knew he sounded eager. He had no quarrel with that.

She chuckled, and he could see her get set to swing into action. When Brigitte wanted to, she could move very fast. "Two hours to pack, four to drive down. I'll drive fast."

"Yes," he said, "I know you will. But you'll have to pack for me too. I have only a couple of business suits with me."

"You'll need ski and après-ski clothes and a dinner jacket."

"I guess so."

"Where are we staying?"

"I don't know yet. I haven't made any reservations. I wanted to talk to you first. I wasn't sure you'd be there."

There was a short pause. He's trying to make me feel guilty again, Brigitte thought. He knows you can't make last-minute bookings in St. Moritz in February. "We can stay with the Kertners," she said. "I'll call Christine and tell her Morocco was getting to be a bore."

"Oh no you don't! I don't want to be a house guest. I don't want to meet anyone's schedules. I want to have breakfast in bed and make love before and after. Without anyone waiting for us to catch the first funicular up the slope. Or the second. Or the third."

"Mmm," she said. She stretched the *m*, almost sang it. It sounded luscious. If I were there . . . he thought.

"But we can't sleep in the funicular," she said. "It's too cold. And they don't run it at night."

"How about Suvretta House? It's toasty warm, and they've been running it around the clock for a hundred years."

"Mmm, mmm!" This time the *m*'s were a gurgle. Suvretta House was an incontestably fashionable establishment in St. Moritz, ranking second only to the Palace Hotel, where the world's beautiful people congregated in the winter, and dressing rooms were as large as the bedrooms of hotels for more mundane mortals. But the Palace was in the center of town. Suvretta House was up on a hill, surrounded by pine trees and its own skating pond, with a view of the mountains that was breathtaking. Sitting

218

on its terrace, or looking out the windows of its numerous lounges, one felt almost as if one were in a funicular halfway up to the peak.

What made him think that he could get a booking at Suvretta House was another matter. One of the pages in Ken's diary reported on a deal with a young Saudi who kept a permanent suite at Suvretta House. Jim hoped the prince was off falcon-hunting in the desert, or was living it up in Paris. Anywhere, in fact, except in that snow-wrapped pied-à-terre he maintained in St. Moritz. Jim was determined to wangle that suite at Suvretta House, even if it meant calling Riyadh. He had, after all, six hours in which to operate. There was a lot a determined VP international could do in six hours.

9

It snowed the first two days, big star-shaped flakes that hid the sky, whirled in the air and stuck to the windows. Only the most fervent skiers tackled the mountain. Jim and Brigitte settled for long walks. Wrapped in their matching Bogner parkas—hers red, his blue—they explored the woods around Suvretta House. The only sound they could hear was the crunch of their thick-soled après-ski boots on the pine needles. They walked with the same stride, in the same rhythm, and shared the deep white silence. On the way back they saw the fresh tracks they had made in the fluffy new snow.

Most of the time they spent in their suite: in bed rediscovering each other, and over long meals alone in their private sitting room catching up with what had happened in their lives during the time they had been apart. It had been almost five months. To both, that suddenly seemed like a long and arid period.

On the third day, the snow stopped and the sun came out. Brilliant and caressing, it made the piste look like streamers of gold foil from late morning to early afternoon. They caught the earliest funicular and came down the slopes feeling as if they had wings. Afterward the glow of the fireplace in their sitting room made their skin tingle. They poured twelve-year-old brandy into snifters of thin Swedish glass, piled up pillows in front of the fireplace and made love. When the logs smelling of pine, sun and snow had turned to embers, they went to bed and slept deeply and beautifully in each other's arms.

Much of the week was gone before they were spotted. Hugo Kertner discovered them, to his delight and their disappointment. They had put in a long morning on the slopes and were lunching late in the gourmet restaurant on the mountain. The restaurant produced the kind of meal that discouraged serious skiing afterward. They were going to come down in leisurely traverses. The cozy suite negotiated from its royal absentee landlord had very quickly become a private nest.

Hugo came crashing over in his custom-made mold-poured boots. "The Lindner twins!" he exclaimed, holding out two hands, one to Brigitte and the other to Jim. "When did you arrive?"

Brigitte fudged graciously. "Jim was on a business trip. We just caught up with each other."

"Why didn't you let anyone know? You could have stayed with us. We've pots of room, as you know. Christine will be angry." He paused and frowned. "In fact, she'll be furious. The last she heard was that you weren't coming to St. Moritz this year. You'd better present yourselves for cocktails this evening to make amends. And explain." He looked at Jim briefly with a question in his eyes, then turned to Brigitte. "You know how Christine feels about her circle. Especially in the winter."

Brigitte did know. Christine Kertner thought of herself as a kind of snow queen. The Kertners were estimable social lions during the season in Bonn, but there they were outshone by couples with more solid claims: important diplomats, senior deputies, the politicians who really counted. Christine came into her own in the winter. Her house in St. Moritz was large and her parties famous. She worked at them assiduously and full time. That was one reason Hugo Kertner was alone on the mountaintop looking for a good lunch and, more important still, good company.

Toward the end of the cocktail party, having done his duties as a host to about fifty people speaking half a dozen languages, Hugo beckoned Jim into a corner. He was fondling a glass of Glühwein, the hot and spiced red wine for which he had concocted a personal recipe that was as delicious as it was potent. Both of

Hugo's large hands were wrapped around the top of the tulip-shaped glass, which he rolled gently between his palms. The scent of the steaming wine tickled Jim's nostrils. He sneezed. With a magician's sleight of hand, Hugo produced a large immaculate handkerchief. "That's a good sign," he said.

"Of what?"

"Of the health of our new venture."

Jim had tucked away Hugo's handkerchief into the pocket of his maroon velvet blazer. Brigitte had bought it for him in Rome when she was on her way to Capri. It was superbly styled and he looked marvelous in it. Three ladies at the party had already told him so, and at least a half dozen more had telegraphed messages to that effect with their eyes.

"I'll send it back," Jim said, indicating the handkerchief. "We haven't produced very much for you so far, I'm afraid."

Hugo smiled into his glass. "Not yet. But you will. The Saudi sale shouldn't take long to complete."

Jim stared at Hugo. He had agonized over the Iranian transaction ever since the revolution broke out a few weeks after he had left Teheran. The word from Rezvani had been to put everything on hold. Rezvani himself was lying low, but Sharif apparently had come out on top by joining the anti-Shah forces at a strategically opportune moment. Still, nothing definite had happened, and Rezvani's advice notwithstanding, a plant with two thousand employees couldn't be put on hold. Max and Günther had been demanding decisions from New York for a couple of months now, and Jim had been thinking hard about finding a new customer for the five hundred copters Mainz was ready to produce. That was not easy to do. Five hundred helicopters were a big order.

The answer had come to him when he had spoken with the Saudi prince in Riyadh about the suite at Suvretta House. Jim had acted on a hunch. The young prince had been cordial and decidedly interested in helicopters. But all that had happened only four days ago. How had Hugo heard about it? More important still, Jim had not yet discussed this promising turn of events with anyone, so how come Hugo knew anything at all?

Jim stuck both of his hands deep into the pockets of his blazer.

Hugo's gray eyes had been fixed on Jim's face and now followed the movement of his hands. "The answer to your question, my dear Jim," he said very quietly, "is that German economic intelligence is very good. Always has been." He paused briefly, and the usual almost professionally amiable expression on his face suddenly turned hard. "Always will be," he added.

The following night Jim and Brigitte received an invitation to a dinner dance at the Palace. Full dress. Ball gowns for the ladies, orders and decorations for the men.

"You'll have to get tails somehow," Brigitte said.

"The hell I will. If they want us, they'll have to settle for a man in a tuxedo." A frown flew over her face. He picked up her chin and kissed her on the mouth. "You'll be such a knockout," he said, "no one will notice me." The doubtful look lingered, but then she shrugged. "Americans can get away with it." There was a trace of contempt in her voice. And envy. Jim grinned. "Yes," he said. "They don't know any better. Can't really be expected to." He pronounced the "can't" the English way, with a long, flat emphasis on the *a*. They both decided to leave it at that.

He was right about Brigitte. She chose to wear black—a chiffon gown with an intricate skirt cut like a collection of veils of various lengths and shapes, and flashing a scattering of tiny diamonds as she moved about or twirled in a dance. The top of the dress was a draped halter displaying the best of Brigitte: her beautiful neck, her creamy shoulders and the luscious curves of her breast. Her décolletage was very deep, and the diamond clip at the bottom of it distracted no one, certainly none of the men.

At three o'clock in the morning, when what was left of the party descended to the swimming pool to drink, talk or flirt seriously on the lounge chairs that surrounded the water, the suggestion was made that the ladies shed their gowns and dive in. Jim watched half a dozen men undress Brigitte with their eyes.

But Brigitte was oblivious. She was deep in conversation with one of the former wives of the Shah of Iran, whose reportedly happy marriage had ended in divorce when she failed to produce

223

a successor for the Pahlevi dynasty. The divorced queen had left Iran and plunged into the hectic pursuits of the European jet set. In February she usually came to St. Moritz. Sometimes the Shah was there at the same time. Whether or not the two met in secret was one of the more titillating speculations of the winter season in St. Moritz, laced with additional drama now that the Shah had lost a throne.

For the moment the former queen was immersed in her conversation with Brigitte. She was dressed in a ball gown of blue velvet, with a rich design of beads and pearls running diagonally from one shoulder to the opposite hem of her skirt. She looked regal. She also looked hot, tired and sad around the corners of her eyes. Her manner, though, was always vivacious, and she offered the supreme flattery of concentrated attention on whomever she was with.

Jim hired a horse-drawn sleigh for the ride back to Suvretta House. Tucked in under the heavy wool blanket, Brigitte sighed. "Poor girl," she said. "It really is outrageous."

"What is? She seems to be having more fun in Europe than she ever did in Teheran. In fact, Teheran is not a very funny town right now. Never has been, Heinz Herbert tells me, and he is pretty good at finding what fun is going."

Brigitte pulled the blanket to her chin, moving a few inches away from Jim in the process. "You disapprove of Heinz Herbert?" she said. There was an undertone of frigidity in her voice.

"Disapprove? No. He has his talents. He also has what I imagine is known in the von Stolzenfels family as his Weltanschauung. It's different from mine."

He looked at her. He wanted very much for her to add, "And mine." She did not. The iron-shod hoofs of the horse thudded against the cobblestones covered with well-trodden, hard-packed snow. The driver snapped his whip.

"She did look a bit sad," he said after a while in a conciliatory tone.

Brigitte, who had followed her own furies during the silence, flared: "How would you feel if someone treated you like . . . like a cow whose milk he just didn't care for anymore? Or maybe just wanted a change of foam or flavor?"

224

Jim thought of his first evening in Basel. Changing flavor was what the fjord-eyed blonde was likely to be doing right now, and he really couldn't care less. "The analogy doesn't quite apply," he said reasonably, "but I agree. It must have been painful. From what I hear, for him as well as for her."

"The initiative was his. He decided. He disposed. It was a brutal, primitive thing to do."

Jim recalled Rezvani's prophetic description of the anarchy still threatening the fragile structure of Persian society, Rezvani's daughter and her passion for the white revolution, a passion hidden under a black chador. "It may have been an act of responsibility," he said. "Perhaps even a real personal sacrifice."

She pulled at the blanket so that it slipped off his knees. "How can you?" she shouted. The driver turned around and pointed his whip up the hill to the next turn of the road. "Minute," he said. He had assumed Brigitte was complaining about the frigid night air.

She lowered her voice, but it was still bitter. "How can you defend such meanness?" she demanded. "Such vulgarity!" She looked past him to the tall pines that were just beginning to reflect strips of light from the windows of Suvretta House. Her eyes followed the golden slivers. "I don't understand you," she said sullenly.

That's true enough, he thought. But . . .

"European dynasties did as much and worse," he said, "not so very long ago." She stared at him. Her lips parted slightly. The fingers clutching the blanket went slack.

"The next generation won't have that problem," he added consolingly, "anywhere in the world." He put his hand over hers and looked into her eyes. "We hope."

When the door of their sitting room had closed behind them, he bent to kiss the nape of her neck. She shivered. "Hold still," he said. They had not switched on the light, and by the milky luminescence of the moon he undid the tricky hooks that held up the halter of her dress. That's what all those other men wanted to do, he thought. The thought made him hard. He swung her around, bent her backwards and, with his arm under her curved

225

waist, ran his tongue over her nipples, between her breasts, down to the sinewy hollow above her bellybutton. Then he snapped her upright. "You'd better do the rest," he said. "I'll get lost in all those veils."

Her lips quivered. "Ah," she murmured secretively. "That's what it's all about."

Late the next morning—they woke when the sun was almost straight overhead—they agreed that Brigitte would pack up the house in Mainz and come to New York in the spring.

Jim had no difficulty arranging a meeting with Russel Knight on the morning of his return to New York. This time it was Jim who suggested that Morse Clark join them. He wanted to discuss a financial matter that concerned Morse Clark directly.

When Jim opened the door to Knight's office, however, Morse Clark was not there. Knight seemed pleased to see Jim. "You're looking good," he said. "How did it go?" The etched lines that ran down Knight's cheeks and across his forehead appeared benevolent in the gentle light of a shaded desk lamp. Despite the pervasive gray of the day outside, the lamp made a yellow-pink pool of Knight's office.

Jim regarded the Lincolnesque face, and for a moment he was tempted to spill everything that was in his mind and heart: Cathy Quon's ledgers, Ken's diary, the mess and misery buried in both. Then Knight reached for a cigar, and Jim checked his intention. Not here, he judged. Not now, not yet.

"Thank you," he said. "It went well. Southeast Asia's in good shape. As everyone told me, Cathy Quon really knows her business."

Knight puffed. "Ken certainly thought so." The statement was emphatic, but had no under- or overtones. Or did it? When Knight wanted to play poker, he was very good at it. It was hard to read his mind or follow his calculations. If Knight knew of the real relationship between Cathy and Ken, he clearly did not intend to discuss it. But he also did not intend to appear ignorant of anything it was his job to know.

226

Instead of volunteering information, Jim resolved to wait for the president's questions. None came.

"I may have a solution for our Iranian problem. I picked up a new Saudi connection."

Knight looked pleased. "I'm glad to hear it. There's a lot going on in that part of the world. We might as well get our piece of it."

"And I made a change in Nigeria. The guy we had is a crook and a phony. He'd never produce for us, and if he did, he'd grab half of it before we were through."

Knight tipped the ash off his cigar. "Yup," he said. "I've been concerned about that situation for a while. Who did you get instead?"

"A guy the embassy recommended."

This time Knight did not look pleased. "I've not found the judgments of our embassies to be very sound in business matters," he said. He drew deeply and exhaled a cloud of smoke, which hung for a few seconds in the pool of light covering the side and center of his desk. "Nor in political matters either," he added.

Don't let yourself get caught in a political discussion with Knight, Jim warned himself. We're probably miles apart, and there is no point in digging yourself that kind of a hole.

"I checked him out," he said. "He looks pretty good. And he'll work on the same terms as our agent in Amsterdam."

The displeasure disappeared from Knight's face. "That sounds all right," he said. "It's certainly a change. How d'you swing it?"

"He offered."

"Did he? Unusual for Lagos, isn't it?"

"I guess so."

"What's he after?"

Jim conjured up in his mind a picture of Michael Smith Oni and the sculpture of the lovely Ife girl in the corner of his office. Was he being naive? Was Knight a cynical bastard? Or was it the voice of experience emerging from the man on the other side of the lamp? There were, after all, fifty-six pages of experience registered in Ken's diary, with Knight privy to each one.

227

"I don't know," Jim responded. "I guess we'll find out."

"Yup," said Knight. "We will."

The knock on the door was brief and sharp. The door opened a split second after Knight had growled, "Come in." Morse Clark sauntered through the room with the exasperating combination of primness and ease that characterized all his movements. The combination probably made customers as well as bankers feel that they were in the presence of an expert and a gentleman, and that was precisely what Morse Clark wanted them to feel. Nevertheless, it made Jim uncomfortable. The man never gives, he thought.

As always, Morse Clark was superbly attired. He wore a light brown suit of very fine worsted, a cream-colored silk shirt with French cuffs and a buff tie with a pale green spattering of tiny horses.

"Sit down," Knight said. "You've come just in time, I think." He looked at Jim.

"Yes." Jim turned in the direction of Morse Clark and nodded. "Morning, Larry."

Morse Clark sat down without replying. He moved back his chair so he was facing Knight but could look at Jim if he chose to do so without changing his position.

"I saw Zwirli," Jim said.

Knight and Morse Clark regarded Jim. Neither one spoke.

"He suggested we move the account for all our European operations to Basel."

"A waste of time," said Knight.

Morse Clark cleared his throat, carefully placing three fingers in front of his mouth. Knight turned to look at Morse Clark, then again addressed Jim. "Did he give a reason?"

Jim felt cornered. I don't have to sit still for this cat and mouse game, he thought. These men know what Zwirli is doing for us. He's been covering their asses for years. They're just giving me the business. "Zwirli wants our account," he said, "in his bank, under his personal management."

Knight shifted his eyes to Morse Clark, who responded with a curt inclination of his head. It revealed that Morse Clark had

228

an incongruous cowlick near the crown of his skull, which made one strand of his very straight hair stand up in a rebellious curl.

Knight's eyes narrowed behind his glasses. "Are there any operational reasons that would justify such a move?" he demanded.

I'm not going to get caught in that squeeze play, Jim resolved. "There are operational reasons that make it plausible."

"Let me have a memo on it," Knight requested. "If it makes sense, you can proceed."

I can proceed? Jim demurred angrily. You know damn well we're doing this for very good, if somewhat soiled, corporate reasons. And you're okaying it because Morse Clark thinks you should.

So far Morse Clark had not uttered a word.

"Right," said Jim. "I'll let you have the memo before the end of the week."

"What's the matter with the end of the day?"

Jim got up. "Nothing." As he walked out, he had to control himself not to slam the door. Morse Clark remained seated and silent.

Not, however, after Jim had left. "Lindner will take handling," he said when the door had closed.

Knight picked up his cigar. "You can leave that to me."

"Certainly."

"I'll send you a copy of Jim's memo. I'll want your recommendations. In writing."

Morse Clark ran his right hand lightly over the top of his head, found the cowlick, tried to smooth it down and gave up. "My recommendation," he said, "will be that if the operational arguments check out there is no financial reason why the move should not be made."

Knight's eyes bored into Morse Clark's face. Morse Clark did not blink or move.

"That's what I thought you'd say," Knight said.

By mid-morning on Friday Jim had disposed of most of the paperwork that had accumulated in his absence. He picked up

229

the phone and dialed Anne Gregory's extension. "This is Jim Lindner," he said. "I just realized I'm back. How about lunch?"

He could hear her catch her breath at the other end of the line. There was a brief pause. "Sure," she said. "When?"

"Today. Soon. I've dug myself out from under a mountain of paper and I'm as hungry as a miner."

She laughed. He had forgotten how deep and free her laugh was. He suddenly felt awfully good.

"Name it," she said.

"Noon. I'll meet you in the reception area. Bring an appetite. And no folders. I don't think I want to see another piece of paper for as long as I can presently imagine."

"Or at least until after lunch."

"That's right, Anne," he said. "You're as smart as you were when I left."

They walked to Delmonico's. The day was raw and somber, but she was well wrapped in a camel's hair coat with a nutria lining. He liked walking in New York, even on a day like this when particles of grime mixed with particles of frozen moisture in the air.

He had settled on Delmonico's because he was ravenous and had his teeth set for a steak. He also wanted to give her a treat.

He had not been to the restaurant since the evening he had spent there with Knight. It looked different in the light of day. The velvet, rich and red under lamplight in the evening, looked sleazy now. The wood that had emitted such a comforting glow in the semi-dark showed chips and cracks in the daylight. The brass was tarnished in spots and streaked with caked polish. No one fawned or fussed over them.

When they were seated at a small table near the center of the room, Anne looked around. "Like?" Jim inquired. "But you've been here before, haven't you?"

She flicked back the hair that had fallen forward to frame her chin. It had looked lovely, the soft brown with its auburn glint clinging to the cheek, then curling under softly. "The answer," she said, "is yes, and no. Yes, I've been here before, and no, I don't particularly like it." The green eyes swept the room.

A number of men looked up. "My father," she added, "would say, 'It looks like a gussied-up saloon.' "

It occurred to him that he had never thought of Anne as having a family. For some reason, he could not imagine what her parents would be like. "Where is your father?" he asked.

"Rhode Island. Providence."

"What's there?"

"His law office."

It made sense. She was a lawyer's daughter. That could account for her disciplined, analytical mind. "Lawyers don't see all that much of saloons, do they?" he pursued. "Not the kind of lawyers I know. They might be more pleasant to deal with if they did."

"You meet the wrong kind. My dad is also in politics. And he used to be a cop."

That was a surprise. He had thought her to be Irish, but with at least a couple of generations of finishing school on the female side. That's what she looked like.

"But," she said, "they do produce a good steak here."

When he had polished off his main course—she had chosen broiled bay scallops—he filled her in on his trip. She listened attentively, asked some perceptive political questions and was intrigued by his encounters with Udoyen and Smith Oni. Every aspect of the trip for which Knight had had neither the time nor the patience enthralled her. He found himself telling her about the way houses looked, streets smelled, people smiled or shouted. With those green eyes watching him, absorbed, he felt as if he were unpacking all the mental luggage he had stashed away during his journey. He had not known how much of it there was until he began to display it in response to the prodding of her questions, the stimulus of her interest. It occurred to him that with Brigitte he had talked only about the surface of everything, culling not what had intrigued, baffled, stirred or moved him but what Brigitte would find entertaining and repeatable. She had been entertained and he had felt scintillating. Now he felt as if he were digging down and reaching up.

"To be continued," he finally said. "How about—"

231

She interrupted him quickly. "Wow," she said, picking up and squinting at the old-fashioned watch she was again wearing on the gold chain around her neck. "I had no idea it was so late."

He grinned at her. "That's all right," he said. "This is work. A debriefing of the VP international by the head of strategic planning."

"True. But there are other high-fliers back in the office with claims on the planning department. The Copter Company is a high-flying organization."

She sounded flip, but there was a brittleness in her voice that he did not recognize, that seemed wrong on the Anne he knew. Or thought he knew. It came to him that he did not after all know her very well.

She had risen. Her face suddenly looked harassed and underneath the harassment disappointed.

He did not complete the sentence he had begun, in which he was going to ask her to spend an evening with him so they could talk at leisure, as they had before he left. He really had no right to her private time. Not with Brigitte coming in the spring.

The invitation arrived two weeks later. It was delivered to Jim's apartment in the east seventies, a modern two-bedroom establishment in a luxury high-rise that The Copter Company maintained for senior executives in transit, either from one location to another or, as in Jim's case, from one assignment to another. The engraved card requested the pleasure of Jim's company for dinner at the home of Mr. and Mrs. Russel Carlysle Knight, 810 Park Avenue, New York City, on Friday evening, February 24, at seven-thirty P.M. The dress instructions in the lower left corner said, "Formal."

Knight ambled into Jim's office late the next day. It was an unusual occurrence. When the president of the company wanted to speak with anyone at headquarters, the person was usually summoned to his office. Equally unusual was the fact that Knight seemed embarrassed, almost shy. "About the party," he said, "it's for some folk from Pittsburgh we've known a long time. Elaine

232

is serving them up Manhattan on the half shell. So it's bib and tucker. Hope you don't mind."

Jim had risen from his chair when Knight appeared in the door. "Of course not. I'm used to it from Europe. Thanks for asking me."

Knight regarded Jim obliquely. He looked as if he were about to voice a thought, then changed his mind. "Okay," he said. "See you Friday then. Good night."

When Jim arrived, looking effortlessly elegant in his dinner jacket, most of the evening's guests were already assembled in the Knights' library. The room was furnished in Biedermeier style, honey-colored wood and petit-point upholstery in old rose, leaf green and pale blue. Bookshelves covered two walls all the way up to the ceiling, displaying sets of uniform leather bindings. The color of the bindings matched the greens of the upholstery and the light brown of the wood. The handsome volumes were carefully dusted but looked as if they were, in every other way, untouched by human hand.

The Gerbers, the Pittsburgh couple for whom the party had been arranged, were telling a circle of polite but inattentive listeners about the world tour of archeological sites from which they had recently returned. The trip had been designed and guided by a museum in Pittsburgh to which Jack Gerber contributed time, thought and considerable funds as a member of the board. The Gerbers had therefore been star members of the tour, a role both of them enjoyed. Jack Gerber had had an additional reason for taking the trip. "Wanted to see how they handle real estate over there. There's a trick to every trade, and you can always learn something new." Jack Gerber had made his money—there was a lot of it—in real estate.

The Gerbers had brought their daughter, a big broad-shouldered girl with a full figure who regarded her parents with a slightly bemused maternal affection. When the party went in to dinner, Jim discovered why he had been asked. He was seated next to the Gerber girl, and it was clear that he was meant to squire her through the evening. That turned out to be less of a chore than appearance had led him to believe. Margaret Gerber had started out as a schoolteacher in Pittsburgh but had decided to move on. She had settled in Manhattan five years ago and since then had become a literary agent specializing at first in books that were intended for school libraries. She was competent, friendly and knowledgeable. She had moved up quickly in her agency and had broadened her interests, her expertise and her circle of authors and editors. She knew a great many people in the arts and in the Manhattan social scene that revolved around the arts. She was the only one at the long and narrow dinner table, set for fourteen, who did not drop names that evening.

The party was exactly what Knight had told Jim it would be: Manhattan on the half shell. There was an earnest young diplomat from the Pakistani Mission to the United Nations, who had been seated next to a thin and lively girl from *Vogue*. He was telling her about the beautiful brocades that were still woven by hand in the villages of Pakistan and how well these fabrics would lend themselves to high fashion. Since the girl's job at *Vogue* was to cover the Seventh Avenue market, her initial flicker of interest expired long before the young diplomat had completed his discourse. The stilted way he spoke English and his obviously rehearsed promotion of Pakistani products made the *Vogue* girl's eyes glaze over. The young diplomat sounded as if he had written out this spiel and learned it by heart. She was used to men and women who lived and breathed their trade.

The couple sitting opposite the diplomat and the girl from *Vogue* got along much better. Elaine Knight had agonized over that combination. The man was a well-bred young banker from Salomon Brothers who, undoubtedly at the direction of his bank, served as volunteer treasurer for the social productions Elaine masterminded for one of Gotham's more fashionable charities. This season's ball for the charity had made the social pages of *The New York Times*, both before and after the event, and had rated a whole column in *Town and Country*. Thanks to the young man from Salomon Brothers, the money made for the charity was respectable if not fabulous, and there had been enough glamour and publicity to please everyone involved. Elaine believed in paying her debts. The reward she had come up with for the young banker was a ballet dancer on the cusp of moving into the first rank, not yet a prima ballerina but slated to become one. Top-seeded, as they said in tennis. Tagged by Balanchine. Anyone who knew ballet knew what that meant. The young man from Salomon Brothers knew ballet.

Another Elaine-designed pairing also worked out surprisingly well. Elaine had snagged for the evening—and considered it a minor triumph—a titled young man from London who worked for Sothebys. In addition to his title, he was genuinely knowledgeable about European antiques, including paintings. Elaine's stroke of genius had been to match him up with a woman who was not only handsome and chic but a Wall Street broker of considerable repute. The two were immersed in animated conversation about the value of paintings as an investment and antiques as a hedge against inflation.

The last of the couples—they did, in fact, look like the afterthought they had been to complete the requisite fourteen who, in Elaine's book of etiquette, constituted an appropriate dinner party—were a redheaded actress who did industrial shows and a middle-aged attorney from the prestigious downtown law firm that handled most of The Copter Company's business. Dinner at the Knights' was obviously a command performance for the attorney. For the redhead, it was a combination of client service and job search. She had been featured in a couple of industrial shows staged by The Copter Company, and the attorney was a likely conduit for recommendations to other corporate clients. A flashy girl with a statuesque figure and very long legs, she was clearly willing to appreciate any such recommendations. It was equally clear how that appreciation would be expressed. The attorney, sophisticated about Manhattan ways, was not uninterested in the bottom line of the redhead's proposition; he just didn't want to work on the negotiations. He knew what the terms and conditions were. It was a bore to have to go through the motions.

The fiasco of Elaine's party was the food. For reasons of her own, Elaine wanted to impress the Gerbers with culinary snobbery. Since the Gerbers and the Knights had started out together in Pittsburgh in a neighborhood of semi-attached small houses where everyone did their own cooking, cleaning and what little gardening was possible in hundred-square-foot backyards, Elaine did not want to have the meal catered. It had to come out of her own kitchen. The result was a palatable boola-boola, with a touch too much pea and too little turtle in the soup's composition. It was the second course—pheasant under glass—that proved to be the disaster. It arrived looking decorative on a bed of lettuce, with sprigs of parsley and whole stewed crab apples, under steaming glass domes. But it was dry, badly overcooked, and no one finished it. The endive salad that accompanied it was fair, but left the guests still hungry. Everyone dove into dessert. Elaine announced that it was a bombe glacé and that the recipe had come from a famous French chef whom she had flown over from Nice to supervise a lunch she had arranged for the board members of her charity at the beginning of the season. It turned out to be good rich American ice cream with a few pieces of candied fruit and a small dose of Grand Marnier, molded to look like a cake. With it came a choice of rolled mocha gaufrettes or star-shaped butter cookies which Elaine had baked herself. The recipe for those came out of a Fannie Farmer cookbook she had been given as a wedding present and had treasured and used for forty years. The cookies vanished in no time.

It was close to eleven when Elaine declared the dinner over and Knight, trying to hide his relief, led the party into the large living room with its splendid view of the avenue. Only Elaine and Connie Gerber had liqueurs. The rest of the guests settled down to serious drinking, following the host, who set a splendid pace.

The redhead and the attorney were the first to leave. Their evening was not yet over. Their departure made it possible for the others, after a carefully timed interval, to follow. The Gerbers stayed, and when all the half-shell people had gone, the talk turned to the old days in Pittsburgh. Jim had tried to take his leave with the other guests, but Knight had prevented him from doing so. "I want to talk to you about something," he had said.

By the time they were all gone, Jim was groggy and Knight

236

was not altogether steady on his feet. Knight could hold his liquor. He had learned to do so at engineering school with beer and cheap wine. He had improved his capacity during his stint with the Army Corps of Engineers in World War II, when PX bourbon took the place of beer—if a PX was within jeepable distance— and rotgut the place of college wine—if no PX could be tapped. Later, at The Copter Company, he had improved the quality of his alcoholic input, as he now referred to booze in the presence of Elaine. There had been a lot of input this evening.

The room to which Knight guided Jim was at the far end of the apartment. The door leading to it had the same interior decorator gloss that had been imposed throughout the residence. Everything behind the door, however, was pure Knight. There were two large club chairs, very well worn, and an old desk cluttered with papers and smudged with cigar ash. Near one of the club chairs a small side table was piled high with books: new novels in shiny covers, tattered paperbacks, a volume of Gibbon. An old-fashioned stand-up lamp was placed so it shed a comfortable light exactly where a reader sitting in the chair would want it. Placed with equal precision for the same reader's comfort was a leather hassock that had seen a great many, if not necessarily better, days. An old chest of drawers in the corner turned out to be a bar. Knight headed straight for it.

"One for the road," he said. "What was it you were drinking?"

"Scotch, please. Soda."

"I don't keep dilutions in here. Will you take it straight?"

"I will if I can sit down."

"You can sit down. You can take off your shoes. You can take off that idiot thing they choke us with. I will." He pulled at his black bow tie and let it dangle, then opened the top button of his shirt, which had been starched too heavily. "Whew," he said. "That's better." He poured himself three fingers' worth of Remy Martin.

"How d'you like the Gerber girl?" he asked when they had settled down with their drinks. Knight had put his stockinged feet up on the hassock. With the question hanging in the air, he proceeded to light a cigar. He snipped off the end with a

237

small silver gadget, poked at the cigar with a big silver toothpick and finally lit it with a bullet-shaped lighter that looked as if it belonged in his hand.

While he was going through these ceremonial motions, Jim considered the question. Surely that was not what Knight wanted to talk about. Margaret Gerber was not a fascinating topic at any time, and certainly not an appropriate one for a conversation at one o'clock in the morning between the president of The Copter Company and his VP international. So what was Knight leading up to?

"I liked her fine, and I thought she had her head screwed on right. Which is a lot these days."

"You can say that again!" The response was instantaneous and heartfelt, a rare combination from Knight.

Is he trying to matchmake? Jim wondered. He couldn't be. He knows I'm married. In fact, he knows Brigitte and knows she'll be here next month. So what . . .

"We haven't been so lucky." For the first time since he knew Knight, Jim heard the edge of his voice disintegrate. The edge was replaced not by gentleness but by a blur that might be due to the sizable quantity of liquor Knight had consumed in the course of the evening. There was a limit even to his capacity.

"Our Carol," Knight said, and the blur in his voice spread inward and thickened, "is shacked up with some guy close to twice her age who lives in a cold-water flat down below Houston Street and has introduced her to dope."

"Serious stuff?" Jim was shocked and concerned.

Knight stared into his cognac. "I wouldn't know. But there is a lot of it. All the time. She doesn't make much sense when I talk to her."

"D'you see her often?"

"No. Once in a long while. Elaine doesn't know about it. She's written Carol out of our lives. We meet downtown in one of those SoHo places. Carol lets me buy her a meal. She needs it."

Under the light of the lamp, Jim could see that Knight's eyes had picked up some of the blur that had corroded his voice.

"Nothing wrong with needing a meal," Knight said. "I remember times in Pittsburgh when I needed one. But I was a lot younger, and the reasons weren't the same. That makes a difference." He stared into his glass. "I was just poor. She's . . ."

Jim could not tell whether Knight did not know what was wrong with his daughter or whether he knew and could not bring himself to say it. "Can you pry her loose?" Jim asked. "Bring her here for a while and put her back on her feet?"

Knight looked up from his glass. One of his legs on the hassock jerked. "She wouldn't come here. *She* thinks this is a den of iniquity."

"This room?"

"No. This place. Everything and everybody in it. You see, she thinks *we're* on dope. Elaine and I. Moral dope." Knight shook his head. He looked bewildered.

Jim's mind darted to Ken's diary. What would Carol Knight think if she saw that? If she was on angel dust now, the diary would send her to heroin. In fact, what would Knight think if he knew about Ken's diary? The notion electrified Jim and made him sit up.

Knight interpreted Jim's move in his own way. "Look," he said, "I didn't mean to saddle you with my problems." His voice had coalesced again. "I'll take care of them, one way or another. What I wanted to tell you"—Knight's eyes were suddenly as bright and sharp as his voice—"is that I like the way you handle yourself. You do your job. You don't ask fool questions. You pick up a ball and run with it. Therefore . . ." He let his voice drop, deliberately this time, while he leaned back in his chair and regarded Jim. "Therefore"—the voice picked up volume and bounced around the room—"I'm submitting your name to the board as an inside director. The next meeting is in April. We'll go through the motions then, but I'll have briefed everybody. I've already discussed it with the chairman. You know Claude Asherton, don't you?"

"Not really. I've heard a lot about him, but we met only once, when he came to Germany while Ken was breaking me in. I was only an understudy. He wouldn't remember me."

"Oh yes he would. He has a sharp eye for comers. Anyhow, I've taken care of it. You'll be item nine on the agenda. They'll all have your background and record. I expect no problems." He crossed his stockinged feet on the hassock. They were long feet, with prominent ankles, the bones jutting out. Knight looked at Jim, then past Jim into a dark corner of the room. "This is one company," he said, "where the CEO still calls the shots."

The biting air of early March cleared Jim's head. There was a subtle but important difference between Knight's neighborhood of old and rambling Park Avenue houses and his own blocks of sleek but tight high-rises that looked as striving and eager as were most of their tenants. Nevertheless, the two neighborhoods were only about ten blocks apart. Jim decided to walk.

So he had made it! That had been the gist of Knight's message. They would negotiate an increase in Jim's remuneration, as it was called at his level, which would include not only a substantial raise in salary but a whole new package of fringe benefits. There would be stock options, tying Jim to the company with a financial umbilical cord to reinforce the existing one of ambition. The directorship meant that he was in the running for the top spot. Unless he stumbled somewhere along the way, or failed to take the hurdles. There would be plenty of those.

He could think of one right now. Ken's diary. Should he tell Knight that it existed and that he was in possession of it? Should he put it away and bide his time until an opportunity came to make use of it? Should he destroy it and betray not only Cathy Quon but Ken himself and all the good and solid things that Ken had stood for, even if he had not finally known when to say no? Was he capable of saying no himself? Apparently not, and did that mean that Knight's daughter was right and they were all on moral dope? Was her freaking out on mind-and-body-destroying drugs in a cold-water flat on the Lower East Side a better, purer way to live? That made no sense. At least the Kens and Jims of this world were producing. The Carol Knights were just destroying—themselves and everybody else who blundered into their world.

240

A chill gripped him, cramping his fingers and making his eyes sting. He felt a stab of pain in his chest. He looked up and realized that he had been standing still on the deserted avenue. He began to walk at a steady but accelerated pace for an additional couple of blocks, then turned east to the apartment he currently called home.

Brigitte arrived in early April. New York was slushy and damp, but Brigitte was radiant. She had stayed in St. Moritz for another couple of weeks as a houseguest of the Kertners and had thoroughly enjoyed herself. The weather had remained glorious, and a collection of her friends and acquaintances had arrived late in the season from all over Europe. Even Heinz Herbert had managed to detach himself from turbulent Teheran for a spot of home leave and had turned up for the better part of a week. They had skied together from sun-up to sundown. It was their favorite form of communication.

In Manhattan, where most people had the sallow pallor and brittle weariness of a long hard winter, Brigitte's rose-colored tan and her rested vivaciousness stood out like a delightful harbinger of spring. People turned around to look at her in the street. A few of the stares expressed envy; most registered appreciation.

The first task Brigitte set herself was to overhaul the apartment in the seventies, which the company had told them they could occupy for the rest of the year. It needed to be civilized, she said. Jim conceded immediately and with pleasure that she had a point. Living in the place alone, he had not noticed how sterile it was. The perfect corporate environment: functional, fashionable, neutral, adaptable. Brigitte adapted it. Within a month it had paintings and pillows; soft silks where there had been tweeds; scatter rugs on top of the wall-to-wall carpeting; daffodil yellow pots and pans in the kitchen replacing the anodized aluminum; and a copper kettle that sang instead of demanding attention with an ear-splitting whistle. And flowers everywhere.

Brigitte also overhauled Jim's life. The twelve-hour days at the office that had become routine slowly dwindled to ten, nine and eight. There were cocktail parties to go to now, and while

Brigitte never insisted that Jim appear anywhere at a specific time, her pleasure at his arrival was so tempting that he happily made the effort to participate in the social occasions that seemed to agglutinate around Brigitte wherever she found herself.

The quiet evenings he had spent before her arrival—reading, listening to music, halfheartedly watching television or, most often, thinking about the office—were replaced now by dinner parties; by evenings at the theater, the opera and the ballet; by previews in the major museums and important art galleries; and occasionally by big balls or intimate nightclubs. Brigitte discovered and tasted the joys of Manhattan with a vengeance. At her side, Jim too indulged in a New York that he had never had the time, money or dedication to explore before. As in those first heady months in Mainz and Bonn, he ran short of sleep and loved it.

When Brigitte told him about the telephone call from Patricia Morse Clark, her nose wrinkled. "Dinner in Bronxville," she said. "What is Bronxville? It sounds awful."

"It is, and it isn't. Actually I think you'll quite like it. At least to look at. It has a lot of nice houses in well-kept grounds, all attractive, some beautiful."

They were having coffee in the living room. They had been to a long and lively cocktail party and had consumed too many hot oysters on beds of spinach and cheese, slices of pink prosciutto wrapped around honeydew melon, mushrooms stuffed with crabmeat, and bite-sized quiche with crumbled bacon on top. They had washed it all down with Bloody Marys, on the theory that tomato juice was better for you than an all-alcohol cocktail, and had subsequently switched to wine. By the time the party dwindled down, they had sworn that they would never eat or drink again. Their dinner would consist of black coffee.

Now Brigitte was stretched out on a chaise longue she had acquired, which was upholstered in blue silk. She had kicked off her shoes. Her form-fitting jade green silk sheath had ridden up to mid-thigh. Her long beautiful legs, in their very sheer pale stockings, looked like marzipan creations against the soft blue that surrounded them. Jim, sprawled out on the wide leather sofa with some of the Brigitte-procured pillows tucked under his head, was delighted with what he saw and the prospect of what would follow.

"But the people," Brigitte said. "Patricia Morse Clark sounded pretty discouraging. To begin with, I have trouble understanding what she says. She seems to be speaking through clenched teeth, so she has to push out the sound through her nose. It sounds terrible, and it's very hard to follow."

Jim grinned. Patricia Morse Clark had been educated, if that was the word, at Finch College and had never shed the voice, manner or habits of thought that this eminently proper and equally pretentious finishing school implanted in its graduates. She had no reason to dispose of these legacies. They were precisely what was required of her by her husband, her social milieu and, apparently, her children. Jim had heard of no rumblings of revolt from the Morse Clark household. Carter, the son, was at Yale studying government. Jennifer had made it through Vassar with respectable grades and considerable social aplomb. She was now secretary of the Bronxville chapter of the Junior League and had managed to turn that volunteer assignment into a full-time occupation, with the unmitigated approval of both her parents.

"The people're all right too, if you like that kind of thing."

"What kind of thing?" Brigitte looked doubtful.

Jim set down his coffee and returned to his sprawl on the sofa. "You're making me think, darling," he said, "which is not a nice thing to do at this hour of the evening; but I'll try."

She put her cup on the floor and blew him a kiss. "All favors are hereby acknowledged and gratefully received."

He closed his eyes. "I would think better, I suspect, if you were over here." He moved against the back of the sofa and patted the empty space he had created on his left.

He heard her get up and opened his eyes to watch her wriggle out of her dress. Beneath the dress, her breasts flowed out of a minimal construction of white lace. The lace was matched in the deep hem of her taffeta half slip. Between the two garments gleamed a hand's span of unobstructed, creamy, silky Brigitte. When she came to lie next to him, he wrapped his arm around that tempting midriff.

"What kind of thing?" he repeated meditatively. "Well, they

243

have the best of all possible worlds. They have money but not in excess. Not nasty kind of money—just the right amount and the right kind. They have position—social, professional or both. The combination gives them status, the kind they approve of, not brilliant or ephemeral but solid and enduring. Prestigious, not glamorous. They flirt with glamour but they don't think it becoming. Their contributions to society are sounder and more subtle. They once were the cement that held it all together. Nowadays they are the high-grade oil that makes it move. Without them the gears would grind against each other, and after a while the entire mechanism wouldn't work. That's what they believe."

She had piled three pillows under her head and was lying parallel to him with her face a little higher than his. She could watch him as he spoke.

"Are they right?"

Jim's mind leaped to a vision of his father in his machine shop, his mother making the daily rounds of her house, her garden, her kitchen and her farm. Unexpectedly, another image appeared: Anne Gregory's father, whom he had never met. The man who had been a policeman and was now a lawyer and politician in Rhode Island. The man who had raised a daughter who handled strategic planning for The Copter Company. "I'm not sure," he said. "Maybe they were, once. I don't think they are anymore. This is really a miraculous country. It transforms people. At least, it gives them the opportunity to transform themselves."

He opened his eyes and caught a bemused look on Brigitte's face. "You sound like the Voice of America," she said. He tightened his arm around her waist and let his fingers slide up and down the strip of bare skin. Then he leaned over so his lips could follow suit. "I warned you," he said, before he covered her with his body, "that it was wrong of you to make me think."

The evening at the home of Lawrence and Patricia Morse Clark was unexpectedly pleasant. The house was filled with books and bric-a-brac from all over the world, well chosen and assembled over generations. There was a great deal of chinoiserie that had been hauled home by the seafaring skipper who had been Larry

Morse Clark's great-grandfather. Larry had a store of anecdotes about this adventurous ancestor who, it seemed, had lived a life of great propriety at home but had managed to spice that life with less respectable savor in other ports. Patricia listened to her husband's tales with a polite tautness on her finely chiseled face. She was a Boston Brahmin. Her antecedents had been governors of Harvard College, while her husband's had, well, plowed the seas.

What astonished Jim was that Larry Morse Clark told these stories, self-deprecating by implication, with wit and grace. He was altogether an excellent host—attentive, amusing and worldly.

Dinner was served at two round tables seating six each. Patricia had produced an abstruse explanation for seating what she called "the visiting couples" together instead of splitting them up. Perhaps she wasn't certain they were really married. As a result, Larry presided over a table that included an Argentine industrialist with a very attractive wife, whose brother was a member of the ruling junta; a banker from Italy with a fascinating face, whose lady looked like a sister of Sophia Loren; and the considerably less dazzling but interesting spouse of the president of a nearby college, who turned out to be an expert on Peruvian textiles. At Larry's table the conversation was conducted in a mixture of English and Italian, in which Larry Morse Clark turned out to be, if not fluent, certainly adept—adept enough to stage-manage a heated conversation about Euro-Communism: what it was and was not, what it could be expected to become, how it would change the face and fortunes of Europe. The Italians were sanguine; the Argentines vehement. Larry and the lady with the exotic knowledge of embroidered mantles from Paracas attempted to mediate.

At Patricia's table, conversation revolved around Woody Allen and Ingmar Bergman. Who had a more profound sense of humor, a more telling vision of life? Brigitte argued for Bergman, the college president for Woody. Patricia and Jim kept out of the debate. Jennifer Morse Clark, attempting to please her young man, came down on the side of the European. She was devoted to Bergman, she asserted, had been ever since she really immersed herself in him at Vassar. The young man reciprocated. He found Woody Allen superbly sympathique. The young man was French, worked for Crédit Lyonnais and had arrived in America only a few weeks earlier for a three-year assignment with the bank's branch in New York. He had met Jennifer at a Junior League benefit arranged to raise money for an organization that supported cross-cultural education. In Jennifer's circle, cross-cultural was defined as French and American. To Patricia's wary delight, the two young people had taken to each other and were setting an example of what cross-cultural education was all about. The young man's name was Alain de Turenne.

When Brigitte caught the name, she interrupted her spirited defense of Ingmar Bergman. "I know Hector de Turenne," she said. "Are you . . . ?"

The young man's concentrated politesse gave way to pleasure. "Mais sure," he said. "Hector is the son of my father's older brother. We are, uh . . ."

"First cousins," Patricia finished the sentence for him. She sounded vaguely tutorial and very relieved. She turned to Brigitte: "Have you known the Turennes for some time?"

Brigitte was irritated. The name was de Turenne. It was an old family, with excellent credentials for its title. There was no reason why its nobility should be buried in the democratic swamp of Bronxville. Bronxville, for god's sake! Even the name of the place was atrocious.

"Quite," she said. "The families of de Turenne and von Stolzenfels have been friendly enemies for about five hundred years."

Alain de Turenne looked enchanted and immensely grateful. He reached across the table to pick up Brigitte's hand, bent over it and made the motion of a kiss without touching her. *"Merci, madame,"* he said. "I could not have explained it nearly so well myself. It is not easy to convey . . ." He hesitated and came to the conclusion that it might not be politic to continue. "When did you last see Hector?" he asked.

Brigitte looked at Alain de Turenne, a half smile hovering about her lips. "In February," she said. "In St. Moritz."

On the way back to the city Jim commented, "That de Turenne bit was neatly done, darling. But who the hell is Hector de Turenne? I don't remember ever meeting him. Should I?"

She looked at him sidelong. To Brigitte's chagrin, Jim had so far resisted acquiring a car. It made no sense in Manhattan, he had pointed out, and while he had access to company cars when necessary, he was careful with the use he made of this perquisite. He had his eye on more substantial rewards. The subject of stock options had been broached. As a result of this calculated reticence, Jim and Brigitte were driving back to Manhattan in a rented automobile. It was a Lincoln Continental, but it annoyed Brigitte to know that the license plates made it clear to anyone who cared that this was a car for hire.

"No," she said slowly. "You haven't met Hector. But I really have known him a long time. Hector de Turenne, Armando Guido-Contini, Renate Kertner and I used to see a great deal of each other."

"I don't remember meeting Renate Kertner either. Is she related to Hugo? He, incidentally, dropped some interesting hints in St. Moritz and had an extraordinary amount of information about a negotiation I had only just begun with Saudi Arabia. Do you have any idea how he came by it?"

Jim did not take his eyes off the road, but he could feel Brigitte stiffen in the seat beside him. "No," she said sharply, "I don't."

He wondered what she did know about the Kertners. Keeping his tone conversational, he prompted: "Regale me with the tale of the fascinating foursome. I need to keep awake until I return this Avis treasure to its rightful owners."

He could sense Brigitte making an effort to control herself and to end the evening harmoniously. When she spoke again, her voice had the gay gossipy tone she used when she reported on the international society she observed but of which she was also a part. She weaves in and out of it, Jim thought. I never know where she belongs. I suspect she doesn't either.

"Renate is Hugo's sister—half sister, really, from a first marriage. Like Heinz Herbert and me. They're very fond of each other."

"And?"

"Renate, Hector, Armando and I saw a lot of each other in the sixties."

"Saw?"

"You'll find this hard to believe, but we were all Maoists for about two years. Or thought we were. We actually built barricades together."

Jim's hand slipped on the massive steering wheel. The Lincoln Continental described a wide curve on the highway. He got it back under control. He had known Brigitte for five years. She had never mentioned that part of her past before. What else was there in her life that he knew nothing about?

"I really do find it hard to believe. You? Armando Guido-Contini? I wouldn't have thought he ever looked much farther than his own navel. And maybe other people's."

She reached for the shoulder strap of the safety belt and held on to it. "You don't really know us very well," she said. "And you'll never understand us." She was silent for a moment, recalling the time. "We were in Paris together, starting things off in 1968." She sounded wistful, a little bitter and very nostalgic. *"La vie en rose,"* she added.

In bed that night they followed their divergent thoughts. Jim had been tired driving back, but he was wide awake now. "What was that huddle you got into with Patricia?" he asked after a while. "You looked like two mother hens clucking over their eggs. At least she did."

Brigitte's voice was constrained. "Not a very gallant description," she said, "but you're right. She was quizzing me, in her clenched-teeth way, about Hector."

"Why?"

"Don't be dense, Jim. She couldn't care less about Hector. What she wants to know is how safe her snippy little Jennifer will be in that continental nest of vipers into which she seems determined to crawl, and how much cachet those vipers will add to Patricia's own bid to become the dowager queen of Bronxville." A deep sarcasm made Brigitte's voice curdle.

A minute later she reached over to touch him. As always, he responded. She rolled on top of him. As she opened her legs, she looked down on him with a triumphant smile. "Don't worry, darling," she said. "My knowing Hector de Turenne will do you no harm at The Copter Company. *Au contraire.*" Her head came down to bite his lip, gently at first and then very hard.

10

In the last week of June, Anne Gregory was kidnapped in Italy.

A tense meeting had been held in Knight's office two weeks earlier, attended by the three men who had become known at The Copter Company as "the HQ Triumvirate"—Russel Knight, Lawrence Morse Clark and Jim Lindner. In little more than six months, it had become clear to all watchers of corporate politics that Jim was now a member of the top team.

The moment the door closed behind Morse Clark, who as usual had arrived a calculated three minutes after the time for which the meeting had been set, Knight came to the point. He did so in his own succinct style. "We're up the creek," he said, "with half a paddle."

Morse Clark looked annoyed. He disapproved of earthy expressions from the president of the company. Morse Clark's mind ran to lucid and precise statements, preferably buttressed by numbers. Unlike Knight, Morse Clark was not a seat-of-the-pants executive. He loathed the phrase and detested the breed.

Jim sat in silence. He knew Knight would come up with an explanation of his cryptic comment.

"The Italians are investigating the Libyan deal," Knight said. "The US Department of Justice has asked us to cooperate in the investigation."

He squinted at the two men sitting opposite him. Both looked concerned. Morse Clark's nose went white. Jim's face was openly troubled.

"They sent a man up to talk to me privately a couple of weeks ago. I didn't tell you because I thought I could get rid of him. It didn't work. This morning I got a call from Washington"—Knight's lips stretched into a grimace—"high up in Washington. The call made clear that they won't take no for an answer."

"But the executive responsible for the transaction . . ."—Morse Clark coughed and placed two fingers on his mouth—"is no longer with us."

Knight regarded his senior VP with irritation. "I told them Ken Ward was dead," he said curtly. "That didn't cut any ice. They pointed out that in a public corporation as well managed as The Copter Company"—once more the grimace seemed to split his thin face into two parts—"surely there was back-up knowledge both up and down the line." The grimace disappeared and was replaced by a hard look. "They intimated that should this assumption turn out to be inaccurate, they would feel compelled to advise the SEC that the quality of management at The Copter Company might warrant investigation."

The pallor that had earlier invaded Morse Clark's nose now spread over his cheeks and crept up to his forehead. Jim whistled. "They play rough," he commented.

"That they do," Knight acknowledged grimly.

"Your suggestion?" Morse Clark demanded. He managed to sound piqued. The implication of his question was unmistakable: Your sloppy management got us into this. It's your responsibility to get us out.

Knight's eyes went flinty. For a moment the innate antagonism between the two men, usually hidden under corporate congeniality, was out in the open, naked and ugly. Jim shifted in his seat.

Knight moved his eyes from Morse Clark to Jim. "I thought we could send Anne Gregory to assist the Italians," he said. Before Jim could reply, Morse Clark broke in. "She doesn't know anything." This time Morse Clark's voice was contemptuous.

251

Knight ignored the comment and kept his gaze fixed on Jim. "She's a competent, clever girl and knows plenty. In this matter she knows just enough to satisfy the Justice Department that we're doing our best, and not enough to get us into trouble."

Jim opened his fist and discovered that his palm was moist. "Isn't it dangerous?"

"For whom?" Morse Clark interjected nastily.

"I hope not," Knight said. "I'm hiring Justinius Lorenzo, who's the best corporate counsel available in Italy, to hold her hand." His eyes locked with Jim's, and Jim thought he saw sympathy soften the steel blue tinge. Sympathy and a trace of affection. "She's a spunky girl," Knight added.

Jim had difficulty commanding his vocal cords. When he managed to get them under control, his voice seemed to come from his solar plexus. He did not recognize it as his own. But he heard it say hoarsely, "Yes, that she is."

The message from the prestigious Roman counsel Knight had hired, reporting the kidnapping of Anne Gregory, was on the telex when The Copter Company's offices opened on Monday morning. Mary, Jim's secretary, saw it and left a photocopy on Jim's desk. When he arrived, it was prominently placed in the center of his blotter with a paperweight to hold it down. His eyes moved over the message three times before his mind accepted what it conveyed. Then he reached for the phone to call Knight. Before he could do so, Knight's secretary rang his extension. "I'm putting you on a conference call with Washington," she advised him. "Mr. Knight and the Department of Justice."

The man from Justice sounded contrite. "Anything the embassy can do?" he offered. Knight cut him short. "The best thing you people can do for us," he snapped, "is to stay out of our affairs."

The man from Justice hung up and Jim said to Knight, "I'll handle this personally." Jim did not ask; he told the president of the company what he was going to do, and Knight did not demur. "There's a direct flight to Rome leaving Kennedy at six P.M." Knight said. "I'll have Grace book you."

When Jim arrived in Rome the next morning, the sun was just coming up in a caressing dawn. Leonardo da Vinci airport was its customary anarchic self, the hectic mess of its daytime operations intimated by a sleepy early morning confusion. Luggage took almost an hour to come down. At passport control, only one window was open and the line of red-eyed arrivals stretched at least three hundred yards. The uniformed immigration officer manning the sole functioning counter looked like a film star and did his work in slow motion. He was evidently wearier than the travelers.

On the way into the city, Jim noticed nothing. The Tintoretto colors of air and sky, the rose and ochre loveliness of old churches, and the subtle smoky green of the city's famous pines swam in and out of his vision. As the taxi deposited him at the entrance of his hotel at the top of the Spanish Steps, the first of the exotic vendors of necklaces, belts and bracelets, beads, carvings and paintings were just beginning to set out their wares. Waiting for the doorman to receive the luggage from the driver, Jim stared at the vendors but did not register who they were or what they did. To the polite inquiry from the dignified gentleman behind the reception desk as to how long he planned to stay, Jim replied, "When does the American embassy open?"

The concierge shrugged. "They are Americans. Probably in another half hour. Exactly." Jim adjusted his watch. It was eight-thirty A.M., Rome time.

The senior political attaché of the US embassy in Rome did arrive in his office at nine o'clock sharp. Jim sent in his card and scribbled across it, "This is urgent." Behind the closed door of the attaché's large office three minutes later, Jim did not have to explain what his urgent problem was. Saunders already knew all about the kidnapping of The Copter Company's chief of strategic planning.

"She disappeared from her hotel the day before yesterday. The concierge sent word to us yesterday morning, Rome time." A trace of embarrassment colored the attaché's cheek. He was an older man, with white hair and a very white complexion. His mouth curved down at the corners in a world-weary line that indicated he had seen it all—more than he wanted to, more than he had bargained for. "We have an arrangement with the concierge of the Excelsior, where she was staying. We have the same arrangement with a number of other hotels."

"What arrangement?"

"Hotel staff informs us when any American seems to have run into trouble. Americans do, you know." Saunders ran a very white hand over his eyes. The blanched hair below his knuckles glistened in the Roman sun. It was a tired gesture. "Hotel staff, for a reasonable pecuniary consideration, inform us before the police do. That can create awkward situations."

So that's what worried Saunders. Not that a twenty-eight-year-old American girl had been kidnapped, was being held in an unknown place, probably under horrendous conditions, and was conceivably in mortal danger. Saunders problem was the diplomatic embarrassment created by the fact that in Rome a network of bribed hotel clerks was more efficient than the metropolitan police.

"What did the man tell you?" Jim managed to keep his voice even.

Saunders studied the carefully trimmed fingernails on his left hand. "That Miss Gregory had not appeared in her room for eighteen hours. He had not called earlier, because she was a most attractive lady and might have chosen to spend the night somewhere else. But American girls, he pointed out, always come back to their rooms in the morning. To freshen up." Saunders looked up from his fingernails. "I suppose that's a compliment to our national passion for hygiene," he said. The thought seemed to please him. Jim pressed his hands flat against the top of his thighs. "And?" His voice sounded constricted.

"And . . ." Saunders was obviously reluctant to dismiss his contemplation of the oblique obeisance to the Stars and Stripes rendered by the concierge of the Excelsior Hotel. "And we informed the police. They claimed that they were already aware of the case and pursuing it. They did, in fact, get back to us within the hour."

"What did they have?"

Saunders peered at the fingernails of both hands and did not look up as he replied, "They said she was kidnapped at the instigation of the Libyans, who wanted the inquiry into the helicopter transaction stopped. You know all about that, of course." Saunders had torn his gaze away from his fingernails long enough to lock eyes with Jim. He sounded accusatory.

Jim ignored the tone. "At the instigation of the Libyans, you say. I take it that means someone else actually did it. Do we know who?"

Saunders' mouth pulled down. The myriad of tiny lines, spread over his face like a road map, seemed to follow. "Unfortunately, the options in Italy are varied." He managed to sound weary, wise and snide at the same time. "It could be the Mafia or the Red Brigades or permutations of either one. Italy has hit teams for hire willing and able to take on such an assignment for financial reward or political compensation. The Libyans would have access to both. Tripoli has enough money for the first and sufficient political appeal for the second. Those helicopters did wind up in Eastern Europe, didn't they?" Something in Saunders' voice made clear his conviction that whatever problems The Copter Company now had it had assuredly created for itself.

"I don't know," Jim said carefully. "We had nothing whatsoever to do with those arrangements. We sold a consignment of craft to a perfectly reputable firm in Bologna. With US government approval, and encouragement."

Saunders looked past Jim to the door that led to the outer office, where his American secretary sat. "Well, yes," he said, then added, "You're aware of the official US attitude on kidnappings, I assume."

Jim pressed his hands hard into his thighs. "No."

Saunders sighed, a modulated gentlemanly sigh. His eyes remained on the door behind Jim's back. "Our policy is that we do not involve ourselves officially in kidnapping cases outside the United States. Our position is that such acts are the responsibility of the government of the country in which the kidnapping has occurred."

Jim took his hands off his thighs and gripped the fragile arms of the chair he had been offered. "Are you saying, Mr. Saunders, that there's nothing you either can do or will do in this matter?"

"The former, Mr. Lindner." Saunders was polished and polite. "Regrettably, it makes the second an inescapable consequence."

Jim pivoted out of his chair with a motion so forceful it startled even him, kicking the chair in which he had sat with one foot. The chair trembled and fell. Saunders looked horrified. He was about to come out from behind his desk to rescue the endangered piece of furniture when a look at Jim's face stopped him. Jim's feelings were plain. They were fury and disgust for a man prepared to be solicitous about a chair while he dismissed from his concern a human being in the clutches of murderers. Jim turned abruptly and without a word strode to the door.

Dr. Justinius Lorenzo received Jim in a fifteenth-century palace that had been exquisitely and efficiently restored. It was situated just off the Piazza Venezia, whose ancient beauty even the monstrosity of the Mussolini-built monument—dubbed by Romans the "wedding cake"—had not been able to demolish. A cobblestone courtyard served as a driveway for the attorney's opulent office. A small elevator had taken Jim smoothly and quickly to the third floor. There a young woman in a long-skirted gray suit, with a deep red carnation pinned to her breast pocket by an antique golden brooch, greeted him. She led him through a marble corridor lined with busts of ancient Romans to the library, which Lorenzo used for consultations. The room was enormous and dark, and all its walls were lined with folios. The heavy velvet drapes were drawn, and massive chairs were arranged haphazardly around a thirty-foot table. In the chair at its head sat Dr. Lorenzo.

He made a gesture at rising and motioned Jim to take a seat. He was a short and stocky man, dressed in a navy blue suit, white shirt and conservative dark tie. His cheeks were fleshy, and his jowls sagged. His face looked like a battlefield on which many wars had been waged—some lost, some won.

"Anna Gregory," he began. He pronounced the family name

with the accent on the *o*, like a chant. "We have some information."
Dr. Lorenzo had a deep basso voice that reverberated in the dark
chamber.

Jim's vision had not yet adjusted to the hushed dimness of
the room after the noisy glare of Rome in mid-morning. He narrowed his eyes to see more clearly the dark figure at the head
of the table. It was a face that inspired, if not trust, responsiveness.

"Yes," Jim said eagerly. "What is it?"

Dr. Lorenzo lowered his eyelids. They were puffy and reminded Jim of Taher Rezvani. "The news we have is not good.
The kidnapping was carried out by Palestinians."

"Palestinians? How did they get involved in this?"

Dr. Lorenzo's eyelids lifted slowly. "It's the Habash group
of Palestinians. They're Marxists. At least they've proclaimed
themselves as such. This means that they're politically close to
the Red Brigades. The Habash group also has strong links with
Libya. Colonel Qaddafi believes himself to be a man of the left.
The Islamic left. The reasoning is tortuous, but the action is clear.
Libya provides terrorists of the left with arms and diplomatic papers. In return, if Tripoli has a terrorist assignment it wants executed, it need only ask. The reciprocity is unquestioned."

Jim's head began to spin. I don't need expositions of the
political ins and outs of the world's lunatic left, he thought. I
need Anne Gregory. "In the matter at hand," he said, "what difference does it make who did the kidnapping? The point is to get
back the victim."

Dr. Lorenzo's heavy head fell forward twice, asserting agreement. "That is true. But who the executing party is does make
a difference. The Palestinians are very experienced and very competent. That makes the work of the police more difficult." He
looked at Jim balefully. "It diminishes the chances of timely rescue."

"Can anything be done to . . . uh . . . motivate the police?"

Dr. Lorenzo leaned back in his chair. "I've already done what
you suggest, Mr. Lindner. But it is not so simple. Our metropolitan
police used to be one of the best in the world until it was attacked
remorselessly by both the right and the left for a decade. The

barbs found their mark. Many people were removed or removed themselves. Only the mediocre remained, men who do not care, who have nothing much to gain or lose. Now the public despises the police. The people of Rome do not cooperate with police officers. Morale among the men of the force is very low. This cannot be changed with a gesture, however generous."

"What happens next then?"

"We wait, Mr. Lindner."

"For what?"

Dr. Lorenzo raised his heavy shoulders and let them fall. "For developments."

He rose, walked to the window and pushed aside one of the drapes. A brilliant sliver of sunshine darted into the room and fell across the table like the blade of a dagger. Jim stared at it. His heart cramped. "The executing party," Dr. Lorenzo had said. For Palestinian terrorists, that was not a figure of speech. They were convinced of the righteousness of their cause and killed without compunction. They would have no hesitation about disposing of Anne in any way they saw fit. The speculation of what the minions of Dr. Habash might consider fit made Jim's blood pound against his temples. He put his hands on the cool surface of the old table, which seemed to act as a conductor for the nervous energy that was throbbing through him.

There was a soft knock at the door, and the woman who had received him at the elevator entered the room carrying a note. *"Scusi,"* she said with a brief nod in Jim's direction. She walked to the window and laid the note on the windowsill. Dr. Lorenzo studied it, wheeled around and moved toward Jim.

"The first waiting is over. We have notification from the kidnappers." Lorenzo's prominent brown eyes fixed on Jim. "Do you know the Signorina Gregory personally?"

"Of course. She's a valued member of my staff."

Dr. Lorenzo reached for the knot of his tie, began to loosen it, then thought better of the idea. "Then you know perhaps the color of her hair."

Something in the lawyer's expression warned Jim that while the question seemed odd there was a good reason for it. "Yes," he said. "It's brown, with an auburn tinge."

"Auburn?"

"Dark red."

"*Ecco!* That is how I remember it also." Dr. Lorenzo looked at Jim sadly. "They have sent a lock of her hair. For identification. But it is also a warning, of course."

"Of what?"

"Criminal terrorists in Italy have adopted the habit of cutting off their victim's earlobe, or the tip of a finger. They say it is for identification, but the message is more gruesome. They will cut off any part of the body to get what they want."

Jim's bowels had turned soft. He felt as if he were about to vomit. Dr. Lorenzo rang a bell under the table with his foot. "A glass of water," he ordered when the woman with the carnation appeared. *"Presto."*

When the water came—a tall modern glass on a heavy tray of chafed Renaissance pewter—Jim gulped the first few swallows. Dr. Lorenzo reached across the table and caught Jim's wrists. "Easy," he said. "You must be careful now. About everything you do. We must not let them acquire a second victim."

Jim put down the glass. The advice he had just been given was sound. Control was what he needed, full control and total attention to whatever had to be done. He took a deep breath and willed his bowels to firm, the pounding of blood to ease. After a few seconds he picked up the glass again and sipped at it slowly. This time he could feel the water trickle down his gullet, moisten his parched throat and cool his body. He looked up at Dr. Lorenzo and nodded.

"They've given us their terms," Dr. Lorenzo said.

"Which are?"

Dr. Lorenzo spoke slowly, keeping his eyes on Jim. "They want the Italian government to cease and desist from its investigation of the transaction between Libya and the company in Bologna. If the government complies, they will release Miss Gregory unharmed." Jim felt relief sing in his mind and echo in his ears.

"If the investigation has not ceased within a week," Dr. Lorenzo continued, "they will kneecap Miss Gregory. That is, they

259

will shoot her in both knees and splinter the bone. If it does not cease within a fortnight, they will kill her." He had hurried the last sentence, almost stumbled over it. It took Jim several seconds before he fully comprehended what Dr. Lorenzo had told him. Then he gagged. Dr. Lorenzo indicated the water. Jim reached for it.

When his mind had cleared, he saw his hand clutching an empty glass and heard Dr. Lorenzo pronounce, "I can attempt to intercede with the government. It will cost a great deal of money."

As in a dream, Jim listened to his own voice respond: "What's a great deal of money, Dr. Lorenzo?"

Once more Dr. Lorenzo got up and walked to the window. This time he did not lift the curtain. He just stared at it. When he swung around, his basso voice boomed across the room. "To arrange this we would have to risk the career and reputation of a cabinet minister. I try to put myself into his heart. I would say we are speaking of five million dollars at least. Perhaps ten."

The vision of a check danced across Jim's mind. The check was made out to cash, read $10,000,000, was signed by Russel Knight and countersigned by Lawrence Morse Clark. Jim shook his head. Knight couldn't do that, and Morse Clark wouldn't. Jim could threaten to quit. They would manage to survive. He could force their hand by telling them he would talk to the press or even go to court to sue them for negligence. They would outmaneuver him one way or another. And it would take time. Meanwhile Anne could be dead.

"Would it work?" he asked in a shaky voice.

Dr. Lorenzo moved to the table. He flung up his hands in a dramatic gesture. "I don't know," he said. "I will try."

In the dark room Jim's blood-drained face looked ghostly. Dr. Lorenzo walked around the table and put his hands on Jim's shoulders. "You should go to the hotel and rest," he said. "Try to divert yourself a little, but carefully, please. Until you hear from me." An idea crossed his mind. "How are you registered at the hotel?" he asked.

"James H. Lindner."

"Of New York?"

"Yes. Why?"

"Do you speak any language other than English?"

"German."

"Do you speak it well?"

"Reasonably well. I lived in Germany for three and a half years, and I'm married to a German."

"Ah." Dr. Lorenzo's mobile face registered surprise. Then he said, "I think we will change your identity for the moment, or rather obscure it a little. You will become Johannes Lindner. Of Hamburg. I will notify the hotel myself. You are at . . . ?"

"The Hassler."

"Good." Dr. Lorenzo waved his hands in approval. "When the roof garden opens, go there and have lunch. Look out over our eternal city. It'll give you a sense of proportion about the smallness of man, the largeness of history and the predictable unpredictableness of fate." He patted Jim on the shoulder. "I'll be in touch as soon as I have anything to tell you."

Jim obeyed Lorenzo's instructions. He took a taxi back to the hotel, rested until one, then went to the hotel's roof garden for lunch. The view below was soft, ancient and utterly beautiful. He saw it as through a faceted glass. He ate what the waiter suggested but paid no attention to what was put on his plate. When he signed the bill, he had to look at his key for his room number. He did remember to slant his handwriting and make it read "Johannes Lindner."

As he put down the pen, a thought flashed through his mind. German . . . Hugo . . . the hint Hugo had dropped about intelligence during their peculiar conversation in St. Moritz. Possibly, just possibly, Hugo could help. Should he tell Lorenzo about Hugo? No, he'd better deal with Hugo himself.

The waiter who had wondered idly just who that dead fish of a customer was now watched Jim jump out of his chair and rush to the elevator. By the time the waiter had decided that the roof garden of the Hassler Hotel really did get some peculiar people nowadays, Jim was already in his room and on the telephone. Five minutes later he was speaking to Hugo Kertner.

261

"Jim, what a pleasant surprise!" Hugo exclaimed. "You keep turning up in my hours of need. Christine just took off for a long weekend in Italy."

"I'm in Italy myself."

"You are? Why are you sounding funereal then?"

"Am I?"

"Yes." A note of caution had crept into Hugo's voice.

"You have a good ear, Hugo. I do have a problem. A serious one. I would like to talk to you about it. Would you mind if I came to Bonn?"

"Not at all, my boy. Always glad to see you." The bonhomie had returned to Hugo's voice. "When would you like to come?"

"Now. First plane I can get."

There was a short silence. The line hummed. "Of course." Hugo sounded matter-of-fact, as if Jim had called from around the corner to ask whether he could come up for a drink. "I have a timetable for planes to and from Italy out in the hall. Christine used it this morning. Hold on just a minute."

Waiting for Hugo to pick up the phone again, Jim could hear his heart hammer. Why am I doing this? What am I getting us into?

Before he could answer his own questions, Hugo's voice was back on the wire. Jim moved the receiver farther from his ear. "There's a plane at 1605," Hugo announced. "Stops in Milan, gets to Cologne at 2015. Can you make it?"

Jim looked at his watch. It was two-thirty P.M. It would be difficult, and he would have to fight afternoon traffic to the airport. "I will," he said.

"*Gut!* I'll meet you at the airport in Cologne."

On the autobahn from Cologne to Bonn, Jim told Hugo what had happened. Hugo kept his eyes on the road and his face impassive. He listened without comment. When Jim had finished, Hugo said only, "We'll discuss it at home." His voice was even, but Jim sensed in it an undertone of anger.

Hugo was angry. After they had settled down in his study, a bottle of brandy between them, Hugo said, "This is a nasty business, Jim, and I'll try to help. But I must tell you that personally I do not find your—what shall I call it—casual approach to political realities very appealing. And not at all amusing."

Jim blinked. "I probably do take my politics more lightly than I should. But what does that have to do with this affair?"

Hugo reached for the bottle. "I was not referring to your personal politics," he said sharply. "I was referring to the casualness with which American businessmen conduct themselves in a dangerous world. I prefer to be charitable and to assume it is a matter of naiveté, perhaps even innocence. It is nevertheless a menace to civilized mankind."

The vehemence of Hugo's tone and the intensity of his anger were unmistakable. "Hugo," Jim said desperately, "I don't know what you are talking about. I really don't."

Hugo poured two snifters of brandy and pushed one at Jim. He looked at the floor in an attempt to get his anger under control. When he spoke again, his voice was a mixture of compassion and contempt. "I'm sure that's true," he said. "But let me ask you a question. Why did you let that craft with nuclear capability go to Libya in the first place? And to Eastern Europe in the second?"

Why did we? The question made Jim feel miserable. "The answer is," he said, both to Hugo and himself, "that we had nothing to do with it."

"That's not good enough, Jim. Not in the world in which we live. They are your craft."

Jim shook his head. "We sold the copters to an Italian company, Hugo, a respectable established Bologna firm."

"Perhaps you should have checked a little more carefully before you made the sale."

"Checked what? We have no way of running a security profile on our customers."

Hugo sighed heavily. The sigh settled in the space between them, and Hugo allowed it to hover there for almost a minute. Then he said in a conciliatory tone, "Perhaps not, Jim. I just want you to understand, and bear in mind, that your laissez-faire approach to business can make life very difficult for others, whose mission it is to protect you."

When Jim reached for the brandy, his hand shook so badly

he needed his other hand to keep the liquid from spilling.

"Drink it down," Hugo ordered gruffly.

Jim obeyed. The brandy seared his throat, and his stomach heaved twice, then settled. He poured himself another.

Hugo nodded approval. "Keep going," he said. "I'll make a few calls meanwhile."

Jim could follow Hugo's heavy tread down the corridor to the entrance hall, where a telephone was perched on a stand. He heard Hugo conduct three conversations, two in German and one in English, and caught enough to determine the language but not to understand what was being said. On the last call Hugo raised his voice at the end. "Right," Jim heard him say, "I'll bring him round tomorrow. Thanks very much."

When they got into the car the next morning, Hugo was laconic. He did not volunteer any information about who it was he had spoken to the previous night, nor where they were headed now. Jim resolved not to ask. It was an exercise in self-control.

They drove through the center of Bonn in determined silence, then on to a residential section where embassies were spotted among large private homes. They pulled up at a house that looked like a fortress surrounded by a high wall topped with barbed wire. Two heavily armed guards flanked the entrance gate, acutely watchful. Hugo spoke to them in German and flashed a pass. They examined it, gave an order, and the gate opened. Jim and Hugo drove into well-maintained grounds. Atop a medium-sized building in the center flew a blue and white flag with the Star of David. "The embassy of Israel," Hugo said.

The security man at the door of the building as well as the receptionist inside indicated that Hugo and Jim were expected. The security man was young and blond, dressed casually in a pair of tan trousers and a white shirt open at the neck, the sleeves rolled up. He spoke both German and English with a pleasant but slightly guttural accent. He nodded to Hugo. "You know where to find Colonel Elan." It was a statement, not a question.

Colonel Elan's office in the back of the embassy's second floor was attractive but sparsely furnished. The colonel himself

264

was tall and slim and sported a well-trimmed mustache. He looked vaguely British, except for a prominent aquiline nose. There was an English intonation to his voice.

Hugo went through the formalities of introduction. The colonel stood and put out his hand to Jim. "I'm sorry, Mr. Lindner," he said. "However often it happens, it's always dreadful. One never gets used to it." The colonel's eyes strayed to a photograph on the bookshelf to his left. It showed a lanky young man in fatigues and paratrooper boots. "One should not get used to it," he added quietly.

Colonel Elan had been briefed. After they reviewed the salient facts, he addressed himself to Hugo. "There's nothing we can do officially," he said.

Hugo nodded. "Of course."

The colonel's deep-set brown eyes moved from Hugo to Jim. "But," he said, "I can recommend a man who would take on the assignment on a private basis."

Assignment to do what? Negotiate with the Italians? Lorenzo is already doing that. With the Libyans? The Palestinians? With what instructions? Under whose authority? At what price?

Before Jim could ask any of these questions, Hugo said, "That's splendid. Where do we reach him?"

The colonel moved his gaze back to Hugo. "The number," he said, "is Tel Aviv 463–285. The name is David. You can reach him now. Use your secure phone."

Hugo stood up. "Thank you, Colonel. We appreciate." For a moment the eyes of Hugo Kertner and Colonel Elan locked. The colonel ran a hand through his salt-and-pepper hair. "Any time."

The man who answered the telephone in Tel Aviv sounded cheerful and innocuous. "David Ari-el," he said, accenting the second syllable of the first and last names. He did not volunteer any additional information, not even a "good morning" or a "hello." The only words to come across the wire were the name.

Hugo, handling the call, was equally cryptic. "Reference, Colonel Elan," he said. "An assignment in Rome." The bouncy voice

265

in Tel Aviv registered no change. "When?"

"Immediately. The sooner the better."

Jim had stood close to Hugo when he placed the call, but Hugo had waved him away. Now Jim was watching Hugo draw his eyebrows together and listen intently. "Right," he said and hung up.

He turned to Jim. "Ari-el will meet you in Rome at seven o'clock this evening, on the twelfth of the Spanish Steps counting from the top. He says there's a blond hippie on that step with his hair in a ponytail who sells copies of Gucci link belts. You ask whether the belt can be adjusted easily, because you are not certain of the size of your wife's waist. Ari-el will join you and complain that he has the same problem. You'll buy a belt each, then walk down the remainder of the stairs together, discussing the problem of keeping up on the shoe, belt and blouse sizes of one's wife."

"Do we have any idea of what Ari-el looks like?"

"No." A tinge of exasperation colored Hugo's voice. "He didn't ask me what you looked like." Hugo made an effort to get his irritation under control. "If Elan recommends him, the man knows his business. Under the circumstances that's all that matters, isn't it?"

Jim thought of Anne, the auburn lock the terrorists had sent and the message that had come with it. Once more his heart began to hammer. "Yes," he said.

David Ari-el resembled a graying teddybear. He was dressed in a nondescript suit that was too loose and not very well pressed. His manner was open and amiable. He bantered with the hippie and looked happily confused when discussing the waist of his wife. The hippie liked him. Jim found him comforting but improbable. David Ari-el did not look like the bronzed and tough Israeli Jim had imagined. Nor did he look like a man who could deal effectively with a group of richly financed and well-equipped professional terrorists, fanatic in their convictions and unscrupulous in their methods. David told Jim he was a grandfather and pulled out a photograph of three strapping youngsters in their early teens at whom he beamed with pride.

Together they walked down the steps to the fountain at the bottom. David fished out of his pocket some small coins and began to toss them slowly and systematically into the fountain. He was designing a pattern and the coins landed precisely where he wanted them. He did not miss once. The design in the end turned out to be a six-pointed star. "Talk to me," he instructed Jim while he was seemingly engaged in his coin-tossing game. "Tell me everything you know." He flung out another coin. "Everything," he repeated, without changing the tone of his voice. "Leave out nothing. Even if you consider it unimportant."

When Jim had finished, David looked at Jim and chuckled. He raised his voice from the carefully controlled conversational pitch he had used earlier and indicated to Jim that he wanted his altered manner copied. "Well," he said, "now that we've made sure we'll be back, let's see what we can find for our wives this time around." He turned and headed for a street lined with some of Rome's most fashionable shops.

They ambled along, halting occasionally to look at store windows displaying crepe de chine shirts and silk scarves, finely knit dresses and suede coats, handsomely designed handbags and cleverly crafted high-heeled boots. Every so often, David would gesture and exclaim, "Nice, eh!" He would then step closer to the window, peer and shake his head. "Too expensive."

In between this charade he said quietly, "We need to discuss terms. I understand this is a corporate matter."

Jim looked into David's twinkling grandfatherly eyes. "Yes. But we are very concerned personally as well. All of us."

They walked to the next store window, and David stopped to point out another lovely scarf. "Your company makes helicopters. We'll accept one as compensation for this"—he hesitated and inclined his head—"venture, I believe you would call it."

The request was worth about a million dollars. Would Knight spring for that? Dr. Lorenzo's proposition ran a lot higher. But Lorenzo's plan involved only money, payable outside the US. Morse Clark would devise some legerdemain to cover it. David was asking for product. That demand was a lot harder to meet. You couldn't just make a helicopter disappear; not with the kind

267

of quality and inventory control The Copter Company had. No one monkeyed with those. And how would they deliver the craft, even if they could shake it loose somehow?

"How would we get it to you?" he asked.

David had stopped at another shop. "Don't worry about that. We'll find a way to collect it."

Jim stared at the store window. Behind it, beautiful mannequins in extravagant poses were wearing eye-catching clothes. He did not see them. What he saw instead was Morse Clark's pinched face. He could hear Morse Clark say, "That means tampering with our books here in the US. I consider that highly inadvisable."

David had watched Jim's eyes riveted on the window. The expression in them told him that Jim was not admiring the models. David was an experienced man. He knew what was going through his client's mind.

"You can tell your company," he said, "that some very good men are risking their lives in this enterprise. Young men, younger than Miss Gregory."

Jim was not used to inactivity, but there was nothing he could do except wait for word: from Dr. Lorenzo, who sent reassuring but meaningless messages to Herr Johannes Lindner; from David, who telephoned at odd hours to report, "We're tracking the merchandise." "We're still tracking, still tracking." Late in the third day David said, "We have a lead. Stay put."

That night Jim did not sleep at all. Would David and his team succeed? Would they get to Anne before the kidnappers maimed or killed her? Would some of David's boys die? Would the terrorists? And where was right and wrong in all this for The Copter Company? Was Hugo right? Or Russel Knight? Larry Morse Clark? Jürgen Zwirli? Max Feld? Who? And how did it all relate to flesh and blood—earlobes and the tips of fingers, pieces of people's bodies—carrying a message of blackmail and murder, premeditated and random. He couldn't remember what Anne's earlobes were like. They had always been hidden by her hair. The steel hoops he had felt encircling his heart when he first heard the kidnappers' terms pressed closer. Someone was tightening them. He sat up, stretched his hands over his head and tried to breathe.

The phone rang. "I have your goods now," David said at the other end of the line. His cheerful voice had an edge of harassment. "I'd like to transfer them as soon as possible. Can you meet me in a couple of hours to complete the transaction?"

"Of course. Is the merchandise in good condition?"

"As good as can be expected. You'll need to be careful with it though after you accept delivery." Relief and apprehension chased each other in Jim's mind. "When can I take delivery?"

"Six o'clock sharp. Our original meeting place."

He was at the Spanish Steps by five-thirty. The place was deserted. It was still dark, but the first touches of postcard pink were beginning to streak the eastern sky. An occasional sound of wooden shutters being flung open and the tolling of a church bell in the distance indicated that the city was beginning to stir.

At six o'clock Jim's stomach started to churn. At 6:01 he began to stare at the section of his wristwatch that registered the seconds. At 6:03 a small taxi swerved around the corner by the fountain below and screeched to a halt. Jim raced down the stairs. The door opened and David's grizzled crew cut stuck out. He lifted his head and smiled. "Special delivery," he said. He turned and with his two hands underneath her elbows, gently guided Anne from the car to the sidewalk. When she stood by the fountain facing Jim, David let go of her elbows. "Take care of her. She'll need looking after for a while." He turned and climbed back into the cab. Before he clanged the door shut, he leaned out once more. "We'll be in touch," he called as the driver gunned the motor. The driver was brawny and bronzed with curly blond hair. He looked like a twin of the security officer who had directed Jim and Hugo to the office of Colonel Elan.

Anne had remained standing where David had left her, her face white and drawn, the green eyes luminous with the lifeless brilliance of neon lights. She was swaying slightly.

He took a step forward and lifted her in his arms. She had

always been a thin girl, but now she seemed terribly light. Her clothes were loose and her body felt brittle. He climbed the steps slowly, trying not to jolt her, to maintain a steady rhythm that would make her feel secure.

At the top of the steps he put her down gingerly, then slipped her arm in his and held it close. He guided her to the hotel entrance, past the drowsy doorman, to the desk of the concierge. "Mrs. Lindner," he said as he requested his key, "has had a trying journey." The concierge regarded Anne and nodded sympathetically. "I'll send up some bouillon," he promised.

When the bouillon arrived, Anne was huddled in the armchair of Jim's room. She had collapsed into the chair the moment they entered and had sat there, numb, ever since. When the waiter knocked at the door, she jumped and looked around wildly. Jim walked over to her, stood at a pace's distance and smiled. "It's all right," he said softly. "It's only room service." She stared at him, scared and distraught. "I'll be right back," he said.

He went to the door, took the tray from the waiter and returned to Anne with the cup of broth in his hands. Carefully, to prevent the soup from spilling, he knelt with it in front of her chair. He ladled out a spoonful and held it up. "Open," he said cajolingly. She flinched. "Say ah," he urged, raising the spoon to her lips.

Her eyes went dark and her mouth clamped shut. "No," she said behind clenched teeth. "No."

He took the spoon and placed it on the saucer. She watched him, then reached for the broth with both hands, steadying her trembling fingers by clamping them around the cup.

"I'll do it myself," she said in an almost inaudible voice that nevertheless shook with vehemence. "I don't need to be spoon-fed. I'm not helpless."

"A noble try," he said when she put down the cup after a few sips. He forced himself to sound jocular. "This is a full-service establishment. What can we offer the lady next?"

He saw her eyes clear for a moment, then darken again. "I feel crawly. I haven't washed in a long time. Could I have a bath?" Her voice was frightened and pleading. It pained him to hear

270

it. "Sure thing," he said lightly. "I'll run it for you."

He went to the bathroom and turned on the tap, testing the water with his finger to make certain it was neither hot nor tepid. What do I give her to wear? he wondered when the water was just right. He had brought only one pair of pajamas and had worn those since he left New York. It occurred to him that a shirt of his would cover her to mid-thigh. He returned to the room, took a shirt out of the drawer, rolled up the sleeves and laid it out on the bed. "Why don't you change?" he said over his shoulder, "while I finish running the bath."

He took longer than was necessary in the bathroom. When he returned, her clothes lay beside the armchair in a pathetic little heap. She was wearing his shirt, which came to just above her knees. Her knees were long and thin, with curves that looked fragile. An image froze him. The terrorists' first term would have been up in two more days. They would have shattered those knees if David and his boys hadn't got to her in time. A storm of fury and gratitude, anxiety and tenderness whirled inside him. He held out his hands. "We're ready for you, madam," he said.

When she came out of the bath, her eyes seemed to have lost some of their dullness and her cheeks had a tinge of rose. But she looked exhausted, and as she walked from the bathroom to the bed her legs seemed barely able to hold her up. He had turned back the top sheet and blanket and propped up both pillows against the headboard. She sat at the edge of the bed, paused to gather strength and slowly swung up her legs. Then she leaned against the pillows and closed her eyes. After about half an hour, during which he willed himself not to pace, he bent over the bed and, with one finger, lifted her chin. "How about some breakfast?"

She opened her eyes and the trace of a smile played at the edge of her lips. "I'm dreaming," she said, "of orange juice and cornflakes, eggs and bacon, and three cups of coffee."

"That's an intelligent dream." He picked up the telephone on the bedside table and put it within her reach. "Why don't you order it? Make it two. I could use a respectable breakfast myself."

271

She moved to the edge of the bed and lifted the receiver. "Pronto," said a masculine voice. The unknown voice and the foreign word were too much for her. The receiver clattered on the table. He picked it up and put it back in the cradle.

When she had stopped trembling, he ordered breakfast. He prepared her bowl of cereal, poured her coffee, uncovered her dish of eggs and bacon and placed everything within her reach. He did not offer to feed her, and she managed to handle her cutlery without rattling it and to hold her cup without shaking. When she was done, she said, "I'll never touch minestrone again." He blinked. "That's what they gave me, three times a day, every day." Her hand flew to her mouth as she gagged.

He pushed away the trolley, laid one of the pillows flat, picked up her legs by the ankles and put them under the blanket. Then he tucked her in. "You should sleep," he said.

"Will you stay with me?" Her voice quavered.

"Of course." He sat on the bed beside her, his shoulders pressed against the headboard, his legs on top of the cover. When he picked up her hand, it was dry and tense. "I'll be here," he said. "Right here."

He could feel her hand relax and go limp. Her head sank deeper into the pillow. A minute later she was asleep.

He sat very still watching over her, but after an hour his muscles began to cramp. He lifted the hand he was holding and looked at the thin wrist. He could see the pulse there, throbbing against the very white skin in which a tiny network of blue veins showed. He touched his lips to the wrist, then put her hand under the blanket and got off the bed.

The movement woke her. Half awake, she clutched at him. "Don't leave me," she sobbed. He held her and the tears became a torrent, flushing out, in a jumble of words, the memory of the past five days.

They had grabbed her as she walked out of her hotel: two dark young men who simply pulled her arms into theirs as if the three of them were old friends going for a walk. At first she thought they were just another couple of adventurous Romans

272

making a pass. Before she could protest, they pushed her into a car—a large Alfa Romeo—and drove off in the direction of the sea. That was the last she saw. In the car they quickly put a bandage over her eyes, which they did not remove until she found herself in a tiny room that had nothing in it except a mattress on the floor and a naked electric bulb on a cord that hung from the ceiling. They kept her wrists and ankles chained at all times, even for meals, when a man in a stocking mask brought her a tin bowl of thick soup, which he pushed into her mouth with a wooden ladle. His thrice-daily appearance was the only way she had of determining what time it was and how many days had gone by.

They did nothing to injure her physically, but shortly after they deposited her in the room, the man with the stocking mask approached her with a pair of scissors. "No need to fear," he said. "Not yet. I will only cut a little hair." He snipped off a large curl from the bottom of the pageboy, then tucked the chopped strand of hair behind her ear. "Nice ear," he said with a throaty laugh.

For three days following, he pretended not to understand anything she said to him in English. On the fourth day he entered the room accompanied by two comrades. She was lying on the mattress, and the three men, all wearing masks, stood against the opposite wall.

"We'll tell you now what will happen," her chief jailer said. "We have presented our demands. If they are not met within three days, we will"—he put his index finger against his thumb and popped it up as if he were using a pea shooter—"shoot your knees. You will not walk for a very long time." He smiled triumphantly. "If they do not listen to us after that, you will become a martyr to the revolution. Our revolution." His voice went somber, but underlying the darkness of the tone Anne had heard the bright edge of ecstasy. "It's a fine way to die," he added. "Some of our comrades have died so. We worship their memory. We will perhaps die in the same way."

The two men flanking him nodded and murmured assent. Then her jailer, in a changed tone, spoke to his comrades in a language Anne did not know. They laughed, and he turned to her, his dark eyes sparkling behind the slits of his mask.

"If you will be a comrade martyr, we should have a good time together before you die." He kneeled on the mattress and his hands touched her breasts and traveled down her body between her manacled legs. "We will have to take away the chains when the time comes," he said almost contemplatively.

Anne did not know what had happened on the morning of her rescue. She had been aware that she was near the sea, because late at night and in the early hours of the morning she could sometimes hear the murmur of the waves. She was straining for that sound—it was her only communication with the outside world—when she heard a commotion and bullets piercing the wall very close by. The door was flung open and her jailer stood there without a mask, a submachine gun in his hands with the barrel trained on her face. He was going to kill her. Her mind froze around the thought as she watched him pull the trigger. Suddenly a fist came down on the crook of his elbow. He screamed and the gun crashed to the floor. Two hands snapped back his head and dragged him out of the room. There was more scuffling, more shots, and seconds later David walked into the room. He had a small key and knelt to unlock the chains on Anne's legs and arms. With expert motions he massaged her ankles and wrists, red and raw from the chains. "Try to get up," David said. He watched as Anne made the effort to stir, sit and finally stand.

"Good girl. Now come with me." He flashed his grandfatherly smile. "It's all over."

He led her down two flights of narrow stairs to a small taxi waiting below, helped her into the back seat and climbed in beside her. When she turned to look, all she could see was a white apartment house two blocks from the beach. "Ostia," David said, sounding like an avuncular tourist guide. "The beach of Rome."

He did not speak after that while the driver of the car moved expertly along the nearly empty roads, turned corners and crossed squares at high speed, until they pulled up at the foot of the Spanish Steps.

"And there you were." She moved away from him, far enough to be able to look into his face. Her eyes glistened.

"Yes, and if you behave yourself today, I'll take you home tomorrow."

She smiled, the full delicious widening of the generous mouth that he remembered from the first time he had seen her. "That sounds like a great idea. What do I have to do to behave myself?"

Her voice had recovered some of its vibrance. He felt a surge of happiness. "First," he said, "you sleep some more. Then we decide what comes next."

She let go of him, rolled on her back and snuggled her head into the pillow.

When she opened her eyes again, dusk was beginning to settle over the hotel's classic garden and over the faded walls, balconies and cupolas that looked down on it. At first her glance swept the room, searching and puzzled. Then she saw Jim sitting in the armchair, and her eyes sparkled, clean and clear.

They agreed that she should not yet get up and that they would have a light supper in the room.

When he had pushed the supper cart outside into the hall, he returned to find her looking perplexed and a little sheepish.

"What is it?"

She rubbed her eyes. "I'm sleepy again."

He bent down, lifted her face and kissed her forehead. "Good," he said.

After she was asleep, he changed into his pajamas and lay on the bed beside her, on top of the covers.

When she felt him close, she murmured something but did not wake. He put his arms underneath his pillow and stretched. He felt shaken to the core and at the same time happier than he had ever been in his life.

He woke to find Anne's head on his chest and his arm around her shoulder. Her mouth had made a small wet spot on the breast pocket of his pajamas. Her hair spilled over his jacket and strayed underneath the jacket between the two top buttons. It tickled his skin.

Anne was still unsteady on her feet when she got up, but

managed to wash and dress herself without help. "Short-term plan," she said when she was ready. "We see whether we can get tickets home and we go get my things at the Excelsior."

Jim grinned. "That answers my question. I was going to ask whether you were ready to travel."

She swung around, wobbled and reached for the bedpost, looking surprised. "I think so," she said, "and I'd sure like to."

"I booked us on the one o'clock flight to New York. I'll have to let Dr. Lorenzo know that you're here and that we're leaving."

She looked distressed. "I talked to him a couple of times before . . . it all happened. He was supposed to guide me on my testimony. I didn't feel very comfortable with him."

"Why not?"

"He wanted me to lie, or at least to evade. But there really wasn't anything to lie about. Besides, I'm not very good at it." Her pale green dirndl skirt was rumpled and her blouse was soiled. The T-strap sandals, once white, were covered with stains. She wore no makeup. Jim wanted to hug her.

"Still," he said. "He is our counsel. And he did his best, as far as I know. Besides, I'm not sure we can get out of here without his help, or at least his consent."

Jim's hunch proved correct. When he reached Dr. Lorenzo on the telephone and started to explain, counsel cut him short. "I've been informed," Dr. Lorenzo said heavily. "I am personally delighted of course, but it creates a difficult situation."

Had Dr. Lorenzo reached the persuadable minister he had mentioned, obtained and made commitments that were now unnecessary? Had The Copter Company's Italian counsel gone far enough to create political and financial embarrassment for the minister or for himself? For the company? Jim decided not to pursue the topic. "Is there anything I can do?" he inquired.

"The police will want to question Miss Gregory."

"Why?" Jim demanded.

"Kidnap victims are always debriefed. The procedure provides the police with leads to the kidnappers and their techniques."

"The leads don't seem to do the victims much good," Jim retorted acidly.

276

Dr. Lorenzo sighed. "We have discussed that topic, Mr. Lindner. Nevertheless, the law requires a debriefing."

Jim clenched his teeth, making certain the sound could be heard at the other end of the line. "Miss Gregory is in no condition to be questioned, Dr. Lorenzo." When Anne had heard him say "victims," she had gone white. Now she looked at him imploringly. He nodded at her and gripped the telephone tightly. "I'm afraid it really is not possible, Dr. Lorenzo. But we do want to cooperate with the law. Perhaps you can ask the police to let you have the questions in writing and when Miss Gregory has recovered she will answer them." Jim let his voice drop and added meaningfully, "You do have good connections with the police, don't you, Dr. Lorenzo?"

Dr. Lorenzo did not miss the inference. "Yes, Mr. Lindner. I will arrange it and forward the questions to you at the company address in New York. You will guarantee that the police get the most exact and comprehensive answers possible. Is that correct?"

"It is."

"I will accept your word. Failure to keep it would make future operations in Italy difficult for The Copter Company."

"There's no need to threaten me, Dr. Lorenzo. I'm in the habit of keeping my word."

"I will need Miss Gregory's deposition in full. Five copies, each duly notarized."

"You will get them, Dr. Lorenzo."

"Goodbye then, Mr. Lindner. And"—there was reluctant admiration in his voice—"my felicitations."

At the airport and in the queue moving through passport control, Jim kept a sharp eye out for anyone in uniform. He did not quite trust Dr. Lorenzo's professed connections, and the idea of having Anne detained and questioned by Italian police enraged him. His worry proved wasted. No one cared. The man at passport control looked neither at Anne nor at her name on the passport. He leafed through the document until he found an empty page, then carefully placed his exit stamp in the exact center of the page. "Grazie," he said politely.

Their flight was equally uneventful, and they arrived in New York by mid-afternoon. When they got to Manhattan, it seemed strangely empty. Then Jim remembered that it was the weekend preceding the July fourth holiday and people were at the beach, in the country, anywhere except in town. He turned to Anne. "Shall I take you home to Rhode Island? You really should have someone look after you for a while."

She shook her head. "Rhode Island no. Home yes. And I do have someone to look after me."

Jim's stomach suddenly turned to lead. Of course. She had a boyfriend. Probably lived with him. Why hadn't he thought of that? When he found his voice, it sounded husky. "Where are we going then?"

"East Thirty-eighth Street, please, between Park and Lexington."

They pulled up at a drab-looking four-story with a handsome iron railing leading up a flight of stairs. Anne pushed the bell three times: short, long, short. They could hear it ring inside. Footsteps came racing down the stairs. A lock was turned and the door pulled open. They were facing a young man in cotton corduroy trousers and a tattersall shirt, wearing enormous tortoiseshell glasses with thick lenses. He looked shy and friendly.

When he saw Anne, he picked her up and swung her around. "Anne!" He raised his voice and shouted, "Heh! Anne is here. Come on down." He put her back on the floor and turned to Jim. "I'm sorry to have been rude, but we've been awfully worried about her." He held out his hand. "I'm Courtney Hayden."

Jim took the proffered hand. Who the hell is "we"? he wondered. "Jim Lindner," he said. "There was cause for worry. Anne's all right now, but"—he forced the rest of the sentence out of himself—"someone needs to take care of her."

Courtney nodded emphatically. "We will." He turned to look affectionately at Anne, then up at the curved staircase with its polished wooden balustrade, which was resounding with the clatter of footsteps.

A tall, extremely good-looking young man appeared, with starlike blue eyes and deep black hair, dressed in a white shirt

278

and blue linen slacks. Behind him was a girl almost as handsome as the boy, with much the same coloring. She was barefoot and wore a pair of torn jeans and a man's shirt tied above the midriff. "This is Neil," Courtney said, turning to Jim, "and Barbara." But the two racing down the stairs were oblivious to anyone but Anne. Barbara pushed past Neil to reach and hug Anne, then propelled her away to look her up and down. "Christ, we were worried about you. You look awful."

Anne swiveled her head slowly to smile at the girl and the two young men. "I don't feel awful," she said. "Not anymore."

11

The apartment was cool and silent. While the central air conditioning hummed reassuringly, the last orange-red rays of summer sun streamed through the windows, making stained-glass patterns on the white walls of the empty living room. The curtains were half drawn.

Jim put down his travel case and looked at the chaise longue from which he had pictured Brigitte rising with delight on her face as she heard his key turn in the lock. The plump upholstery was undented, and the glare of blue silk hurt his eyes. He closed them and felt a mingling of fatigue, sadness and peace.

He was startled out of his reverie by a small thud from the room that served as a combination guest room and study. When he opened its door, Brigitte was there, lying on the sofa with her feet, elegantly shod in white Amalfi sandals, thrown up on the sofa's arm. An open paperback lay on the floor beside her. She was wearing white jeans and a pale blue silk blouse with very wide sleeves and a large poetic collar. The blouse had no buttons and an enticing sliver of bare skin showed from throat to navel.

Jim contemplated his wife with admiration. It came to him with a shock that the admiration he felt was not for Brigitte herself but for nature, for the random confluence of genes that could produce a Brigitte. Although he was grateful and appreciative, his heart did not race and nothing in him stirred.

"Hello there," he said. "How're you?"

She turned to look at him but made no move to get off the sofa or change her position. The beautiful face was marred by its expression. Of what? As usual, he was not certain, but it laid a film of darkness over her skin and distorted the symmetry of her features.

"Terrible," she said. "If you really want to know, I'm bored out of my skull. This is a ghastly city in the summer, a ghost town. No one's here. There's nothing to do." The exasperation in her voice came close to hysteria. She caught it and made a visible effort to get herself under control. "How was your trip? Successful, I hear. Exciting, I imagine." She sounded envious and eager. "Tell me about it," she begged.

But he could not tell her what he had done or how he had felt.

"It was a hell of a week," he said, "but it worked out all right in the end."

She wanted more than that and moved her legs on the arms of the sofa to make room for him to join her. He did not take the bait and remained at the door.

"Who kidnapped the Gregory girl," she demanded, "and why? She never struck me as a particularly intriguing type. What did they really want?"

He propped himself against the doorpost. "You're right about Anne. She was just a chip in a game. What the kidnappers wanted is a long story. The men who did it were Palestinians."

"Palestinians!" She swung her legs off the sofa and sat up. "I think they're fascinating. And so attractive."

Jim thought of the man in the stocking mask pushing a wooden spoon into Anne's mouth, running his hands over her supine body and finally aiming a submachine gun at her face. He put his hands against the two posts of the door to steady himself. "A matter of taste, I suppose," he said coldly. "Anne Gregory did not find her encounter with them either attractive or fascinating."

Brigitte tossed her head, dismissing the intrusion into her fantasy. "They're marvelous," she pronounced. "Real revolution-

281

aries. Gallant. Brave. They have a cause and they risk their lives for it."

He could not help wondering, as he had so many times before, where Brigitte picked up her peculiar, almost perverse notions. Was it from the paperbacks she devoured that were written to titillate rather than tell the truth? Or did it all come out of her own head? She had brains and imagination but nothing solid to work on, so her ideas festered and every so often blew up. Since they were made of air they just blew into bubbles, but the bubbles were poisonous.

He walked to the desk that could do double duty as a dressing table when they had a woman visitor, and turned around the chair so that he could sit on it and face her. He stretched his legs and permitted himself a small sigh. "Look," he said, "I had to deal with these heroes of yours. I don't want to discuss their politics. I suppose there's room for disagreement on that, although I find it hard to understand anyone who wants to drive three million Jews into the sea. Again." He looked at her levelly. "I thought we all had our fill of that particular enterprise."

She shook her head. "Oh no you don't," she said. "You're not going to make me feel guilty about the Nazis. I had nothing to do with that. And it was very different."

"Not for the people on the receiving end it wasn't, and isn't. I know about that now. Your gallant revolutionaries were hired guns and acted exactly like the murderous goons they are: prepared to kill anyone, anywhere. They were quite ready to blow Anne Gregory's knees to smithereens. She would not have been able to walk for years. They were also ready to shoot her dead. In fact they tried. And Anne, as I—and you—know, has nothing whatsoever to do with any cause of concern to them."

She pouted. "You're just mad because they got your precious Anne. But in the big picture the Anne Gregorys of this world don't matter; they really don't." She ran her right hand through her hair and added defiantly, "You have a very apt phrase"— she paused to smile at him conspiratorially—"that tells it like it is: 'You can't make an omelet without breaking eggs.' "

A wave of disgust washed over him. How did she get that

way? This casual cruelty, where did it come from? He had seen her behave like that once or twice with people she considered her inferiors. He had thought at the time that it was just absent-mindedness, or one of her moody days. He had been wrong. It was a fundamental attitude, a way of looking at life.

"What happens," he said, "when one of the eggs is someone you know? Someone in your care? Someone for whom you are responsible?"

She pulled up her knees and hugged them. "That doesn't change anything. History is history. A cause is a cause."

It occurred to him that she sounded very much like her father when he was deep enough in his cups to talk about the good old days when Germans knew who they were and what they wanted. But Brigitte had always hated those liquor-soaked ruminations in which her papa occasionally indulged. She had hated not only what he said but everything it implied in memories and convictions. He watched her hugging herself. "I don't understand you, Brigitte," he said disconsolately. "You sound like your father."

She pulled her knees closer to her body. "Don't be silly," she retorted vehemently. "I'm talking about the future, not the past. I'm talking about the way the world has to go."

"What way is that, Brigitte?"

She looked at him proudly. "The way we showed in 1968, Jim, in Paris, when we built the barricades."

He remembered then the hint she had thrown out the evening they had driven back from the dinner at Morse Clark's house in Bronxville. He had not quite taken in what she had said at the time, had not really believed it. He had been wrong. It was true and the memory, alive within her, had a meaning he could not understand.

"What happened to those barricades, Brigitte? And to the people who built them?"

Exultation flushed her face. "We served notice on the world, and on the generation that handed us that world."

"Of what?"

She propped her elbows on her knees, fists balled, her chin

thrust out, and almost spat out her reply. "That we would not—will not—live with their hand-me-downs. Not their system, not their values, not their aspirations. They just aren't good enough!"

"And where is it now, that notice you brandished from your barricades?"

Triumph danced in her eyes. "It's there, Jim, never to be forgotten. It has infiltrated the consciousness of the world. Our barricades stopped, once and for all, the smooth progress of the fat ones, individuals or nations. Those barricades put an end to the smugness and security of the bourgeoisie. Forever." Her face glowed.

He leaned back further into the chair and stretched out his legs as far as they would go. "Come off the soapbox, Brigitte," he said. "You don't look good on it, and you make no sense. Answer my question. There were four of you in Paris, right? I know what happened to Armando Guido-Contini and so do you. He does nothing, with a panache of sorts. What happened to the others? Where are Hector de Turenne and Renate Kertner now? How do they *épater les bourgeois* today?"

For a moment she looked contrite. "They do their best," she said defensively. "Hector works for the French Ministry of Planning. He specializes in the Middle East, where the French make a real contribution." She underlined "real," hesitated for a second and could not resist the temptation. "Hector's an under-secretary, the youngest man in the French government with that rank."

Jim crossed his ankles and regarded her neutrally. "Bully for Hector. I'm sure his illustrious relatives are proud. The Middle East is undoubtedly a romantic place in the eyes of the French aristocracy. There aren't many reigning monarchs left who do things in the style of which the de Turennes would approve. I just don't see where the revolutionary fervor finds a place in Hector de Turenne's undoubtedly impressive career." He made no effort to hide his sarcasm.

She uncurled herself and with one foot kicked the paperback across the floor. "You don't understand," she said sulkily. "It's not what he does. It's the esprit, the élan, with which he does it. That infuses everything. It's the only thing that really counts."

"Like the Palestinians," he said. "What counts isn't that they kill. It's the inspiration that matters. Their inspiration."

She stared at him sullenly. "That's right."

He uncrossed his ankles. "I see. And what inspiration propels Renate Kertner these days? To do what?"

She tucked up her knees again, put her elbows on them with the palms open and cupped her face. The blue eyes flashed. "Renate," she said, scoring a point, "is a journalist."

"For whom, Brigitte?"

"Any publication with the intellect and integrity to print what she writes."

"Name three."

The slim fingers that had framed her face once more cramped into fists. "You wouldn't know these journals if I named them. They are the voices of the new consciousness."

"Do these voices pay Renate Kertner enough to eat?"

"What has that to do with anything?"

"She does eat. Well, I gather. Someone has to pay for it. Who does?"

Brigitte lifted her head off her fists and shook it in disbelief. "The questions you ask. I don't know who feeds Renate Kertner and I don't care. More to the point, she doesn't care. The family has money."

He took a deep breath. It really was hopeless. Brigitte simply did not see the connection. She had never learned to be responsible for what she did and she never would. She wanted what she wanted when she wanted it, and that was what her life was all about. For a while, he conceded, what she wanted had been him and he had no complaint. It had been mutual. But it wasn't anymore.

He looked at the distance between his feet and her elegant toes in their white kid sandals, now placed flat on the sofa. The distance was no more than three paces. And a world.

"I see," he said.

She looked at him and shook her head slowly. "No you don't."

He let go of the support offered his back by the edge of

285

the desk and sat up very straight. "That's right, Brigitte," he replied quietly. "I don't. And I don't think I ever will."

She put her forehead on her knees and kept it there for several seconds. When she lifted it, the defiance, the exultation and the sulkiness had all disappeared. Sadness had replaced them. "It's true, Jim. I've come to the same conclusion. You see, darling"— a half smile turned up the corner of her lips but the eyes remained clouded—"while you were gallivanting in Europe, I was here alone. I had time to think things through."

"What things, Brigitte?"

The trace of smile vanished. "Things like myself, Jim. What I was doing, and not doing."

He allowed his body to go slack. "I know what you're not doing, Brigitte. It's a pity. I have long thought so."

Her eyes narrowed. "You're talking about the child."

He put his hands on the back of the chair and let them rest there lightly. "No. I'm not talking about the child. Not anymore. I'm talking about you. You have beauty and you have brains. You're very good at anything you make up your mind to do. You have abilities that you've never explored, never even tried to explore. If you did, there's no telling where you might go."

The laced fingers on her shins opened and began to slide up and down the bare legs. "I don't want to go anywhere, Jim. Not the way you mean it. I don't want to be the perfect corporate spouse like poor Edith Ward. I don't want to command the good ladies of Bronxville like Patricia Morse Clark."

He bent forward, his hands now clasped loosely around the back of the chair. "That's not what I am talking about, Brigitte. I don't need anyone to play those kinds of roles for me and wouldn't want them for you."

"What are you talking about, Jim?" She had stopped caressing her shins and looked up expectantly.

"You. What you could do with yourself."

The half smile returned to her upper lip. "You make it sound like work," she said teasingly.

"What's so wrong with work?"

The blue eyes opened wide and swerved from Jim's face to her exquisitely manicured pale pink toenails. "Nothing," she said, addressing her toes, "for those who like it, but I'm not one of them. I don't want to get anywhere. Nor do I want to do anything with myself, as you put it. I just want to be."

"Be what?"

She looked up from her toes and turned to face him. This time the smile returned and stayed. "Wrong question, darling," she said sweetly. "Not what. Who. And the answer is me. Brigitte von Stolzenfels. For whatever that's worth." Briefly, sadness clouded her eyes once more. "Or not worth."

She let go of her knees and stretched out fully on the sofa with her arms behind her head. Her eyes roamed the ceiling until they seemed to find a spot that held her attention. "And that, I suppose," she said calmly, "is in the eye of the beholder."

He looked at her beautiful face, composed now in self-satisfaction, and let his eyes run over her body, so handsomely proportioned in every aspect, so alluring, so perfect. She was right about the eye of the beholder. But for this beholder it was not enough. Not enough to build a life that made sense, a life that made one sing in the shower in the morning.

The image had brought the beginning of a grin to his face. She had seen it and smiled in return. He got out of his chair, walked to the sofa and held out his hands. "Up you get, beautiful," he said. "We need to talk and settle a few things." She held on to the proffered hands and put her feet on the floor. He pulled and she stood. He had forgotten how tall she was.

She stretched up and brushed her nose against his. "Yes," she said. "But how about a little Inbiss first? I don't think I had lunch. I know I haven't had dinner."

He did not want to eat. When they had brought around the trays on the plane, something about the precooked smell of the food and the segmented plastic of the containers had made his stomach revolt. He had controlled himself because he had wanted Anne to take what nourishment she could. He had succeeded in persuading her to eat her portion of meat and his, and to finish part of his dessert in addition to her own. It had been a delicate maneuver. He had to be careful not to make her think he was forcing her in any way. She would be sensitive about that for some time.

"Okay," he said. "But make it light, will you please? The flight got to me this time."

Still holding on to his hands, she arched her back. Her eyelids fluttered. "Light and bubbly, as befits a celebration."

In the kitchen she handed him napkins, plates and silverware to put on the coffee table in the living room. "I'll bring the rest," she said. "Why don't you take it easy meanwhile. Turn on the hi-fi."

The push of a button delivered a typical Brigitte selection. A rock tape first, which reminded Jim of Basel and gave him a headache. That tape was mercifully short. Next came arias from Wagner operas. He thought of the row they had had so long ago and smiled ruefully. I should've known then, he told himself. The rest was repetition.

When Brigitte came into the living room, Wagner had been succeeded by her choice of oldies and goodies. Edith Piaf warbling huskily about "La Vie en Rose" was followed by Marlene Dietrich voicing sexy regret over a man she had treated badly and lost, when he had, after all, been the best of all her "items." The Dietrich lament was followed by a song of sultry promise to a man called Peter, whose birthday she promised to celebrate by being his guest for the night.

Brigitte stopped to listen, nostalgic and amused. *"Tue ich auch,"* she said when the song had ended.

"What?"

"Be your guest for the night. On your birthday."

She set down the tray she had brought. It held a bowl of caviar, another bowl piled high with sour cream and a third containing hard-boiled eggs and onion, chopped fine. There was also a plate with thin triangles of pumpernickel and a bottle of Taittinger blanc de blanc.

"What exactly are we celebrating?" he inquired.

She picked up the bottle and busied herself with the cork.

288

They had agreed early in their marriage that he would serve hard liquor, but wine would be her domain. She was particularly adroit at handling champagne.

When she had worried the cork loose enough to pop it, she looked up and fluttered her lashes. "Our divorce." She pointed the cork toward a place in the ceiling and let it fly. It made a sharp sound. Like a bullet, he thought, and shivered inside. She handed him a glass and raised her own. "To a lovely, bubbly divorce."

The first sip was cold and dry and set his teeth on edge. But the wine became warmer and more congenial to the system as he got to the bottom of the glass.

He patted the seat on the sofa beside him. She had finished her drink quickly, refilled her glass and drained it. As she sat down next to him, she poured herself a third.

"What would you like to do, darling?" he inquired. "What arrangements would you like me to make?"

She looked into her glass and watched the bubbles burst one by one. "I want to go home, and there is really nothing you need to do. Papa has a neighbor who is a judge. They've known each other for ages. He can take care of the divorce. The laws are civilized now. If the divorce is uncontested and there are no property problems, it can all be done in less than two months."

He looked at her in open admiration. You had to hand it to the girl. She had style, first and last.

"Don't you want anything? Paintings? Carpets? Silver? Furniture? Money?" He stumbled over the litany, then grinned. "Divorcing couples are supposed to fight over such things."

She reached for the bottle and refilled his glass. "I know. That's why we won't. *Èpater les bourgeois!*" She raised her glass and clinked it against his.

He entwined his arm with hers so they could drink in the traditional German way. "Brüderschaft," he said.

"Und Schwesterschaft," she replied. "And on your birthday
" She left the sentence unfinished.

He laughed. "My birthdays are mobile."

Her lips trembled and pushed out. "You wouldn't by any chance have a birthday tonight?"

He nodded solemnly. "It just so happens . . ."

Their lovemaking was languorous and seemed to last most of the night. In the morning his eyes felt grainy and his body limp. He turned to look at her. She was awake and apparently had been watching him for some time. A teardrop had formed on the side of each eye.

After breakfast she disappeared into the guest room. He heard her make telephone calls and repeat instructions to overseas operators in German, French and Italian.

When she returned to the living room, she looked contrite. "I know what I want for a divorce settlement," she said.

He looked at her encouragingly. "Speak, girl."

She shook her head. "I won't have to. The telephone company will. That bill will be the biggest even we've ever had."

While she had been on the telephone, he had skimmed the newspaper. It had made him anxious to get to the office and find out what had happened in his absence. It seemed as if he had been away a very long time.

He rose. "If that's the case," he said lightly, "I'd better go downtown and make some money to pay off Ma Bell."

She looked at him briefly and inclined her head in assent. "That's a good idea."

It was the last thing he heard her say. When he returned to the apartment in the late afternoon she was gone. In the bedroom he found a note fixed to the pillow with a pin. It said, "Auf Wiedersehen." There was no signature. Only the imprint of her mouth in a lipstick of dark rose. The paper smelled of lilies of the valley.

He ran his fingernail along the rosebud outline of the mouth.

Monday and Tuesday were bridge days for the July Fourth holiday and the offices of The Copter Company were closed. Jim was the only one there. On Thursday, though, the place crackled. At nine o'clock sharp everyone was at their desks with only two exceptions: Morse Clark, who, keeping to his principles, did not appear much before ten, and Knight, who had been in the office since shortly after eight. Some of the younger people at the company claimed that Knight spent his evenings supervising the cleaning crew, because he did not believe anything could be done right unless he kept an eye on it.

Also on hand at nine o'clock sharp on Thursday morning was Anne. About nine-fifteen she stuck her head into Jim's office. Mary, who was not generally given to displays of affection, had hugged Anne when she appeared and had not prevented her from walking into Jim's office unannounced. Anne closed the door. "I'm here," she said, the old pixie grin lighting up her face. There was an undertone of defiance in her voice.

"So I see." He regarded her with evident pleasure. She was wearing a tailored suit of lime green linen, with a white shirt open at the neck and cuffs that folded back over the sleeves of the jacket. White pumps and her watch on its chain completed the costume. She looked crisp and subtly lovely. But her jacket hung too loosely, and the lime green of the suit emphasized the pallor of her skin. Jim tried to keep out of his voice the gnawing concern he felt. "The question, Miss Gregory," he said lightly, "is, should you be here?"

She sensed the care he had attempted to hide and remembered then, for the first time, how he had held her when she emerged from the taxi that had sped her away from the horrors of Ostia and how he had carried her up the long flight of steps. She could feel the weakness in her knees and found herself swaying slightly once more. She leaned against the closed door. "I think so, Jim," she said softly.

He nodded. "In that case, let's go see the boss. I'm sure he'll want to take a look at you himself and hear all about it." He looked down at his desk and unnecessarily rearranged two neatly stacked piles of papers. "If you're up to it," he added in a throwaway manner.

291

"I am." Her voice was clear and firm, but he thought he detected a constriction where the vibrancy used to be.

Knight rose when they walked into his office. That was a rare gesture, reserved as a rule for the kind of visitor whose VIP status was certified by a potential or actual price tag that had at least six zeroes. Knight's way of dealing with staff was from behind a cloud of cigar smoke surrounding his leather recliner like a mammoth halo. Among most of The Copter Company's staff, Knight's office was known as Olympus.

Knight walked toward Anne, put his hands on her shoulders and propelled her toward the window. "Let me take a good look at you," he said gruffly. He pushed aside the vertical louvers that covered the expanse of glass in his office during the summer. The harsh sunlight revealed the granite texture of his face and the deep lines of his cheeks and forehead. In contrast, Anne looked young and vulnerable. The auburn glint in her hair, reflected by the window, threw delicate spots of color on her brow, her cheeks and her chin. Knight closed the louvers. "You've got no business being here," he pronounced.

Jim watched Anne struggle for control. "I'm fine, Mr. Knight," she said. "I really am."

Knight strode back to his desk and picked up the telephone. "Grace. Get me Dr. Nelson." He motioned Anne and Jim to take the chairs facing his desk. "I'm sending you to my personal physician for a check-up," he said. "You look peaked."

"I did lose some weight," she conceded. "But—"

He waved her into silence. "But nothing. I want you to take care of yourself. That's the first item on the agenda. The only item, until I am convinced you're okay."

Anne looked crestfallen. There was no way to buck Knight when he had made up his mind. Everyone in the company knew that. Jim thought he saw her tremble. With the best of intentions, Knight was bullying her. It was not what she needed.

"We're ready to report," he said.

Knight looked surprised and, for a moment, disconcerted. Then he picked up his cigar. "Go ahead."

292

Jim's account was terse. He knew Knight did not like detail, except when it involved an engineering problem and the old fascination surfaced. Knight could happily spend hours huddling over a piece of machinery.

Jim's judgment of what Knight did and did not want to know proved accurate. Knight asked no questions about how Anne had been snagged by the terrorists, where they had held her or under what conditions. Jim was not certain whether this was because Knight was not interested or whether he was being protective in his curmudgeony way. Jim carefully arranged to leave some sections of the reporting to Anne. It was like a tennis game, Canadian style. The two of them—Jim and Anne—on a doubles court playing against Knight covering a court for a singles match. Jim took the groundstrokes from base line and encouraged Anne to handle the net. She caught on to the tactic quickly and got in a couple of very effective shots. One of them bounced hard off Dr. Lorenzo. "He has a twisty mind," she said.

" 'Subtle' is the polite word for it," Jim endorsed her comment.

"He knows Italy," Knight came back.

"One kind of Italy," said Anne. "There are others."

Knight moved his glasses down the bridge of his nose and peered at Anne over them. "That's an interesting comment," he said. "Let's talk about it when you are . . ." He stopped to rephrase what he had been about to say. "When the doctor's given you a clean bill of health." He pushed his glasses back into place and picked up his cigar. "And me just a bill." It was as personal a crack as Knight permitted himself in the office. It was also the end of the conversation.

Jim had barely returned to his desk when the phone rang with Knight at the other end of the line. "Come back," he said. "There're a couple of things we still need to talk about."

Knight got to the point without preliminaries. "What's the bottom line on this? How much? To whom?"

Jim sat in the chair, his legs stretched forward, the heels dug into the carpet. "No money."

"How come?" Suspicion edged Knight's voice.

"I mean no cash." Jim tried to convey reassurance.

"It sounds worse by the minute, Jim. Cut out the mystery. What's the deal?"

Jim braced himself. "One copter. D-One. For the Israelis."

"What?" Knight snapped forward. "We can't do that! How the devil did you get us landed with such an arrangement?"

"I didn't have much choice."

Knight sank back into his chair. "I guess that's true." He reached for the octagonal humidor on his desk and carefully chose a new cigar. When he had lit it, Jim said, "Lorenzo's price was a lot steeper and riskier."

"For whom?"

"For Anne. For The Copter Company. For the Italian government."

"Screw the Italian government," Knight said sharply. "They're in bed with the communists anyhow. But why the company? And Anne?"

"Lorenzo's deal might not have come off in time. In fact, I don't think it would have. Not in sufficient time to get her out in one piece. I didn't think we should take a chance on that."

Knight carefully lit his cigar. "No," he said when it had begun to glow. "That wouldn't look good in any way I can think of." He puffed. "But what about the company? Handing over a D-One to the Israelis for free and, I take it, without an export license, is not the kind of transaction I'm happy to report to our stockholders. Or to our board, for that matter. Asherton would hit the roof."

Jim felt the blood rise in his cheeks. "I don't believe we should report the transaction. To anyone."

"Of course not. If word of it goes beyond this room, we're in trouble." Knight swiveled in his chair. "How much did Lorenzo want?"

"He didn't know yet. He was guessing."

"What was the guess worth?"

"Between five and ten."

"What?"

"Million. Dollars. It involved a cabinet minister."

"And those don't come cheap, do they? Anyplace." Knight sounded bitter. "Cash?" he inquired.

"Yes."

"Where?"

"Switzerland."

Knight sighed. "It would have been easier to arrange."

"Yes," Jim said neutrally.

"Larry is pretty good at that kind of thing."

Their eyes met. "I know," said Jim.

"Can you work out a cash deal with the Israelis instead?"

"I don't think so. They know what they want." Jim recalled David's caution: "If the company gives you a hard time, tell them that some fine young men risked their lives. Younger than Anne."

"And need," he added.

"Yup." Knight signified his recognition that this ploy led up a blind alley. "How do we swing it? I see no way of doing it from here."

"How about—"

"Mainz." They said it together. "You'd have to let Feld or Westphal in on it," Knight continued. "But if I read those two guys right, they're big boys who know when to keep their mouths shut."

Jim nodded. "That's right."

Knight put down his cigar and began to tap the top of his desk with his now unencumbered right hand. "That Iranian sale you switched to the Saudis. Maybe we could lose a copter on a test flight, or through some local trouble. They have enough of that down there. We can tell them the pilot got shot at and bailed out, but the copter crashed somewhere in their desert." His eyes suddenly became very bright. "That way, the Saudis could even pick up the bill for it. God knows they've got the money. And we could recoup a small piece of the horrendous commission we pay that guy in Abu Dhabi."

"The commission is figured into the price," Jim blurted.

Knight gave him a searching look. "I know that. Nevertheless, one lost copter represents less than four percent of the money our friend in Abu Dhabi will collect on the shipments from Mainz. He is not exactly going hungry these days."

Jim thought of David, of their session at the fountain at the bottom of the Spanish Steps, during which David had laid his successful plans. He thought too of the harassed look on David's face when he had handed over Anne, and of the screeching of the taxi as it tore off down the morning-silent Roman road.

"No disagreement there," he said.

A silence fell between the two men, each pursuing his own thoughts.

Jim pictured in his mind the talk he would have to have with Max Feld. They would sit in Jim's old office in Mainz, at opposite sides of the desk. Not that Max would give him a hard time. He wouldn't have to. They would both remember only two well their conversation on the subject of morality. Jim would look as hypocritical as Max had accused him of being. Worse than that, he'd look silly, and that was no way to look in a line relationship. He was, after all, still Max's boss; and when you had to supervise someone across the Atlantic, especially someone as smart and agile as Max, respect and trust were ingredients you really couldn't do without. At minimum, it was awkward as hell. At maximum, it could be very damaging to his authority.

"I think," he said deliberately, "I can work it without Feld or Westphal. I'd prefer that." He looked at the tips of his shoes. The heels were still dug in. "Greatly."

Knight's eyes narrowed. "So would I. What d'you have in mind?"

Jim's mind assessed Hugo Kertner, Colonel Elan and David's seemingly casual comment when they had discussed delivery of the copter. "Don't worry about that," David had said. "We'll find a way to collect it." Jim had cause to believe that if David said, "Leave it to me," that was a reasonable thing to do. But did he want to explain this to Knight? Could he? Jim suspected that in his heart of hearts Knight didn't see much difference between the Libyans who ordered the kidnapping, the Palestinians who executed it, and the Israelis who got Anne out. To him they were all one wild bunch whose antics any sensible man could not possibly figure—and if he knew what was good for him did not try.

"I've made some contacts," he said, "who can arrange it. I think."

Knight puffed twice, releasing two large clouds of pearl gray smoke that obscured his face. "Okay," he said from behind the shifting curtain. "It's your baby. Just don't put anything in writing."

Jim did not reply. He had no objection to seeing this affair through, and at this point he really did not have much choice. But was Knight right in passing the buck this way? He was president of the company, its chief executive officer, and responsible for the policies that had led the company into this maze in the first place. Hadn't the time come for him to fish or cut bait?

When the smoke of the two giant puffs had curled up to the ceiling and Knight's face was again clearly visible, Jim saw the lines that ran from the nose downward deepen into clefts. "It's a hell of a way to do business." Knight's voice was filled with resentment. "It used to be simple. Before . . ." His voice trailed off.

"Before what, Russ?"

"Before we got mixed up," Knight said vehemently, "with all those loony, lousy . . ." Once again he paused in mid-sentence.

Jim looked down at his feet. "We can't turn the clock back, Russ. They're customers."

"That's right. Sometimes, a lot of times lately, I wish we could." Knight blew a triple ring of smoke and watched it dissolve. "The customer's always right. That's the law. You break that law and you're dead."

Are you? Jim wondered. Or do you just have to slug a little harder? Come up with a better product, better service, a better price. Beat out the competition with inventiveness or quality and run with that. You can't win them all anyhow. And the ones you lose because you don't want to play that kind of game you may be better off losing. In the long run certainly, maybe the short run as well.

"I'm not so sure," he said.

"Of what?"

"That the customer is always right." He forced a smile. It came and went quickly. "Seems to me that some customers are more right than others. Like Qaddafi, for instance. I know I'd feel a lot better if our D-Ones hadn't wound up in his hangar." Jim looked at his boss. "We all would, I guess."

Knight's fingers, which had clamped hard on his cigar, seemed to relax a little. "That's right, Jim," he said quietly. "We would. But who decides what customer is right? And on what basis?"

Jim shifted his feet. His heels had made noticeable dents in the carpet. He dug them in again. "We do. It's a business judgment like any other. It's what we get paid for."

Knight's fingers tightened and once more clamped on his cigar. "We get paid, Jim, to make decisions that show up on the bottom line. Our shareholders want dividends, not sermons."

There was no mistaking the finality of Knight's judgment. Jim pulled back his legs and rose from his chair. As he turned to go, the phone rang. "Hello, Doc," Knight said. Involuntarily Jim hesitated halfway to the door. He heard Knight explain to Dr. Nelson the case of Anne Gregory. Jim turned with a question in his eyes. Knight nodded brusquely. As Knight listened, the lines on his face deepened until they looked like cuts made by a knife. When he replaced the receiver, his face was the color of the cigar ash.

"Nelson says a physical check-up isn't enough. He'll have to send her to a psychiatrist as well. A shrink, in my daughter's vocabulary. He says an experience like that can leave a trauma for life."

Jim's heart began to race. Yes it could. And whose fault was that? He made an effort to still his anger and think soberly. He did not believe that what had happened to Anne in Ostia would permanently maim her, emotionally or mentally. It would leave a scar perhaps, but not a wound. She was too sound for that, too healthy in mind and spirit.

But Knight did not believe that. In Knight's mind there was a line that ran from his daughter, freaked out in her cold-water flat, straight to Anne Gregory. They were the same age. He felt responsible for both and did not know, did not understand, would never understand, where he had failed, or why. It was eating him inside, corroding him.

"I'll keep tabs on Anne," Jim volunteered. "I think she'll come out all right."

"Do that," Knight said in his customary tone of command. But his eyes had gone blurry, and the ashen hue of his face had settled in like a coat of paint.

12

"I've had a lot of time to think," Anne said, "during that fringe benefit vacation our president wished on me."

Jim and Anne were sitting in directors' chairs in the backyard of the house on Thirty-eighth Street, a handkerchief-sized garden with a wrought-iron railing separating it from its similarly sized neighbors. The main features in the garden were the heart-shaped ivy that curled around the wrought-iron fence, a large elm tree that looked like an enormous green umbrella at this time of the year, and a small stone fountain splashing limpidly in the far corner. It was a muggy July day in the heart of Manhattan, but Jim, sitting under the elm tree in the early evening with Anne beside him, felt comfortable and at ease.

"You have to watch that stuff," he said teasingly. "It's dangerous." She shook her head emphatically, her hair swinging with the motion. "Mm-mm. My mother and uncles tried to lay that one on me. It didn't take."

He looked puzzled. "You lost me, Anne. Who tried to lay what on you that didn't take?"

She waved her hand. Watching it dance through the darkling air made his heart jump. "Oh," she said, "the folks on my mother's side of the family sent messages, overt and covert, that it wasn't really nice or useful for a girl to think. By my dad fed me the antidote, so they didn't do too much damage. Besides, I discovered when I was about four years old that I liked thinking. I mean, I really enjoyed it. It was fun and didn't do anyone else any harm. So I kept doing it, and it got to be a habit."

He looked at her out of the side of his eyes. The pageboy framed her cheek, with a piece of hair still missing where the kidnappers had chopped it off to accompany their message. The missing piece revealed the line of her chin, articulated but gentle. "I wasn't serious about the thinking," he said carefully. "I'm kind of partial to the exercise myself. D'you want to tell me what you were thinking about?" He winked at her. "On Copter Company time."

"I've been wondering . . . ," she said and stopped. Her eyes fixed on the fountain with a look that managed to merge clarity with dreaminess. Something warned him that he would not like to hear her complete the sentence. She did not. "It's a personal quandary," she said. "I haven't quite figured out the answer."

"Can I help?"

She regarded him in an assessing way, but her voice was affectionate. "Thanks, Jim, but no thanks. I have to get out of this one myself."

His mind raced. "Get out of," she had said. Did that mean she was planning to leave the company? New York? He did not like speculating what the answer to either of these questions would be. "If there's anything I can do, just yell," he said. He had reached deliberately for the casual phrase, but his voice was tense and reverberated with the anxiety he felt.

Behind them a door squeaked. They heard the soft tread of sneakers, first on the flagstones, then on the grass. Courtney Hayden appeared, balancing a drink in each hand. "The usual," he said, handing Anne a glass of chilled white wine and Jim a scotch and soda. Jim raised his glass in a thank-you gesture. "Neil wants to know," Courtney responded, "whether you're staying for dinner."

Jim mumbled a perfunctory demurral. He wanted to stay, but Anne's housemates had been hospitable to the point of embarrassment ever since he had returned Anne to their care. He had called at the house a couple of times a week, after work, presumably on his way home. The first time they had been attentive, polite and unabashedly grateful. Anne had evidently told them everything she knew about his role in her rescue. They had offered drinks and dinner, and he had accepted. The evening had been pleasant and interesting for him, and apparently they had felt the same way. Whenever he came to call thereafter, drinks appeared unbidden and the invitation to dinner was proffered as a matter of course. If he had not yet quite become a member of the household, he had certainly become a friend of that congenial if somewhat unorthodox family.

Anne sipped at her glass. "Gee, that's refreshing." She smiled at Courtney. "You make the best Almadén spritzer I know." Her eyes traveled from Courtney to Jim and back to Courtney. "He's staying," she said. "I just twisted his arm." Her head swiveled back to Jim. "I did, didn't I?"

He grinned. "Yes you did. You just didn't hear me say ouch."

The housemates liked having dinner in the kitchen. It was a large old-fashioned room, equipped with a coal stove as well as an electric range; two refrigerators, one of which rattled rhythmically; and a spacious wooden table, its planks scrubbed to a mellow near-white. The kitchen took up half the basement. The other half was a dining room which was furnished formally and used rarely. The dining room door led into the garden. With the door ajar and the kitchen's large window wide open, a pleasant through draft made air conditioning unnecessary.

The four permanent chairs grouped around the kitchen table did not match. Each housemate had provided the kind of seating he or she liked best. Neil's was an old-fashioned kitchen chair with a very high straight back. It came from his parents' cattle farm in Wyoming. Barbara sat in a modern creation of chrome and cream-colored Naugahyde that looked like suede. She had bought a match for Anne. Courtney's choice was a rocking chair with a hard red pillow on the seat and a red bolster tied to the back. For guests who shared the housemates' preference for eating in the kitchen, chairs were hauled in from the dining room. These were cane-bottomed oak, had arms and, their very proper looks notwithstanding, were eminently comfortable. Jim certainly had no complaint.

He had no complaint about the food either. It was as interesting and unconventional as everything else about the house. The two boys did the cooking. They liked doing it, and the girls were articulately appreciative customers. This evening Barbara praised the gazpacho. It was spiced just right, she said, and hailing from Texas she ought to know. Anne clucked over the casserole and, to everyone's evident relief, requested a second helping. Unobtrusively, Jim let his eyes travel over her body. She had filled out since he had brought her back from Rome. The face had more color and the clothes didn't hang loose anymore. They fitted now, indicating lines and curves that moved him and made him want to shelter her. From what? He wasn't sure of the answer to that question and knew better than to ask her for the answer. She would have said she didn't believe in shelters except for the needy, and she wasn't needy.

"What I was thinking," Anne said when they had finished their salad—it had watercress in it and dandelions and a tangy taste of mustard—"is that we have to do something about it."

Neil looked up from the bowl of berries he was ladling into dessert dishes. Conversation at the dinner table in the house on Thirty-eighth Street was erratic, intimate and wide-ranging. Neil's eyes were expectant. Barbara handed her dessert dish to Neil and Anne passed it on. The girl's eyes met. "Do something about what?" Barbara asked.

Anne settled back in her chair and brought its springs into play. The motion made her look wobbly. Instinctively Jim leaned in her direction, his arms ready to hold her. Anne caught the reaction and halted the motion of the springs. "From where I sit," she said with a grin that vanished quickly as her face grew serious, "the time has come for us to clean house. It's imperative and urgent."

Courtney looked distressed. "I cleaned the house last week. Top to bottom. With one of those big vacuum machines the hardware store rents out. You must have heard me."

Anne blew him a kiss. "I don't mean this house," she said, looking around the table. "There isn't much wrong with the way this house lives. I was talking about the country."

Neil laid down his ladle, his starlike eyes fixed on Anne. "That's right," he said. His voice was quiet, but there was in it a passionate intensity that sent a tremor across the table. Jim felt as if he had touched a live current.

Neil turned and reached for the coffeepot on the stove. As he poured, his tapered fingers shook. He tightened them around the pot's handle. "That's what our fight in the sixties was all about." He pushed a filled cup in Jim's direction. "I was in the SDS." He added the explanation in the same tone he used a second later when he asked Courtney to pass the cream. Then his voice started to shake again with an inner reverberation. "The fight wasn't really about Vietnam, although I still think we had no business there; you can't fight other people's civil wars for them. It wasn't even about what happened at Kent State, although that comes a lot closer. It was about being lied to by people we had been brought up to trust. About being manipulated, pushed around, when what we'd been taught to expect—had every right to expect—was that we would be treated like adults, or at least potential adults, in a democratic society."

"Meaning?" demanded Barbara.

"Meaning," said Neil, "individuals who are both free and responsible." He had paid no attention to what he was doing but had automatically continued to pour. When he had finished speaking, four cups of coffee surrounded the pot in front of him.

Courtney reached for one of the cups. A look of unabashed affection suffused his face. "I know what you mean," he said. "I run into it, in my own small way, at the library."

Barbara nudged Anne to pass her coffee. "How?"

Courtney exuded concern. "Kids borrow books and don't return them. They produce excuses that are imaginative but untrue. They keep a book because they want it and maybe can't afford to buy it. It shows they love the book, and that's what the library's all about. But I can't let them keep it, all the same. If I did, we wouldn't have a library after a while."

Neil turned to Courtney, added two spoons of sugar to his coffee and stirred. "It's a difficult balance," he said. "Freedom and responsibility. You have to keep fine-tuning it all the time."

"Correct," Anne concurred. There was a tautness in her voice that made Jim's heart skip. He looked at her, but she was unaware of his attention. The green eyes swept away from everyone at the table. "The balance has to be struck in our lives and in our institutions, within them and among them." She sounded remote, as if she were talking to someone far away from this circle of friends around the kitchen table.

Jim felt an overwhelming desire to bring her back from the distant place to which her thoughts had strayed. An ache in his chest made him realize he did not want to lose her—physically, emotionally or intellectually.

"That's a tall order," he said.

"They told me to stand tall when I was two years old," Neil said hotly.

Barbara grinned. "Or at least ride tall."

Anne did not seem to have heard either comment. When her eyes left the spot in space on which they had fastened, they concentrated on Courtney. "What do you tell a child who wants to keep a book it can't afford to buy?" she asked.

Courtney brought his rocking chair forward and leaned across the table toward Anne. "It's a terrible problem. It breaks my heart every time I have to do it. But I do it." His mouth set. "I tell them that when they take a book and don't return it, they take away a piece of the library. It's a small piece, but the pieces add up, and when you get enough people hauling away little pieces the building comes down."

Anne sat back in her chair and closed her eyes. "That's right," she said. "Letting people get away with it often looks tempting, but it always turns out to be dangerous in the end."

"Yup." Barbara's head bobbed. "I see it at the bank. Someone starts messing around . . ." She sniffed. "They do, you know, and sooner or later everybody's in the soup." She held out a hand in Neil's direction. "I don't mean your gazpacho, baby. I mean . . ." She stopped and waved her hand. "Banker's discretion. I can't tell you any more. But it sure is dumb." She shook her head.

Jim had only half heard Barbara. His eyes were riveted on

Anne. It always turns out to be dangerous in the end, she had said.

"Let me play devil's advocate." He could hear the harshness in his voice. Anne looked at him, and he plunged. "There really is such a thing as competition. If we don't do what is needed to seize an opportunity, to run with the ball, someone else will. With fewer scruples and more success."

Four pairs of eyes seemed to be pinning Jim to his chair. Neil had turned very pale. "Some people kill to get what they want," he said tonelessly. "Would you?"

Jim felt the blood drain from his face. "That's a hell of a question," he retorted angrily.

Neil refused to back down. "Then where do you draw the line?" he demanded.

Where did Jim draw the line? It was a fair question. The answer was that the line had become blurred. By what? Pressure? Yes, some of that, but a good manager didn't crumble under pressure. Ambition? Some of that too. Ambition to get where, exactly? Be what? A success like Cathy Quon, who had to be counted a true success in the terms of her world? Like Russel Knight, who had achieved everything he had set out to achieve and had wound up with a life that was coming apart at the seams? Opportunity then. The kick of the challenge, the stimulus of the possible. Dealing with the Max Felds and Taher Rezvanis of this world, men with dreams of their own, and who was he to gainsay them.

"You want a simple answer, don't you?" he said. "But the truth is that the answer is not simple. The world we live in really is small and interdependent. Other people have other values. Should we—in fact, can we—insist that they're wrong and we're right?" His eyes went around the table, hung for a moment on Anne's face, then swept on to lock with Neil's. "Where do you draw the line on that?"

Neil placed his hands on the arms of his chair and sat up very straight. "Where I have standing," he said. "That's what we call it in law. What it amounts to is where I've earned the right to make a stand for what I believe."

306

"Earned how?"

"In personal terms, by accomplishment; in community terms, by my contribution to society."

"And in moral terms?" The query came at Neil like an arrow. From Anne.

Neil pressed his back into his chair. "That's the hardest part. The only answer I know is that you've earned your moral standing if you can live with its results when you wake up at four o'clock in the morning in silence and solitude. If you're at peace with yourself then, you're on the right track. If not . . ." He shrugged.

The faraway look invaded Anne's face again. There was pain in it, and doubt. It made Jim feel desperate.

"I know," he said urgently, "you're talking about the encounter with oneself. It takes courage."

He succeeded in his effort to bring Anne back from the place to which her mind had wandered. She had heard his comment and turned to look at him. "I've been thinking," she said, "that there are two kinds of courage—the courage to act and the courage to be. The first kind tells you what to do, and you know all about that." The green eyes, radiant now, pulled at him like magnets. "The second kind," she pressed on, "tells you why. For the lone encounter at four o'clock in the morning you need both."

The housemates had fallen silent. They were attentive to Anne and Jim and to the vibrations that flowed between them.

"Yes," Jim said. It came out almost a shout. He felt his pulse pound in his throat. Yes, it pounded. Yes. Yes. Yes.

13

"Come with me. I want to show you something." Jim held out his hand to Anne. She took it and followed him as he headed for the bedroom. He switched on the light, let go of her hand and bent to rummage in the bottom drawer of his dresser. He found what he was looking for under a stack of evening shirts.

When he straightened up, he had in his hands a loose-leaf exercise book with a marbled cover. He regarded it for a moment, his face remote and drawn. Then he walked to the bed, stacked two pillows against the headboard and laid down the notebook alongside the pillows. He picked Anne up, swung her through the air and deposited her on the bed. "I want you to be comfortable," he said, "while you read this." He pointed to the notebook. "You'll need the solace, and I need . . ." He wanted to say "you." That was the truth. "Your reaction, your advice."

She reached for the book eagerly. "What is it?"

His eyes darkened. "You'll see. I'll leave you to it."

He pulled the door closed behind him but did not shut it. The sliver of light from the reading lamp over the bed pointed in the direction of the living room. He followed the arrow and walked to the window. The curtains were open and skyscrapers glittered beyond. I love this town, he thought, and this girl. I just have to find a way . . .

They for dinner earlier in the evening, and this time he had picked his favorite restaurant, the Coach House on Waverly Place. He liked its intimacy, its fine unpretentious service, its excellent home-style American food. He had taken Brigitte there once, but that had been a mistake. Brigitte had pronounced the place tolerable but uninteresting, and something about her had made her look exotic in this setting. Heads had turned when they walked it and had kept turning. When Jim arrived at the Coach House with Anne, no one paid any attention. Seated at their table, Anne looked and felt at home.

Over coffee he said, "I wanted to take you out not only because it's my turn many times over. I like your folk on Thirty-eighth Street a lot, but I want to talk to you about something that really isn't their business." She looked at him. She was wearing no lipstick, and he wanted to hold her and taste her lips. Instead he said, "It concerns the company . . . and Ken."

Her soft mouth did not change, but her eyes dimmed. "What about Ken? Has anyone come up with the answer?"

He put his hand on hers. The touch sent a glow through his body. "No. But I have some questions."

She did not move her hand, and he could feel it tremble. He tightened his hold. "I want you to tell me everything you know about what happened when the news of the Libyan mess first reached the company."

Her fingers cramped. "I'm not a tattletale," she said hotly.

He bent to kiss her. She did not flinch. "I have a reason for asking. A good reason."

"Tell me."

"I want to do something about it."

"There's nothing anyone can do about Ken; not anymore." Bitterness distorted her voice. The mouth turned down in a curve of despair. He had never seen such an expression on her face or heard her speak in that tone, not even when she had told him about her days and nights in Ostia. Seeing her so, and hearing her, sent through him a shock of compassion and regret.

Her hand under his had gone dry. He picked it up, brought it to his lips, then gently placed it on the table. "If you'd rather not talk about it," he said.

She looked down at her hand, at the spot where he had kissed it, and back at him. The curves at the edges of her mouth were gone. When she spoke, her voice was low but even. "I would rather not talk about it, but I think we should."

The compassion he had felt changed to understanding, the regret to hope. It was good to have her with him in this enterprise, even if he was not yet sure what the enterprise would entail. "You're right about Ken," he said. "Nothing can be done about that anymore. But something can be done about the company. And I suspect there is a connection."

She heard the news of what happened to the Libyan copters within ten minutes after she reached the office. The telex containing the information was addressed to Ken, but Anne had laid down a network of sources on matters of concern to her, both outside and inside the company, that functioned dependably and quickly.

The moment she had absorbed the content of the message and considered its implications, she picked up the phone to call Ken, but he was already in conference with Knight and Morse Clark. She left word for him to get in touch with her as soon as convenient.

He called just before noon. "Let's have lunch," he said. "Upstairs. I need a drink fast. In fact, I need three."

The elevator that sped them to the 107th floor was large—Anne thought of it as a subway car moving vertically instead of horizontally—but it was also crowded, and they did not speak. The shiny aluminum doors sprang open with a breathless swish. The redheaded lady maitre d', in her tight-fitting tuxedo trousers and short white jacket, waved at them. Windows on the World, a fabulous restaurant at night, functioned during the day as a club for the executives who had offices in the building. The redhead knew them all, most of them by their first names. She crooked a finger, beckoning to Ken and Anne.

310

When they were within earshot of her, Ken said, "I need the quietest table in the house." The redhead gave Anne an appraising look. "Can do, Mr. Ward," she said and led them to a table in a corner on the upper platform of the restaurant.

Ken sat with his back to the window, and Anne concentrated on Ken. Ken, always clean-shaven and trim, managed that noon to look stubbly and rumpled. Tiny red veins swelled and pulsed in the whites of his eyes.

"You've heard, of course," he said.

Working together closely and well, they had developed a verbal shorthand.

"Yes."

"You've figured out what it means."

"Some."

"The SEC already called. Also the IRS."

"Justice?"

"Not yet, but they will."

"What did Knight say?"

"In short, that it's my baby." He turned, his bloodshot eyes searching for a waiter. The redhead saw the motion and sensed its urgency. She sashayed to the table. "I'll take your order, Mr. Ward," she offered.

"You're a great kid and there are few of us left." He remembered the required joshing. He was a disciplined man. "I want a double bourbon now. No water. Another in ten minutes. Please."

The redhead clicked her tongue. "That kind of a day," she said.

Ken nodded twice. The gray bristles of his crew cut lit up flame-red under the midday sun. "Yup, Rosemary," he said, "that kind of a day." He turned back to Anne.

"And Morse Clark?" she inquired.

"Ditto. With delight."

She reached for a glass of water and sipped. "That figures."

"Correct."

"Where do we go from here?"

He eyed her warily. "Not we, girl. I."

The bourbon arrived. He gulped it down in two large swal-

311

lows. "Hell," he said, "another ten minutes for the next." He signaled the waiter, who had not yet moved out of sight. "Repeat, please."

When he had demolished the second double bourbon, he leaned forward and put his hands on the table. They were broad hands, competent and workmanlike. The fingernails were clean and trimmed straight across, but the palms had never lost their calluses and the occasional cut or stain that came from hunching over a workbench and handling tools. "I want to go over the options."

She eyed the dependable hands and the bloodshot eyes. Sympathy welled up in her. "I'm not sure we have very many. I think we have to level with the SEC, file an Eight-K, tell the truth about where we paid off and how much. And, of course, clean up our act." She looked straight at him. His eyes, filmed over now, looked more serene. "I know this isn't the best time for what I'm about to say," she added, "but I'll say it anyhow. I've thought for some time that our act needs cleaning up."

For a moment he stared at her, a flush rising in his cheeks. It revealed a network of veins as intricate and highly colored as the red lines that had earlier bulged in his eyes. But his hands did not move and his voice remained steady. "That makes two of us," he said.

She looked at him hopefully. "In that case—"

"No," he interrupted. "Russ wants me to stonewall, admit nothing to anybody."

Her eyes narrowed, and her face went white. "How can we? Now?"

"Russ and Larry think we can. And should."

"But . . ."

"That's right, Anne." He turned, caught the eye of the redhead and held up two fingers. Within a minute, the waiter brought another double bourbon. This time Ken did not gulp it. He looked into its amber depth, then slowly and methodically took three swallows and stopped. "The marching orders are that if I don't stonewall, or can't, I take personal responsibility. Alone."

She stared at him, horrified. "That could mean a fine of a million dollars and five years in jail."

Ken concentrated on the depth of his bourbon and seemed to find assurance in the earth-colored tumbler. "They'd come up with the money," he said, addressing the glass. "I don't have that kind of dough anyhow. Going to jail would be my contribution." He looked up and added grimly, "I can retire when I get out at full pension."

Anne's face sagged. "I don't think you should do that," she whispered.

Ken's eyes wandered to the bourbon. "I don't either. It would kill Edith. She'd be so mortified, she couldn't look anyone in the eye. I don't know what it would do to Lisa and Stephen, but it would certainly throw a monkey wrench into their lives."

Anne grasped the table. She could feel her palms stick to the cloth. "Why don't you tell the truth?" she said.

"To whom?"

"The SEC, the Justice Department, whoever needs to know. Against immunity from prosecution. They'll make a deal. They're not interested in getting you. They want the information."

Once again his eyes strayed to the bottom of the glass, where a thumb's thickness of liquid still undulated calmly. "That's true," he said, his voice husky. He moved the glass off the napkin on which the waiter had placed it and took two felt-tipped pens from the breast pocket of his jacket. They were the kind of markers engineers use to draw blueprints, one blue, one red. With the red one, he sketched a neat triangle on the napkin, the three sides perfectly even. Then he picked up the blue marker and slowly, with deliberate calibration, drew three perpendicular lines. They were of varying length, but none touched the triangle's side or apex.

"My life," he said, indicating the triangle, "and my options." His square-tipped index finger ran along each one of the blue lines as he explained. "I go to the SEC," he said, touching the first line. "That doesn't connect with what my life is all about. If I learned one thing from the man who taught me engineering, it's 'If it ain't broke, don't fix it.' The Copter Company isn't broke. It doesn't need fixing—by me, or the SEC."

The middle line was the longest but stopped short of touching the top of the triangle. "That's what Russ wants me to do. Doesn't

313

quite connect either. Comes close, but . . ." He shook his head. The finger moved to the last line, which was shorter than the first. "That one," he said, "is the Justice Department. Can you see me go that way?" He looked up.

She did not reply. They both knew the answer was no.

It was the last time Anne had seen Ken or spoken to him. He had returned to his office after lunch, gone home as usual and worked the next day. She had come in the following morning to hear that he had been found dead at this desk.

When Anne had finished giving Jim her account of that final, fatal encounter, she had looked as weary and wan as she had when she sat in the chair in his hotel room in Rome. He had taken her face into his hands. "I'm sorry," he had said. "Let's go home."

She had not demurred when he gave the driver the address of his apartment. In the taxi he had put his arm around her and she had lain against him quietly. Neither one had spoken until they were in the apartment and he had led her to the bedroom and given her the diary.

He moved away from the window and toward the bedroom. He thought he heard a sob and quickened his pace.

She was lying on the bed, curled up like an infant and crying bitterly. Her hands still gripped the notebook, and as the sobs shook her she clutched at it. He lowered himself on the bed beside her, kissed her closed tear-sodden eyes and stroked her tangled hair. "Anne," he said urgently. "Anne. My love. Look at me." The mascara had smudged and made small blotches on her cheeks. He licked them clean with his tongue. Her body straightened, and she opened her eyes. She let go of the diary, and her arms reached out.

At last, he thought. Anne. Love. My love.

In the morning when they sat down to breakfast, he looked at her speculatively. She was wearing the top of his pajamas, the same pair he had had with him in Rome. She looked loved and

314

lovely. "It's a very sensible arrangement," he said.

She blinked. He had not managed to dispose of all the mascara. A small smudge remained under one eye, like a beauty spot, and set off the alabaster of her skin and the sea green of her eyes. He leaned over and circled the smudge with his tongue.

"You mean this?" She gestured vaguely about the room. "I don't think it's sensible, but it is very nice."

He sat back in his chair. "No," he said. "It is very nice, but it's not what I was talking about. I meant the division of the pajamas: upper half for you, lower half for me. Full utilization of available resources. First-rate management." He felt his chest expand. "It doesn't even have to be the same pair all the time. I'm rich. I have six pair. You can have half of each one."

Her nose twitched with amusement and pleasure. He had not seen that happen since the first evening they had dined together, in the booth of that converted parish house where he had watched her lap up her Irish coffee.

"Your nose is twitching," he said. "That means either that we're about to get some interesting news or that you need a handkerchief."

"The former," she said.

"Oh." He leaned forward and kissed the tip of her nose. It stopped twitching and her mouth came up to meet his. He took a deep breath and held it. It seemed to fill his lungs with love. After he had let out his breath, he asked, "What makes you so sure?"

She crossed her bare legs under the table. "I have the news."

"That doesn't count."

"Oh yes it does. I just made the news."

"Let's have it then."

She put her elbows on the table, concentrated on turning back the cuffs of the pajamas so that she could pick up her cup without the edge of the sleeve dipping into the saucer. "I'm leaving The Copter Company."

The glow that had suffused his chest dimmed. She saw the change and added quickly, "Only during the day."

Happiness surged through him. He reached for both her

315

hands, turned them palms up and placed a long kiss in each hollow. "In that case," he said, "you have my permission. Reluctantly."

"Thank you, Mr. Vice-President."

He tightened his clasp. Her fingers felt cool and light. "And where will you be spending your days?"

"In politics."

"Come again."

She took her hands away from him and turned up the pajama sleeves two more folds on each arm. "I've decided to go into politics. I think it's where I can do most effectively what I want to do."

"Which is?"

Her answering smile was thoughtful and radiant at the same time. How does she do that? he wondered. It made him feel wonderful.

"Clean house," she said.

The conversation at the kitchen table on Thirty-eighth Street leaped back into his mind. He looked at her approvingly. "Good."

This time she bent forward to kiss him. He reached inside the pajama jacket, felt her fragile collarbone and let his fingers play on it. Harmony seemed to flow from the collarbone, through his fingers, to his mind.

When she had moved away, he asked, "How're you going to do it?"

Unconsciously, her hand went to her hair, searching for the swatch that was still missing. "I talked to Dad after we got back from Rome. He and I have always been very close. He'd never say so, of course, but in his heart of hearts I guess he always hoped that I would join him and go into politics too."

Jim felt a stab of anxiety. It came and went quickly. "You're not moving to Rhode Island?"

She heard the worry in his voice. "No, I'm not. I'm going to run for office from Brooklyn Heights. It'll take a while, of course. I'll have to establish residency, get connected with local organizations, build a constituency. But I like the district. It's interesting from many points of view, one being that it just happens to have a Copter Company plant."

316

He whistled. "I see."

She looked at him expectantly. "I hope so."

Her eyes made his head swim. "Let's go back to bed," he said. "I think better horizontally."

In bed she turned on her side to face him. The expectant look had turned into a searching one. He realized that her declaration of hope had really been a question. She wanted an answer, and she wanted it now. He rolled on his back and closed his eyes. "I can't go to the Justice Department either," he said. "Or to the SEC. What I thought I might do," he continued tentatively, "is to set up an appointment with Claude Asherton. Tell him everything I know, firsthand and secondhand, and see what he'll do about it."

"Our chairman doesn't strike me as the kind of person who goes looking for trouble. Not this kind of trouble, anyhow. He's Main Line Philadelphia, isn't he? He'll worry about his reputation if anything unsavory about the company becomes public."

"My plan is not to give him much choice."

"How're you going to do that?" He could hear the excitement in her voice and did not dare look at her face. Doing so would blow Claude Asherton clear out of his mind.

"I'll take along Ken's diary."

He heard her draw in her breath. "Yes," she said, "that should do it."

He felt her hand on his chest caressing him, moving from the chest down. A moment later her mouth was on his, and he forgot all about Ken Ward, Claude Asherton and The Copter Company.

"I'm hungry," she said afterward.

"*You* are hungry!" He sounded aggrieved. "I'm ravenous. We never did eat any breakfast. After I fixed it too!" He sat up and looked down on her face. Love shone out of her eyes. "We could have lunch," she said. "We can both fix it—and eat it."

They made sandwiches and poured two glasses of milk. She found plums and peaches in the refrigerator and piled them into a bowl. They put everything on a tray and took the tray back to

317

bed. With pillows stuffed behind their backs and the tray between them, they had lunch.

"You know," he said when the plates, glasses and bowl were empty, "there's a downside risk to Operation Asherton."

She dabbed at her mouth with a corner of the pillow and ran her tongue over her lips to remove the last trace of crumbs. Like a kitten, he thought, and wanted to stroke her.

"You mean he'll do nothing and we're back to square one."

He let his shoulders sink more deeply into the pillow. "Yes. And fire me first. If I say anything to anyone after that, I'm just a disgruntled ex-employee trying to get his own back."

She nodded assent. "If you went to the SEC at that point, or to Justice, you wouldn't have much credibility."

"I would have Ken's diary."

"If Asherton didn't destroy it."

"That would be tampering with evidence. He's a lawyer. He wouldn't do that."

She shook her head. "I wouldn't count on it. He may be a lawyer by training, but what makes him go is power. I've only met him a couple of times. Not really met him either; he doesn't condescend to small cogs. But for reasons of his own, Knight introduced me to the chairman shortly after I became head of strategic planning. Maybe Knight had to convince him that I didn't have horns, or wasn't Farrah Fawcett-Majors in disguise. Anyhow, he bestowed on me the benign dynamism of the chairman of the board. He stank of power. Of addiction to power. I have a nose for it. Dad trained me."

He looked at her in surprise. She was probably dead right. He would have to watch over the diary, and that would not be easy. Asherton was not only addicted to power, he knew how to wield it as well. "If Asherton decides to play hard ball," he said, "I could be unemployed very quickly."

She shook her head. The pageboy swung. "Quickly maybe, but not for very long. Not you." The beginning of a grin pulled at her mouth. "If you're unencumbered by more remunerative employment, you can always help me campaign. I could use a competent campaign manager. You'd be just dandy."

318

He pressed his hands together and inclined his head in a New Delhi salute. "Thank you, the Honorable Miss Gregory. It's the best offer I've had all day. Coming to think of it, though, that isn't true. I had a better offer right after not eating breakfast." He put his hand under the sheet, found the inside of her thigh and ran his palm down the soft, cool, slightly moist incline. Like snow, he marveled, fresh snow on the farm at home.

The curve of the knee stopped him. He could feel the bone of the cap. His stomach tightened. That had been a close call. He did not want another. Not if there was anything he could do about it. And he could. At least he could sure as hell try.

"I'll call Asherton's office tomorrow," he said.

When Jim telephoned Philadelphia the following Monday, a mellifluous male voice informed him that Mr. Asherton was not available. The chairman was away in Scotland for a couple of weeks of fishing and golf, staying with Lord and Lady McAllister. He could, of course, be reached in an emergency.

"No," Jim said to the male voice that had identified itself as Mr. Asherton's secretary. "This is not an emergency, but it is important. When do you expect Mr. Asherton back?"

"The week after Labor Day."

"I would like to see him then, as soon as possible."

"Just a moment, Mr. Lindner. I'll look at his engagement book." The voice was not only mellifluent. There was artifice in it, as though its owner had deliberately modeled his voice after someone else's. To convey what? Class? Style? Distinction? Before Jim could decide, the secretary was back on the line. "I see Mr. Asherton is free on Tuesday, the eleventh, at ten o'clock. For half an hour. May I tell him what you want to see him about?"

The pseudo politesse of the phrase irritated Jim. "The Copter Company," he said curtly.

"Any particular, uh, aspect?" The secretary had hesitated to reach for what he considered the proper word. "Mr. Asherton will want to know the topic of the interview."

Jim felt his gorge rise. "A criminal matter."

On the night of September tenth, Anne stayed with Jim. Knight had allowed her to come back to work in the middle of August, and she had given notice the day of her return.

She was still working with her successor, a man in his middle forties, settled and experienced, who was polite to Anne but not overly attentive to what she had to say. He would handle things his own way when she was gone.

The changing of the guard at strategic planning was awkward for Jim. Anne was at the office every day, which was nice, but Jim's business dealings had to be with the new man. It took handling.

Their evenings also still operated on a split level. They met after work and had dinner together. But at night Anne went home to the house on Thirty-eighth Street.

The night of September tenth was different. They slept in each other's arms, and in the morning she made breakfast and insisted that he eat it. "Sustenance. You'll need it today." She watched him dig into the eggs and bacon she had cooked.

The toaster popped and she forked out two English muffins, buttered them and put them on his plate. "My problem is," she said, "that I don't know whether to tell you to keep your head up or down. Asherton's a dangerous man, in his supersmooth way. If you give him reason to think that he can trample on you, he will."

He moved one of the buttered muffins to her plate. "You eat too. I don't want to marry a wraith."

Her eyes grew wide and she swallowed. He watched her Adam's apple skip, then settle. "It may not always show," he said, "but I'm a big boy myself. It takes two to tango—or trample."

14

The eight o'clock train to Philadelphia was half empty, and the passengers on it looked either sleepy or disgruntled. The car smelled of spilled coffee, flat soft drinks and stale cigarettes. The roadbed was bumpy, and the train jerked. The ride was not designed to calm a turbulent mind or to settle a slightly queasy stomach.

It was odd about Claude Asherton, Jim mused as the train slogged from the concentrated ugliness of Newark to the messy sprawl of Trenton. C. R. Asherton, Esquire, had, in the Lindner family, been the very model of a Main Line gentleman. An old family, the Ashertons, Jim had heard his dad expound, wealthy and public-spirited, social only in the most restrained and responsible sense of the word. Claude Asherton himself was not a fritterer of the family's assets, not frivolous in any of his pursuits. He was successful in his own right and had arranged his affairs so he could add to his highly reputable practice as the city's top corporate lawyer, service as a director on the board of a number of companies and carefully chosen public enterprises: the Board of Education, the Fine Arts Museum, a hospital noted for its research.

Claude Asherton had accepted the chairmanship of only one corporation, The Copter Company. No one quite knew why. He could have had others. It was known, however, that Asherton and Knight had met during the war when Asherton was at the

Pentagon and Knight a colonel in the Engineers. The two men could scarcely have been more different in appearance, outlook and background, but something clicked between them. Launching The Copter Company after the war had been Asherton's idea, and in his judgment Russel Knight was the man to run with the concept and make it work. That had proven to be a sound and profitable judgment.

Jim was not certain whether his father's admiration for Claude Asherton had not settled subliminally in his own mind, so that when he saw The Copter Company advertisement after he got out of MIT something came together in his unconscious. Certainly Dad had been more than pleased when Jim had called to tell him he was going to work for The Copter Company. To J. H. Lindner, Sr., this meant that his son would be working for Claude Asherton, and a man couldn't do better than that.

The offices of Asherton, Philips and Gersten took up the top two floors of a venerable office building in the section of downtown Philadelphia that had once been the heart of the city's wealth and power. It was still an address of repute, and the building was beautifully maintained and carefully serviced. Claude Asherton himself saw to that.

Asherton's firm had more than fifty partners, but only the most senior had suites in the penthouse, to which access was provided by a private elevator. Visitors had to be announced and personally escorted by a receptionist with lacquered blue-gray hair who looked as if she had stepped out of the pages of an old copy of the *Saturday Evening Post*.

The penthouse itself was a mixture of sumptuousness and solidity. It had old furnishings in mint condition, desks that were either English or French eighteenth-century antiques. Walnut parquet floors gleamed against deep-toned carpets from Persia, and small etchings of hunting scenes or of barristers in powdered wigs decorated the walls. Three large oil portraits of the firm's founders, framed in gold, looked down on the visitor as he stepped out of the elevator.

Asherton's secretary opened the heavy oak doors to the senior

322

partner's domain. The secretary's own office was sizable and car- peted. He turned out to be a spare, brittle man in his fifties, with a pink complexion and a prim look about the mouth. He wore a dark blue suit, a white shirt and a discreetly figured narrow tie. His black shoes had a high shine.

The secretary looked at the large clock on an ormolu stand that commanded his desk. The clock showed ten o'clock. "Mr. Asherton will see you now," he said.

Asherton's suite consisted of two rooms, with a connecting door that was ajar when Jim entered. The room in which Jim found himself made a gesture at being an office. It had a desk, a Louis XIV beauty, without a single piece of paper on it. Behind it was a row of walnut cabinets that might or might not have held files. The view through the door was of a gentleman's study: easy chairs, small tables, bookshelves on four sides and, in one corner, a library ladder with broad steps and brass railings. Jim caught a glimpse of a crystal decanter and matching glasses on a mantelpiece of dark green marble.

Asherton did not usher Jim into this inner sanctum. He sat immobile behind his desk, his eyes strafing Jim. "I'm seeing you," he said without preliminaries of any kind, "because you're a direc- tor of The Copter Company. I received your inexcusable message. I consider it both indiscreet and maladroit. Get to the point."

Asherton had not asked Jim to sit down. Deliberately, Jim looked around among the available chairs, slanted two of them together so that they faced Asherton at an angle and sat in one while putting his briefcase on the other.

Asherton watched the proceedings without a sign of reaction. His hands were still. There were daggers in his ice blue eyes.

Jim made certain his voice gave away nothing. "The point," he said, "is that the message I left is accurate. The Copter Com- pany has procedures which, I am convinced, must be reported to the SEC. In addition, the company has made moves that are actionable under the Foreign Corrupt Practices Act; criminally actionable." The chair Jim had chosen for himself had tall arms. He rested his elbows on them and let his hands hang loose at the end.

Asherton opened the top right-hand drawer of his desk and came up with a pince-nez. He had moved only one hand to reach for the eyepiece. The hand was heavy and pinkish white, with white hair just below and above the knuckles. Incongruously, the hair looked silken.

He clamped the pince-nez low on his nose. It was a small nose for a large man, but not out of proportion to his face, which tended to fleshiness and floridity. His features were symmetrical, and enough of the bone structure showed to indicate that Claude Asherton must once have been a handsome man. He was still unquestionably impressive. Now his eyes pierced through his lenses. "Example," he demanded.

Jim willed himself not to change his position. "Payoffs," he said, "to senior government officials in Thailand and Kuwait; to generals in Indonesia; to members of the ruling families in Abu Dhabi, Sharjah and Saudi Arabia. These are some examples from a long list."

Asherton's eyes had not moved from Jim's face. Jim saw them blink once when he cited the generals in Indonesia. Asherton had held a general's rank during the war.

Jim tightened his stomach muscles taking care the pull did not show in his posture or alter the tone of his voice. "The amounts involved are substantial. In the aggregate, they are large enough to leave us open to SEC action and class suits from stockholders, as well as to prosecution by the Justice Department under the Foreign Corrupt Practices Act."

Asherton's response was swift. "I know the law, Mr. Lindner," he said contemptuously. "I need no lectures on it from upstarts who consider themselves experts." He took the pince-nez off his nose and laid it on the desk. He had seen all he wanted to see of Jim Lindner. "The question," he said, his voice now as icy as his eyes, "is how do you know this? Did you make the payments?"

The instinct that had prompted Jim to tighten his stomach muscle proved to have been sound. Asherton was going for Jim's gut. "No," he said. But I came close, he admitted silently. He clamped his teeth against each other, hard but without a sound. Only a muscle in his jaw indicated what he had done.

Asherton had a sixth sense for the vulnerability of anyone who entered his orbit. He had perhaps been born with that sense. Certainly he had observed its effects and rewards in both of his parents and had cultivated it carefully throughout his life. It had been a useful tool over the decades.

"If you did not make these alleged payments yourself"—Asherton let his voice resonate to underline the "if" and allowed an ominous pause to separate the word from the remainder of the sentence—"you're dealing in hearsay." Something about the way he threw out the phrase "dealing in" made it sound cheap and suspect. "Or gossip." The voice had in it a tone of dismissal. "Highly irresponsible behavior in either instance for the director of a public corporation." He picked up the pince-nez and ostentatiously returned it to the desk drawer. Addressing himself more to the desk than to the man sitting opposite him, he added, "Clearly that appointment was premature. I thought so at the time."

Jim's nomination as a director of the Copter Company had been submitted and approved in April. The board met four times a year. The first meeting Jim could have attended took place in June, but he was in Rome when it was held. Asherton was now saying that Jim would not attend the next board meeting of The Copter Company either. He would have Jim kicked off the board before then. The session was scheduled for the end of September. That gave Asherton two weeks to act, which was more than enough. All he had to do was to place half a dozen phone calls.

Right, Jim thought. That takes care of the directorship and leaves only the job to go. "Not quite," he said.

Asherton did not move. "I'm waiting, Mr. Lindner." He looked at a thin watch on his wrist. "You have three more minutes."

Jim turned away from Asherton to the chair he had placed at a convenient angle to his own. He bent over the briefcase and twirled its combination lock. It clicked open, and he lifted the top of the case, reached for Ken's diary and held it up so Asherton could see it, flipping its pages in the air. A phrase flashed through his mind. "Show and tell"—convince the teacher, impress the class.

Asherton was neither convinced nor impressed. He was as close to apoplectic as he ever allowed himself to get. "What," he sputtered, "does this absurd exhibition . . . ?" He did not deign to complete the sentence. His foot found a bell under his desk and pressed it. Within seconds the secretary appeared at the door.

Jim shut the notebook and put it back into the briefcase. He paid no attention to the secretary. "This is a diary kept by Mr. Ward," he said. "It records in accurate and complete detail a large number of transactions of the kind we discussed." He allowed his voice its normal cadence but indicated with a motion of his hand that this was probably not a matter Mr. Asherton would want his secretary to be privy to. Asherton's face had turned a dark pink. He nodded at the secretary. "Thank you, Mr. Webster," he said. "I've found what I need." The secretary withdrew, and the door closed noiselessly behind him.

Asherton held out an imperious hand. Jim turned to the briefcase once more and came up not with the notebook but with a sheaf of papers stapled together. He rose, took a step forward and laid the sheaf on Asherton's desk. "These are photocopies," he said, "of the diary's pages."

Deep red blotches formed on Asherton's cheeks. Jim had made clear that he did not trust the chairman with the original document that would prove Jim's case. Asherton pushed aside the papers that had been placed before him. "How did you get this?" he demanded, pointing at the notebook in Jim's briefcase.

Jim had returned to his chair and carefully reassumed his original posture. "I found it in Switzerland, in the bank we use in Basel." His eyes tracked those of Asherton, caught and held them. For several seconds the two men stared at each other.

Asherton was the first to speak. "Does Morse Clark know about this?" He flicked a finger at the sheaf of papers, unwilling to dirty his hands by touching them.

Asherton was on the scent, smelling blood. "I don't believe so," Jim said. "Mr. Ward kept the diary in a safety deposit box at the bank. It was a private arrangement."

The high color on Asherton's face receded. The bright red

spots that had made him resemble a malevolent Santa Claus paled into a profusion of pink veins. He did not inquire how Jim had found out about Ken's private arrangement, nor how Jim had managed to get access to the notebook. The man knew how to handle himself, as well as others.

Asherton's voice was measured and polite when he said: "It's ten-thirty, Mr. Lindner. I have another appointment."

Jim rose and closed the briefcase. The combination lock clicked into place. "Thank you for your time, Mr. Chairman." Asherton did not reply. As Jim turned to leave he could feel Asherton's eyes on his back. It was not a comfortable feeling.

Anne and Jim sat in the backyard of the house on Thirty-eighth Street. September was almost over. The leaves on the elm tree were beginning to turn. Two weeks had gone by since Jim had been to Philadelphia, and so far he had heard nothing from the chairman, nor, as far as he knew, had anyone else in the company.

It was twilight. Anne had left the company and Jim had resumed his summer habit of stopping at the house after the office. Sometimes he stayed to dinner with the housemates, sometimes he and Anne went out. Once in a while they would go to his place and whip up a meal together there. They had never discussed this, but neither of them was particularly fond of Jim's apartment or felt at home in it. It belonged to the company, a fact that became increasingly evident as Brigitte's touches faded. What was left of those touches inserted a subtle wedge between Anne and Jim that both of them sensed.

Anne was house hunting in Brooklyn Heights, looking for a studio or a one-bedroom apartment at a reasonable price. It would take a couple of years for her to put down the necessary political roots in the district. She could manage the economics of this if she was careful. She had saved a fair amount working for The Copter Company, and her father had happily offered to stake her to the rest. Since Jim was still legally bound to Brigitte, he had not felt free to say anything about participating in Anne's living arrangements.

327

They were reclining in the canvas chairs under the elm and talking about her plans. Over the roofs in the west, pale pink clouds scudded across a Wedgwood blue sky. The blue deepened, turned marine, then shaded to a lavender-gray. The outlines of the leaves on the elm tree began to fade. Dusk was settling over Manhattan.

"Why don't you get a floor in one of those nice old brownstones?" he suggested. "I had one of them when I worked for the company in Brooklyn Heights. They make great apartments."

Anne and Jim had moved their chairs close together and her hand lay on his where the corners of the chairs touched. Her fingers started a jig on the back of his hand. "I've seen a couple of them and loved them. But they're out of my reach." She sounded regretful.

"They were affordable in my days."

He could hear her chuckle. "That, my love, was ten years ago."

She had said it lightly, teasing him. But she had said, "my love," and the words echoed in his heart. "Mine had two bedrooms," he said. "I used one as a den. You'll need a study if you're going to work from home. And we can share the bedroom"—he picked up the dancing fingers and brought them to his lips—"as soon as my divorce comes through. I heard from Brigitte last weekend. It shouldn't be long now, and we can get married the next day." He put Anne's hand back on the chair. "That way," he said, "we can split the rent."

He could hear her draw in her breath and let it out very slowly. It was a happy sound, delighted and delightful. "Yes," she said, "we could."

He insisted on taking her out to dinner that evening, and they went back to the place where they had shared their first meal. The proprietor recognized them and led them to the same booth. Over coffee, Jim said, "That offer to split the rent isn't altruism, you know. I may need the split myself. I'm not at all sure I'll have a job next week. Asherton wasn't exactly appreciative of the information I gave him."

Anne pushed out her lower lip and worked it over with her teeth.

When she stopped gnawing at her lip, it looked bee-stung and tempting. "Claude Asherton doles out his cordiality," she said. "I think he measures it out in the morning before he gets up and assigns an appropriate quantity to each person he's going to meet that day. Being appreciative is not one of his gifts either. Not of people like you. He doesn't need you enough. But he can't just sit on those papers you left him. They're dynamite, and he knows it. Unless I miss my guess, he's doing some high-powered maneuvering right now. He can't afford not to."

Jim put his arms on the table, thinking what an unwelcome and unnecessary obstruction it was. Eating off a tray in bed made a lot more sense. "I sure hope so," he said. "After all, that was the purpose of the exercise. But it doesn't necessarily mean that I stay in my job. Asherton already as much as told me he's going to kick me off the board."

She was wearing a two-piece ensemble of putty-colored cotton corduroy, with a shirt of green Swiss cotton. The green matched her eyes. The rest of the outfit consisted of a pair of tailored trousers and a vest with two small pockets. She sat back and stuck one thumb in each pocket. "Yes," she conceded. "You'd be un-comfortable to have around." Her eyes went luminous. "For Claude Asherton, that is."

He had trouble detaching himself from her eyes. "I could always go to work for Taher Rezvani," he said. "I hear he's landed on his feet. If I worked for him I'd make enough money to finance your compaign all by myself."

Taher Rezvani, it turned out, had saved not only his neck but a good part of his fortune by the failure of the helicopter deal to go through. Jim had succeeded in switching the entire consignment to Saudi Arabia, to the relief, indeed the delight, of Max Feld and Günther Westphal. And Rezvani was serving as an industrial adviser to the new regime in Iran. Jim did not know how he had arranged that feat; perhaps it was the Sharif connection. When he had heard about it, he had wondered what was happening to Rezvani's daughter. She was probably wearing her chador all the time now.

He had made his remark about Rezvani in jest, but the comment changed the luminosity in Anne's eyes to hard green fire. "No. You can't work for Rezvani!"

"Oh?" The flat firmness of her tone astonished him. Did it mean that she hated the idea of his working for Rezvani because he would be away much of the time? But if that was what disturbed her she would have said so and her voice would not be edgy and keen. "Why can't I?"

She pushed her thumbs deeper into the pockets of the vest. "That would be worse than working for The Copter Company if it doesn't straighten out and fly right!"

"But Rezvani is an interesting man with intriguing plans, and he's got himself squared away with the new government. They need people like him."

"Intriguing is right. Too intriguing."

"For what?"

"For his own good, or anyone else's. I know how Rezvani operates. Or at least I know something about it. It's flaky, and it can't last. Sooner or later, men like Rezvani are bad news. If you team up with them, you become part of the gang. And I do mean gang. The men who make up these gangs exist everywhere—the US included. They cut deals, cut corners and in the end cut throats. It's not for you. It shouldn't be for anybody." She hunched forward. Her voice changed from vehemence to a quiet insistence. "There really is such a thing as doing things right or doing them wrong."

She took her thumbs out of her pockets, put her hands on the table and splayed her fingers. "I think the work you do is important, and it's important to do it the way it should be done. Working for Rezvani would make you a mercenary. Getting The Copter Company cleaned up makes you a fighter. There's a big difference between those two."

She fell silent and seemed to be ruminating. Slowly the radiance crept back into her face and moved from her eyes up to her forehead and down to her chin. "You know the difference," she said softly. "I remember."

15

The following morning—it was Wednesday, the twenty-sixth of September—Jim arrived at the office to find an envelope carefully placed in the center of his desk. The envelope was thick, had a heavy linen texture and was marked "personal and confidential." He turned it over. Engraved in dark gray on the back flap was one line: "Claude R. Asherton." He ripped the envelope open.

It was not, as he more than half expected, notification that his employment with The Copter Company had been terminated. It was a memorandum consisting of three paragraphs and typed in the lean letters of the latest model IBM executive typewriter. At the top it read, "From: Chairman of the Board, The Copter Company. To: James H. Lindner, director." The memo informed Jim that The Copter Company's president, Mr. Russel Knight, had decided to take early retirement; that a successor had been selected by the chairman; that the chairman would present the successor to the board for its approval at the next meeting, on Friday, September 28; that there would be another important matter for discussion at that meeting; and that the chairman therefore expected all members of the board to be present.

Jim read the memorandum three times. When he was certain the contents were indeed what they purported to be, he put the memorandum back into the envelope, pushed the envelope into the pocket of his jacket and headed down the corridor to the corner office. When he got there, the door stood open and Grace

Hartung was staring through it. There was no one at the desk, which still had most of its accouterments; only the humidor was gone. The ashtray held the cold stumps of two cigars.

Jim felt as if a fist had slammed into his stomach. "Where is he?" he demanded. Grace's voice was acid. "You're the second one who wants to know. Men in a hurry, aren't you?"

Jim's mind did not register the sting of her comment. "You haven't answered my question, Grace."

"He's gone." Her voice shook. "He was here this morning, early as usual. He cleaned out his desk and left before I got in."

Jim stared at her. That's how it was done. After almost thirty-five years of work. Half a lifetime. He kept staring at Grace Hartung without seeing her. In a way, he reminded himself, this was his doing. It should have felt good, but it didn't. It felt godawful.

The sentiment must have registered on his face. Grace Hartung reached for a handkerchief and dabbed at her eyes. "You mark my words," she said sententiously. "This company will miss Mr. Knight."

"It will," Jim agreed quickly. In the commiserating silence that followed, her initial remark swam into focus. "Who else knows?" he asked sharply.

Bitterness came back into her voice. "Mr. Morse Clark," she said. "Of course."

Of course. Without considering what he was about to do, Jim strode to the next office. Morse Clark was not usually in at this hour. Why was he here today? Jim opened the door without bothering to knock. Morse Clark looked up, displeasure on his face. He was not used to anyone entering his office unannounced except for Russel Knight, and Knight was not with The Copter Company anymore.

"Good morning, Jim." He was being civil, but barely, and made no attempt to conceal his annoyance. "What can I do for you?"

"*Is* it a good morning?" Jim blurted.

Morse Clark looked at the slim gold cigarette holder lying in the indentation of its Chinese jade ashtray. "Not particularly. Mornings rarely are at this hour."

"You know Russ quit," Jim said.

Morse Clark picked up the cigarette holder and twirled it twice between his thumb and his index finger. "Of course I know. He didn't quit. He was fired." Morse Clark could easily have found a more gentlemanly way to say this. He chose not to. He wanted Jim to get the full impact of everything he intended to convey: that he, Lawrence Morse Clark, knew all there was to know about anything and everything that occurred in The Copter Company; that he was tough; that the inside track for the top spot was now his; that Jim had therefore better mind his p's and q's.

He stopped twirling his holder. "Anything else?" he asked.

Instinctively Jim had touched his pocket. He could feel the heavy envelope. "No," he said, turned on his heel and walked out.

On Friday morning the tension in the boardroom was palpable. When Jim walked in, the customary easy pre-meeting exchange among board members—of interesting events on yachts in the summer or intriguing incidents in hunting lodges in the fall—was minimal and strained. The outside directors were clustered around Asherton. Jim hovered for a while, but they were intent on what Asherton was saying, and Asherton did not acknowledge the presence of Jim Lindner.

Jim sauntered to the sideboard, picked up one of the china cups of black coffee that were set out on a silver tray and looked around. He had not been in the room before. It had a simple, almost austere elegance, with a large round rosewood table in the center, surrounded by matching chairs placed at precisely calculated distances. The rosewood sideboard that held the coffee tray displayed a steel model of The Copter Company's first aircraft. Two charcoal drawings framed in copper hung on the wall above the model. They were artistic renderings of the latest company product. No other furnishings or decorations marred the sweep of the room.

At ten o'clock sharp, Asherton called the meeting to order, and eight men took their seats at the table. There were chairs for nine. The empty seat gaped like a missing tooth.

333

Jim noticed that although the table was round, there was no mistaking where the head of the table was. It was where Asherton chose to sit. The outside directors took the chairs nearest the chairman. The inside directors sat below the salt—in this instance a pewter pitcher containing iced water, which no one touched.

Asherton was encased in a superbly cut suit of dove gray flannel with a very fine chalk stripe. A pale blue silk tie with a crest at the bottom matched the blue of his eyes. Seated, he exuded the air of the top of an iceberg: massive, smooth and impossible to shatter. His voice reinforced the impression. It was sharp and clear and carried without his making any effort to raise it, bouncing against the expanse of glass that constituted one complete side of the room and echoing in the seven minds intent on his words.

Asherton waved a large pink hand at the empty chair. It was a gesture of dismissal. "Gentlemen. You have all received and read my memorandum. You know, therefore, that Mr. Russel Knight, president and chief executive officer of this company, is no longer with us. He chose to take early retirement. For good reasons."

There was no comment. Everyone at the table had taken notice of the fact that the chairman did not say that Knight's reasons for retiring had been personal. In the arcane shorthand of boardrooms, that meant Knight had been forced out because his continued presence was considered undesirable for the company. They all knew that the reason for this distasteful development would emerge in the course of the meeting, subtly but transparently.

The chairman had paused after his announcement. It was a matter of corporate punctilio, but he did not expect anyone to speak up at this juncture. When he had taken note of the silence, he continued: "To deal with this emergency"—this time only his eyes strayed briefly to the empty chair—"I have conducted an intensive search and have a successor candidate to present to you today." He had emphasized "today," and the meaning of the emphasis was clear to all present. For the good of the company, Asherton had taken time off his many other pressing duties and

334

had devoted his attention to finding a replacement for Russel Knight. He assumed that the board would express its appreciation of these efforts by approving his candidate. Today.

"Good work," said Mark Lennert. Lennert was the chairman of a capital goods company well up in the ranks of the Fortune 500 and had agreed to serve on the board of The Copter Company as a personal favor to Asherton. Their business and personal association dated back four decades.

"Thank you, Mark." Everyone at the table realized that the two words from Lennert and the three-word response from Asherton meant that the candidate, whoever he was, had been approved. There would be some pro forma discussion in the half hour set aside on the agenda for the purpose, but the comments would be polite and would raise no objections. The new man was in.

Asherton lowered his voice so the directors around the table had to strain to hear him. He wanted some tension, some suspense. Meetings had no flavor otherwise. "The man I propose to you as the next president of The Copter Company is Putney Carrington. You will find his qualifications in the materials before you." The chairman indicated the folders on the table in front of each chair. The folders, of a sturdy grained plastic, were embossed in the center with the legend THE COPTER COMPANY and with the company's logo: a pair of wings with a circle of blades connecting them. No one bothered to open his folder. Asherton's voice picked up volume. It became assertive, making clear that contradiction was not welcome. "Putney is a young man, but I believe this company needs young men to carry on"—he allowed a tone of self-deprecating whimsey to touch his voice—"when we of the old guard hand over."

Lennert nodded and smiled thinly. "Right."

The chairman acknowledged the one-word consensus the way an actor accepts the applause of the house. Asherton's bow was a minimal inclination of the head. His eyes swept the table, going cold and dead, Jim observed, when they reached him. Jim felt his hands go clammy. Asherton's going to fire me today, he thought. At this meeting. He's just building up steam, getting

335

the important things out of the way. Jim's eyes strayed to Morse Clark. In the light pouring through the window, Morse Clark looked sallow and sphinxlike.

Asherton's voice came at Jim from what seemed like a long distance. "I've known Putney," Asherton was saying, "and his father over a considerable period of time. As you are all aware, Carrington Senior is a bulwark of the business community, one of the best corporate counsels this country has. Nevertheless, young Put did not join his father's firm. He had the gumption to go out on his own. He's with Whitney, Fenton and Garst, just up the road here on Wall Street. He became a partner when he was not yet thirty. He is a very competent young man." Asherton let his voice subside, then gave it volume for the significant announcement to follow. "I suggest we elect Putney Carrington president of this company but not chief executive officer. For the time being, I will accept that responsibility myself." He paused briefly, offering obeisance to the amenities. "With your concurrence," he added.

As he had assumed, no one demurred.

"I have also spoken with the chairman of the SEC." Asherton had had the attention of everyone at the table before. Now he commanded their total concentration. Lennert looked pained. The chairman's voice hit like a hammer. "There have been certain procedures in this company that will have to be eradicated." He stared at the three inside directors sitting opposite him: Grant Barlow, the company's inside counsel; Lawrence Morse Clark; and Jim Lindner. "They will be eradicated. Promptly. I made that commitment to the SEC. We will also have to file an Eight-K with the agency."

Bill Worthing, the outside director sitting on Asherton's left, tried to assuage the unease that had settled in the room. "More than four hundred companies have done that already. Most of them were in the family of the Fortune 500. At least we're in good company."

As chairman of a medium-sized steel company in the Midwest that supplied The Copter Company with a substantial amount of its raw materials, Worthing had every reason to try to restore calm and confidence to the meeting. The fortunes of Worthing's firm were heavily intertwined with those of The Copter Company.

Something about the self-serving ostrich quality of Worthing's remark got under Jim's skin. What the hell, he decided. I might as well go for broke.

"Do we name countries," he asked, "and people?"

The silence that followed Jim's question seemed to lower the temperature in the room by thirty degrees. Everyone around the table knew that the problem the chairman had negotiated with the SEC was bribery, or acquiescence in extortion. They also knew that citing the countries in which such payments had been made would close the markets of those nations to The Copter Company, and that revealing the names of payoff recipients would at the very least cause a sequence of minor international scandals and at worst would endanger careers and perhaps even lives. They had not raised any of these points, because Asherton had intimated that he had come to an understanding with the commission. Why then was this young inside director making a fool of himself? Well, he was new to the board and obviously had a great deal to learn. They could depend on the chairman to teach him, quickly.

Asherton did exactly that. He did it by ignoring the question, and when his eyes once more traveled around the table, they skipped Jim Lindner. As far as Asherton was concerned, the chair in which Jim sat was as empty as the one that had once been occupied by Russel Knight.

Grant Barlow disposed of Jim's question. "I'll take care of it," he said. He sounded sure of himself and a trifle smug. He would never be guilty of the kind of gaucherie the VP international had just perpetrated.

The chairman placed his hands on the folder before him obliterating the company's name and logo. "The agreement with the SEC," he said, "also calls for the constitution of an audit committee of the board. That committee will investigate corporate missteps of the past and will police procedures in the future. The audit committee will consist of outside directors only." He looked sternly and with unconcealed disapproval at the inside directors at the bottom of the table. His expression changed to

337

one of confidence and intimacy as he turned to the outside directors on his right and left. "I need," he said, "three good men and true. Mark?"

Lennert's mouth set. "Count me out, Claude, on this one." His irritation was evident. But there were old debts between Lennert and Asherton, and while they had long ago been settled, one never knew what the future might hold. "I don't really have the time," Lennert added.

Asherton's eyes became impenetrable. "Of course." He turned to his left. Worthing acceded hastily: "I'll serve." Asherton inclined his head. "Thank you."

"Graham?"

Graham Caulder was a prominent Philadelphia banker with useful international connections, social as well as financial. A note from Graham Caulder opened not only the doors of exclusive castles and haciendas in Europe and Latin America but also the even more elusive doors of boardrooms in companies and banks where the decisions were made that got much of the world's work done. The Caulder and Asherton families had been neighbors on the Main Line for five generations.

Caulder said easily, "I'll take it on, Claude. You'll want someone with financial expertise."

Jim sneaked a glance at Morse Clark. Morse Clark sat stock still, but his nose had gone very white. Caulder had not intended to be disparaging; he simply did not consider Morse Clark in the same league as himself and his peers. Nevertheless, the manner in which Caulder had agreed to serve constituted just about the cruelest cut anyone could have administered to The Copter Company's chief financial officer. It was the kind of slap in the face that in another age would have made a man demand a duel to remove the stain on his honor.

"Professor Maartens?" Asherton said. Robert Henry Maartens had been a surprising choice for The Copter Company board. A professor of government and political science at Princeton, Asherton's alma mater, Maartens had joined the board at the chairman's persuasive invitation in the early 1970s, when it had become evident that international business would play an increasingly important part in The Copter Company's future.

"The way the world is going," Asherton had said at the time, "most of our international business is likely to be with governments. We should have someone on the board who understands political ins and outs here and everywhere else."

For Professor Maartens the offer had been flattering, remunerative and intellectually tempting. Not many academics, especially in his field, got the opportunity to see from the inside how multinational companies conducted their affairs.

All the same, Professor Maartens chose to decline the additional insights the chairman was proffering now. His brown eyes peered at Asherton from behind a shock of wavy gray hair that fell over one eye. He took a puff on his pipe. He was the only member of the board who smoked in the chairman's presence. "I'll pass." he said, "Don't know enough about it." Another puff of the pipe caused Asherton to wave at the sweet-smelling cloud that had begun to float in his direction. The cloud had an aroma of figs, and Asherton detested the fruit. "I can recommend a colleague from the economics faculty," Maartens offered.

Asherton dismissed the offer. "Thank you," he said curtly. "that won't be necessary." He looked at Caulder. "We can tap Wharton, can't we? The School of Finance." Caulder put his index finger on the table in front of his seat. It came to rest in the circle of blades between the wings. "Yes," he said. "I know most of the trustees."

At five minutes before noon Asherton closed the fall meeting of The Copter Company's board. "Our new president is joining us for lunch," he announced. "Thank you, gentlemen." He nodded at the outside directors and rose. They followed suit.

The Copter Company's boardroom was about fifty feet by thirty, divided in the middle by a pair of Japanese screens. Beyond the screens were two additional rosewood tables, smaller than the one at which the morning session had been held. In that part of the room, which was also rigorously uncluttered, the corner near the window featured a glass-topped, scimitar-shaped bar, amply stocked. The directors now congregated there. The two tables were set for lunch. The snow white cloths that covered them were Belgian, the silver English, the crystal Irish, the china Limoges. A quality company. It struck Jim that he would not like

339

to leave it. The possibility that he might have to felt like a rip in his brain.

When Asherton headed in Jim's direction a half hour later, Jim was certain the time of severance had come. The company's new president had appeared at twelve o'clock on the dot, and Asherton had spent the past thirty minutes directing all his dynamism and much of his charm at the young man and the four outside directors who were getting to know him. Jim had watched the chairman orchestrate the encounters with enormous skill. By the time everyone was on his second drink, Putney Carrington had become a peer.

Jim was standing alone near the window. As he walked toward Jim, the chairman's face closed up tight. The joviality had vanished, the dynamism had turned to a quietly smoldering menace. This was the man Jim had challenged in his penthouse office, sitting behind his spotless antique desk. Asherton's voice was very low and his message brief. He stopped a pace away from Jim, his broad back turned to the other men in the room. For all they knew, he was having a friendly word with Jim, perhaps even handing out avuncular advice to this young new member of the board, who clearly needed it. What Asherton offered Jim was advice of sorts, containing threat as well as counsel. "I've done what had to be done for the company," Asherton growled, "but I've never liked whistle blowers, and the last two weeks have deepened my distaste. Your behavior has cost this company the valuable and loyal services of Russel Knight." Asherton's icy eyes drilled into Jim's. "That's a very high price. You'd better make sure this company does not suffer from the transaction."

He did not tarry for a response. He seemed to pin Jim to the window with his gaze, turned and walked back to the bar.

Jim waited for what he judged to be an appropriate interval, then headed in the same direction. He picked up the bottle of twelve-year-old Ambassador scotch and poured himself half a glass of unadulterated whiskey. He drank it down in one steady gulp. It felt mellow on his tongue and warm in his gullet, his throat and his stomach. "You'd better make sure," Asherton had said. That meant Jim was not going to be fired. It implied even more:

340

the charge that he, Jim Lindner, was to make the new system work. The company's procedures would be cleaned up, but it was Jim's job to see to it that the process and its consequences did not wind up being more costly to the firm than they had been already. It would take doing, but the rend in Jim's brain had disappeared, and he was suddenly feeling no pain, no pain at all.

At one o'clock lunch was served. Asherton managed the seating. He ushered the outside directors and Grant Barlow to the larger table, then asked their leave. Steering Putney Carrington to the second table, set for four, he beckoned to Jim and Morse Clark. When all were seated, he turned to Carrington. "Put," he said, "now that you're aboard I thought you should start out by breaking bread with your top team." He reached for the crystal carafe of wine in the center of the table. The dynamic charm came on like a klieg light, dazzling the three men at the table. He tilted the decanter, filled everyone's glass, then raised his own facing Carrington. His voice was vibrant and paternal. "To your stewardship, Put. You know how much I appreciate it." He sipped at his wine ceremoniously and immediately replenished the small quantity he had consumed. Then he raised his glass a second time, signaling Jim and Morse Clark that he expected them to do the same. "To the caretaker of The Copter Company," he said. "I expect you to give him all you have." The raised glass described a circumspect flourish that encompassed Putney Carrington, Morse Clark and Jim. "And to the three of you," he added, "good luck."

Jim did not get back to his desk until well after two. His head felt light. He had drunk considerably more than he usually did at lunch and was unquestionably high. The high was not only alcoholic; it was a state of mind. The precipitous scenario he had written in his head was at the very least premature. Whatever plans were being hatched in Asherton's labyrinthian mind included Jim for the time being. Asherton had made that quite clear during lunch, reinforcing his calculatedly extravagant toasts. He had made it equally clear, if somewhat more obliquely, that

341

there were three men whom he considered qualified for the presidency of The Copter Company. Two, after the caretaker president returned to his own duties. Who would succeed Putney Carrington, and when, remained to be seen; but the candidates he had in mind were sitting at his table now.

Jim reached for the phone and pushed the buttons for the house on Thirty-eighth Street. The phone rang six times. No one picked up the receiver. The housemates were at work. But where was Anne? Tracking down a suitable apartment in Brooklyn Heights. Nice thought, but he wished she weren't doing it right now. He wanted to talk to her and tell her what had happened. He also wanted to run by her analytic mind the implications of the day's events. What exactly was the portent of Asherton's barb about whistle blowers? And how did it relate to the double track the chairman had so deliberately laid down for the presidential race, with one of the tracks marked Jim Lindner? I wish, he thought, and then the receiver was lifted at the other end and a voice, slightly out of breath, said, "Hello."

"Hello to you. I'm glad."

"Good. I raced in from the garden to catch the call. What exactly are you glad about?"

"I'm glad you answered the phone. I'm glad you're there. I'm glad you are."

"Wow! All that in the middle of the afternoon."

"I have a brilliant idea," he said.

He heard her chuckle. "I'm susceptible."

"How would you like an Irish coffee?"

"When? Where?" She sounded nonplussed.

"Now. In the tallest building of the world. Floor 107 of the World Trade Center. The dining room is probably closed, but the bar's open. I've a feeling we could persuade them to come up with Irish coffee for two."

"I'm not dressed for such a towering occasion."

He felt what he had come to describe to himself as the "Anne glow." He clamped the receiver between his shoulder and ear and stretched. In his mind's eye he saw Anne wearing the jacket of his pajamas.

"You look good to me," he said, "in whatever you wear."

His voice must have carried his feelings across the telephone line. "Rank prejudice," she replied, but he could hear the catch in her voice. She cleared her throat. "The choices," she said, "are: One, I come as is, in fifteen minutes. Two, I change, which gets me there in about thirty minutes."

"One," he said. "It's urgent."

She laughed and hung up.

When he walked into the bar, the last of the lunch stragglers were on their way out. Only about half a dozen customers were left when Anne arrived barely fifteen minutes later. Those customers looked up, did a double take and smiled. Anne was wearing a pair of overalls made of what looked like mattress ticking, with a white broadcloth shirt underneath, the sleeves turned up in two-inch folds just above the elbow. Everything seemed large on her. The effect was of a little girl who had put on her big brother's work clothes.

He rose when she came in and, as soon as she was close enough, took her face in his hands and kissed her. "I'm glad someone in the family is working," he said. "What were you doing?"

She looked at her hands. There was dirt under her fingernails. She held them up for inspection. "I was saying goodbye to the roses in the yard. With fertilizer."

"Oh. Are you ready to leave Thirty-eighth Street?"

She looked at him sidelong. "Not quite. But I've found an apartment. The apartment. There is a problem, though."

"You're speaking to one of the world's better problem solvers. I hope."

"It's expensive," she blurted.

He waved his hands in a dismissing gesture. "That's all right, love. You're about to marry a man with a brilliant career before him."

"I am?"

"You are. Listen to this." He put his head close to hers and told her how the morning had gone and what had happened thereafter. She listened without interrupting him. When he had finished, she said, "So Carrington isn't meant to last. He's just a stand-in for Asherton and knows it. It was part of the deal."

"That's what I figure too. Asherton as much as said so at lunch."

"Then it's a rat race between you and Morse Clark."

He reached for her chin, pulled it close and kissed the tip of her nose. "I'll thank you to remember," he said, "that there's only one rat in this race. The other animal is a pussycat."

Her lips widened in the beginning of a grin, then became very soft. "Yes," she said in a tone intended to sound judicious. "That's a reasonably accurate observation." Her hands went to the straps of the overalls and began to play with the metal clasps. The face turned serious. "All the same," she said, "it isn't going to be easy. Morse Clark is—"

"A slippery customer," he finished the sentence for her. "Subtle and smart."

Her fingernails made a scratching sound on the tin clasps. "And unscrupulous. And ruthless."

That was true, and vital to keep in mind, especially since Jim could not count on either the president or the chairman to back him up if push ever came to shove. Carrington could not, and Asherton would not. If Asherton ever found out that Morse Clark and Jim were having at each other, he would, metaphorically speaking, hold their coats, and urge them on and enjoy the spectacle. Let the best man win.

Jim had spoken the last sentence out loud: "Let the best man win."

Anne's fingers stopped playing with her buckles. She reached across the table and caught both of Jim's hands. "That's right," she said. Her fingers were soft and dry and had the effect of making him feel infinitely confident. He held on to them. "I've just decided," he said, "what I will do first thing Monday morning."

She winked. "Get cards printed to read, 'James H. Lindner, Vice-President International and Director.' "

He shook his head. "Uh, uh. That's Tuesday. On Monday

344

I'm going to do something with that cartoon from *The New Yorker* that Lisa Ward sent me early this year. I told you about it when it came."

Her eyes darkened. "Yes, I remember. It showed one of those chairmen of the board who look like Asherton ringing for his secretary during a board meeting."

"That's right. Asking her to send in whoever in this company—"

"Knows right from wrong," Anne said.

He tightened his hands around hers. "I'll have the cartoon blown up and framed and hung in my office where anyone who walks in can't help but see it."

For a moment she looked doubtful, then her nose twitched. "Asherton isn't going to like that," she said, sounding pleased.

He grinned. "There're things Asherton does that I don't like."

She rocked in her chair, pulling his hands with her. "Morse Clark is going to absolutely hate it. Ostentatious and juvenile." The last phrase was pronounced in a manner that mimicked Morse Clark's nasal, toneless delivery, with the words pushed out from behind clenched teeth. The imitation was perfect.

Jim laughed. "I know. That's one reason for putting it there."

A waiter ambled over. He had watched them out of a corner of his eye and decided not to disturb them. They seemed ready for him now. "What'll it be, folks?" he asked.

"Irish coffee. Two."

He returned with the hot glasses, sugared at the rim, their deep brown contents topped with a frothing of cream.

She flicked her tongue at the cream, then through the cream to test the temperature of the coffee. It seemed to satisfy her, and she picked up her glass with both hands and held it in the air. "To The Copter Company," she said. "Clean and shiny."

He raised his own glass. "To the Lindner residence in Brooklyn Heights." The spiked coffee was hot, fragrant and delicious. "When does the lease start?"

"November first."

He clucked approvingly. "Good timing. I had word from Germany yesterday. The decree will be final the middle of October."

He saw her face light up before she bent down to have another sip of her coffee. When she looked up, a dollop of cream had settled on her nose. He stretched across the table and licked it off. "Mmm," he said. "Delectable. Where do you want to get married?"

She brushed the back of her hand over her nose, then turned the hand over and examined her fingernails. "I'd better get a manicure first. After that, what are my options?"

He caught her hands, held up one finger at a time and kissed the nail of each. Between kisses he said, "Rhode Island, Pennsylvania, New York."

Her fingers lent themselves to his game. Her eyes, enormous now, melted into his. "I like New York," she said.

"So do I. Look." He stood and, taking her by the elbow, propelled her to the long stretch of window in the front of the bar. She leaned against his chest as they peered together at the scene below. The river and its bridges, people and cars looked like a display in the windows of a toy shop. Across the water they could see the high-rises and brownstones of Brooklyn Heights and, at the water's edge, the old Navy Yard that had become The Copter Company's first plant. Out in the bay the brilliant sun of a New York fall afternoon gilded the Statue of Liberty. The bright light showed up a smudge of dirt across the statue's brow and a streak of grime running down its torch. Anne and Jim, gazing in the same direction, noticed the spots together. "Too bad we aren't rainmakers," he commented. She did not have to ask what he meant: Rain would wash them clean—the lady and her torch.

"But we are," she said.